Halo of Fires

The Dark Harbour Tales Book 1

By Joseph Kiel

Copyright and Legal Notice

"Halo of Fires" Copyright © 2020 Richard Joseph Dutton

Cover design by Zaph copyright © 2020

ISBN: 9798668571345

Previously published as "Dark Harbour: The Tale of the Soul Searcher" by Joseph Kiel (ISBN: 9781533501073). Copyright © 2016 Richard Joseph Dutton.

The right of Richard Joseph Dutton (writing as Joseph Kiel) to be identified as the Author of the Work has been asserted by him in accordance with the Copyright, Designs and Patents Act 1988.

All rights reserved. No part of this book may be reproduced or transmitted in any form or by any means, electronic or mechanical, including photocopying, recording, or by any information storage and retrieval system without the written permission of the author, except in the case of brief quotations embodied in critical reviews and certain other noncommercial uses permitted by copyright law.

This book is a work of fiction. Names, characters, places, and incidents are products of the author's imagination. Any resemblance to actual persons, living or dead, is entirely coincidental.

All trademarks are the property of their respective owners.

www.josephkiel.com

Get a Free Dark Harbour Novella and Exclusive Dark Harbour Material

Somewhere in a parallel universe, *Dark Harbour* is a sensational bestselling series and they've made epic Bafta-winning films of all the books starring all the national treasures (true story). The exciting thing for your dimension is that this hasn't happened yet so you're getting in on this world before everyone else, before it's become the next big thing.

And what better way to do that than to sign up to my mailing list? If you do that, I'll email you more stuff from the shadowy seaside world of Dark Harbour:

> 1. *Into The Fires: A Dark Harbour Novella*, the story of a man on the run from the city mob who ends up in town. An exploration of the genesis of revenge in the Halo of Fires organisation and the strange characters of this mysterious place (eBook version). Not available anywhere else.

> 2. Classified profiles of the Halo of Fires operatives (a character sheet to this book), exclusive to the mailing list. No one else gets this either.

Signing up to this list won't result in endless spammy emails, so don't worry. To get your hands on this bonus material, please follow the link at the end of this book.

Part 0: Jeremy and the Black Widow

Chapter 0.1

There's a certain place in England that you've never been to. It's tucked away in that distant corner of the country that you've always thought about visiting but never got round to.

You've quite possibly travelled up and down these roads, amongst the clouded hills and satanic mills, and concluded that you've seen all there is to see in this green and pleasant land. But when you next have the map book opened up on your knee, try having a look for this particular town.

Once you've found it, you'll wonder why you'd never heard of it before. Some things only come into your awareness when the time is right though, and here the universe has brought you to this very moment where you've picked up this book and for some reason the town of Dark Harbour wants to make itself known to you. Perhaps it knows there's already a part of you here.

There are things you will read about this place that may surprise you. Certainly you can come here for a seaside holiday of sitting on a deck chair in a cool breeze while you lick an ice cream and watch Punch and Judy shows, but this book isn't a tourist guide.

There are many colourful tales to tell about these murky shores, beyond the red and white curtain of the puppet show. Visit a pub and the locals will enchant you with plenty of delightful yarns: tales of sea monsters and outlaws, stories about the mysterious characters that have come and gone over the years. Spooky stuff, too.

Perhaps the most well-known story concerns a group of pirates that once set out for a faraway land to search for treasures. Many a child has been kept amused by this tale at bedtimes, and a common playground game is to re-enact how these mariners struck misfortune as they sailed towards the harbour in their ship. In a thick fog, the helmsman became quite disorientated and was unable to find the lighthouse. The vessel cut into some rocks barely covered by the waters, tearing open the hull. Some of the pirates managed to swim back to shore. Most of them drowned.

In an attempt to keep them in line, certain mischievous children here receive the lecture about the wicked creature Night-Shines Nick (or Old Shiner as he's also come to be known). 'Don't stay outside too late else Night-Shines Nick may get you,' is a line often heard from worried parents. It's good advice really, for it is said that the creature liked to tear the skin from your face while your shrill screams woke the entire town. Reports of encounters ended many years ago, and so his devilish legacy of fear is now unfortunately dwindling.

There is one story that you probably won't be told about in the pubs these days, not in much detail. It might be worth reminding the locals about it because it was big news for a while, as stories of missing children often are. The child in this case was a boy called Jeremy, an outsider like you.

His tale began a number of decades ago, but it isn't clear where it all ends. Some individuals know what became of the boy and, quite rightly, they've kept the secret to themselves. But even they don't know everything. The abject morbidity of it all. The devastation.

The pain.

***

Jeremy remembered his arrival clearly. He was only six years old on that grey day, sitting on the back seat of his grandfather's battered Volvo, action figures clutched in his clammy hands.

He and his brother were on their way to start a new life after their mother had lost her battle against pancreatic cancer. She'd managed to hold on for a remarkable amount of time, adding over a year to the doctors' best prognoses. The outcome was inevitable though, no matter how much willpower Jeremy had put into sustaining her life.

The orphaned child found it a struggle to get his head around this, that he would never see his mother again. She was dead forever and forever was a very long time. For a short while after her passing, there had been some uncertainty about who would look after them. That responsibility had eventually fallen to their grandfather though, as he was the only known living relative they had.

Being the eldest brother by a clear seven years and four months, Simon sat in the front passenger seat. His seniority over Jeremy apparently gave him such privileges, but the junior sibling was not one to argue. Simon knew best. Simon knew a lot of things, in fact. He was the first person to go to whenever Jeremy had a question, and even though he would reply in an irritated tone of voice, Simon was always forthcoming with explaining things to him.

There hadn't been many questions on the journey so far as none of them was feeling talkative. As the vehicle reached the edge of a mist, the passengers' thoughts were being projected towards the unknown future ahead.

Jeremy decided to break the silence. 'How many more miles is it, Granddad?'

'Oh, not far now.'

Simon tutted. 'Didn't you see the sign back there? It said it was only two more miles.'

'Missed it,' Jeremy replied.

Simon glanced over his shoulder and then rolled his eyes at the fistfight that his little brother was orchestrating between Han Solo and Darth Vader.

Jeremy had lost Han's blaster the other day. The things were so small and so easy to lose. Vader still possessed his lightsaber, however, and just as he was retracting it from his arm, Luke Skywalker intervened in the nick of time to block the Sith Lord's swipe. He could really do with Yoda's help right now, but unfortunately the Jedi Master was stuffed in a box somewhere in the boot of the car.

'Playing with his toys again,' Simon said.

'They're not mine; they're yours.'

'You can have them.'

Simon was a teenager now, had been for the past two months. Arriving at that milestone evidently meant that you could no longer play with your action figures. These days Simon had advanced onto comic books and had an unread edition of *The Incredible Hulk* resting on his knee. Jeremy would possibly follow that same progression in seven years' time.

'Damn coastal weather,' their grandfather muttered as he flipped on the wipers, driving them into a bleary drizzle. Ulric Helliwell never spoke a great deal, as he wasn't the type to exert his tongue for the sake of filling silences. His grandsons could often tell there was something going on in his head, but he would rarely let them know what. He was talkative when he wanted to be though, and especially when he'd had one or two whiskies.

It often entertained Simon and Jeremy when his mouth got going and he spoke of his past, of the times he skipped school and stole apples from the orchard. Or his times in Europe when he'd shot at Germans and dodged bombs on the docks. So far on this car journey their grandfather had seemed like a man with the weight of the world on his shoulders. Or maybe he'd just had a bad day at the bookies. Either way, the boys wouldn't have been able to tell the difference.

The ethereal mist fluttered by the windscreen like a legion of ghosts. By the roadside, what looked like cloaked figures would slowly blur into view before manifesting as old, crooked trees. It almost felt as though they'd somehow veered from the roads of reality into a supernatural vortex, sucking them into another dimension.

And even though it was misty, it was still very dark, unnaturally dark. So much so that as Simon finally looked down to read his comic book, he had to squint to read the words.

'I guess they don't call it *Dark* Harbour for nothing,' he said.

The other two people in the car failed to acknowledge his wittiness. Jeremy was too busy saving the galaxy in the back, and his grandfather just sighed wearily.

'You haven't heard the start of it, my boy.'

***

Originally a Harbourian, Ulric Helliwell had recently moved back to the town after a long time away. He still had a handful of friends here, and one of them had set him up in a retirement flat in a quiet area. It was just what Ulric was looking for, not that he was getting old. At sixty-three years of age he could still get up at seven each morning and drink until it was light. He wasn't buying vests and thermal underwear from Marks and Spencer just yet.

If anything, it was now a case of having to rein in some of his energy. It was time to live more modestly, amongst the pension-collecting bingo players of his new neighbourhood, amongst people who didn't *know* how to spend a lot of money.

Ulric had been there when his daughter was suffering. He was the one who'd driven her to the hospice where she'd withered away in a bed of blood and vomit. There he had been at her bedside when the feeble rise and fall of her bedsheets had finally, and mercifully, stopped.

The grandsons had been in the television room, Simon's protective arm around his little brother, yet both the poor boys fast asleep. He'd woken them up and told them she was gone. As Simon had wept, Jeremy had looked out of the window towards the heavens with his big, brown eyes. Looking for a passing angel.

At that moment it hit Ulric that he would have to get rid of social services and take on the guardianship of the boys himself. What else was he supposed to do? Let them be fostered or abandon them to an orphanage? Ulric wouldn't have dreamt of it.

During those painful days, the memories of which he now had to choke back, Ulric had decided to accept his responsibility. It appeared that it was something he was doing a lot of these days. The only thing was that at this particular point in his life, it wasn't a brilliant time to be bringing them into his fold. Given his circumstances, was it really the right thing to do after what he'd done?

Barely wiped the blood off your hands, Ulric.

Of course it was. He definitely wasn't going to abandon his grandsons when they needed him most. No, this was the only choice he had.

***

Jeremy peered out of the raindrop-mottled window. Whilst he saw the road sign that welcomed his arrival to Dark Harbour and knew that the car journey would soon be ending, in many ways he sensed that this was only a beginning. As they drove into the town, the young boy put his action figures aside and peered closer.

This place usually makes a strong first impression on people, but it isn't really anything you see here that makes this impression. You'll know that *something* has hit you, but you won't know what it is, no matter how hard you search for it.

What most people eventually put it down to is the town's atmosphere, a brooding yet seductive ambience that pervades every corner you tread. You can literally feel it in your footsteps, as if you're walking over tombs as you anticipate the zombified hand that will burst upwards and drag you down into its abyss. Oozing out of the pathways are the painful thoughts of citizens long since departed, ghostly whispers still carried in the wind, the presence of dark muses that influenced the gothic architecture floating around you and drawing your reflections inwards to the more morbid and bleaker corners of your soul.

As the car sloshed through the drenched streets into the heart of the town, it felt as though this *something* was waiting for Jeremy. An odd sensation buzzed in his tummy after they turned each corner, as if the thing he was looking for would suddenly reveal itself to him.

'Ah, cool,' Simon chirped, wide-eyed. 'You've got an amusements arcade here.'

'Oh yes,' Ulric replied as they drove along the seafront. 'Plenty to keep you two occupied. I'll take you there this weekend.'

Jeremy looked the other way and saw the jaded lights of a seaside playground: a big wheel spinning into the soaked sea air, the twisting slide on the helter-skelter that stood like an alien temple, the tortured face of a cadaver as it burst through the wooden sign on the ghost train. It reminded him of the Land of Play in *Pinocchio*, and the young boy feared that he might turn into a mule should it beguile him into pursuing these wayward pleasures.

Beyond the amusements he saw the wild waves that crashed against the promenade, the edge of another world where sea-swallowed skeletons might dance by their aquatic grave. The place seemed peculiarly familiar to Jeremy.

'Where's your house, Granddad?'

'I don't live in a *house*, Jeremy.'

Simon tutted again. 'He lives in a flat. He told you that.'

Jeremy now remembered and felt a bit silly for having asked his question.

'It's just along this road and up the hill a bit. Near Moonlight Cove.'

'What's Moonlight Cove?' Jeremy asked. That was a safe question. He wouldn't be shot down for asking that one.

'Well, then,' Ulric began, 'it's a bit of a beauty spot. It's crescent-shaped. You know, like the moon.'

Jeremy listened in fascination.

'Quite a magical place, so I'm told. It's somewhere unhappy people go.'

'Why's that?' Jeremy asked.

'There's a legend, you see. You're supposed to go there at midnight, stand in the middle of the cove and watch the moonlight dancing on the waves. If you gaze into the reflection of the moon, then the spirits will appear to you and reveal how to find the things you dream for.'

Simon rolled his eyes and turned his head away. He wasn't going to be taken in by a story that was quite clearly for kids.

Jeremy's eyes went out of focus as he chewed on his thumbnail. 'Have you ever been there, Granddad? Have you looked into the waves?'

'Don't be stupid,' his brother quickly cut in. 'It's not real.'

His grandfather made no reply. He had slipped back into his silent mood.

Chapter 0.2

Over the following weeks, Jeremy and his brother slowly orientated themselves into their new life. It was during the first days of June when they moved in, not long before the end of the school year.

Simon was admitted at one of the local secondary schools but a place could not be found for Jeremy at either of the crammed primary schools. However, one of them agreed to accept him for the start of the following academic year. For the next couple of months, Jeremy was to spend a lot of time with his grandfather.

Though not quite of retirement age, Ulric Helliwell was apparently not in employment either, not that the boys had ever been clear on what his line of work was. Since moving in with him, Simon was eager to find out exactly what his grandfather did. He was usually so curious that, after school while they sat around the tea table, he would persistently dig away with questions. The answers he received from his grandfather tended to be vague and were promptly followed by the sound of the air whistling through his moustache.

Ironically, it was the disinterested younger brother who had the best insight into their grandfather's occupation, but Jeremy couldn't understand what all the fuss was about. What did fascinate him were all the different places in his new hometown. Each morning after Simon had gone to school, Ulric would take Jeremy on a walk to a different corner of these shores.

One of the first places they visited was Moonlight Cove. Ulric knew of a secret way of getting there, through a woodland area not far from the flat.

As they walked through the trees, Ulric recounted to his young grandson how evil spirits once haunted the woodland. His story went that a mysterious traveller had wandered into the area a couple of years ago and made a home within the wilderness. The ghosts and ghouls weren't happy about this, and so they tried to scare the poor man away.

However, this cunning traveller made sure he had the last laugh. Casting a spell in the woods, he strode to the giant tree in the centre, a great English oak that was hundreds of years old, and on a branch he carved an angel that would keep the evil spirits away.

Jeremy couldn't see any ghosts as they walked deeper into the woods, but, even so, he clasped his grandfather's hand tightly.

'Take me to the angel, Granddad! I want to see the angel.'

'Okay, I'll take you there. We have to go right to the heart to find her.'

'Do you know the way?'

'Of course I do, my boy. But you can't tell anyone about her. She's a secret.'

Ulric led Jeremy off the main path and in amongst the trees. After beating a path through the thick growth of bracken and branches that all seemed to reach out and pull them back from their route, they eventually reached the magnificent oak.

'Here she is,' Ulric announced. 'The oldest tree of the woods. The oldest and the wisest.'

It was very majestic, its monstrous limbs reaching for the heavens like the arms of an almighty ogre. It didn't take Jeremy long to find the carving; his enthralled eyes magnetised to her before Ulric had even raised his finger to point her out.

Two feet tall, dressed in flowing robes, her wings were unfurled as though she was magically floating within the timber. Despite the shadow of the canopy, the carving was at such a point where the sunlight trickled its way through the leaves to illuminate her. She looked radiant, almost as if she was generating the light herself, shining her protective spirit over the woodland.

As they left the angel behind them, Jeremy wondered how his grandfather knew so much about this place. He just seemed to know *everything*. The young boy hoped that one day he could be like his grandfather, that he would be so clever and insightful. He hoped that one day people would be in awe of him.

On the other side of the woods was the cove, just a short walk through some wildflower meadowland. Ulric had trailed through the trees with spirit, but by the time they arrived at the shore he was a little solemn.

The ageing guardian led Jeremy to the top of a cliff that looked down onto the sea. For about a quarter of an hour he just stood there watching the waves dancing over the rocks. Jeremy did not speak.

The whispering sound of the crashing surf drew the boy into a comforting corner of his mind. He felt lulled by the soothing sensation, cleansed of the unhappy thoughts that were polluting his life.

In this trance, he continued to gaze on the effervescent waves as they swept over the beach, making the grains of sand glisten in the brilliant sunshine as though the sea was scattering jewels across the shoreline.

Jeremy glanced over to his grandfather and it seemed that the salty air was stinging the old man's eyes. Ulric ran his fingers through his thinning grey hair and then circled his palm over the back of his head, almost like he was trying to massage his own mind.

So many questions filled Jeremy's head. He thought about all the other broken people that had presumably come to Moonlight Cove over the years, and he wondered whether they found what they were looking for. He wanted to know how these moonlight-reflecting waters could perform such magic. And just what other secrets were waiting to be unveiled in this town?

Just as a question seemed to find itself on the tip of his tongue, Ulric drew in a deep breath of sea air and turned to his grandson. He took his hand and then led him away towards home. But Jeremy would soon be back here. Sooner than he would have wanted.

***

Ulric went out that evening and left Simon to keep an eye on his brother. He told them he was going to see a friend and that he would return around eleven. Jeremy was easy to baby-sit though. With his *Star Wars* action figures and *Knight Rider* on television, the young lad was in a world of his own.

As he continued his battles against the Empire, Simon was back to playing Sherlock. That was until he came into the living-room and slunk down onto the settee. He shifted around in his seat for a moment as though he couldn't get comfortable and then stood up again and switched off the television.

'Granddad's in trouble. I've found something out.'

'What sort of trouble?'

'Doesn't matter.'

Jeremy didn't know whether to leave it at that or to risk being berated for asking another stupid question. Not understanding what his brother was on about anyway, he got back to the galactic battle.

'I found a letter in his bedroom.'

Jeremy placed his figures down. 'You read it?'

'I shouldn't tell you really,' Simon replied, facing the window as though talking to a six-year-old was beneath him.

There was a strange tone to his words, a new timbre within it as though his developing body had suddenly broken his voice that little bit more. Jeremy could feel his heart thumping. 'Simon, what did it say? Who was the letter from?'

'I don't know. He just put his initials: T.H.M.'

'What does that stand for?'

'I don't know, Jeremy!'

Simon lowered his head like he was praying, but then Jeremy noticed the letter was in his hands. Simon unfolded it.

'It goes like this: "Dear Mr Helliwell, I understand the angels lead us to paradise, and the martyrs greet you and lead you into the holy city of Jerusalem. Is this not how it goes for you? Do the angels greet you? Did not Lazarus, once also a poor man, find eternal rest? Perhaps you chose to dwell in Dark Harbour for another reason. Perhaps you thought someone else might be able to save you. Alas, you cannot hide under my eyes. Adieu." Signed T.H.M.'

Simon folded the letter up again, and there was a cold silence. Jeremy's mouth had suddenly gone very dry. He didn't understand what it all meant, but he could feel the sentiment of it, the seething threat hanging over the words, a picture of an angry deity lurking behind Biblical allusions.

'What should we do?' Jeremy asked.

'I think Granddad needs our help. Well, my help at least.' Simon got up to return the letter.

The younger brother looked back at his action figures, what now seemed like silly pieces of plastic. What did he mean? How could *he* help him out? He knew that these were no idle words. Simon always meant what he said.

***

Jeremy did not sleep very well that night. Despite having an enjoyable day in the sunshine of Moonlight Cove, it seemed that an ugly presence had floated along in the form of that sinister letter. He was even a little angry with his brother for reading it to him. Why did he have to go and dig it out?

The youngster had wanted to know happiness again in his new life, yet the clouds of misfortune had followed them over here. He could see it in his grandfather, the ponderous way he stroked his moustache all the time, the way he drummed his fingers at the dinner table, the fact that he could never sit still for longer than five minutes.

During the next week, there was further unfurling of their grandfather's secret problem. One afternoon, around the time they'd usually set off to meet Simon out of school, Ulric said they would remain at home instead as a visitor was on his way.

'Who's coming over?' Jeremy asked.

'Someone I've known for a very long time.'

'Is he a friend?'

'A good friend.'

Just at that point, there was a knock at the door so Ulric got up to answer it. Standing in the doorway was a very smart and commanding gentleman dressed in a black suit and hat. Jeremy guessed he was a fair bit younger than his grandfather by around twenty years.

Furtively the boy tried to peek over his grandfather's shoulder at the tall man's eyes, but the brim of his hat cast a shadow over them. He was smiling gently to Ulric. A gentleman in the true sense of the word, Jeremy thought.

He was handsome, too. He wouldn't have been out of place in a film playing the role of Superman or Flash Gordon (if he had blonde hair). Stepping into the flat, he removed his hat and shook hands with his grandfather.

Jeremy could now see that he had warm blue eyes, just like Superman's funnily enough. Suddenly those eyes were peering directly at him. The man crouched down.

'Hello there, young man. You must be Jeremy.'

How does he know my name? Jeremy thought.

'That's him,' Ulric said. 'His brother Simon is at Harbour High but the other schools were full.'

'Oh, you should have had a word with me. Not that he minds starting his summer holidays a little early, eh Jeremy?' The gentleman flashed a smile and his apprehension eased, even daring to step up to his grandfather's leg.

'I've been taking him to see the places round here,' Ulric said, ruffling his grandson's hair.

'Do you like your new home then, kiddo?'

'Yes.'

'Different from where you came from, isn't it? Outsiders often feel out of place.'

'Not Jeremy,' Ulric vouched. 'He's already got that Harbour kick in his voice.'

'You know what they say. You can't take the Harbour out of the boy, but you put the boy in the Harbour...'

'...and he'll drown.'

They both laughed, but Jeremy frowned at their joke.

'Jeremy, do you want to go and play with your toys for a bit? Alan and I need to have a chat.'

'Here, maybe I've got a sweet for you,' the gentleman, Alan, said. He rummaged into his jacket and brought out a bag of mints. Jeremy saw on the packet they were mint humbugs, whatever they were. He took one.

'What do you say?' Ulric asked him.

'Thank you, Mr...'

Alan laughed. 'You can call me Alan. Only people I don't like call me Mr Hammond.'

Ulric patted a hand on his back. 'Come through.'

The mint humbug was quite a hard sweet at first and so blandly minty that Jeremy thought about spitting it out. As he continued to suck on it, he eventually got to a gooey, sweet centre that made the initial hardness worthwhile.

The two old friends conversed over coffee for well over an hour, so long in fact that they had not finished by the time Simon returned from school. As soon as he stepped inside, he heard the muffled voices beyond the kitchen door.

'Who's he yapping to?' Simon asked his brother.

'Alan.'

'Who the hell's he?'

'A friend, a good friend.'

'What are they talking about?' There was an urgency in Simon's voice, but none in Jeremy's.

'I don't know.'

Simon rolled his eyes, then approached the door. He immediately cocked an ear to it. Jeremy didn't think his brother should have been doing that, but he did not dare voice his disapproval.

Jeremy saw the frown form on Simon's heavy eyebrows, and they betrayed the growing fiery emotions that festered within him. He didn't bother asking him what he could hear. He didn't have to anyway, because once Alan had left, his brother was ready to burst.

'I want to help you, Granddad. Tell me what to do!'

What the heck is he saying? Does he think he's a gangster?

'Oh, Simon,' Ulric replied and then sighed.

'Let's go get them. We can take them on.'

Them? Who are them?

Jeremy looked to his grandfather.

'Just because you were eavesdropping doesn't mean you know what you're talking about.'

'Yeah? I saw that letter. The one from T.H.M.'

Their grandfather's moustache stiffened. 'And do you have any idea who *he* is?'

'Well... no.'

'Let's keep it that way.' He wandered over to the cabinet and took out a bottle of whisky and a glass. 'I appreciate your concern, my boy, but someone's already giving me help.' He poured out a generous tot. 'This isn't a problem with the playground bully I'm having here, Simon.'

'I know. I just want to help you against this bastard,' Simon shot back at him.

Jeremy's eyes opened wide. He'd never heard him use such a word, not in front of an adult. Maybe that was his way of making himself seem more grown up so that their grandfather would take him more seriously.

'Don't you have some homework to do?' Ulric asked before knocking back a mouthful of the amber spirit.

Chapter 0.3

A few days after the visit of Alan Hammond, Ulric took Jeremy to the park to play on the swings. It was a drab morning and the slate clouds were threatening to unleash their venom over them. Ulric pushed Jeremy but the little lad wasn't swinging that high at all. He just didn't have the energy today.

'Granddad, who is T.H.M.?' Jeremy asked him.

Not this again.

Ulric remained quiet for a moment. 'He's just an important man who lives in this town.'

'Does he not like you?'

'Jeremy, these are not things for you to worry about.'

It seemed that Simon was starting to rub off on his little brother, the curiosity burning behind his eyes.

'Is *he* not a very nice man?'

'No. Not very nice at all.'

The old guardian knew that it wouldn't help matters by talking to a young child about his problems, yet it was tempting to just be able to talk to *someone* about them. He sat down on the swing next to him.

'Unfortunately, Jeremy, there are unfriendly people everywhere you turn in life, people who like to do others harm. And the way these unfriendly people go about it is very devious so they're able to get away with what they do. And you don't have a Superman or a Batman to help you against them. At least...' he paused for a moment and ran his bottom lip over the thick bristles of his moustache. 'At least not how you would imagine your superheroes to be. The reality is there are no heroes. They're only on the same level as the enemy.'

Ulric could detect from his smooth tone of voice that he was getting a little philosophical. He guessed that the little lad was most probably lost by now, his face etched into a frown.

'What about the police, though? Can they help you?'

Ulric smiled at his grandson. 'No, they can't. But someone else is helping me, someone who knows how to deal with these sorts.'

'The man with the mint humbugs? Alan?'

You don't miss anything, kiddo.

He knew the boy was perceptive. He had sensed an astounding brightness from him since the very first moment he'd laid eyes on him wrapped up in his daughter's arms in the hospital.

'That's right.' Ulric looked towards the heavens. 'Looks like it's starting to rain. Come on, let's go home and have some lunch. I'm getting a bit peckish.'

***

By the time they arrived back at the flat, they were soaked by the unrelenting shower. It wasn't just a few spots that the sky had been threatening, it was a virtual cloud burst.

'That's the thing about clouds, isn't it?' Ulric remarked as he towelled Jeremy's fair hair. 'Sometimes they drizzle and sometimes they pour buckets. Can't always tell what they have in store.'

When Jeremy had dried off, he walked over to the living-room window and peered outside. It suddenly seemed a tremendous view. He scanned the vista and picked out some of the landmarks he'd come to know: there was the Lafford monument poking above the buildings on the High Street, the run-down theatre near the seafront, and there were the mule-making arcades. Their colours were even more washed out as the rain continued to lash down on the gloomy structures.

It felt like he could see the entire town from there and he could sense some sort of underlying turmoil emanating from it, manifested in the form of this vicious rainstorm that attempted to cleanse a tortured world.

As he could imagine the waves of Moonlight Cove sweeping through him the other day, so too today he could sense the town's shadows creeping into his being, blending his colours into their own, like a black cat as it absorbed the falling dusk.

The young boy knew that this was where he belonged. This was where he was supposed to be. A stranger to the town at first, it had not taken long for Jeremy to feel a part of Dark Harbour and the shady world of his grandfather.

***

During the final days of term, Jeremy continued to walk around in his grandfather's shadow while Simon sat it out at school. Being the new kid there he struggled to make many friends, but there was one lad called Oliver whom Simon had taken a shine to, quite possibly because the boy had a yellow belt in karate.

The more Simon clenched his fists and the more his grandfather bashed his fists against his own head, the more fragile life seemed to young Jeremy. He felt as though he had to hold on to everything so tightly for fear of them slipping away through his fingertips, as had happened with his mother.

Jeremy had sensed for a while that something was waiting for him, a poisonous brume lurking in his mind, slowly creeping in to eclipse the light of his soul. It was just a matter of when it would come, but he knew its arrival would fulfil his dark metamorphosis.

The ringing of the telephone signalled its arrival. It was a Wednesday evening in July, and Simon had just completed the last day at school. He and Jeremy sat in the living-room watching *Blue Peter* while Ulric prepared bangers and mash for tea in the kitchen.

And so the telephone rang.

'Can you get that, Simon?' they heard their grandfather call out.

Simon was already picking up. 'Yeah?' he answered the caller.

The voice on the other end spoke firmly. 'It's time we talked, Ulric. Meet my man down on the beach in ten minutes. And make sure you leave those boys of yours locked up while you're down here.'

The line went dead. Simon slammed down the receiver. His eyes shifted towards his grandfather in the kitchen, his mind in overdrive, eyes sparkling like firecrackers.

'Who was it?' Ulric called out.

'No one,' Simon replied. He disappeared into his room but soon returned. 'I'm going out,' he muttered to his brother. 'I'll be back in a minute.'

'Where are you going?' Jeremy asked.

'Stay here.'

Hearing the front door go, Ulric popped his head around the door. 'Where's he gone to? Tea's nearly ready.'

'I don't know,' Jeremy replied.

A timer in the kitchen sounded.

'Can you go after him for me?'

Jeremy stood, grabbing a couple of his action figures. He just felt that he needed them.

It did not take him long to spot his brother. It was a muggy evening, but Simon had still gone out wearing his coat. From the promenade, Jeremy could see him standing far across the sands. It suddenly struck him that Simon's coat looked a little too big for him.

He ran over to him, calling, 'Simon! Simon! Granddad says tea is nearly ready.'

Simon pulled something from his mouth before turning round to face him. He looked pale, his hand shaking as it held a small box. As he slid it into his jacket pocket, Jeremy squinted. Was that a pack of cigarettes?

'What are you doing here, Jeremy? Someone's coming in a minute and I need to sort something out.'

'Sort what out?'

'Look, bugger off home, you stupid little shit.'

Why is he so angry? Jeremy could feel his flesh vibrating, as though the ground trembled as the leviathan of disaster approached.

Simon peered across the beach. There was a man in the distance walking in their direction.

'Go and wait over there,' Simon instructed his brother as he pointed towards a row of multicoloured beach huts lining the promenade.

'Why don't you come back and we can play with these?' Jeremy said as he held up Luke Skywalker and Boba Fett.

'I will later.'

Jeremy didn't know what he should do, but with Simon's heavy glare on him, he reluctantly did as he was told. Slumping down beside the beach hut, he looked back towards his unhinged brother.

The lone figure eventually walked up to him. He was a grown-up, but not the same as those you pass on the street. He had such a black aura and emitted a poisonous charge in the air, like a demon summoned from the underworld. Jeremy wanted to go back to his brother and just pull him away from him.

This isn't a movie I'm watching. I can still do something. I can save him.

The man folded his arms and began circling around Simon, words exchanging between them. Jeremy watched as he suddenly tore off his T-shirt and stood there flexing his hulking muscles, growling at Simon as though he were turning into a monster.

The next moments shot by in a flash. The man pushed Simon slightly and he lashed out, attempting to push him back as he might the playground bully.

Stop it, Simon, stop it! Just run away!

But his brother was oblivious to Jeremy's thoughts and the sick feeling that was swelling in his stomach. Suddenly the bare-chested man had a flick-knife in his hand. Suddenly he thrust it into Simon's chest and he toppled to the ground.

Now Simon was oblivious to everything.

But Jeremy instinctively ran to his aid, coming to a halt as the bare-chested man reached down to pull the knife out of Simon's guts. And it was at that very moment that an image was permanently etched within Jeremy's mind, a vision that would haunt him for the rest of his life, an image that would represent the darkness that had suddenly exploded within his soul. On this man's back was a tattoo of a spider. A black widow spider.

On removing the knife, the man turned to face Jeremy, but the young boy could only stare at his pale brother lying still on the ground.

Lifeless. Gone. Forever.

'Get out of here, kid,' the black widow man said, but all Jeremy did was sink to his knees in the sand.

He heard the man breathing unsteadily before taking a deep snort through his nostrils. The demon muttered some curse words before suddenly darting away, melting back into the ether.

Jeremy's mind was blank. He knelt rigidly, staring at Simon's eyes. There was nothing within them, and it pushed him over the edge into the abyss.

An abyss of such penetrating darkness.

***

For a good ten minutes Jeremy was numb, rooted firmly to the ground beside his brother as if some invisible force were holding him there.

He had no idea how much time had passed before he was able to stand up again. Wiping his eyes, he turned back towards home to tell his grandfather of the terrible thing that had taken place.

It all seemed normal as Jeremy returned to the flat. He slowly tiptoed into the living-room and saw Granddad sitting in his favourite chair, facing the television as though he was having a rest.

Something wasn't right though, and it took a few moments for it to register with him. In the kitchen, one of the pots on the gas stove was boiling over. Froth sloshed everywhere so Jeremy reached to switch off the flame. His hand burned as soon as he touched the handle and he instantly recoiled.

The dead feeling in his stomach suddenly turned back into one of dread. Couldn't Granddad hear the stove was on?

Looking at his grandfather's head as Jeremy made his way back to the living-room, he could see that his wiry grey hair was ruffled. There had been some commotion here. As the young boy tiptoed closer, he saw that Ulric's face was all bruised and bloody. On the left side, just above the temple, there was a deep wound from a very heavy blow. It had ripped apart the skin, and Jeremy could see the skull bone beneath. A thick line of crimson blood dripped from the gash onto his shirt.

Ulric was staring ahead at nothing, but when Jeremy peered closer, he noticed that there was still life in his eyes. In fact, they were slowly shifting round to look at him.

'Jeremy...' Ulric wheezed. His voice was thin and raspy, fading.

'Granddad, what happened?'

'You have to leave here. Go away.'

He struggled to speak, a queue of words battling to get out before his life was fully extinguished.

'Come with me, Granddad. Come with me. I'm alone,' Jeremy pleaded.

'Simon... Your brother?'

'He's dead, Granddad. Simon's dead!'

Ulric groaned as he closed his eyes, his grasp releasing in devastating failure.

'What shall I do, Granddad?'

His guardian's eyes opened again and focussed on him. He drew in a few more wheezy breaths as he stared within his eyes, but such was the fascination in his face, it seemed like he was staring far beyond him, into the far reaches of space.

'Find that man,' his grandfather said, his voice softening as peace came over him. 'The man... with the mints.'

'Alan Hammond?' Jeremy asked.

'Such a bright boy, you are. Find him. He will take care of you. He will take care of this...'

He fell silent, his final gaze fixed on the boy.

'Granddad?'

Jeremy didn't expect any more from his grandfather, and he didn't get anything more either. It was the last question he was ever to ask him. The fading light in his eyes now diminished into nothingness.

Now he had absolutely no one. Every single person he had ever loved had been taken away from him. A cold and cataclysmic rage erupted within him, and he sank to his knees and clenched his fists tightly. He closed his eyes and as his face turned purple, he roared out the most chilling scream he would ever hear from his lungs. Every other resident in that block of flats must have heard him.

An emotion he had never experienced before overcame him. Hate. Raging, destructive hate, engulfing his being. The image of the black widow spider with that hourglass of blood again flashed within his mind. He pounded his fists against the carpet so hard that his knuckles went red. His left hand began to ooze with blood.

When that wave of rage had passed, Jeremy was again rooted for another ten minutes or so. He expected someone to come knocking on the door to see what was going on, but nobody appeared. He knew that he had to leave the flat, but he had no idea where he should go. For now, he would collect some things together into Simon's school rucksack.

He went into his grandfather's bedroom and lifted the carpet in the corner. This was Ulric's secret hiding place, something he had shown him one day. The young lad had naturally never taken any money from it before, but now was an entirely different matter. There seemed to be quite a lot of notes there, but Jeremy didn't really have any idea how much. He grabbed it all and stuffed it into the rucksack. On the sideboard sat his grandfather's penknife next to some old leather-clad book that he'd often seen his grandfather reading. He took both the objects.

After a careful rummage, the rucksack was eventually full of things that Jeremy thought he might need. One thing there was no room for were his toy figurines. He would never need them again.

Just as he was about to leave, it suddenly occurred to him that he might require a torch to light his way through wherever he was to go now in Dark Harbour. As Simon had pointed out that time, it was a very dark town. Ulric had a torch beside his bed, so Jeremy grabbed it. There was just enough room in the bag for it.

He returned to the living-room to look on his grandfather for the last time. A tear rolled down his cheek.

'Goodbye, Granddad,' he said aloud, then left.

Chapter 0.4

Jeremy felt so empty as he wandered the town streets, like cinders from a bonfire blowing aimlessly in the wind. Although his grandfather had told him to search for Alan Hammond, he did not have the slightest clue where to begin.

When it reached eight o'clock, Jeremy had been walking around for over an hour, going wherever his little feet would take him. Despite the fading light, it was still stiflingly warm outside as though an inferno were raging nearby. As he walked along the seafront, tiredness began to set in his aching limbs. He slumped down in front of a café, hugging his knees to his chest.

The occasional faceless stranger passed by, but no one paid him any attention, this lost little boy out alone as night approached. He started to believe he might be invisible. No one was going to help him. No one cared about him. Everyone who *had* ever cared about him was dead, and the one person in the world that might lend a hand in his turmoil was hidden somewhere within the never-ending shadows.

A few feet away from him, under the glow of a street lamp, Jeremy noticed a red telephone box. A flash of inspiration suddenly hit him, a flicker of hope. Why not look up Alan Hammond in the telephone book and call him?

He darted inside the kiosk and rifled through the directory. There were a few Hammonds listed, but none with a first name beginning with A. He scanned through them all again, thinking perhaps he'd missed him. Nothing. He eventually closed the book, and then trod back onto the lonely streets.

His heart began sinking even lower as the sun disappeared below the horizon into the blackness of space. Nerves sparkled in his stomach like static. He had to get out of this place and he had to do it immediately. There was only one place in the world to go to now, one place that could help him: Moonlight Cove.

Night had fallen by the time Jeremy arrived at the woods and the young boy was dreading the walk through them. Alas, this was the only way he knew of to get to the cove. He reached into his rucksack and brought out his torch, feeling so relieved that he'd thought to bring it. He took in a deep breath as he shone the beam ahead.

Jeremy had not been so frightened before in his entire life as he walked through the stirring trees. He thought back to the story his grandfather had recounted, about the evil spirits that had once inhabited this place. The glimmer of torchlight quivering in front of him, he hoped so much that his grandfather was right and that the angel in the tree had warded them away. He prayed that she still floated there.

The leaves on the trees rustled in the faint breeze, sounding as though they were all whispering to each other about this little waif walking amongst them. He heard the eerie sound of an owl calling but Jeremy aimed the light straight ahead, not daring to point it into any unnecessary direction for fear of what it may illuminate.

The woods seemed to go on forever. As his heart pounded faster and heavier, he began running, the penetrating darkness creeping into his mind and dragging him into madness. The dread was turning into panic and as he strayed into the thicket and thorns scraped over his skin, he imagined they were the claws of witches and they were tearing him to pieces.

Thankfully, the branches began to recede and Jeremy could see the haven of Moonlight Cove. He had made it to his sanctuary.

On this night, of all nights, the cove was living up to its name. A gibbous moon hung in the sky above the waves that gently crashed against the rocks. Jeremy wandered over to the tree that his grandfather had stood beside and looked down onto the dim shoreline.

Having had so many emotions surging through him this evening, now, as he gazed on the reflection of the moon dancing on the inky expanse, he felt a sense of calm. It seemed as though everything that had ever happened in his life had all led up to this very moment.

Jeremy wasn't going to wait any longer, and so began clambering down the cliff. It wasn't a particularly steep escarpment but for a young boy in the dead of night it was a considerable challenge. It didn't help either that the batteries in his torch were dying after having used it so much in the woods.

When the bulb gradually faded to a feeble orange glow, a blaze of anger flickered within. With a shriek he threw the torch away and it smashed to pieces on the scree below. He would now have to rely solely on the silvery light of the moon that shone unnaturally bright tonight in its incompleteness.

He'd soon had enough of carrying the rucksack too and decided to cast that aside. As it sailed down the cliff, Jeremy no longer cared if he should need any of his supplies. He no longer wanted *anything*.

As he jumped onto the fine sand of the beach, he peered back up the cliff. It seemed a lot taller from this viewpoint, towering above him, making him feel cocooned within the cove. Here he was safe, and he knew that the threat he felt in the town was now far away from him, unable to infiltrate him here.

The young boy slid his hands into the tiny crystals of the beach and he held a sand-filled fist before his face. The warm grains slithered smoothly between his fingers and it felt very comforting until the salt caused his wound to sting.

He picked himself up and gazed over at the rustling waves. It was time to go and ask the place to work its magic for him, time to commune with the spirits. He began making small footsteps towards the shoreline with a strange sensation that something, possibly, was waiting for him over there.

The terrible events of his life replayed in his mind: poor Simon getting stabbed, Granddad with his head ripped apart, his mother slowly dying in a hospice bed. How he missed her right now, more than he'd ever missed her before.

The black widow spider...

By the time he reached the water, the end of the world, the young boy looked into the watery lunar reflection and then realised what he was really here to do.

This wasn't the end of his walk and he wouldn't be asking this place to help him. Jeremy knew he had to keep on walking, that he had to trudge his way into that murky pool and let it wash him away. There was nothing in this world for him any more, and Jeremy wanted to become one with the limitless expanse before him.

Tears rolled down his cheeks. He knew that he shouldn't be having these thoughts. Someone as young as he should not have to deal with such extreme emotions. However, he also knew that he wasn't just any little boy. He was different to everyone, as his grandfather had always said to him. There was a special light within him... or rather there had been.

He took one last look at the world around him. Across the cove, the swaying surf crashed around the skerries, sending up clouds of mist into the night air that danced over the sea like aqueous ghosts. Maybe it wasn't sea spray, maybe these were the benevolent spirits that lived here and who granted fortune for the lost souls that visited. They moved very strangely, and for a moment Jeremy wondered if they were floating their way over to him.

Suddenly there was an almighty crash of roaring froth to his far left. As he turned to look, he could see something across the cove from him, something... someone... standing over there on the rocks.

He now felt very different as curiosity diffused his bleak feelings. Who was that person and why was she standing all the way out there? He could tell it was a woman as she wore a flowing skirt which gently fluttered in the wind.

The tide was far out, and many of the cove's rocks were visible, dotted all around the watery vista like tiny islands. As Jeremy looked upon the mysterious lady, he wondered why she was standing on one that was a considerable distance out, one you'd have to swim to.

His heartbeat quickening, Jeremy stared at the lady on the rocks, seeing how the moonlight appeared to be a spotlight for her. She had long flowing hair, tasselled and tangled like seaweed. He guessed she was probably fair-haired but it was hard to tell from where he was.

Her clothes were unusual. They looked the sort of garments that someone out of a fairy tale would wear, old fashioned. Yet, her appearance did not seem out of place to Jeremy. It all seemed right somehow.

The bowing of her head as she looked down upon the waters seemed to convey such a heartbreaking sadness. Even though he knew nothing of her, he could feel her pain. Perhaps she would share the anguish with him, perhaps she might understand the torment in his own soul.

She turned to face the beach. Jeremy realised she'd seen him and an uplifting wave of emotion surged through him, sending him to the verge of more tears. She dove gracefully into the water, out of sight for a few moments. He saw her reappear about twenty feet away where the sea was shallow enough for her to stand.

As she walked towards him, her features gradually came into view. She was incredibly beautiful. In fact, Jeremy could not imagine there to be a more beautiful woman anywhere else in the world. It was difficult to guess her age, but her skin was soft and her body slender. The colours of her flowing garments were a warm mixture of mauve and turquoise.

Jewellery adorned her body: earrings dangling from her ears, bracelets around her wrists, necklaces, even silver chains ringed her naked feet, a rainbow of different jewels within them. She seemed so vivid, so celestial. She must have been one of the resident spirits coming to help him, perhaps even one of Neptune's servants rising from the depths of the sea.

She walked over to him and sank to her knees so that her eventide sky eyes were directly in front of his. A gentle breeze swept by them, but it did not disturb her soaking clothes and hair which clung to her. Jeremy looked deeply into her eyes that must have absorbed the light of an infinitude of orchid sunsets. At this moment, as they took each other in, Jeremy could see they were filling with tears.

'Hello there,' she spoke to him.

'Why are you crying?' Jeremy asked her.

She did not answer the question. She just stared at him as the tears streamed down her cheeks. At the same time a smile was appearing, a smile which completely lit up her face.

'I've found you,' she whispered to him and then took him into her arms.

In the comfort of her embrace, Jeremy now felt complete. He had gone from such despairing darkness to this uplifting rapture. He had tasted both extremes within the same night.

Both ends of the spectrum, and indeed everything in between, would be within him for eternity.

'You were looking for me?' Jeremy asked.

'I was.'

'But... I don't even know you.'

'We have met before.'

Jeremy released himself from her embrace. 'Who are you?'

Part 1: The Akasa Stone

Chapter 1.1

That's about all there is to tell about the story of young Jeremy Helliwell. After seeing his brother stabbed and then going home to discover his grandfather murdered as well, the poor boy went to Moonlight Cove to seek help. If you were to talk to your typical Harbourian know-it-all, as in that guy that sits on his own at the end of the bar and is an expert on whatever the topic of conversation is, this is all he would tell you.

Jeremy's rucksack and broken torch were discovered on the beach, leading people to think he'd walked into the sea in order to end his life. His body never washed up on the shore though. But neither was it in common knowledge that the living-breathing Jeremy had turned up anywhere.

Over the months following that fateful evening, pictures of the young lad were splashed around the town proclaiming his disappearance. With no legal guardians pressing the story, and with it being before the days of the internet and Facebook and plastic bracelets and 24-hour news channels, the search for Jeremy eventually fizzled out.

They still talked about the two brothers in the school playgrounds, and with an unhealthy degree of morbid curiosity. Some of the pupils who had known Simon even fraudulently bragged about 'What we do to the new kids round 'ere.' The more timid would speculate on what became of the missing brother. A rumour soon formed that the malevolent being Night-Shines Nick had returned to the town and taken him away. You can't really pay much attention to what kids tell you though. They do talk a lot of crap.

As the years went by, even the chatter within the playgrounds dried up. A decade or two later, as a new generation passed through the schools, Jeremy was largely forgotten about... Yet not completely.

The thing about this town is that there are many other exciting things to look for. And who really wants to discover a dead body? Face it, when kids go missing, how often do they turn up alive?

You see, people would rather spend their time searching for treasures than corpses. If you want to get to know this place and understand it properly, then you also need to be told about the story of the Akasa Stone. The search for this particular treasure has gone on for decades and has disappointed many would-be adventurers. Even so, they rarely lose their belief that somewhere in the area the stone is out there, waiting to be found.

And the other thing that people like to search for here is love. They like to search for *the one*. The mystery of this town seems to inspire such heart-bleeding romance in people here.

***

After dowsing his chips with vinegar, Danny picked up the saltcellar and sprinkled a generous helping of salt over them too. Working at the chippie this afternoon had been agony on an empty stomach. He would have eaten some breakfast this morning if one of his roommates hadn't kindly helped themselves to the rest of his Cheerios. Fortunately, his job had its perks. Being a hungry, hard-up student, he often took home free food.

Danny grabbed a wooden fork, picked up his jacket, and shouted goodbye to his colleague in the back mopping the floor. A short walk down the street he found a lonely promenade bench to sit on so he could satisfy his hunger at last. By some strange perversion, though, he was actually glad he'd been so hungry today. The ravenous sensation eclipsed other feelings.

For that same reason, he didn't turn up the collar on his jacket against the bite of the February air, the sea wind breezing in off the icy waters. The teasing grey clouds had been sweeping over the town one after the other, each threatening to unleash a storm but only spilling the odd drop. Not that Danny would have been bothered.

Now he was in the second year of an English Literature course at the college in Dark Harbour, Danny Adams's appearance had fully evolved into one of a tortured poet. The crumpled black jacket he wore over his work clothes made him look like he'd walked out of a charity shop a couple of quid worse off, mainly because that is exactly what he'd done.

He'd forgotten his striped brown scarf today. Typical when it was actually bloody freezing out there. The reason he usually wore a scarf was because that's what other intellectual poets seemed to wear, and Danny wanted that same badge. He supposed that writing actual poetry would help on that matter too, of course, but that was something he'd been doing a lot of recently. It had been necessary, a form of therapy, all to help with his problem.

After guzzling down the majority of his chips, Danny was now feeling quite full and somewhat bleh. He poked idly at the remaining ones with his fork, wondering why they looked so appetising ten minutes ago.

It was a good thing he wouldn't be working at that place forever. When his college days ended, he intended to move on to a job of higher esteem. He hoped to amount to something, that his life would have meaning.

Worrying about his future was nothing compared to the other thing that was on his mind, which had been ever since September. It was something that was getting more and more tormenting for him, but something he'd kept to himself. That was the best way.

He felt he was starting to get things under control now. It was silly to let these thoughts dominate his mind so much, but, being the poet, he could use his talents to tackle this issue and then hopefully move on with his life. At last.

The chilly wind picked up even more so Danny summoned the energy to start walking back to the flat. He stuffed the wrappings in a nearby dustbin and then pointed himself toward home.

As he sauntered along the pavement, his eyes to the ground, his thoughts soon came to his latest composition and he suddenly felt the inspiration for another couple of lines. The fervour had been intense, like static building in a storm cloud.

It had all begun the first week back after the summer break. Danny had met up with his two friends and, as it was freshers' week, they'd gone out on the town to try their luck with the new intake of students. It was all Larry's idea, really. The other two just wanted the chance to catch up with each other over a few drinks.

While Larry had been going through his chat up lines at the nightclub, Danny and Michael watched on with amusement, talking about their summer boredom of bunching flowers and catching chickens. Danny remembered being happy he was back with his friends, looking forward to the new year of study ahead. Everything was comfortably straightforward. Life was simple.

That was until she walked in the room: Stella, the best-looking girl in the whole of the town. Michael hadn't noticed her and neither had Larry. Even he would have known better than to go and ask her if she was a parking ticket or if her father was a baker. She was way beyond his league. And way beyond Danny's too.

Completely under her spell, he hadn't been able to keep his eyes off her. Suddenly his whole life had seemed to transform, as though all the lights within him had been switched on. They'd illuminated parts of himself he'd never known before, inspiring him to want to shine like she would shine.

Six months on, Danny was still haunted by her, waiting for whatever random encounter fate would manifest for him next, whether that would be passing her in the street or seeing her a few rows ahead in the theatre. That was the magic of this town. She could suddenly appear again at any moment. Each time she did, his heart would beat faster and he would be aware of nothing else in the universe. He was sure it wasn't healthy thinking so much about one person, someone he'd never even spoken to.

He'd thought about plucking up the courage and going up to her, introducing himself, channelling a bit of his mate Larry and attempting to chat her up. But what were the chances she'd take any interest in him, some Mister

Average student?

Maybe it was best she was confined to his imagination. If nothing else, she was certainly the inspiration for some great poetry.

Chapter 1.2

The tap started to drip again. At half-past three in the afternoon Devlan was dreaming he was beneath a giant cathedral bell, but when the sound woke him he realised it was only the plinking of dripping water. He'd been sleeping a lot in the day recently. There just wasn't anything else to do, but unconsciousness was a good way to escape.

Devlan sat up on his mattress and made a long grumbling sigh, annoyed the disturbance had brought him back to the dank greyness of his reality. He'd been there a week, a place out of the way so nobody would find him. No one in their right mind would surely want to come to this dump.

Before the incessant dripping would turn into torture, he got to his feet and walked over to the rusty sink in the next room. He gave the leaking tap yet another hard twist and wondered how long it would be before the bastard thing started up again. Being gifted at repairing things, he wished he had the tools to fix it properly. It wasn't as though there was a landlord to call to see to it. Then again, fixing a dripping tap in this place would be like putting a plaster on someone who'd jumped in front of an express train.

He glanced at the cracked mirror over the sink and saw his enervated reflection. Through the filthy sheen he could see the tiredness within the grotesque features that peered back at him. It was a visage he'd kept hidden throughout his life, for it was a sight that induced revulsion in everyone he met. He'd felt their thoughts so many times: *My God, what on earth is that thing?*

Devlan broke his gaze and picked up the shades on the side of the sink. He put them over his eyes and pulled up the top on his tattered hoodie. That was better. Now he looked acceptable, if he kept his lips sealed.

He shivered as a bitter draught whipped through the gaping hole in the roof. The building really was a complete wreck, but then it had been a while since it was in use. Devlan could remember those days. He'd even known one or two people who'd worked there, their names now lost in the haze of time. He recalled it had been a confectionery factory, and they'd made quaint little boxes of fudge and sticks of rock that were sold on the seafront stalls. Then the war had come and the facility was repurposed. By the fifties, operations had declined. Eventually the workers moved out and the rats moved in. And then, most recently, Devlan.

Looking back towards the other room, he noticed one of the rats now sitting on the mattress. Propped up on its hind legs, it looked towards him with its arms in front, as though begging, wanting more of the food Devlan had been handing out earlier in the week.

'I'm sorry, little one. No more.'

Just as he spoke those words, and just as the pangs gnawed his stomach, he crouched down and pursed his hand forwards. The rodent twitched its whiskers as Devlan slowly edged towards it, hoping he'd earned its trust enough to get close. Just as he readied himself to pounce, the rat scampered away.

Devlan sighed and sat down on the grubby mattress, feeling hollow. How miserable could life get? Forced to live in the most dismal hole in Dark Harbour. There had been only vaguely better days though, the occasional times when others wanted to hire him. Since being here, he hadn't spoken to another soul at all. Perhaps everyone had forgotten about him now. He'd never felt so meaningless in his whole life, a life that was as big a shambles as this old building.

His phone started ringing. Not expecting to get any calls, he'd put it away somewhere and completely forgotten about it. He was surprised there was even any charge left in it. Where was it? His hearing, which was as exceptional as his sight, swiftly pinpointed the location of the sound.

He reached under his pillow and pulled out the phone.

The name on the screen triggered a myriad of old thoughts and feelings that all screamed out like victims in a gas chamber.

'Hello, Floyd.'

'Devlan, my old friend. You hiding again?' boomed Floyd's gravelly tone on the other end of the line. His voice always came at you like a slab of ice.

Devlan angled the phone away from his ear. 'I've moved.'

'I assumed so. Got yourself a nice place?'

'Oh yeah, a real palace. I was about to call Henry Maristow. See if he's got any work for me.'

'You're that desperate? Things must be bad.'

He could hear the irritation in Floyd's voice as it was no secret that he despised that man. He enjoyed winding Floyd up though. 'No one else seems to have anything going.'

'Then maybe we should have a little chat.'

His mobile beeped. 'Phone's going dead. Want me to come down?'

'Yeah, why don't you meet me in an hour?'

'Your place?'

'Of course.'

'What's it all about then?' Devlan asked him.

'Oh, this one's an absolute beaut. Grade A stallion. I can feel the big time calling us because this is really gonna...'

Although his phone had picked a teasing moment to die, Devlan stood staring at it as though it might reveal the scheme that Floyd was concocting. No doubt it would be sheer lunacy. That man's schemes always were.

Many people saw the two of them as a good team, for both were very much feared within the underground of Dark Harbour, albeit for different reasons. Devlan could illicit fear in people through his natural appearance, whereas Floyd had been quite the monster at heart in his younger years. However, these days Floyd was floating the mainstream of business enterprise, and only hired Devlan for his engineering abilities. Judging by this call though, it didn't sound like another mechanism he wanted repairing.

He had to admit the phone call had lifted his spirits. Suddenly he felt wanted again. It seemed so long since he'd known that feeling, not that he'd ever really been that much of a friend to it in the first place.

The twinges of apprehension were there, however, as he remembered the troublesome roads he'd been down with Floyd in the past. But Devlan had to follow this road of intrigue. Whatever was round the corner, he'd deal with it. He hadn't got this far without being able to cope with serious adversity and hardship. Devlan was a survivor.

And it sure would be good to get out of this place, he thought to himself, as the tap in the next room began to drip again.

Chapter 1.3

Chasing a breeze of inspiration, Danny arrived back at his flat in no time. Although he'd been searching intently for the right words for his poem to convey his feelings, no matter how hard he tried, whatever he found didn't seem to be good enough.

He stepped into the porch and hung up his jacket. He had to close his eyes tightly and clear his head. Judging by the muffled voices he could hear, his three roommates were all in and he didn't want to bring the weight of his thoughts into the room with him. In a moment he'd no doubt be dragged into a more mundane conversation topic: which Bond girl was the most shagable, or which teams would be relegated from the Premier League this season.

After a few deep breaths and a rub of his forehead, Danny made his way upstairs to their lounge area. Michael and Larry were both there. His other roommate, Eddie, was probably in his bedroom as usual. He didn't really have a lot to do with any of them.

Wearing his sunglasses as he often did indoors, like he was attending some Hollywood pool party, Larry was sprawled over the settee shooting off whatever rubbish happened to be floating around in his head. Some empty crisp packets and two empty coffee mugs were dotted around him, and it looked like he'd been having a heavy gaming session this afternoon.

Michael sat opposite him reading a journal, or rather he was *trying* to read a journal by the looks of things. There were few moments when he wasn't studying.

'Hey, Danny,' Michael said, noticing him enter.

'All right, guys?'

'Completed your stupid game already, Danny Boy,' Larry proudly bragged. 'How long have you had it now? Only took me two days.'

'Larry wants to put this fantastic achievement on his C.V.,' Michael said.

'Damn straight I do.'

'Looks like we're all having a thrilling time then,' Danny muttered as he wandered over to the window.

'What do you expect from students in a dead end town?' Larry whined. 'I can't help that Dark Harbour is such a boring hole.'

'Come on, it's not *that* bad,' Michael said, quick to defend his hometown of which he was very fond.

'Yeah, not bad if you're into bingo or ballroom dancing, that is.'

'Maybe you should spend more time studying.'

'Oh, give it a rest, homeboy...'

Danny could tell this was going to turn into another Larry versus Michael bickering contest, so he mentally switched off and peered out of the window.

Far up the street he immediately caught sight of a woman. Although she was in the distance, Danny knew who she was.

It was *her*.

He could sense her, just tell by her aura. Her beauty charged the air, and now, as it always did with him, Danny was entranced. It was becoming a little eerie. Recently she seemed to be everywhere he went and everywhere he looked.

Larry suddenly interrupted his private moment as he waltzed over and lifted his sunglasses. 'Hey look, isn't that Stella Connoly down there?'

The intrusion startled Danny, as though his friend had no right to eye up his shiny thing. He wanted her all to himself, untarnished by Larry's smutty comments.

'You know her?' Michael asked, still sitting on the settee. He wasn't interested in ogling her as he only had eyes for his sweetheart.

'Sure as hell like to,' Larry said. 'She goes out with a mate of mine, Sam Allington.'

That was indeed the truth of it, the cold fact that tormented Danny deeply. Although she was only a matter of yards from him at this moment, she may as well be lightyears away. She was untouchable to him. Only special people like Samuel Allington were in her league.

'Get out of here. You're not friends with him,' Michael protested.

'I am.'

'Really? How so?'

'Oh, I know people, my friend. I know people. I tell you, he's one lucky chap, that lad,' Larry went on. 'Got his father's business empire to inherit and got the best-looking girl in the whole town.'

'And he's got some fine looks himself too,' Michael added.

Larry laughed. 'I didn't realise you were that way inclined. Did you write that to your beau?'

'I don't think I'm his type. Just as none of us is her type.'

Larry looked out the window again and shrugged. 'You never know...'

'Okay,' Michael said, 'you guys want to hear the rumour about her?'

They both turned simultaneously to face him. Being the only one of the students who'd lived here all his life, Michael told many intriguing tales about the town, and he delivered them all in a curiously sincere tone.

'Another one of your half-arsed stories?' Larry asked.

'My brother told me it a while back. It's a bit weird.'

They listened patiently.

'Yes?' Larry prompted him.

'The story goes that Stella is a siren, you know, like a sea nymph. She fell in love with someone, found her long lost love, so that's why she stayed in Dark Harbour. You know, with Sam Allington. Maybe she might take him away one day.'

For a moment or two, no one said anything. Usually when Michael told them a local tale, they would wait for him to say *juuuuuuust kidding!* even though it never came.

'A siren? You're certainly full of it, mate,' Larry said. He finally sat back down, his interest now waning.

'It's true.'

'I thought sirens were supposed to lead men to destruction.'

'They do?' Michael asked. 'I thought that was just women in general.'

They both laughed, but Danny did not join in. He was lost in his moment again, gazing on as Stella walked away down the street.

Larry yawned. 'Anyway, who's coming down *The Cape* with me to play pool?'

'I'm not sure,' Michael replied. 'There's a documentary on Channel 4 I was going to watch this evening.'

'Oh, come on. It's the weekend. How about you and Dan take us on at doubles again?' Larry persisted.

'You and Eddie?' Michael asked, slowly starting to consider it. He was never one for making decisions of any sort. 'I suppose it's about time we gave you a good kicking again.'

'What do you mean? We thrashed *you* last time.'

'No, you didn't. Me and Danny beat you five-nil.'

'Now you definitely are talking crap,' Larry said as he got up.

'Come on then, Diamond,' Michael said. 'Let's grab ourselves a table. Where's Eddie?'

'In his room?'

'I'll go get him.'

Michael, being the diplomat, was always keen to include their elusive flatmate on things. Even though Eddie was clearly a young man who wasn't bothered about fostering friendships, Michael still saw him as a part of their circle of friends, or the 'square' as he referred to it. He put his book down as he made a move.

Danny remained rooted to the window as he watched Stella finally disappear from view. He still couldn't think of the right words for his poem, couldn't even remember the lines he'd been composing earlier. It was as though a hurricane had twisted through his mind and scattered his thoughts everywhere.

Every time he saw her, the problem just seemed to get worse.

Chapter 1.4

Devlan felt edgy being out in public again. Hidden underneath his hood, he looked reasonably normal: a short and muscular body as sturdy as any tree trunk, his back forming into a slight hunch as though he'd been carrying a great weight most of his life. He wore blind man shades and woollen gloves; both were necessary to conceal his strange features. Without them, he might blend in with the garish ghouls and monsters painted on the panelling of the ghost train that he stood beside.

Friday evening in late winter and most of the rides were boarded up or covered in tarpaulin. The arcades were kept open all year so there were always people trailing through the grounds of *Floyd's Amusements*: old age pensioners who would visit at off peak times, fruit machine addicts, skivers. Nobody was paying Devlan any attention though, which was just how he liked it.

In recent years, Floyd had seemed quite tame and dispassionate as he'd laboured on with his business. The effervescence of danger had fizzed out of him with age. Devlan supposed that, at fifty-seven, Floyd was starting to get on a bit, starting to mellow and slow down, if indeed that was possible for a man like him.

At first it had been plain bizarre to see him take on these amusements, but the story went that he'd acquired the business in a card game and quickly appreciated the money to be earned. Without such a quirk of fortune, he'd surely be up to his usual tricks. Or he'd be dead by now.

'Still busy then, Floyd?' Devlan asked his old associate

creeping up behind him, as though he had eyes in the back of his head. He knew it unnerved him.

'Yes, matey. Yeah, soon be getting the new rides. I'm expecting a busy summer.'

Devlan turned round and Floyd towered above him, all six feet and six inches of him. His beanpole figure had deceptive strength to it, as powerful as his coarse, bag-of-gravel voice. That voice of his could hit you as hard as a punch from his right fist. It was not enough to intimidate Devlan, however; nothing ever did any more.

The skin on Floyd's face was rough like sandpaper, and his eyes were small and shifty, constantly jittering around so that nobody could focus on them. They were coloured a murky brown, like a stagnant swamp that would swallow you away.

He brought out a hand from his grey leather trench coat and stretched his long, bony fingers. They were inscribed with faded tattoos across his knuckles: 'fear' was written on this particular hand, 'pain' across the other. He was probably suffering a bit of cramp from the pen-pushing he'd been doing today, an activity his hands were simply not meant for.

'All right for some,' Devlan said in his quiet, gruff voice. By habit, he rarely opened his mouth very wide when talking, and Floyd was automatically leaning in closer to hear him.

'I'm sure you've looked after yourself, Devlan. Anyway, this new gig should keep you busy for some time.'

'Go on then. Spill.'

A grin of self-satisfaction formed on Floyd's face. 'You know the real reason you didn't get in touch with Maristow?'

'What?'

'Because he's on the downward spiral. Everyone knows it. It's not going to take much to push the bastard over the edge for good.'

'So, what? You want him whacked?'

'Too simple. Too pointless. You know, it's taken me a while to learn what I was taught, but these days I think I'm finally getting it. Cat has a mouse, he likes to play with it.'

'You sound so refined.'

'And it doesn't take a genius to know a bullet's too crude an option.'

'So, what do you want me to do?' Devlan pressed.

Floyd twitched his head to beckon him over towards the promenade. 'You're aware of Henry and the Akasa Stone, right?'

Devlan nodded. He already knew where this was going, but he wasn't going to let on. 'I've heard things. Heard he's looking for it.'

'For a long time.'

'So what? A lot of people have. No one is ever going to find that thing. I don't care who the hell claims they've seen it.'

'There's one place nobody has looked.'

They stopped walking as they reached the seafront. Floyd began gazing out across the grey waves.

'And now you want in on it?' Devlan asked, although it was more of a statement.

Floyd smiled an impish grin as though he was so pleased to unleash the great plan in his brain. 'Henry has invested so much hope in finding it. And if I were to find it before him... Oh sweet baby Jesus!'

'I can imagine.'

'It will finish him, Devlan. Destroy him. And hopefully his stupid organisation will go down with him.' There was a chill in his voice all of a sudden.

'I suspect that's not all though, is it, Floyd? You don't just want to rain on your rival's parade here.'

'What makes you say that?' There was a note of protestation in his response.

'The legend says this stone can give you... *abilities*, and knowing you, you probably think it might be some sort of weapon.'

'Well... we'll see about that, won't we?' His eyes blinked slowly and Devlan half-imagined a serpentine tongue was about to flicker from his mouth to lick his lips.

'We have no hope of unearthing it, Floyd.'

'I know where to find it, old friend. Do you? Come on, you know this town far better than I do. Tell me what you know.'

He could detect Floyd's resentment and determination bubbling away under his surface, as though he'd been keeping it dormant until the time was right for it to erupt once more. For years he must have plotted how he could bring down Henry Maristow, but then it had to be expected after what had gone on between those two. On one hand, Devlan found it reassuring that Floyd still had a bit of go in him, but he wasn't going to be swept into it all that easily just yet. Not until he'd properly assessed this bronco of an idea.

'I have no idea where that stone is. Nobody does.'

'Interesting,' Floyd said, smirking.

Under his shades, Devlan rolled his eyes. 'Okay, what do you think you know?'

'It sank with the *Tatterdemalion*.'

Devlan certainly didn't need any further explanation about that matter. Every Harbourian knew the tale of the pirates who'd sailed that doomed vessel.

'Your daddy told you this at bedtime, did he?'

Floyd snorted. 'I missed out on the bedtime stories. So the *Tatterdemalion* was before your time, huh?'

'Do I really look that old? That thing sank two and a half centuries ago.'

Floyd grinned back at him. 'You're always so cagey about your age. Anyway, I just want you to find that shipwreck for now. Are you in?'

Devlan pondered for a moment, stroking the coarse bristles on his chin. It all seemed straightforward: a couple of months at sea, perhaps he could even do some fishing again while he was out there. What could possibly go wrong? Apart from the fact he'd be working for Floyd again, the same man whose schemes came with self-destruct mechanisms that blew up in their faces every time. The same guy that would see an iceberg straight ahead and put the throttle at full.

'Yeah. I'm in.'

'I know you know the right people, Devlan. Your old buddy Harp. But whoever you bring in, just remember you're the only one *I* can trust with it.'

'This will cost a lot,' he said, already his guts sinking with what he'd just agreed to.

'Yes, yes,' Floyd said as he reached into his trench coat pocket and brought out a bundle of notes. 'Here's something to start on. Looks like you could do with a proper feed. And some new clothes, too. I'm sure you were wearing those same rags last time I saw you.'

A sweetener, Devlan thought. Because it all gets sour from now on. 'I guess rat soup won't be on the menu tonight,' he muttered so quietly that Floyd didn't catch a word of it. It might be a crackpot idea, but he had no choice. He couldn't have just stayed in his hole all the time. He had to take whatever opportunity the universe sent his way.

'This stone can do a lot for us, Devlan.'

'That's a bit of an understatement.'

A loud silence passed between them. Floyd's eyes were jittering with excitement, but Devlan couldn't pick up on anything else in them.

'If the miracle happens and we find the thing,' he added, and then felt the hairs on his neck stand up as he remembered Floyd's other strange quirks of fortune.

'Okay, I've got to go now,' Floyd said as he stuffed his bony hands into his coat pockets. 'Got some calls to make. Make sure you charge your phone up. I'll be in touch.'

Floyd walked back to his office while Devlan gazed towards the murky sea that had swallowed this famous pirate ship.

'Do a lot for us?' he said to himself. 'What are you looking to do with it, you old snake?'

Chapter 1.5

'Best of three?' Danny asked his fellow pool players as he racked up the first set of balls in *The Mermaid's Cape*.

It was their favourite haunt, an olde-worlde tavern that captivated tourists and students, like something out of a Tolkien novel. The establishment celebrated its history as a former brothel. Legend went that one of its ladies was actually a mermaid with a magical cloak that could grant men the ability to survive with her in her aquatic domain.

'Why don't we make it interesting?' Larry replied. 'How about best of seven?'

Slumped on a bar stool, Larry's doubles partner Eddie rolled his eyes. 'That'll take forever,' he muttered. Although they'd coaxed him out of the flat to make up the numbers, Eddie clearly didn't want to be there.

Danny rummaged into his pocket for his wallet. 'I'll get some more fifties at the bar,' he said. 'What are you all drinking?' Being the one who worked, he was used to getting the first round in. Before he got an answer from any of them, Larry caught sight of someone.

'Hey there. How are you doing, man?'

They all turned round. Danny's heart sank. It was Samuel Allington, Stella's boyfriend. Of all the people.

'Good evening, Larry,' Samuel replied cheerfully as he approached. 'Where were you last week?' He shook his hand warmly, as though Larry was suddenly the most important person in the world.

Danny so disliked him. Samuel Allington was too damn nice and sincere to everyone that it had to be fake. Or maybe he disliked him because there was nothing to dislike him about.

'Sorry about that. Had a bit of a sore head,' Larry replied, distinctly proud of it.

'We could have done with you, man. We lost 7-2.'

'Damn. Well, I'm getting in some practice with these amateurs. Usually do on a Friday evening. Hey, do you want to play?' Larry asked as he lifted the triangle from the pool balls.

What a sycophant. Danny wasn't starstruck by the high flyer at all. Samuel Allington may drive around in a real BMW Z4 Roadster while Danny only drove them on his PlayStation games, but that was no way to judge a person.

'Take my place if you want,' Eddie said as he offered Samuel a cue.

'No, no, I can't tonight. Meeting some friends shortly.'

'That's all right. I'll kick their arses on my own,' Larry

said.

Eddie rolled his eyes again.

'Be careful,' Samuel said. 'Larry's our star player in the league, you know.'

'Ah, we taught him all he knows,' Michael replied. Seeing that Larry wasn't going to introduce them, Michael took it upon himself to do so. 'My name's Michael, by the way. This is Danny here, and that's Eddie.'

Samuel nodded a salutation to them each, a bright smile on his face as he did so. 'Nice meeting you guys. You not drinking anything?'

'Yeah, Danny was just about to get them in,' Larry replied.

'Let me get them. What do you want?'

'Nah, you don't have to, man,' said Larry.

'Sure, no problem. You're all students, yeah? What do you guys want?'

He wouldn't be doing this to *try* to be nice, not with a bunch of guys he'd only just met. Danny figured it was easy to be generous when you had money to burn like he did, and when you had a girl like Stella to make you happy.

'Cheers, Samuel. I'll have a Bass,' Eddie took no hesitation to say.

'A Fosters would be great,' Michael added.

Samuel then turned to Danny. There was something of an irony in asking for his usual drink, so Danny opted for another.

'Yeah, Fosters too,' he said.

'Coming right up.'

As soon as he was out of earshot, Eddie shook his head. 'Man, that guy's a dick,' he muttered, and was promptly ignored. Danny, however, had to suppress a grin.

He had to be honest with himself, Samuel Allington really did seem to have an uplifting quality to him, leaving you with that same feeling you get on meeting a celebrity. As he began chalking up his pool cue, he gazed on as he walked across the room, like a magnificent eagle soaring above a field of turkeys. Danny realised he was a million miles away from being anything like him, a million miles away from being the sort of guy Stella would be interested in.

And would anyone ever want to leave a person like Samuel Allington? Was he, perhaps, as perfect as Stella was, the yang equivalent? Man, the two of them were like Brangelina.

But there was one positive to be taken from this little encounter; if Samuel was here, then maybe *she* would be too.

***

After Samuel the Saint bought them all a drink, they got on with their pool match. It turned out to be quite an epic contest. Despite his indifferent demeanour, Eddie played very well and they had Michael and Danny at three-all as they went into the final frame.

Victory was either team's and the four of them had their total concentration on the table.

With all the yellows and the reds potted, Michael had the first shot on the crucial black. He lined himself up at the rim with delicate precision, still unsure if he should attempt the difficult angle or play a safety.

'You can do it, Michael,' Danny said, anticipating the face-rubbing Larry would give them if they messed this one up.

After a very long pause, Michael gently tapped the white towards the black. The black slowly rolled towards the pocket, bounced off the edge and back against the other, teetering over the hole. Michael stamped his foot on the ground, but the ball wasn't going to fall.

Larry started chuckling to himself. 'Lo-sers. Lo-sers,' he chanted like a schoolboy as he walked over to the pool table.

'Miss this and you really are a knob,' Eddie said to him. It was probably his idea of encouragement.

Instead of playing the simple tap in, Larry blasted the cue ball at the black and smashed it in, the white proceeding to bounce off all the cushions. No in-off transpired, because that sort of misfortune didn't happen to cocky gits like Larry, whose pool cue now turned into an electric guitar as he performed his victory celebration.

'Bad luck, chaps,' he said as patronisingly as possible.

'Well played,' Michael gracefully conceded.

'We thought we should let you win, you being the star player and everything,' Danny said.

'Don't give me that. You were trying so hard. I could see it,' Larry replied.

He was right, but Danny didn't want him to know it, so he changed the subject. 'So that was nice of Sam to get us all a drink earlier.'

'Oh yeah, he's a top bloke,' Larry replied.

'Didn't realise you were so friendly with him.'

'You've got to get in with them, haven't you? He'll own one half of this town one day. Never know when you might need your connections.'

'Yeah, with a little luck he'll get you a job in his dad's factory when you finish college,' Eddie muttered.

Larry threw him an unimpressed look. 'Nah, I'm going to live the highlife with him, hanging out on his yacht, women on our arms.'

'And you reckon I talk crap,' Michael said.

Larry gaped at Samuel who now sat across from them with his fellow big shots. 'You see. One day I'll be going round everywhere with a permanent smile on my face just like him.'

'Yeah, right,' said Michael.

Eddie stood up, his attention clearly strained by now. 'You guys are obsessed with him. Jees. Want me to go ask him if he swings the other way?'

'Michael might want to,' Larry muttered.

'Anyway, that's enough happy hour for me. I'm off.'

'Okay. We'll meet you back at the flat, yeah?' Michael asked, but Eddie had already grabbed his coat and was leaving.

'See you later, dude,' Larry called after him.

Eddie didn't reply, sauntering out of the pub as though he were being chased away by a rain cloud.

'He's a ray of sunshine as ever,' Danny said.

'That's Eddie in a good mood,' Larry replied.

'What's up with him?'

'I don't know.'

'He's your friend.'

'Yeah, I'm not his shrink, am I?'

'It's like living with a teenaged Emo girl on the rag.'

'He pays the rent. We were struggling before. Want me to get him out?'

'No, we just need to be patient,' Michael said diplomatically. 'Come on, one for the road, guys?'

'Absolutely,' Larry quickly replied.

They had a little tradition of getting whisky shots at the end of the night, right before they made their way home. As they stood at the bar sipping their drinks, Michael and Larry were back to their eulogising of Samuel Allington, repeating how great he was, admiring all the wonderful things he did in the community. Being familiar with the fundraising at his church, Michael had heard about Samuel's efforts, how he would volunteer a lot of his time to an organisation that helped disadvantaged children, taking them out on trips and such.

It was yet another area where Danny felt he didn't measure up to that man. The student could barely look after himself properly, let alone lend his hand to good causes. Could anyone really be that perfect, though? Surely there had to be some blemishes to Samuel's character. Maybe he snorted cocaine or secretly downloaded child abuse images. Isn't that what all the heroes did these days?

Larry slammed his shot glass down with a belch. 'I gotta go shake hands with the devil.'

'Me too, I think,' said Michael.

'Whoa. You ain't shaking anything of mine, Mikey.'

'I meant *mine*, you idiot.'

Their bickering slowly faded as they walked towards the toilets, leaving Danny alone at the bar as he dragged his stubborn thoughts through his head. He looked down at the glass in his hands and swirled the amber fluid around. No matter how much he drank, it was never enough to numb his feelings. There didn't seem to be any escape from them.

Sometimes he wished he never knew of her, that she never even existed. But what kind of world would it be without her in it?

He took another sip then spontaneously looked up towards the main entrance. The door swung open and in she walked.

Most of the time she would be walking by on the other side of the street, or Danny would spy her out of the bus window. Since that night in September, there hadn't been that many times when she'd been in the same room as he, so this was clearly about to be one of the closer encounters.

Everything slowed down. The clamorous chit-chat and the jukebox music seemed to fade. Danny was only aware of her shiny-happy beauty and his heart beating rapidly in his chest.

She walked up to Samuel, naturally. He got up and kissed her hello. They both looked so happy to see each other, so full of love. He seemed so perfect for her and she seemed so perfect for him.

After some inaudible small talk, Danny continued to read their body language. Samuel was encouraging her to sit down as he would go to the bar for her, but she insisted it was okay for him to carry on chatting with his friends. He conceded as she zipped open her purse.

Danny's heartbeat quickened even more as he realised she was walking *directly towards him*. This was definitely a close encounter, the closest there could be. His legs felt weak. His skin flushed. At the last moment, she looked up from her purse and her body softly collided against Danny's arm.

'Oh, sorry,' she said to him.

Danny smiled nervously, his power of speech failing him. She had spoken to him. He had entered her world. His existence was within her awareness.

But that's all he was. Some random stranger she accidentally bumped into. That was his introduction to her life. Surely there had to be more to it than this.

He leaned back against the bar. He could feel her arm still pressing against his. She was *touching* him, and she felt electric as Danny's skin tingled.

Danny was rigid, trying to retain that physical contact with her for as long as possible. Such a long bar too, and of all the places she could have stood at, she was right there next to him.

He peered out of the far corner of his eye to see what he could of her. She seemed to be looking at her hand... at one of her fingers. And was she smiling?

Eventually she received her drink and the link was broken. Watching her walk away, Danny felt gutted, like he'd suddenly woken up with a crushing hangover. That was it. That's all he would be in the story of her life. Not a star-crossed lover of hers but some random nobody in a pub.

He knocked back the rest of his useless whisky in one. Michael and Larry were returning. Danny breathed in deeply.

He saw Stella standing above the table of friends. She was holding her hand out in front of them and they were all looking at it with gasps of delight. Of course, they were all looking at a *ring* on her finger.

An engagement ring.

***

Seven frames of pool were about all that Eddie could stand. Larry wasn't so bad, but Danny was just plain boring while Michael had his nauseating *I have to be nice to everyone else I'll be going to hell* attitude that was incredibly tiresome.

Eddie didn't believe in God, didn't really believe in anything. He didn't even believe in having a dream, or think he would ever discover the key to what he wanted to do with his life. It was a waste of time trying to find it, anyway. He hadn't come to Dark Harbour through choice. It was just that he had nowhere else to go. His worthless mother had dumped him here, if anything. She'd wanted to get him out of the way. Eddie knew it.

He stood outside Danny's chip shop eating from a tray of chips, intermittently illuminated by the purple light of the neon fish that hung on the shop sign. Before leaving the pub, he'd noticed there were still a few fifties on the side of the pool table, so Eddie swiped them and came here for his first meal of the day.

The smell of hot vegetable oil and the saline air

swarming in from the sea reminded Eddie of his childhood holidays. They used to come to this town for a week each summer. It was the only token of fun his father ever afforded him, before he left his stupid mother. The resort was local and it was cheap.

Eddie had never liked the place. Shadowed by thick clouds, the rain endlessly fell. Litter floated along the pavements, and the weathered buildings looked like they were all falling apart. Often he'd stay at the caravan park, surrounded by gormless kids who always had dried chocolate smeared over their faces and cherryaid-stained lips.

Then there were all the unpleasant rumours he'd picked up. Stories about kids drowning in the sea, devil worshippers sacrificing people in the woods. It wasn't a place he'd planned to return to, but the sadistic hand of fate had dragged him back to these godforsaken shores.

At least the geeks he was living with now were better than the stoners at his previous place. Now, they really were a bunch of pretentious arseholes. They'd smoke all night and talk to each other about incomprehensible existentialist crap as if they were being so profound. They didn't take proper drugs, didn't have the guts for a pill or the dragon. It had gotten to the point where Eddie couldn't get on with them any longer, so he'd stuffed his things into his bag and slept in a church porch for a week.

Before too long he got talking to some lad at the college football trials. Larry was trying out as a striker, the glory-seeker he was, while Eddie, being tall and lanky, went for goalkeeper. Neither of them made the team, only making occasional reserve for the B team. In other words, it just underlined how they were complete losers. Larry would dismiss it with a joke; it seemed he had the same warped sense of humour as Eddie.

As for the other two pricks in his flat, they were just friends of Larry. He'd heard their wonderful story about a dozen times, how Larry was out getting shitfaced one night because his girlfriend back home told him she didn't think the long distance thing was working out (or in other words she was screwing someone else). Heartbroken, he got trashed on Newcastle Brown and sang *Solitary Man* by Neil Diamond in the streets at four in the morning.

Michael the Good Samaritan and his sidekick Danny were walking back from the club and found him. They sat with him to commiserate about his heartbreak, took him home, made him drink water so he could sober up, and gave him the genius nickname of Diamond. And they all lived happily ever after. Until they dragged Eddie along to spoil their party, that was. Wasn't such a gay Enid Blyton adventure then.

Eddie paused eating for a moment and removed his baseball cap. His head was itching, as it often did with wearing the hat all day. He ran his fingers through his wiry hair, noting to himself that he should get another haircut soon. If he left it much longer he'd be sprouting an Afro like his father.

The neon fish continued to hum as the light flashed off and on. Gazing down the road as he munched on his chips, he could see a string of amusement lights along the promenade. Many of the bulbs had blown and were left to sway pointlessly in the wind. Typical for this dead end town. They left everything to ruin.

As he turned away he saw there was another hungry soul beside him. Eddie replaced his baseball cap, and the dog with the wide brown eyes continued to stare at him.

'Get lost,' he said to it.

The dog didn't move, instead misinterpreting his words as an invitation. He stepped closer to the stranger with the lovely smelling chips and licked his lips.

'I said get lost, you stupid mutt.'

Eddie couldn't see a collar. Despite its gentle nature, it looked a little wild, like a wolf that had trotted out of the woods. He had no idea what breed it was.

'You don't get the message, do you? Stupid animal. Here.' Eddie stabbed a chip and flicked it across the pavement. The dog mooched over to it and quickly licked it up. He then returned to Eddie and looked up with those big eyes.

'Oh, for God's sake. Here you go then.' Eddie placed the tray on the ground and let the damned dog eat the rest of them.

At that point, the chip shop owner came outside. 'Don't know whose he is. Been lurking round here a couple of days now,' he said to Eddie.

'Looks like a stray. Smells like a stray.'

'I'll call the pound in the morning,' the shopkeeper said before turning to go back inside as some drunk-hungry students came stumbling along.

'Hear that, doggy? Tomorrow they'll come take you away and put you to sleep. It's going to be your lucky day.'

The animal had already finished eating and gazed up at Eddie, cocking his head as though he'd been telling him how lovely he was. Eddie shook his head, then set off for home. He soon heard the pitter-patter of paws behind him.

'Look, just go home!'

The dog wouldn't take his eyes off him though, staring at him like he was his best friend in the whole universe. He certainly was a quiet soul too, a bit like Eddie.

'You're not coming with me. I don't want no flea-bitten mutt.'

He turned away once more, but the dog just kept following.

Chapter 1.6

There was barely any light in the rat-infested factory when Devlan returned, not that he needed any. He could see exceptionally well in the darkness, when he wasn't wearing his shades. A pizza box was stuffed under his arm, barbecue chicken and peppers, bought with the money Floyd had given him. He sat on his grubby mattress with a mouth full of saliva and opened it up.

In the gloom he heard scuffles, as though the bricks and rubble were coming to life. The rats were congregating, one of them even sitting next to him on the mattress. A quick flick of his arm and he could have easily grabbed it, but tonight the rats were back to being dinner guests rather than being on the menu. He tossed them his crusts. Neither Devlan nor his rodent roommates had eaten so well in a long time.

When he'd finished eating, he propped himself up against the wall at the end of his bed. He had some thinking to do, had to delve into his vast memory banks and retrieve whatever he could about this treasure that Floyd now wanted him to search for, this Akasa Stone.

After half an hour of meditation on the subject, every corridor he ventured down in his mind had led to a locked door. He'd known a handful of people who'd searched for the stone, but also remembered how they'd only discovered disappointment. It was a game for fools, for rainbow chasers. Deluded by its mystical lustre, the searchers of the illusive Akasa Stone had never fully understood what it was they were looking for. Perhaps this treasure wouldn't allow any old person to find it.

He was certain that Floyd wasn't aware of the true nature of the stone. Hardly anyone was. Devlan didn't actually know anyone who fully knew what *he* knew, no one who was still alive.

Perhaps by some beginner's luck, Floyd had stumbled upon the secret resting place of the stone. Devlan hadn't known anyone else to scour the sea; everyone just assumed the treasure was to be found within the town somewhere. If it was under the waves, how would that explain the people who'd claimed to have seen it? Then again, what value was their word? Who *were* these people?

With his thoughts going round in circles and the pizza laying heavy in his stomach, Devlan's mind drifted away. The room was frigid as it always was at night, but the rugged vagrant was now numb to the sensation. Being in the cold so much, he'd eventually *become* the cold.

Memories still floated around and around in his head, like diseased fishes in a stagnant pond. They'd suddenly dart this way and that as they escaped the larger predators that emerged from the murky blackness, the grotesque thoughts and visions unsettled by his reminiscing.

Devlan was used to bad dreams, had come to accept them as part of himself. He now knew to embrace the harrowing nightmares that plagued his mind like flesh-hungry zombies, wanting to eat away whatever hope and humanity clung to his soul's fabric. The low resonation of his existence was never meant to vibrate higher than the animalistic thought forms that he often meandered within. Devlan was clearly a freak of nature in his body, and the same had to be so for his mind.

Within the nightmarish sensations, he submitted himself to sleep, facing the deathly, decaying visions of people he once knew but were now long gone, now rotting within the grim recesses of his aberrant mindscape.

Chapter 1.7

'Where did Eddie get to?' Michael asked Larry as they sat down in the lounge back at the flat.

Danny had gone to get himself a glass of water before going straight to bed. Larry held a can of cheap lager as he would often keep drinking until the moment he finally went to bed. Michael wanted to wait up until everyone was home and safe.

'He'll be back soon. Stop worrying. You sound like an old woman,' Larry replied, taking a sip of his beer.

Michael frowned and turned to the window. As he got up, something slipped from his pocket.

'Hey, lost your wallet,' Larry said as he immediately reached over and grabbed it. Instead of handing it back to him, he sat there regarding it. 'You know, you can tell a lot about someone by looking at the contents of their wallet.'

Michael shrugged. 'Go ahead.'

'Hmm... a total of 43p.'

'There you go. Obviously a student.'

'What's with the jewellery?' Larry asked as he withdrew a silver necklace.

'That's the Virgin Mary. You know, that person who gave birth to Jesus?'

'Think I heard of her. Cash cards, library card,

someone's phone number. Want to enlighten us?'

'It was a lad in my video group.'

'Oh, a *lad* then,' Larry said like someone out of a *Carry On* film.

Michael rolled his eyes while Larry smirked. He was about to snap it shut when he saw one last item in there. It was a business card. Although black and rather plain, the name on it was intriguing. In the middle of the card was a red flame with two menacing eyes peering out from behind it.

'Halo of Fires? Who the hell are they?'

'Oh, that. That's something I'm researching.'

'Who are they? I've not heard of them.' He tossed the wallet back to Michael, but kept hold of the card.

'They're just another one of Dark Harbour's shady little secrets.'

'Oh, I'm with you now. Do you meet up at a secluded layby and hump each other like...'

'No! Not like that.'

'So, what then?'

'They're an organisation of thugs. They... go and see to people.'

'To...?' Larry prompted him.

Michael pressed his fingertips together in front of his mouth. It was somewhat difficult explaining Halo of Fires to his friend, what with Larry being an outsider. This organisation was in fact the one thing about his hometown that he was not entirely proud of, the black cloud that ruined the tranquil blue sky.

He'd found the card a few months back, at church of all places. As he sat there waiting to receive Communion, it was at his feet, the vivid black colour standing out against the dusty stone floor. He was quite disgusted to think that a member of the congregation had most probably dropped it. Why would they have had such a thing?

As he'd picked it up, he'd immediately felt the synchronicity. The week before, they'd been set their main Journalism assignment for the semester and Michael was deliberating about whether to do his project on the Fires. Over the years he'd heard many lurid stories about them, but there was one story that had stood out in particular, a story about a missing kid, something else passed on to him by his older brother.

Seeing the discovery of the business card as a message that he should pursue this subject, Michael felt that it was more than just a simple college project that he was about to undertake; God had called him for an important life assignment, and Michael had to shine his torch into the darkness.

He detested Halo of Fires, disagreeing with everything they stood for. He'd seen first-hand what they were capable of and, for that reason, he saw them as a bunch of bloodthirsty desperadoes.

'I guess you could call them professional vigilantes,' Michael resumed. 'If you want to get revenge on someone, if someone has done you wrong, then you can call these guys and they'll... sort them out.'

Larry was quiet for a moment, evidently not expecting to have received such a reply. No doubt the town suddenly didn't seem so tame after all. 'I see. And have you ever called them?'

'Hell no. That's not why I had the card. I just found it somewhere and picked it up out of curiosity. But then I did have an idea for something.'

'What?'

'My Journalism assignment. I'm doing it on them. I believe the Fires are involved in one of the town's old mysteries.'

'Cool. Will you need this any more?'

'I guess.'

But Larry didn't hand it back. 'What sort of things will they do? They go and chop people up into little pieces with a chainsaw?'

'I'm not sure. I knew a lad at school who once contacted them. There was a teacher he didn't like. Picked on him all the time. Lad couldn't take it any longer so he calls them... and the teacher gets a knock on the door one night.'

'Fascinating,' Larry said, sincerely for a change.

'Something like that,' Michael said as he peered through the curtains.

'Well, I'll keep them in mind. In case anyone kicks my arse at pool, eh?' He slipped the card into his pocket.

Part 2: The Fires

Chapter 2.1

Imagine you have a teenage daughter and she's recently all grown up, wearing lipstick and breast-hugging tops. She's now at the stage where she's learning how to get attention. One night she gets together with her friends because one of them is throwing a party, her parents away for the weekend. While she's there she meets a player, and he gets a lot more friendly with her than she wants him to. It gets past midnight and you wonder why she hasn't come home yet. Eventually the front door opens and there she is, looking like she reached into the cage of the cute little lion cub and got her hand bitten off. You notice her smudged lipstick, her ruffled hair, and maybe one or two bruises. What stands out most of all, and what sends the raging anger coursing through your blood is her crying. She's sobbing because she never thought her first time would be like this.

So what do you do about it? Call the police? How long would you wait for them to get down from their office that's in some other town twenty miles away? And how much trust would you have in them to actually do something about it? Maybe they'd just tell you she was asking for it.

Now imagine there was another option open to you, another organisation you could contact. Imagine you could go to these guys, tell them what happened, and ask them to visit the tosser in question and beat the living shit out of him. Wouldn't that be a more satisfying response to your problem? It's a service available to people in this town in the form of a skilled vigilante organisation.

Some people here hate Halo of Fires, others laud them. Some of the more philosophical Harbourians see them as a necessary darkness, a presence that encourages folk to stay in line more so than any threat of a hellish afterlife. The organisation has been around for years, and in this dog-eat-dog world it doesn't appear to be a service that will die out any time soon.

Henry Maristow, the man in charge of Halo of Fires, is known as the Seraph. He'd initially been brought aboard a couple of decades ago by a local lawyer, Alan Hammond, who wanted another Seraph alongside himself. Alan had seen Henry as the ideal man for the role, mainly because Henry knew the underground of Dark Harbour very well.

Alan Hammond had been the brains and the heart behind Halo of Fires, creating a morally conscious force that would aid victims by seeking justice through vengeance. His alliance with Henry meant he could recruit the perfect soldiers of karma and ensure their endurance.

When Alan passed away, Henry became the sole Seraph. With age increasing and energy decreasing, Henry still held onto the original tenets that Alan had asked his friend to stay true to. There were many things he'd asked of him. They had made promises.

Henry had needed something to believe in. He'd needed a way to escape the evil Network he'd previously belonged to, and which forged a burdensome tangle of chains that weighed heavily in his memories.

Over the years, Halo of Fires has continued to thrive, mainly due to the exceptional force of personnel the Seraphs assembled. There was one member in particular who brought a special kind of energy to the organisation, taking things to another level. He just had something within him. Something extraordinary.

***

The tolling of the church bells signalled to the town that it was ten in the evening, and to Vladimir that it was time to get moving. He stood up in his darkened room and stretched out his arm as he slid on his long, black faux leather coat. Glancing at the mirror beside the window he took in his reflection, just to check all was in place.

He ran a comb through his hair, his locks almost as black as his clothes. Even his eyes were so dark that they were like black buttons, the iris almost indistinguishable from the pupil.

Before he would gaze too deeply at his reflection bathed in the pale moonlight streaming into the room, he peered out of the window. The moon was full tonight, hanging in the sky above the waves of the harbour like a searchlight looking for wayward souls.

The vigilante lived in an inconspicuous chalet on the edge of town, up on the cliffs where the clouds sometimes hovered. On clear days he had an all-seeing view from his living-room. It seemed apt because this town sure did need looking over.

People never came round to his place, not even the other guys at the Fires. In fact, they didn't even know where he lived. That's how Vladimir wanted it, for he liked to withdraw from the world here and cut himself off from the constant disappointments of humanity. At home he would mostly spend his time reading. Whilst he owned a television set, he would only use it to watch the news to observe the slow erosion of society and the growth of crime. When it came to frivolous entertainment, Vladimir allotted none of his precious time to it. He wouldn't have a clue which song was at number one in the charts or which *X-Men* film they were up to.

The antique clock on the wall chimed. Hanging above the mantelpiece, almost as the centrepiece of his room, the clock was a constant reminder that time was always ticking, and that he had to make best use of it. It was as if he could feel every second of his life go by, listening to the demon that constantly taunted him by pointing out all the work he had not yet done, the endless wrongs that were still to right.

He had plenty of time before he would meet up with his colleagues, but he picked up his keys from the desk, patted his pocket to check he had his phone, then left. Vladimir was eager to get to work. He always was. Tonight was a little different, too; he was especially looking forward to chatting with tonight's target and discovering the true extent of his misdeeds.

In his rank of Throne, Vladimir was leader over the Powers, the guys who worked on the front line. He'd been the Throne for a couple of years now, and he hoped to climb the echelons to become a Seraph one day.

Vladimir lived for his work, the only job he'd ever had. Vengeance was central to his beliefs, central to his very essence, and under the wings of Alan Hammond and Henry Maristow, Vladimir shone in his role as an Angel of Karma, dealing out retribution to those that deserved it. It was, quite simply, a role he was born for.

The supreme energy he brought to Halo of Fires transformed the organisation into a resolute force. The flames of their inferno pervaded throughout the entire town, mercilessly burning down the wrongdoers without compromise and seeping into the conscience of those who *might* commit misdeeds. The Fires was a fate that was best avoided.

He walked briskly down the footpath that ran along the cliffs, the burgeoning blades of spring grass rippling in the sea breeze. At his normal pace, it took him only fifteen minutes to get into the town centre. He would be at the meeting point at least ten minutes before his colleagues, and it was most likely they'd be late, anyway.

Although he was tall with his six-foot frame, Vladimir did not have the action man figure to go with it. Then again, he rarely had to get hands-on with his work. Vladimir just seemed to have such a dense aura to him that when he glared at people with his large eyes, it was enough to intimidate anyone and overpower their self-assurance.

If he didn't have such an intense look on his face all the time, he would probably seem quite personable. He was actually rather attractive with somewhat elfish features, delicate lips, and neat yet heavy eyebrows that sat above his eyes in a fixed frown. His sunlight-starved face only contributed towards his gothic appearance. One could imagine he'd just risen from the churchyard grave, and was about to open his mouth wide to reveal a set of blood-seeking, vampiric teeth.

Walking along in the moonlight which cast his shadow before him, the young vigilante went over the main job they had on tonight. The guy they were targeting was a former major in Her Majesty's Armed Forces. Not that Vladimir was apprehensive by that fact at all. He suspected Jake and

Clint were most probably looking forward to this one. Finding a challenge for them was an impossible task.

Years ago, the major had done something very wrong, and he'd kept on doing it for a long time. It didn't matter how long ago it was though; crimes were never forgotten. Every evil deed sent out ripples of karma, and the Fires was the force that brought that karma back to them.

Vladimir had studied intently the profile of the major that Henry Maristow put together. A native Harbourian, the major had joined the army at the relatively late age of twenty-five. What intrigued the young vigilante was what the major had been up to before he'd enlisted.

The more he thought about it, the more it felt like they had a match. Could it be possible that Vladimir had found the one perpetrator that had evaded him his whole career? Was this finally the one?

In a little under thirty minutes, right after this ex-major felt the full brunt of his karma for the deeds they *did* know about, Vladimir would make that identification and discover whether he was guilty of another particular crime. And if so, things really would go downhill for this guy.

Chapter 2.2

The Legionnaires Club in the town centre is a members only club, traditionally for British service veterans. To get inside, patrons present their card to the person on the desk (although for the recognisable regulars this obviously becomes unnecessary). Non-members usually find that they are politely refused entry. This wasn't the case with the representatives of the Halo of Fires organisation as they discovered on this particular night.

Witnessing the sight of the tall and intimidating Vladimir walk through the door with his muscular Powers: the square-jawed Jake, and Clint, who looked like he could be Lennox Lewis's brother, the chap on the front desk felt it was best not to say anything and just let them pass through.

Heads turned when the three vigilantes entered the main lounge. They brought with them such a heavy atmosphere, and most of the punters hugged their pint glasses tighter as they intuitively sensed trouble.

'I don't see our Kolley,' Clint said to Vladimir who stood in the middle of the room scanning the faces with his gravity-eyed glare.

He eventually spotted him through a doorway where he was playing snooker. Gridley wore a black moustache mismatched with grey hair on his head, just like in the photographs Vladimir had pored over. The guy looked tall, bigger than he did in the pictures. He wore a grey shirt with the top three buttons undone, chest hair sprouting out, a gold chain around his neck, the type that guvnors wore.

'Through there,' he said to the Powers.

The people in the club sipped their drinks for comfort, timidly watching the wolves wander amongst them, wondering which lamb was about to be slaughtered.

Entering the snooker room, Vladimir approached the table and picked up the white ball. 'Major Gridley?'

'And who do you think you are?' asked Gridley as he straightened up, his cue in hand.

'Eva sent us,' Vladimir replied, slithering the cue ball along the tips of his fingers.

'Eva?'

'Yeah. Your daughter. Remember her?'

A prickly silence hung in the room, aggression and adrenaline charging the air like a raw stench. The major studied the three visitors closer, mentally calculating the muscular ratio. He shared a glance with his burly friend who stood across the table. Vladimir could tell what they were both thinking.

'This has nothing to do with him. He should leave the room.'

The other man did not move. He was big but he didn't have the same physique as Jake or Clint, just rolls of muffin fat spilling over his belly and sweat stains under his armpits. As for Gridley, he may have been military trained, but it didn't compare to the training the two Powers had undergone.

'I don't think so,' Gridley said, his voice rising to a bark. 'You know, I thought Eva would have been smart enough to put the past behind her.'

'How can she?'

'The hell's that got to do with you?' Gridley bellowed as he stepped closer to the cavalier vigilante.

'It's my role to ensure that your past catches up with you.'

'You three punks think you're going to do me over, do ya? I'll tell you what *you* should do. You should turn round right now and get the hell out of here, or we'll smash the lot of you to shit.'

Vladimir turned to the big-bellied snooker opponent. 'You really do need to leave the room.'

Gridley's friend was defiant and stood his ground with a stern face. Vladimir shook his head. The fool. If only he knew what happened when people interfered with Halo of Fires.

'Listen fella,' Gridley boomed at Vladimir, 'you need to get out of my face.'

Vladimir stared at him, inhaling long, deep breaths. Eventually the young vigilante nodded, a nod of resignation that could very easily have been interpreted as meekness. He turned around and grabbed the handle to the door. Pausing, he then suddenly slammed the door shut. Gridley raised his cue but Jake stepped in and caught the stick in his hand before it connected with Vladimir's head. Vladimir did not flinch at all.

Jake yanked the cue from Gridley's grip and then hammered it against his head, causing the wood to shatter into sharp splinters. The next time he brought the fractured stub down onto the major, who had now fallen to his knees and was bawling like a dog that had just been hit by a car, it would really tear up his flesh.

The muffin-fat friend tried to intervene, but Clint wrapped an arm round his throat and effortlessly kept him at bay. If it proved necessary, he would send a heavyweight's punch his way and soon end his pointless fussing.

The faces outside in the lounge area stared at the closed

door to the snooker room, and it didn't take much imagination to realise what was taking place on the other side of it. They could hear every hammering punch being delivered, every rib being cracked, the bloodcurdling shrieks, the 'No no no, please stop!' belting out. They knew the major to be a bit of a tough nut so no doubt he would eventually get the better of those three goons.

After about five minutes the commotion died down, yet nobody dared get up and see what was going on in there.

'Okay guys, you know what to do next,' Vladimir said to his two Powers. At his feet, a dazed Gridley lay in a splattering of blood and broken teeth.

Jake nodded, then flopped Gridley's body over with his foot so he was face down. He then produced a five-inch blade from a sheath around his leg.

'Come on, what are you doing to him now?' the muffin-fat man pleaded.

'Shut up,' Clint replied before tightening his meaty arm around the guy's neck.

Jake dug the tip of his blade into the small of Gridley's back. The major was still way too punch-drunk to react to anything.

'Do it,' Vladimir commanded, eager for Jake to get on with it.

With one fluid motion, Jake hacked with his knife, tearing through the back of the shirt like it was paper. Unable to take the suspense any longer, Vladimir crouched down to their prey and pulled the material away from Gridley's torso. Silence filled the room as the three agents stared down at the details before them: hairy flesh, moles, blood smears. One detail missing.

'Shit,' Vladimir muttered as he hung his head.

'Sorry, mate,' Jake said.

Vladimir spat on the guy then stood up. So it wasn't him. He didn't carry the ink of a certain tattoo on his back.

For his entire career with the Fires, Vladimir had searched for a murderer, a cold-blooded child-killer lost somewhere in the town. But Vladimir knew how to identify him, his giveaway feature the black widow spider that crawled upon his back. The search for this particular perpetrator would go on.

At least Gridley had finally reaped the seeds of another crime, the years of sexual abuse his daughter had endured. It was the nature of the universe; things always caught up with you in time.

Vladimir just hoped to address the karma of another certain case soon.

Chapter 2.3

After the trip to the Legionnaires Club, the three vigilantes had a few other minor revenge assignments to attend to. A journalist for the *Harbour Gazette* needed his car spray-painted a vivid pink after insulting someone in his column. A footballer needed to have Jake's fist planted in his face after cheating on his girlfriend with her sister. They then swooped on the town centre to see old Bloated Bluey, the town drunk who was always found by the river wearing his navy raincoat, a bottle of whisky in hand. It was nothing severe. He'd been harassing some people again in the street the other day so Vladimir wanted a quiet little word.

By two o'clock in the morning, they'd finished all their revenge assignments. Wandering back through the town, Jake suggested they all visited a nightclub called *Ice Breakers* to unwind. Although Vladimir felt like going home after tonight's frustrations, he agreed to go there all the same. At least a bit of socialising meant he could keep his finger on humanity's thinning pulse.

'Vlad, can I get you anything?' Jake asked him as he stood at the bar.

'Just a Coke,' he shouted back above the thumping music.

'Of course.'

'Always got to keep your focus...'

'Whatever. You should let your hair down every now and again,' Jake shouted back to him.

He ignored him. They were two different people, and

whilst Vladimir easily comprehended that fact, he did not expect Jake to.

The young vigilante understood a lot about people in this town, what made them tick. He could fathom why, at this very moment, Jake felt like losing himself in drink, that there were deep feelings inside he wanted to numb, and that alcohol was the only resource he knew of to do that. But just because Vladimir understood people, it didn't mean he was *like* other people. He knew he was of a completely different sort to everyone. No one had the same perceptions that he had. Of that, he was certain.

Looking around at the other nightclubbers dancing and drinking in the dazzling disco lights, he could perceive more than what they could. He could see within that kaleidoscope of rainbow lights and observe how they were trying to escape themselves. All around him were broken people and he could see all their lesions, and that, for the most part, they had no idea how to heal themselves.

Floating away in these thoughts, Vladimir's eyes sank solemnly to his feet. A familiar inner voice was kicking in and he did not like where it was leading him. He had to remind himself that broken people only existed because others had hurt them in the first place. People do people harm. He saw that plainly wherever he went. The ever-multiplying degenerates in this world had to understand their crimes, and for Vladimir there was only one way of ensuring that.

'We're going to sit over there,' Jake said as he handed him a drink. They made their way over to a shadowy spot beneath a staircase.

Jake and Clint would probably get so drunk they wouldn't know what they were doing. No doubt Vladimir would be arranging a taxi for them later. He didn't mind. It was all part of his role, looking over people. And besides, as an Angel of Karma he had to protect the other servants who worked within that same field.

They all understood the fatal dangers of working in the Fires, having had a sudden reminder just over a year ago. Quade had been an exuberant terrier, not quite as brutal as his fellow Powers Jake and Clint, and with not as strong an alcohol tolerance either. But he was spirited, a die-hard soldier always with that *What do we do next, boss?* look on his face.

Since Quade's curiosity had led to his untimely death, the guys had coped with the extra workload. Even so, promoting someone from the lower ranks to become a Power was something that had been on Vladimir's mind recently. Although they'd formed a tidy triumvirate, it would be desirable to increase their numbers.

It wasn't like they would put an advert in the local paper for any old jobseeker to answer. They specially selected agents, and they all took years to climb the ranks. They truly had to devote themselves to the purpose.

Vladimir swallowed a mouthful of Coke, the bubbles sparkling in his stomach. He was sure that the universe would bring along new candidates when the time was right. He knew all about the meaningful path-crossing that souls made.

Part 3: Searching Souls

Chapter 3.1

'Predictable,' was the word Devlan muttered when asked how he felt the project was going.

It was the twelfth day of the search for the *Tatterdemalion* as he stood at the back of a vessel with Captain Harp, waiting for the three divers to remove their scuba gear. The sunset-sparkled carpet of sea stretched out before them, seemingly forever, its secrets hidden beneath in the glop of sediment on the seabed. One of its particular mysteries would have to wait another day at least.

Devlan had made some logical deductions going by the general tale of the sunken pirate ship. If the vessel had run aground, then it would have occurred close to the shoreline. Having agreed with Floyd on the length of coast in which they were to scour, the first task was to make an initial sweep up before then working themselves down again. And then going up again, and then down, slowly working their way farther and farther out to sea.

The three divers were Archaeological Oceanography students fresh out of a university in Rhode Island. One of them was a native Harbourian, who in turn brought in his two American friends. They were all very geeky and kept themselves to themselves, or rather away from Devlan, as none of them knew what to make of the strange, hooded man who directed operations.

Along with their social awkwardness, the divers brought in a wealth of fledgling expertise with all their contraptions that seemed ill-fitting in the rusting *Alchemist*. Their multibeam bathymetry system fanned out sonar beams towards the seabed, and from this swath of signals they produced maps of potential shipwreck sites. So far the young mariners had made only a handful of dives, and today's expedition was once again fruitless.

'It's a wide playing field, but if they can find themselves that there *Titanic*, I'm sure we can find our old missus,' replied the old salt dog Captain Harp. He'd spent more time on these waters than anyone else in Dark Harbour, which was exactly why Devlan had hired him. That and the fact he was one of the few friends he had. In his early seventies, Harp had found a new lease of life taking on this job with his faithful companion, the *Alchemist*, a well-used powerboat trawler with flaking blue paint.

'Remind me to dig out my fishing rod, will you?' Devlan said as he gazed across the waves. He needed to get used to the prospect they were going to be at sea for some time.

Captain Harp roared with laughter, or more like exploded with it. He was always brimming with enthusiasm, like a barrel of frothing beer. 'Ha! If we can't find our booty, there's plenty more fish in the sea, eh Devlan?'

He climbed up to the helm and switched on the engines but they stuttered, choking out thick black smoke.

'Come on, my dear,' he pleaded. Perhaps the *Alchemist* wasn't used to being taken out so much, for today she'd been acting stubbornly. Harp gave the key another forceful twist, and then finally she agreed to come to life. 'Homeward bound we go!'

Devlan called up to him, 'What's up with it?'

'Think she must be in a bad mood with me.'

'Let me have a look when we get back. I'll have her fixed in no time.' It was no exaggeration. Devlan had a genius ability to fix malfunctioning mechanics. Getting his hands on rusty engines was what he loved doing more than anything else.

'That you will,' Harp agreed as he began whistling one of his old sea shanties.

His spirit certainly hadn't dampened, even though they were yet to find any clues as to the whereabouts of this shipwreck. On the third day, the divers had come across a wartime-era plane, a Spitfire, that only encouraged their thirst for discovery.

As long as Floyd was willing to pay, then they were all content. Even if they were to be out there for months without success, Devlan didn't care. It was something to do.

His thoughts were interrupted as Captain Harp began singing his shanty:

'Her eyes were as pale as the moonlight's glow,
As she stood by the shore, her heart full of woe,
Her love set sail,
To search for that grail,
And nevermore would he know,
How she loved him so.'

'Not heard that one in a long time,' Devlan said.

'No. Me either,' replied Harp.

He started on the second verse, the boat slowly chugging its way back to the harbour. What waited for them there was something Devlan would not have described as *predictable.*

***

On reaching port, Devlan slid beneath deck to examine the engines. Harp stayed on board while the oceanographers returned home to get their rest.

'Seen what's wrong with her yet?' Harp shouted down the hatch.

'Your injectors are playing up.'

'Blasted things. Want me to fix a brew?'

'Sounds great.'

Devlan heard Harp's footsteps as the captain walked across to the galley. Below deck, the damp air smelt thick with cloying fumes and oil. As he reached for a ratchet, he hesitated. Strangely, he was now picking up the hint of another scent. Aftershave. He knew that Harp didn't wear any, and the deodorants the divers applied to their bodies were too faded by the end of the day.

He stayed still, like a panther waiting for the rogue predator to come closer. As intuitive as he was at fixing mechanisms, he could also sense when there was danger about.

There soon came the unmistakable sound of multiple footsteps creaking on the boards above. He detected three people. Were they the divers? What would they be doing back?

'Hello. How can I help you?' Harp asked them. Gone was the chirpy tone with which he'd been singing his shanties.

'Captain Harp,' one of the intruders said. 'Made any healthy catches today?' His smooth voice was too friendly.

'No. No, we haven't gone a-fishing today.'

'You've been out every day this week. And every day last week. But nothing to show for it. How curious.'

'We been boating on other purposes. Private purposes, if you please.'

The spokesman perched himself on the side of the boat. 'Indeed. We assumed so. Not escaped our eyes at all.'

Devlan's muscles were rigid like cement.

'Thinking of finding yourself sunken treasures out there in those waters, are you?'

'I don't see how that's any of your business,' Harp replied.

The spokesman began laughing, a laugh that would fail miserably in a James Bond villain audition. It certainly did not impress Devlan, who crept closer to the hatch.

'Some things are best remained lost, Captain Harp. You never know what sort of trouble you may uncover if you find them.'

'We don't want no trouble,' Harp replied.

'I thought as much. By *we* you mean...? I'm assuming you're not doing all this off your own back. It would be of great assistance if you could tell me who you're working for.'

That was it. He couldn't risk him spilling his guts to them. It was time to even things up.

Springing up, he landed in the middle of the deck with a rumbling thud that seemed to shake the entire vessel. The spokesman immediately shot to his feet like someone had burst a balloon under his seat. One of the other men involuntarily shouted, 'Oh my God! That's Devlan!' as their cool composures dispersed. Devlan glared hard at the three of them. Looking back at him without the shades was an experience that made anyone's blood run cold.

The spokesman swallowed hard. Although he still had three against two, on account of Devlan being one of the two, he was still outnumbered.

Devlan's mouth turned to a snarl. The man was young, only in his twenties, an air of fancying himself too much.

'Herb,' the man whimpered to one of his companions.

The goon who was apparently called Herb stepped forward. He was at least six foot three. Most probably lifted weights at the gym every day.

He charged towards him, reaching for his throat. He was far too slow, and much too weak. Devlan darted out of reach in a blur of a move and Herb found himself with a hand wrapped round his face. In a monstrous flick of his body, Devlan then tossed him face first into the sea.

He then turned to the young man with the expensive cologne. 'It would be of great assistance to me if I knew who *you* were working for.'

But by now the man and the other remaining thug were backtracking. They hurried back onto the quay and waited for the humbled Herb to drag himself out of the water.

'I thought that you of all people would know.'

With that, they scampered away.

Gingerly, Harp walked up to him. 'Well, I think we handled that well.'

Devlan chuckled. 'That tea ready yet?'

***

'Those bigheaded bastards!' Floyd roared as he kicked his chair across his office. Part of the arcades complex, the room was decorated in a steel grey emulsion, no pictures on the walls, just a cheap paper calendar that was a freebie from a local Chinese restaurant. The air in there always smelt stale, like morning-after beer.

'That's it,' he went on. 'Tomorrow I'm going to see Henry and have it out with him.' He held his bony fingers up in front of his face and stretched them out before clenching them into a fist, as though he could already picture the fight in his mind.

Devlan hadn't seen him so pissed off in years. 'Floyd, if I were you I would just keep quiet. Like I say, I'm pretty sure they weren't the Fires.'

'This has got Henry Maristow written all over it,' Floyd spat.

'I tell you, none of these guys I recognised.'

'Who else could it be?'

Devlan sighed. Did he really want to put the thought out there? 'Come on. You know who else there is.'

Floyd went quiet, his small jittering eyes fixed in one place for a change, as if they were about to bulge out of his head. He stuffed his hands into his pockets as he paced around the room.

'You think they were sent by... *him*?'

'Why not?'

Floyd shook his head as though he were trying to shake the thought away. 'They don't know I'm running the gig?'

'They saw me. I would guess they worked it out from that.'

Floyd scrunched his eyes shut. 'Nah, time I saw Henry. Can't wait to see his face when I tell him what I'm up to.'

Devlan rolled his eyes. Deep down he was still the same old Floyd, reckless and headstrong. And a complete loudmouth, too. He couldn't say anything to him. Floyd was like a runaway steam train when he got going, and nothing he said to him would get past his impulses. The best thing to do was just temper him.

'Okay. But maybe leave it a few more days. At least until we've got the Donna Bank covered.'

'Right. Maybe.'

Devlan got up. He'd had enough. 'I'd best be going. Got another long day tomorrow.'

'Think you're getting close?' Floyd asked.

'Who knows? All I know is, someone out there is worried that we might be.'

'That's good enough for now,' Floyd replied as he picked up his chair. He sat back at his desk, the steam train coming to a rest at the bottom of the hill.

For now.

Chapter 3.2

Wednesday evenings were becoming a masochistic routine for Danny. At five o'clock he had a lecture at college, this evening's being on post-romantic literature. In the warmth of the lecture theatre and with the monotonous tone of the professor's voice, Danny found it a difficult task keeping his eyes open tonight. He never used to be like this. Recently his enthusiasm was like a dying fire.

After his studies he would have normally gone straight home, but a few weeks ago he'd stumbled upon an interesting discovery, something with the same effect as throwing paper onto his fire: it reignited the flames again, but only briefly. After missing the 1823 bus one week and catching the 1906 bus instead, he'd continued getting this later service from then on.

Danny felt a little awkward as he stood at the shelter. The curls of hair on his head were twisting around in the breeze like leaves in a storm. His mind was just as agitated, fixed on the one thing that it always was, that beautiful woman who'd hijacked all of his desires: Stella. Her name echoed throughout his head constantly, as though it beat along with his pulse.

Stella Stella Stella Stella Stella.

Danny was seriously worried. His lust for her had only increased since he'd found out about her engagement. It was all a hopeless cause now, but why couldn't he give her up? Why did he still keep chasing after this silly dream? He'd completed his poem now. That was supposed to straighten out his emotions, but all it seemed to do was make them worse.

He knew he should be up in the lounge with Michael and Larry at this moment, playing on the PlayStation or moaning about how badly their coursework was going. Instead, like a fool, he stood here, waiting to catch this stupid bus.

It arrived early by about five minutes. Danny climbed on board after the half dozen other people congregating at the shelter. After he paid for his fare, he turned and faced the seats. Which one to sit on? He picked one at the back, away from everyone else. Once he made himself comfortable, he then waited for what inevitably happened. *She* would turn up.

He glanced out of the window. Just a little way down the road was a leisure centre that had early evening classes. He figured that Wednesday's class taught yoga because she would have what looked like a yoga mat under her arm.

There she was. Immediately the fire blazed, oxygen feeding the flames. As she approached, Danny closed his eyes. It was a funny thing for him to do. Usually he would be fixated, his senses absorbed in her. Perhaps this was an attempt to cut himself off from her spell.

He heard her delicate footsteps as she alighted, her soft, melodic voice as she said hello to the driver. Coins exchanged, her ticket wound out of the machine, more footsteps.

Danny wished he'd opened his eyes two seconds later, for at that precise moment, Stella was *looking directly at him*. An electrifying surge juddered through his body, his throat going dry, his palms leaking sweat.

He looked aside, instinctively scared about what may have been given away in that fleeting moment, worried that he'd averted his gaze too quickly. Connecting his eyes with hers made him feel naked, like she was able to look deep within him at all the fervour that flowed throughout his being. It was best to keep his feelings hidden. She'd be freaked out if she truly knew about them.

He peered out of the window, but still he could not escape her, his eyes focussing on her reflection as she took the seat opposite. He looked at the pattern of the headrest's fabric in front of him, but that was no good either as she hovered like a nebula in his peripheral vision. There was only one thing for it and so Danny shut his eyes again.

The driver revved the engines and Danny's shoulders vibrated as the bus started moving down the street. Why oh why was he here again? Why would he submit himself to this soul-destroying torture? There was no way in the world she would ever be his now. There was no way that someone like her would take the remotest bit of interest in him.

Just at that moment, a curious thought struck him. Exactly what *did* he want? He knew how Larry would answer the question. What else would he want to do besides going up to her room and having his mind blown by some old-fashioned debauchery? But that wasn't it exactly. These thoughts had gone through his mind, but not *that* often. So what was it?

Maybe he just wanted to *own* her. Maybe she was like some beguiling gemstone that he'd spotted on a beach and just had to have. Perhaps. She seemed too delicate, too serene to be so physical with, like connecting with her in that way was too base, too crude. It appeared there was something higher leading Danny in all this.

Something higher.

Just what was the connection he was feeling with her? Could it be some sort of metaphysical part of him that dragged him along this journey, yearning for her? Danny sat up in his seat a little. It felt like these thoughts were leading him somewhere. Would it really be too crazy to think that he and Stella could be lost soulmates? There had to be a reason the universe kept making their paths cross so often.

He dared another glance over at her. She was staring idly out of the side window. What the heck was he thinking? *I'm nothing to her!* Here was Danny contemplating all these deep and wonderful thoughts and there she was wondering what she would get herself for tea. Or rather, what she would get herself *and her fiancé* for tea.

This had to be lust, so intense that he was mistaking these feelings for something else, something much more down to earth. He would have to deal with this. He couldn't keep catching this bus for one thing. That would be a start. Get lost in his coursework, give his friends more attention. Maybe tonight he would suggest they all go out for a drink, if not tonight, then soon. A lads' night out. Straightforward, no hassle enjoyment. Maybe he should start looking at the other girls out there.

They continued to trundle towards town. He knew how this would go. Stella would get off at the same stop. She would walk one way down the street and he would walk the other. He would casually glance over his shoulder as she got smaller and smaller in the distance, the fire dying down to a pile of meaningless ash.

But tonight when he got off he would just keep walking. This time he wouldn't glance over his shoulder at all. And this time next Wednesday Danny would already be home, arguing with Larry about whose go it was next on the PlayStation.

Chapter 3.3

The spring semester was fluttering along languidly and Michael wondered if he'd made the right decision in choosing the subject of Halo of Fires for his Journalism assignment. But that was the thing with Michael; he was never any good at making decisions. It was the curse of being a Libra apparently, as he read in his horoscope that Friday morning:

Is life becoming a little too predictable? Or have you become a little too predictable with life? You don't always need to take the same train route. Perhaps a change of your mental tracks will open up new possibilities to find the success you're looking for. Don't be afraid to make some firm decisions now and again!

He folded up the newspaper and pushed it aside. Somehow he had to focus himself. He was supposed to be reading the articles, not the extraneous crap that came with them. Still, he might save the crossword for later, until Larry dragged him out to play pool.

He decided to take a break from studying and get a coffee. Friday mornings in the library were usually quiet, the ideal time to get in some quality study, but Michael had other things on his mind.

He wandered down to the canteen, bought a decaf and a

sausage roll, then sat down on one of the stiff, metal chairs. He could hear the radio set behind the till playing a Beatles tune, *All You Need Is Love.*

Lennon. Another Libra.

Michael reached into his bag and brought out the letter he'd received in the post this morning, arriving all the way from Lucca in the Tuscany region of Italy. There were five pages, ornately written words on summer sky blue writing paper. As he flipped through them, he caught the hint of a fruity perfume.

Faridah had been an exchange student at the college and attended church each Sunday. It hadn't taken long for her sophisticated beauty to catch Michael's eye.

During their year of corresponding, they'd bared their souls to each other and grown closer despite the distance. She'd become his sweetheart, the only girl in the world. The only complication was they hadn't had the chance to meet up again.

It would happen one day though. As soon as Michael had the time and the money, or as soon as Faridah was able, then they would reunite. The others, particularly Larry, would rib Michael about it all the time. He was totally wasting the best years of his life on a girl over a thousand miles away.

The days of virtue and trust were gone now, it seemed. Michael was a rare breed. He still held on to his ideals, still imagined similar dreams shared by that certain other Libra whose voice he could hear right now.

Michael stroked his chin as he read over the letter for the third time that day. When he reached her signature and the seven Xs, he folded it up and restored it to the envelope. Time to put her out of his mind for now, to stop trying to solve that eternal conundrum about how they would get together again. Time to concentrate on his assignment. He munched on the rest of his sausage roll and then washed it down with the coffee. Where to next?

He wandered off campus and found himself walking through the town centre, past the shoppers out buying milk and bread, and the school kids queuing outside the chip shop. They were wearing Harbour High uniforms, the same badge Michael had been wearing only four years ago. They all looked so young and so uncouth, constantly scuffling and fidgeting.

Was the story of the Helliwell murders still to be found on their lewd lips, or was it all video games and *X Factor*? Maybe they wouldn't care anyway. Some school kids get murdered? They probably had it coming to them. They were obviously mixing with the wrong sort, young scallies who don't know better. Everyone in this town had been handed the power to judge, the means by which to seek retribution.

Michael continued down Lafford Street and wandered into his church, an empty Saint Anthony of Padua's. He feared before too long the doors wouldn't be left unlocked, but, for now, he could go in whenever he needed some inspiration.

Standing by the ring of votive candles, he looked up at the grand painting of the Virgin Mary. She stood on a mountain and beneath her was a fissure from which protruded a horn: the eternal battle.

He peered closer to the candles and saw their flames bend and cower under his breath. He suddenly pictured himself as six years old, a party hat on his head, a big chocolate birthday cake before him. Blowing out candles and his brother telling him to make a wish.

His wish as a twenty-year-old would be so different. Sometimes it was difficult to see any soul in this town at all. Michael didn't know whether the Halo of Fires organisation was the thing to cause the poisoning of the Harbourian psyche or the Fires resulted from that tainted psyche. Sure they may parade themselves as moral crusaders these days, but back around the time Michael was growing up, their reputation was much different.

They were evil anarchists. *Child killers*.

But how could he present to the world what he knew? He couldn't base an article on a story handed down to him in his childhood, even if his brother had been a credible source. He still needed more information.

After making some prayers, Michael continued with his spontaneous meandering. He found his feet walking towards the market place, opposite which was the town library. Perhaps he might find something in the *Harbour Gazette* news articles, the archives of which were stored at the library.

The rumour at the time, echoed within the local press, was that the Helliwell murders were part of a Halo of Fires hit that got out of control. The vigilantes had gone hunting for the grandfather, the adoptive guardian to the two brothers, but innocent youth was caught in the crossfire, a whole family exterminated. Or so the story went.

They never found the younger brother's body, but, even so, it still felt like a dead end story. No doubt they'd just hidden his body in a good place. So what chance did Michael have of discovering what had happened to him if even the police had failed to find anything?

As he combed through the microfilm at his workstation, he sensed there was something slightly out of reach, a piece of the puzzle that didn't quite fit. But it was waiting, or rather hiding, from Michael's persevering eyes. He'd often wondered what had happened to this younger brother... Jeremy Helliwell.

Jeremy! He saw the name in one of the articles and Michael now remembered. Michael's brother recounted intriguing stories about that young boy at their Sunday afternoon dinners. Within these tales were certain things that wouldn't have made any of these reports, that was for sure.

'I had to go looking, Michael. He was out there somewhere, Simon's poor little brother, lost on the streets. I had to find him so I set out on my bike, riding all over. But I never saw him anywhere.'

Michael eventually came across the article that announced the end of the search for Jeremy Helliwell. It appeared the authorities assumed the boy to be dead.

'But I couldn't believe it. He couldn't be dead. It wasn't supposed to happen.'

The young student paused from his reading and closed his strained eyes. The voice from years gone by still echoed in his mind.

'No, I don't think we'll ever find him now, Mikey. It's always the good that die young.'

He'd done enough research today, done enough thinking. His head felt dizzy, his mood scales unbalanced. Perhaps it was all a little too personal for him. Plus, there was no one around to interview. Not unless he reacquired that calling card from Larry, rang up Halo of Fires and asked them if they wouldn't mind having a chat about these murders. Who else besides them could he talk to?

He left the library and stepped outside into a blustery snap of wind. People wobbled around as they walked past him, but Michael's feet were rooted to the pavement. He didn't know where to go next.

If it wasn't so late in the semester, maybe he would think about finding a different topic. Still, it wouldn't do any good to go against the valuable advice in his horoscope today.

Somehow Michael would have to keep on track.

Chapter 3.4

Captain Harp was clearly getting fidgety. He'd picked up a curious habit of singing the first couple of lines of a shanty and then trailing off, the words seemingly lost. Then he'd wander off and put the kettle on, even though they were still drinking a cup from the last brew. It would have helped if he'd had someone to repeat his tales to, or to give a commentary to on whatever was rattling around in his brain, but often he would only have Devlan to talk to. Devlan wasn't a conversationalist. All he would do was sit there with his fishing line cast into the sea.

Harp now wandered over to him. 'Anything biting today?' he asked him.

'Only little fish.'

As that particular conversation came to an end, a seagull cawed overhead as the glassy waves plinked gently against the hull of the boat. The skies were completely clear, the sun beating down as though it were a midsummer's day.

These repetitive days weren't a problem for Devlan at all. He had purpose again. He had a reason to *be*. So often people had avoided him, and so he'd lurked on the periphery of life. It was only reckless types like Floyd who would take a chance on him, who knew Devlan could be a very useful tool.

It was unfortunate that hanging around with Floyd seemed to perpetuate the rumours, that Devlan was a brute who preyed on people in the middle of the night in order to satiate his craving for fresh human blood.

Just what is that thing? A vampire? A monster? Was he the Old Shiner creature, still haunting the unfortunate folk of Dark Harbour after all these years? Floyd knew how the misfit provoked so much fear in people, and he'd seen how he could take care of himself. Nobody ever got the better of him. He was just too frightening, too savage. Or so people saw him. Devlan didn't mind. Being feared by everyone meant the troublesome sort left him alone.

He sat back in his deck chair and breathed in deeply the sea air, the salty taste attacking his nostrils sharply. He felt a sudden tug on his line. As he stood and wound it in, a very large salmon appeared, flipping and jolting around on his hook.

'Always a bigger fish,' he whispered to himself.

'Devlan! Devlan!' Captain Harp waved his arms around from the other end of the boat. 'I think our friends are returning for their midday snack.'

The reticent fisherman peered over the side as a froth of bubbles sparkled on the waves. A head in black rubber eventually bobbed above the foam.

'Hullo there,' shouted Harp. 'I guess it's time for me to fire up the stove, is it?'

'Hold that,' said the diver, one of the Americans. 'We've got something.'

For a moment or two nobody spoke. Devlan and Harp looked at each other. Both of them could sense that it wasn't another piece of Second World War memorabilia he was referring to.

'What have you found?' Harp asked.

Chapter 3.5

Eastgate is a quiet street just off the bustle of the town centre. It's devoid of swaying pub signs or the razzle-dazzle of amusement arcades. Among the sleek premises of the accountants and solicitor, however, you will find a charming little café called *The Cheshire Cat*. For those in the know, this unassuming establishment is a gateway to something else, a shade within the shadows.

Most people never fail to pick up on the strange atmosphere of Eastgate, the air feeling stale and dead. Like a winding lane out of a ghost town, pedestrians would be forgiven if they thought the rest of the town's population had suddenly died in a holocaust.

But for someone like Floyd, whose perception was limp at the best of times, the vapid ambience of Eastgate did not register at all as he made a beeline towards the cafe.

There was only one thing on Floyd's mind this Friday afternoon, and that was how he was going to tell his rival Henry Maristow about his extra competition in the search for the Akasa Stone. When he reminded him that Floyd always, always got the better of him, it would give himself so much pleasure twisting this knife around in Henry's gut, especially when he told him that Devlan had found undeniable proof that he was closing in on the sunken *Tatterdemalion*. Floyd loved pissing over people's dreams. That's what his life was all about.

As he walked along the narrow pavement, fantasising about the look of despair on Henry's face, another soul appeared. It was in the form of a bright yellow baby duckling, offspring of the early spring.

The lonesome creature stumbled and flapped around as if it had just fallen off an Easter card. It made more of a squeaky chirping sound rather than a quack, tripping over its webbed feet as it did so.

As Floyd approached, the duckling squeaked even louder as if to say, 'Did you see which way my mother went?'

Floyd stamped his size 13 boot towards the pathetic

excuse for an animal. The chick tumbled from his trajectory and Floyd caught only half of its body. It was enough to squeeze out some of its innards, but not enough to kill it. Flapping spastically, it tried to free itself from the tarmac to which it was now welded.

He thought about leaving it to die slowly, but instead he stomped down hard once more to put its survival beyond doubt. The waterfowl population in Dark Harbour had grown unwieldy in recent years and they'd become a nuisance, especially at this time of year.

After the impromptu culling, he walked onwards to the café and entered without wiping his feet. Scanning the room, he saw there were a few customers sipping at tea and munching cherry bakewells.

In contrast to the white marble floor tiles, *The Cheshire Cat* had striking splashes of colour on its furniture. The padded chairs were a gaudy purple, the backs shaped like a wide grin. On the walls hung abstract artwork that didn't resemble anything to Floyd. It looked as if some three-year-old had squirted paint, grabbed her mother's lipstick, and then thrown up for good measure.

Behind the ever-gleaming counter was Nigel Lyons, the young man who ran the establishment. He wore a neatly trimmed beard and thin-wired spectacles. His hair was a mass of wiry strands that all stood like antennae on his head, able to pick up foreign wavelengths from way out in the cosmos.

'Hello, Floyd,' he said with a cheerful smile on his face. 'You've heard about my new blueberry doughnuts, haven't you?' The guy spoke in a way that suggested he loved his own voice.

'Is he in?' Floyd grunted.

'Who?'

'Maristow.'

'In what?'

Floyd scanned the faces in the room again. 'At his office?'

Nigel shrugged, confused. 'Whose office?'

Floyd threw him a blank look before heading for the exit, leaving the disturbed Nigel Lyons with the alien voices in his head. Having ruled out his café, there was only one other place Henry would be so Floyd backtracked to the town centre.

Along the seafront road were many of the hotels staring out across the stirring landscape. A lot of them dated back to Victorian times when the British seaside holiday of promenade strolls and beaches cluttered with bathing tents and deck chairs was in its heyday. Dark Harbour had revelled in that glorious era, as the posh and the riff-raff alike flocked to the shores each summer, indulging in the carnival of fun, building sandcastles by the rock pools, scoffing cockles and candy-floss, and breathing the healing sea air. The seaside was the gateway of mystery, where people could gaze across the waters and only imagine the distant lands beyond the blue horizon. Dark Harbour, like all the other coastal resorts, was like a glamorous movie star with hordes of admirers falling about her feet.

Then came the days of cheap airline flights, her fickle fans looking elsewhere within this ever-shrinking world, and the ever-crumbling Empire. Other countries offered a more exotic environment, even further mystery and better weather. The once popular British seaside town stopped being courted and was left to grow old in resentful reflection. It had been a glorious past, but now the seaside playground just gathered dust like the candlelit dressing room in Satis House.

Although entrepreneurs like Allington Senior had been practical enough to bring in other industries, certain people like Des Floyd and Henry Maristow had kept the tourist industry ticking over, trying to attract more than the daytrippers and working class holidaymakers who still couldn't afford those Easy Jet flights. Not that they ever acknowledged it, but together they formed a symbiosis.

Clarence Hotel, part of the business empire Henry had built up after joining the Fires, was a renovated establishment that stood out amongst the decaying, grimy-faced hotels of the past. It was invariably the place where any visiting dignitary would take accommodation.

Four storeys high, Henry's office was located on the top floor. Floyd made his way up the porch steps and clomped his boots along the marbled lobby floor towards the lift, pressing the unmarked button.

When the doors opened upstairs, he saw the grand mahogany door ahead. A shiny gold plate on it was etched with Henry's name. He stepped towards it, but only got halfway when he heard a voice.

'Hello. Can I help you?'

Floyd turned round. It was Henry's secretary, a woman called Aurelia. She was late-thirties but wore clothes as if she was still in her twenties and had never had any children. She was unfortunately pretty and thought her beauty was a power to wield on everyone. It had no effect on Floyd though who carried on towards the door.

'Mr Floyd? Henry is busy at the moment. You can't go in there.'

Now she was getting downright irritating. She wasn't worthy of a reply. Instead, he strolled over to her desk and towered before her. She was wearing a suit jacket and blouse, and showing off a lot of cleavage. Not that Floyd wanted to ogle her.

'Mr Floyd...'

At that point, he tipped over her coffee mug and the thick liquid poured all over her papers, spilling onto her thighs. She scurried to her feet, gasped, and held both arms aloft.

Winking at her, Floyd turned away and walked through the mahogany door, slamming it behind him.

Henry's eyes immediately shifted over to him but it was as if he was looking through him, not that Floyd expected him to waver from his telephone conversation to mouth him a hello. Already he was now gaping at a random object on his desk instead. A fly buzzing into the room would have received a warmer welcome.

The office was like a showroom: paint that looked like it had been applied only yesterday and a lush royal red carpet that, knowing Henry, was likely the same pile the Queen had in her study.

The large desk and his leather chair with the tall back seemed to dwarf him. He probably redecorated every year, the pretentious tart. Or perhaps surrounding himself with new things was his way of not having anything around that reminded him of the past.

There was one thing in the room that did not look fresh, however, and that was Henry himself. Floyd looked him over. It had been about a month since he'd last seen him. Every time he did, the lines on his face were more pronounced, his hair that little bit more silvered. His ageing wasn't as severe as what happened to the guy in *Indiana Jones and the Last Crusade* who 'chose poorly' but he brought that particular character to Floyd's mind. The fool sure had made some poor choices in life, the overriding mistake being that he thought he was cut out for the Network.

Their rivalry since those days was based on mutual loathing. The reason for the breakdown was down to Henry. It was all his fault, the screw-up he was.

As ever, he was dressed as though he was on his way to some important soirée when in reality he was going nowhere. He was more like a gentleman on board the *Titanic*, smoking cigars and listening to the band, all dressed up ready to sink.

As Henry continued yammering, Floyd hovered impatiently. Just as he was about to plonk himself in the empty chair and put his feet on the desk, something grabbed his attention.

His eyes opened wide as he mentally cursed himself for not thinking of this earlier. How could he have forgotten about Henry's wall display? A collage of photographs of local landmarks, photocopies of old letters, portraits of aristocrats, Henry had created this monument as though he was some sort of historian. Or maybe it had been curated so he would have *something* to show for the many fruitless years he'd spent searching for the Akasa Stone.

He'd only ever given this a passing glance before. But things were a lot different now. As he stepped over to the wall, a picture of Empringham Abbey caught his eye. It triggered a vague memory. Was there a grave here that Henry wanted to exhume? Had he believed that someone was buried with the Akasa Stone? But who? One of the pirates from the *Tatterdemalion*?

It was time Floyd tried to remember all the things he'd been told about Henry's efforts. Now he was in the same game he had to know everything his estranged associate knew. And more.

Floyd looked at the top of the display where a small but magnetising picture hung above everything else. It was a sketch of a tatty-looking necklace. Handmade wooden beads formed the main cord, and dangling from the front of it was a shiny purple gemstone. The stone was a strange shape, like a curved teardrop.

He realised what he was looking at. Deep within, he felt an odd sensation. Why was he so drawn to this stone? Why was he so drawn to even just a *picture* of it?

The room fell silent as the handset clicked onto the receiver.

'Why are you looking for this stone, Henry?' Floyd asked him as he continued to stare at the image.

He could almost hear the cogs ticking in Henry's brain as he tried to come up with a clever answer to a simple question.

'Salvation,' was Henry's eventual reply. 'Silas wasn't the only one who needed to send out an S.O.S.'

'*Captain* Silas?' Floyd asked him, turning around. It was Silas who'd captained the doomed *Tatterdemalion*, and who'd gone down with the vessel when it approached the Dark Harbour shore, and Henry's cheek below his left eye twitched. Floyd had seen that twitch before. 'Didn't do him much good, though, did it?'

'I suppose not. But there's no point in having the Akasa Stone if you don't know how to use it.'

'But you believe you're worthy of owning it, do you?' Floyd put to him as he approached the desk.

He saw Henry's strained eyes fixed on his. 'Why your sudden interest in this treasure, Floyd? Why would someone like you hold it in such regard?'

Floyd smirked as he sat down before him. 'Everyone else has their eye on this thing. Everyone wants to get their hands on it. And you know what I figured, my old matey?'

'What's that?' Henry asked as he rubbed his temples.

'I figured that I want in on the game as well.'

Henry's hand slid down his face and covered his mouth.

'I just came to tell you that it's time you threw in the towel,' Floyd went on. 'Like everything else, you're going to come in second place to me.'

Henry removed his hand and chuckled to himself. 'Well, I'm really up against it now, aren't I? Ladies and gentlemen, Grimsby Town have just entered the Premier League.'

'Laugh all you want.'

'You wouldn't even know where to start. You're too late anyway,' Henry countered, biting his lip after he'd said the second sentence.

'So, they weren't your men I had to deal with the other day?'

'What are you talking about?'

Floyd took a moment to try to read his face. Perhaps Devlan was right; they weren't Halo of Fires agents who'd intruded onto the boat that evening, as much as he'd hoped for that narrative.

'Run into a bit of trouble, did you?' Henry asked as he leaned back in his chair. 'You should make yourself aware what this game is about, who the other players are. It'll make you think differently.' He lectured this to him like some sort of high and mighty priest.

'They weren't much of a concern. Devlan easily saw to them.'

Henry rolled his eyes. 'Devlan... Where there's one, there's the other. So where have you put him on the search?'

'You know, I'm surprised you never went after the *Tatterdemalion*.'

'You're looking for that old thing? Now I know you really are wasting your time.'

'We'll see.'

'Why would it still be at the bottom of the sea if people have seen it in the town? Answer me that one,' Henry fired at him, his voice getting louder. He was rattled. This was going well.

Floyd stood up and admired the view from the grand window next to Henry's desk. Above the promenade he could see the expanse of brine and knew that Devlan was out there somewhere. Maybe they'd even found the ship by now.

'I realise I'm new to this game, but you know what? There's something I'm blessed with that you never had, Henry. Luck. So here's something I have for you, another picture to put on your wall, to remind you of the man who beat you to it.'

Henry sighed but it was overcooked. 'Is that so?'

'One thing first. The picture up there. The one of the stone. Where did you get it?'

'From a book in the town library. George Styleman L'Estrange. He spent a long time searching for the stone early part of last century. Everyone who knows about the Akasa Stone knows about L'Estrange.'

Floyd rummaged into the inside pocket of his trench coat. He pulled out a Polaroid photograph and tossed it onto Henry's desk. Once his former cohort had put his glasses on to examine it, he gasped.

Floyd grinned to himself as he left the room.

Chapter 3.6

As night descended, another life form ventured into the bleak no-man's-land of Eastgate. Blending in almost seamlessly was Vladimir, his pallid complexion the only distinguishable feature in the gloom.

Not far along from *The Cheshire Cat* was a narrow jetty that led to the rear of *Clarence Hotel*. It was the route the Halo of Fires operatives took to get to Henry's office, bringing them to an external fire escape stairway. Vladimir made his way up there.

When he stepped inside and walked through the mahogany door, he saw that the light was on at the desk, but Henry was not sitting at it. Instead he stood in front of his wall display staring up at the picture of the Akasa Stone. He'd probably been there for an hour or more, lost in his thoughts. He often did that.

'What's up?' Vladimir asked him as he sat down in the

chair at Henry's desk, ready for their Friday night meeting. The seat wasn't warm, but he had the sense that someone had been sitting in it recently.

Henry remained rooted to the spot as he stared at the picture on the wall like someone who'd gone on a hypnotist's stage and been compelled into portraying a praying Jew.

It was Vladimir's next question that brought him back into the room.

'What's this?'

Henry lowered his head to the floor. 'Another piece of the puzzle.'

Vladimir picked the Polaroid photograph up off the desk. The image was grainy and badly lit but he saw it depicted the steering helm from a ship. It was missing a few spokes and consumed by rot, but that was not surprising considering that it was from an old vessel. He realised it was a very old vessel indeed when he read the lettering around the rim.

'*Tatterdemalion*... Who gave you this?'

Henry opened his mouth to respond, but then stopped himself.

'Floyd?' Vladimir asked. 'It's Floyd, isn't it? He's found the wreck of the *Tatterdemalion*.'

'So it seems.'

'We need to keep an eye on him. What does he think he's up to?'

'Any excuse to meddle in his affairs. Vladimir, I've never met anyone who was so clear about who they did and did not like.'

'I just know people. I know the black souls of this town.'

He made no secret of the fact he detested Floyd. The guy was a time bomb of wickedness that might go off at any second, and Vladimir could see that, years before his time, he'd already exploded his evil to devastating effect. The dust of those old explosions hung in his aura like a noxious fume, and if it had been anyone else, the Fires would have dealt with them and made them pay for their historical misdeeds.

But nothing would ever be authorised when it came to

Floyd, not officially. Given the company he mixed with, given his connections, he was untouchable.

It was a cause of eternal frustration for Vladimir. It wasn't supposed to matter who you were; Karma was universal.

And still a certain thought dangled in his mind, even after Henry had warned him off.

It's not him. He's not the killer you're looking for.

Even so, he just couldn't categorically scrub Floyd off as a candidate. Vladimir had seen those tattoos on his fingers. He had to see for his own eyes whether the needle had ever gone to the guy's back to accept Henry's word. Although his master knew the man a lot better than he did, still the thought persisted. How was Henry so sure?

And every time Floyd's name came up, he couldn't help the feeling that it was another little nudge from the universe.

'No. You don't need to monitor him,' Henry said. 'Seems someone else is already doing that.'

'So why is Floyd looking for sunken ships all of a sudden?'

'Why do you think?'

'Bought into the fairy tale too, did he?'

'I just hate to think what he'd be capable of if he got his hands on the Akasa Stone.'

'I wouldn't worry about that.'

'Yes. Well, you don't believe that anyone will ever find it, do you?'

'Wouldn't they have done so by now, Henry? After all these years?'

Vladimir felt his master scrutinising him, as though he might find answers, another clue. It was so typical of Henry, always searching, even when it was a blind alley.

'You think,' started Henry, before clearing his throat, 'you think I'm just a stupid old man. For chasing after this treasure.'

Beneath Vladimir's ice hard aura he could feel his profound frustration, amplified by the similar inner demon that burned inside himself, his own search that had eluded him for so long.

'You're not stupid, Henry. Everyone has something they search for.'

'The thing is, in the light of what I've learnt this evening, that Floyd has now joined the race, I think we must act.'

'How do you mean?'

'There's someone I need to talk to.'

Vladimir sighed. He knew where this was going. 'We already have work tonight.'

'I appreciate that. But some things are even more important.'

'We can't just abandon it. This is what we do, seek justice. We're avengers, not archaeologists.'

'I promise I won't keep asking like this. I just fear that if we don't act now, time will run out.'

Vladimir suppressed another sigh. 'You're the Seraph.'

'I heard something the other day. Something that should prove that Floyd definitely is wasting his time scouring the seabed.'

Vladimir cocked his head and squinted his black button eyes. 'Then you'd better tell me about it.'

Chapter 3.7

Floyd walked to the end of the quay where the *Alchemist* was moored, the waves sloshing gently against its hull. In the near distance, a bell from a ship ringed rhythmically to the swaying of the inky black waters. Apart from these sounds it was eerily quiet, and for most people if they had been there at that precise moment and seen what Floyd saw, terror would have clawed at their guts.

He shuddered as he paused to collect himself. A pair of red eyes glared at him from the old trawler. It had been a while since he'd seen Devlan without the shades and it seemed he would never become desensitised to the dread those eyes induced. They were demonic, like a portal to the fires of hell. Gradually he subdued his twinge of fear as carried on up to the boat.

'Not got a home to go to?' Floyd asked him.

'This is my home these days,' Devlan replied.

'A boat?'

'You should have seen my previous place.'

That had always been his way, drifting from one nook of Dark Harbour to the other, dwelling wherever the currents of life floated him. It wasn't straightforward for him to fit in anywhere, not easy to get a normal home and live a normal life. But then there was one blatant reason he couldn't do this: Devlan wasn't normal.

Floyd stepped on board and perched himself on the gunwale.

'What did you want?' Devlan asked him.

'I went to see my old mate Henry at his office today.'

Devlan raised his arm to silence him. 'Why don't you step into *my* office?' He rose and ushered him into the cabin.

Inside he asked, 'What did you tell him?' as soon as he'd closed the door behind them. They both sat down at the table.

Floyd did not hold his gaze, instead looking out the porthole over the harbour. 'Showed him the photo, didn't I? I got him so worried. Can't wait to dangle that stone in his face and crush his soul.'

As he spoke, Devlan buried his head in his gloved hand. 'Floyd, why don't you learn to keep your mouth shut for once?'

It wasn't the reaction he'd wanted. It seemed his accomplice was on a different wavelength, so Floyd suppressed his tongue.

'You already know we're being watched,' the freak continued, 'and now we have even more information. Why are you showing everyone your cards?'

Because I want to taunt the hopeless fool. That was the whole point of this!

'Not that you've actually found the wreck,' he shot back at him. 'All you've given me so far is that stupid steering wheel.' They both glanced across the cabin to where the helm of the *Tatterdemalion* still sat, a token to inspire their continuing endeavours. 'Any closer to finding the rest of it?'

'We discovered a couple of other things that look like they were from the ship. The point is, we're close. Very close.'

'When you do find it, just so you know exactly what it is you're looking for...' Floyd delved into his trench coat pocket. 'I got hold of this after visiting Henry today.' He unfolded the page he'd torn out of a book.

Devlan ran his gloved fingers over it. 'The Akasa Stone. How I understood it to look. Which makes me ask, if someone was able to draw it, wouldn't that indicate it wasn't hidden from view at the bottom of the sea all this time?'

'Oh, not you as well. The pirates on board. They didn't all drown. The survivors would have seen it, described it to this artist.'

'Perhaps.'

'Just face it, Devlan, however long you've been around, you don't know everything about this town.'

For a moment, the way he stared back at him, Floyd wished he hadn't shot that at him.

'Okay Floyd, answer me this one: Do you know why people have been searching for this stone for centuries? Do you know what it is about the Akasa Stone that makes people want to find it? Well?'

'They want glory. Henry wants to achieve something after being a loser his whole life.'

'But this isn't just any old gemstone, is it, Floyd? Not something to stick in a museum or sell on eBay. That stone it... it has powers.'

He noticed Devlan snap his mouth shut. There had been an unmistakable passion to the old freak's voice. Was he being drawn to this thing too? Did he have his own plans for it?

He broke his train of thought and stood up. 'Let's just assume the Fires will be watching us too now. Once we find the wreck, we'll throw them off track. Send the boat out to random areas as a decoy. The only people who need to know the location are you and me.'

Although the conversation hadn't gone as he'd imagined, Floyd felt it had put his mind into sharp focus.

'Harp too, of course. And the divers. They'll know.'

'Can we trust them?'

'Harp yes. The divers? I'll make sure of it,' replied Devlan with a rare grin on his face, an expression that produced yet another twinge of fear in him that evening.

'Good. Okay, I've got to go. I'll speak to you soon.'

As he stood back out on the quay, all he could hear was the tolling of that ship's bell, as though it was sounding as a reminder of all those unfortunate souls who'd drowned in the sinking of the *Tatterdemalion*. It resonated with his being, for Floyd was not just the one who had tolled the bell for others so many times before, Floyd *was* the bell. It was all part of his teaching, his purpose.

He'd been taught to destroy, and as an agent of destruction he'd had to separate himself from the great continent of humanity. It was strange how his old life was coming back to him so much recently. And it was strange how, in his re-membering, he saw how he was a *member* of something else entirely, something beyond the hopeless searchers like Henry who struggled so much at life.

He walked onwards feeling thrilled and more like his old self. It had been a long time since he'd felt this way. He loved destroying people, and ensuring Henry Maristow's soul suffered that fate would be the most satisfying achievement of his entire life.

Of course he understood about the powers of the Akasa Stone. When he found it, his star would irrevocably rise. He'd seen first-hand the rise and fall of an overlord in this town. Acquiring this treasure would surely mean he would step up and take that castoff crown.

Chapter 3.8

Within the majesty of *Clarence Hotel*, within the office of a forlorn man who believed he might finally be stumbling upon his salvation, Henry explained to Vladimir the important assignment he had for him that night.

There was a faster beat to his words than earlier. His eyes had filled with a glimmer of light, inspired by the lead the Virtues had been investigating for the last five months. It was a thread that had finally led to something promising.

'When we put all the pieces together,' Henry said, 'it all pointed to this certain someone in the underground. Someone, it turns out, we know rather well.'

'Who?'

'David Tovar. Remember him?'

'How could I forget?'

'I guess he had no clue how word spreads around in this town. But anyway, he's the one I need you to find. Bring him here and we'll get to work on him.'

'What do we need to get out of him exactly? He knows where the Akasa Stone is?'

Henry began nodding before he could get his words out. 'I don't know how. I mean, this is Tovar we're talking about. The man who tried to sell a chalice back to the church he'd stolen it from.'

'I heard he knocked his front teeth out as well. Did you hear that?'

'Tripped over a bar stool?'

'Wasn't us.'

Henry leaned back in his chair. His gaze returned to his Akasa Stone wall. 'Maybe his arrival in our town wasn't so much of an accident,' he pondered. 'I suspect he'd been told something back from wherever he came from.'

'Yeah, what country *was* that?'

'Don't ask me. I thought you knew.'

'No, none of us could ever place his accent.'

Whilst Vladimir was willing to help his master, he was also careful with his words. Henry may be reinvigorated right now but he had to ensure he was there in the fallout of disappointment when it turned out this was another false dawn.

'We'll be able to find him,' Vladimir said.

'Good. Be careful.'

'You don't need to worry.'

'I wish that were the case, but you know what happened to Quade.'

'I do. And, as I say, you have nothing to worry about.'

'Well, there is one more thing I ought to warn you about, Vladimir.'

'Lay it on me.'

'I don't think we're the only ones looking for him. In fact, it's almost a certainty we're not.'

Vladimir stood up. He knew where Tovar was right at that moment, and already he was itching to meet up with Jake and Clint so they could get it done. They got that task out the way, they could do some proper work.

'We're Halo of Fires, Henry. Nothing gets in our way.' He stepped aside from his chair. 'I'll be back later with one slack-jawed reprobate.'

Part 4: New Dimensions

Chapter 4.1

Dangers forever lurked for those that hovered within the ranks of Halo of Fires. Although Henry Maristow took good care of his workforce, there was still a price they had to pay for dwelling in the flames.

Along with their existing enemies, they also faced the risk of retaliatory attacks with all the bone-breaking revenge they dealt out. They had to be careful who they targeted, something the Seraph Alan Hammond always instilled. 'Never go after anyone bigger than you,' he would often say in his cigar smoke-filled office, an open bottle of gin on the desk. Although Henry had agreed with him on this matter, his stance was more, *whoever you hit, make sure you get away with it.*

These days it felt like there wasn't anyone bigger out there. With Vladimir's tenacity and the brawn of Jake and Clint, they all trod wherever they wanted. What they did have to be mindful about, however, was what they got up to outside work. For someone like the Throne Vladimir, this was not a problem as he rarely bothered to socialise with anyone. His perch on the fringe of society perfectly suited his role. They had each other. That's all he needed.

As for the Power Jake, his interactions beyond the Fires were limited to short-term girlfriends. He didn't go to Sunday afternoon barbecues, didn't offer to mow his neighbours' lawns or fetch their wheelie bins in on bin day. With no children, his was not a life of parents' evenings and sports days and pushing a trolley around the supermarket every Saturday morning.

Not that Jake ever worried about enemies. He'd built a reputation of indomitability even before the Fires. The only person who could master his downfall was himself, but that was a notion he pushed aside on the day Henry gave him the job offer.

'I'd like our organisation to be peerless. The toughest band of bruisers in the whole of this town. As close to superhuman as is humanly possible,' Alan had envisaged one day, back in the excitement of those embryonic days.

Henry listened closely to Alan's vision. It was a time when his words inspired him. It was a time when he *needed* to be inspired by someone. So, taking them on board, he set out to bring this vision into reality.

The first person to headhunt was Jake. Having moved in his circle under the cloud of a powerful criminal network, Henry had seen first-hand what he was capable of, that he was a born champion. He was the best they could hope to have, once they'd properly shaped him, and cleaned him up.

It was on the seventh day of a drinking binge when Jake was passed out on the park bench, reeking of stale booze and dried vomit, his stubble forming a beard. He awoke to find Henry in a smart grey suit tugging at his arm.

The alcohol couldn't quite eradicate his paranoia, and neither had it suffocated his heart. He had no idea if the man before him was an angel, an accountant or an assassin.

His eyes finding some focus, he recognised him correctly as Henry Maristow, but incorrectly as an existing member of the Network. Thinking they'd finally come for him and swiftly shaking his drunken haze from his mind, Jake shot up and put him in a headlock.

'Why are you here? Why are you here?'

'Damn it, Jake,' Henry forced out, 'I can't answer if you're going to choke me.'

After a few moments, and with a nagging thought at the back of his mind that Henry Maristow was a *fallen* member of the Network, Jake released his grip.

'You don't work for *him* any more, do you?'

'No,' Henry wheezed as he undid the top button of his shirt. 'I'm working with someone else now. We got our own thing going. That's why I came looking for you.'

'What is it?'

'Something a little different,' Henry told him as an intriguing smile formed on his face.

That day was his baptism by Halo of Fires and its spirit

of vengeance. Once he'd made his accession, and days after he'd bought himself some new clothes and had a shave, he then helped Henry to bring others to the ranks.

Of the names he put forward, the one that would have the brightest of careers was the Power Clint. Already friends, the two had similar interests: drinking heavily, playing with fast women, and spilling blood.

With bulging muscles packed around his tall ebony frame, Clint held the unofficial record amongst the gym crowd of being the best arm wrestler. He usually got the better of Jake when they competed.

With an optimism that was as low as his droning voice that constantly conveyed his bleak outlook on their operations, Clint ironically appeared to be immune from pain. Jake remembered one incident in the gym when Clint was on a rowing machine and a poorly installed television had crashed onto his head. Clint never even winced.

Acquiring the two gargantuan gladiators of Jake and Clint, Henry was well on his way to fulfilling Alan's vision. Later on there had been Quade, too, a nephew of Alan Hammond. Henry had accepted him into the organisation after the passing of his uncle, yet recently tragedy repeated in the bloodline. Quade had been off on his own investigations, and the reports on who'd killed him were vague, and even vaguer was the reason why. The universe often had a funny way of repeating itself, so perhaps this was just a coincidence.

Of the other members that Henry brought to the organisation, most of them performed non-violent operations as Dominions, or acted as sleepers or informants in the rank of Virtue. But the person who completed the trio of core agents, the chief over the Powers, was one of Alan's, a youngster brought in from out of town.

While Henry searched out the men with the muscle, Alan stumbled upon someone rather unique. Vladimir's involvement with the Halo of Fires organisation began when he was bequeathed the task of a manhunt, an operation he had not yet solved.

Alan never lived to see the finished article. He'd overseen him for a number of years though, as his protégé absorbed his ideas and intentions. He'd seen something within him from the start, raising him on a diet of vengeance to become the Angel of Karma he was today.

Henry initially raised his eyebrows at this recruitment. Vladimir did not appear to have the requisite weight to his physique. He was about as far away from a thug as you could get. There was a distinguishable *gentleness* to the youngster's features. Would he really translate into a viable X factor?

No one would ever now deny how great a choice Alan had made. Although the Seraph had passed away many years ago, his spirit lived on in Vladimir, a spirit of vengeance and retribution burning so fiercely that, without Vladimir, Halo of Fires would not be the force that it was today. Alan had indeed taught him well.

Vladimir's birthplace wasn't as far away as Krypton. He'd never hung out in a chemistry lab in his entire life, had never been bitten by any genetically modified arachnids. He didn't know anyone who could make any kick-ass weapons. Vladimir was just a young man, of flesh and blood, like everyone else.

This particular vigilante relied on something unique in scrapping his way through the underground of Dark Harbour. Jake and Clint could take the punches that came their way, but Vladimir had a much different coping mechanism, as was to be evidenced on the night Henry sent them to obtain a thief called David Tovar.

It was on this night that something bewildering happened with Vladimir, something that would show how Alan Hammond's vision was more fulfilled than anyone could have ever imagined.

Chapter 4.2

'Where's Clint?' Vladimir asked as Jake sat down at the table.

'Making a quick stop. He'll be here soon.'

Vladimir checked his watch, shaking his head. His Powers often did this to him. As they waited, he surveyed the lounge of *The Apex*, a jazz bar he'd picked for tonight's meeting point. Across from them was a stage area, empty tonight. Maybe the band that was booked had been listening to their own depressing music so long they couldn't even be bothered to get out of bed this morning.

The room was lit by neutral blue lights that fought the cloying darkness. Contemplative individuals were scattered around the tables like souls in a purgatorial waiting room, reviewing the trials of their lives inside their minds as they listened to the melancholic jazz number that played over the speakers.

No one was in earshot, which was exactly why Vladimir had chosen this booth at the back of the lounge, not that any of these people would be bothered to pay them any interest.

'Do you come here to drown your sorrows or something?' Jake asked him, looking at the glass in front of him. One of the cool ceiling lights shone directly on it, making it look like some sort of magical fuel.

'Never stray from the Coke...'

'Always got to keep your focus,' Jake finished the stock answer for him. 'And you think caffeine is good for you?'

Vladimir threw him a blank look. Jake had his usual two-day growth of stubble on his face. How did he *always* have two days of growth? It suited him well though, added to his action-hero appearance. With his square jaw and tightly packed muscles, Vladimir could imagine Jake to be the inspiration behind the Action Man toy figure. There was a precision to his body, a perfection to his chiselled handsomeness. If any artist wanted a model to represent maleness or heroism or strength, then Jake would be perfect.

He sometimes wondered whether the gods had created him as a physical masterpiece of creation, but his inner defects had angered them and they'd discarded him to this lowly world as punishment. On Earth he would battle it out with himself and come to understand his flaws.

Jake broke his attention away from the slithering jazz

music and caught Vladimir's gaze. 'Anyway, so what's with the change of plan tonight? I thought we had a job at the rec.'

'We'll have to leave that for another night.' Vladimir explained Henry's request, that they were now urgently searching out Tovar and taking him back for interrogation.

Inevitably, Jake then asked, 'So what does Henry want to talk to Tovar about?'

'The same thing it always is with Henry, that never ending search of his.'

Jake squinted his eyes. 'The uh... the Akasa Stone? Is that what you mean?'

'Yes.'

'That thing that doesn't exist?'

'You're so well trained, Jake.'

Jake laughed. 'I listen to you. About time we told them they're all wasting their time eh, Vlad?' He glanced towards the bar, no doubt feeling the alcoholic temptations.

'You don't know how true that is. But trust me, when it comes to Henry, I've tried.'

'So why doesn't he listen to you? What the hell is so damned important about that stupid thing?'

Vladimir leaned across the table a little, searching Jake's eyes conspiratorially. 'There's something about the Akasa Stone that few people know. There's something that it does to the person who holds it.'

'Does Henry know about this?'

'He knows about its magic powers.'

Jake scoffed. 'What kind of magic are we talking about?'

Vladimir breathed in deeply, wondering how to put it to him. 'Do you believe everyone has a soul, Jake?'

'It's not something I think about. What do you mean by a soul, anyway?'

'The higher part to ourselves, in some unseen dimension. The true essence that we hide behind our surface.'

He shook his head as though his brain had exploded. 'I don't know. Come on, why are you asking me?'

'What about if you could look inside, if you could *perceive* someone's soul? What about if you could look into the force that makes up that person's true being, by looking right into this realm?'

Vladimir's eyes burned. In the reflection of his drink, he saw the glint of empyreal light dancing around in them, like the aurora flickering in the night sky above the frozen wilderness. 'What about,' he went on, 'if you could open up your senses and perceptions and connect with this invisible realm? With your own soul? And everyone else's, and all the souls that have ever walked this earth.'

'Is that what Henry wants?'

'That's the secret with the Akasa Stone, that it has these powers.'

'I can see why you don't believe in it.'

'But you're right. That's what Henry wants. That's how he thinks he's going to heal himself.' Suddenly Vladimir connected his eyes with Jake's again. 'Maybe *you* could do with some soul-searching, Jake.'

'Too late for that, I think.'

The jazz number stumbled to a stop and died. *The Apex* fell quiet for a moment, the melancholic clientele looking around hopefully as though the world had thankfully now come to an end, but the next song eventually pounced on the silence. This one was a cacophonous and jarring dirge, and completely transformed the atmosphere, evoking the eternal pain felt by souls who part from fellow souls. If ever a piece of music could ooze with tears, this was it.

Vladimir checked his watch again, suddenly remembering why they were there. Even in these moments of stasis as he waited around for people, he was sure to make the most of his time.

Seeing him do this, Jake said, 'He should be here any second now.'

A silence came between them for a few moments, both of them lost in their knotted thoughts.

'Anyway, you never said. What's Tovar done?' Jake eventually asked. 'What's it got to do with the Akasa Stone?'

'We'll find out. Don't get excited. Tonight is only going to turn out to be an anti-climax.'

Vladimir was not often wrong about things, but on this occasion he had never been so wrong in his entire life. Then again, he always was so confident in himself.

Chapter 4.3

Once Clint turned up, only twelve minutes late in the end, the three vigilantes made their way down White Horse Passage, an alleyway that led into the town centre.

The pathway was a popular hangout for the local hoodie brigade, evidenced by the graffiti that adorned the old stone wall. A garish scrawl of fat letters caught Vladimir's eye, 'Dark Har*bore*'. It looked to be a new addition, evidently the work of one of the more literate of these socially disillusioned vandals.

He longed to get their hands on these punks. They were most probably teenagers and, like all delinquents these days, would know they were too young for the law to touch them. But no one was beyond the laws of karma; spraying their paint into their eyes would be delicious comeuppance.

Charging on, he pushed that fantasy aside as he tried to anticipate what they would run into when they caught up with David Tovar.

The Fires had visited the rogue three times before so were well aware of his troublemaking, and of his rather strange manner. A foreigner to England's shores, he'd turned up in town just two years ago. His deep olive skin tone indicated he might have originated from any side of the Mediterranean. On occasion he would become jittery and slip into a foreign tongue, but his mumbling was so severe that no one could ever identify what particular language he was actually speaking.

No one determined what had brought him to Dark Harbour either, but he soon acquainted himself with the wrong crowds, often stealing underground cabling and copper piping. As his notoriety spread like a nasty disease, a rumour circulated that he'd escaped from prison in his home country. Presumably, he'd opened up a map of England and looked for the place that best sounded like where he needed to go.

His first entanglement with the local vigilante force was only a 'verbal', or a quiet heart-to-heart as Vladimir liked to describe such occasions. For most people, having such a chat with Vladimir and his two colleagues was as effective as a Jedi mind trick in making them go home and rethink their life. It had not worked on Tovar, however.

The second time they'd visited him, Tovar had come out of the experience minus the index finger on his right hand. That still wasn't enough.

The third visit resulted in him spending a week in a hospital bed. By then he got the message.

With his profile lowered, Vladimir had almost forgotten about him. It had surprised him earlier, hearing Henry bring up his ugly name again. Just what was this loser thief up to this time?

Vladimir led them to the other side of the road from Tovar's favourite haunt. *Sparks* was a nightclub of the roughest kind, that made the Mos Eisley Cantina look like a sophisticated gourmet restaurant.

'We going in?' Clint asked Vladimir who continued to gaze intently at the entrance.

'He's in there.'

'We're just going to go in there and drag Tovar out?'

'That's the plan.'

'Shouldn't we have a couple more of us? I mean, you realise who else hangs out there, right?'

Vladimir ignored him as he began crossing the road.

'Come on, scaredy-cat,' Jake said as he walked after him. 'Down on numbers these days, aren't we?'

'So we have to learn our lesson,' Clint shouted, following at last.

Vladimir suddenly paused. He hadn't abandoned this conversation just yet. 'I've learnt, Clint. Trust me, I have. Nobody else is going to go like Quade. Now start acting like a Power.'

Bypassing the line of people queuing outside the nightclub, Vladimir strode on as though he owned the joint, his companions in tow. Two bouncers on the door looked them over before pretending not to see them.

As Vladimir cut through the crowd inside, he saw what a dredge of humanity this place sucked in. Lowlifes and basket cases, the lot of them.

Bathing in the gloom of sticky-floored clubs in a pungent plume of herb smoke had never held any appeal for him. All these people looked lost.

That was the difference between these sorts and Vladimir. Action was power. Delivering retribution and ensuring people got what they deserved was power, because it was *purpose*. Sure, he'd been lost once, too. He'd had his share of soul-destroying experiences, but resentful victimhood and anarchy were not his destination.

Vladimir delved deeper into the crowds, as the shadows danced around him and the heavy music smothered him. He felt the bass beating in his chest, a death metal song of fear and angst that seemed to engulf his body.

There was Tovar, at the back of the club in an exclusive section, surrounded by a posse of thugs who were all high on their own importance for occupying the 'VIP area'. He was the same scrawny vagabond, a patchy beard covering a rat-like face etched into a devious grin. A sickly nicotine-stained tongue wriggled in his mouth beyond his missing teeth.

They'd soon erase that grin when he noticed who was coming for him. In the special way Vladimir could assess people, he saw how much of a miscreant he was, the laden of wrongdoing that cancerated his soul.

As the vigilante barged into their zone, Tovar's facial muscles suddenly relaxed. He sprang to his feet, waving his phantom finger at him.

In his panic, he began muttering something, but the music drowned it out. Vladimir expected him to make a runner and could not understand why he still stood there.

The details he observed troubled him, Tovar's breathing slowing, the frown on his face morphing into a sneer.

As Clint and Jake edged closer, Tovar's hand thrust behind his back and pulled out a gun. He aimed it at Clint and squeezed the trigger with his middle finger.

Clint clutched his arm, more out of surprise than pain as the bullet lodged into his flesh. Before Jake could grab

Tovar, a thug set upon him. Clint put his wound to the back of his mind as two more attackers swarmed over him.

Jake lifted his thug into the air and sent him crashing onto a table. Clint smashed his fist into his first thug, while he flipped the other one over his back and twisted his arm until it snapped.

Monitoring the commotion, Vladimir turned to face Tovar. He still clutched the gun tightly in his hand and now he brought it up to him. The vigilante swallowed the non-existent saliva in his mouth, focussing every ounce of his attention at that deadly weapon. This was an eventuality he'd prepared for. He just hadn't expected it would come tonight.

Anger erupted on Tovar's snarling face. 'I knew you bastards would come for me again.'

Vladimir shook his head. 'You need to come with us, Tovar,' he tried to roar back at him. 'You're in danger.'

Tovar could not hear him and so continued with the conversation he was having. 'I have a message for you and your pals, Vladimir. You may think you're the most powerful in this town, but you're wrong.'

He pulled the trigger. Again and again and again. Six times in all. Six bullets, spinning through the air at over three hundred metres per second towards their target: Vladimir.

Slugs would cut through his clothes, penetrate his flesh, slice open blood vessels, fracture bones, and burrow into his internal organs. Six pieces of lead compound that within this infinitesimal fraction of time could spell nothing but doom for the person who stood in their way.

But they were only bullets. They were only deadly because of their physical properties, densely ordered material vibrating at a tightly packed level. Beyond an atomic level, they were composed of nothing different from anything else in Vladimir's existence. The clothes on his back, the floor beneath his feet, the air between him and Tovar. It was all energy, just of varying vibrations within the light continuum.

The fact that these bullets were hurtling towards him was only a problem because one particular vibration of energy was about to collide with a significantly different vibration of energy. If only one of those vibrations could momentarily *change* into a different level, a higher level...

The DJ killed the music and the sound of screaming filled the club as people tried to escape.

One person who was not running, however, was Tovar. He was anchored to the spot, staring at the person in front of him who should now be on the ground in a pool of blood. But Vladimir was still standing, just as he was before.

He released the breath that had been a prisoner in his lungs, then stepped up to Tovar and removed the gun from his hand.

'Tovar, it is you who are wrong.'

Jake and Clint appeared back at Vladimir's side, a little ruffled but unfazed. They'd dealt with the thugs swiftly and all nine of them now lay bloodied and bruised on the floor.

They both grabbed Tovar's arms to drag him away, and he was too stunned to put up any resistance. And so, with the same composure with which they'd sashayed in, they now departed with their Kolley.

Chapter 4.4

In the staff car park behind the nightclub, Jake and Clint were making Tovar very sorry for firing his gun at them. Clint held him with his good arm while his partner jabbed away at Tovar's ribs.

'Okay, that's enough, guys,' Vladimir bellowed as he brushed off some fluff from his shoulder. 'Let's save the rest for later.'

Clint released him and he collapsed to the ground, his mouth full of blood. He clambered on to all fours while he groaned and wheezed.

Jake could not resist the opportunity to kick him while he was down, his right foot flying into his already broken ribs. Tovar rolled over, whimpering.

'Jake! That's enough,' Vladimir commanded.

He backed off as Vladimir crouched beside the injured rogue. He'd started to mutter incoherent words.

'What the hell happened in there, anyway? How did he miss?' Clint asked.

'Blanks,' Tovar answered for Vladimir. 'They loaded me with blanks...' His words again discomposed into his secret language.

'This was no sodding blank,' Clint moaned, raising his arm.

Vladimir peered into his watery eyes. 'What's this crap you speak, Tovar?'

As he focussed on his face, the random syllables he uttered slipped into form. 'You would not understand.'

'See, your accent sounds Spanish, but the words don't.'

'Just as you don't sound very Russian with a name like Vladimir.'

'I have my own meaning.'

'As do my words.'

A shudder coursed through Vladimir's blood as he listened to the wild-eyed man continuing to speak in tongues, as though he was chanting some diabolical spell upon his soul.

He broke his gaze and stood up. He was sick of looking into the eyes of such a waster, sick of listening to him. 'Stand up. It's time to go.'

Tovar gingerly hobbled to his feet. 'I know why you came for me. I know what you want from me.'

Vladimir froze.

'My father spoke of it for years. Back home he told me all the stories, everything. Including... where to find it. There was just one piece of advice he gave me which I wish I had listened to: When you find it, don't tell anyone.'

There came a soft thud. A bullet hole appeared in the perfect centre of Tovar's forehead and his eyes pointed inwards as he toppled to the ground.

Vladimir looked to Clint then Jake to see which one had shot him. They were both empty-handed. He peered over his shoulder. There stood a man in a lopsided trilby. He was holding a silenced SIG Mosquito that had a wisp of smoke at the end. His other hand was stuffed casually in his pocket, as though he'd been shooting ducks at a fairground.

Lucas Duffy, or The Dim Reaper as was the name that everyone called him, was usually a private operative in Dark Harbour who provided the ultimate mercenary service that the Fires stopped short of offering.

'Now step aside from the body, you three fine young chaps, you. Don't want to make this look like a Tarantino film set.'

Vladimir didn't move.

'Now, I know they call me dim, but I'm not that dim to know it's not a good thing to have a *facking* gun pointed at you. So, like I said, move away from the pretty boy with the Colgate smile there.'

Duffy always spoke in a dull whine, which was what gave him his nickname. Behind his spectacles, a pair of thin eyes squinted at Vladimir. The Dim Reaper was not really a fool though. He was another one of those black souls, like Floyd, only with a brain. He was a slight of a man, barely five and a half feet tall. With his Mister Bronson moustache, The Dim Reaper looked more like a secondary school teacher than a cold-blooded assassin.

'Who are you working for?' Vladimir asked, the imminent threat before him inflicting no corrosion of the steel in his voice.

Duffy cocked his gun as he sighed theatrically.

'Come on, Vlad. Don't push your luck,' Clint said.

'Well said, Clint. Ever the hero, I see. I'll make sure to kill you quickly.'

Vladimir noticed Duffy still had the gun aimed at him. He wanted to keep it that way.

'I ain't afraid of you, bozzo,' Vladimir said as he knelt down beside Tovar.

Jake edged closer to Duffy.

'No, who's going to be scared of a *facking* gun?' Duffy whined on. 'I say, John? John? You'll give me an autograph, won't you? I say, Reeva? Open the bathroom door, you hear?'

Vladimir zoned him out as he examined the corpse. Tovar's dentally deficient mouth was open, but for once it was not forming a grin. Vladimir grabbed the collars on the corpse's shirt and yanked it apart.

'Hello? Are you listening to me?'

Resting on Tovar's chest was a necklace, a wooden cord holding a dull, indigo-coloured gemstone shaped like a shark's tooth.

'My God,' Jake muttered. 'That's...'

'Mine,' Duffy said.

Vladimir tore the necklace from Tovar's body and held it close to his eyes. He needed a good look at this thing. Right in his hand he held what Henry had been searching for, the culmination of the thread he'd followed for the past five months.

'All right then, Vladimir, old chap, give it to me,' Duffy said as he stormed up to him and rested the gun behind his head.

'Have it,' Vladimir spat back as he threw the necklace on the ground. 'Let's get out of here,' he said to his colleagues as he began walking away.

Raising his eyebrows, Duffy aimed his gun at Jake next. Despite his nonchalant manner, The Dim Reaper was a cold-blooded professional who killed everyone and anyone he was ordered to. Even if an innocent child was in the way he was sure to blow their brains out like he was swatting a fly.

'You heard the man,' Duffy prompted.

Jake and Clint looked to one another before figuring it was best to retreat with their captain.

'So?' Jake asked, jogging up to Vladimir

'So, what?'

'Are we bluffing or have we really finished our business back there?'

'I think we've wasted enough of our evening.'

'But... what the hell are we going to tell Henry?'

'We had no choice.'

'Vladimir, don't you realise what that was? You just gave him the Akasa Stone.'

'Oh, Jake,' he replied, shaking his head as he would have done to a mischievous little kitten. 'It seems I haven't trained you as well as I thought.'

Chapter 4.5

At a quarter to four that morning Henry was still awake. Vladimir and Jake had debriefed him about the operation and then he'd gone to his eighteenth century Georgian home where he'd lived alone for the past thirteen years. It was located in the countryside of one of the quiet villages, a few miles inland from town.

Henry poured himself a glass of Cognac and put on one of his Mozart CDs. He sat out on the balcony of his bedroom, staring out across the clear skies onto one half of the universe. Gazing into the infinity of space helped give Henry some perspective. It reminded him that nothing really mattered, if only he could buy into that notion all the time.

The Andante of Mozart's Number 21 Piano Concerto also helped to comfort him. He often played it, the arrangement he believed was the purest cry from the composer's tortured soul.

From one soul who had died over two hundred years ago, to the soul that sat in a house built during his life, Henry could feel the profundity of frustration that resounded behind each of the punctuating beats of the orchestra, as the gentle, listless music breezed along. That was the genius of Mozart's work: a playful, reverent spirit on the surface that belied the burning frustration that churned within, glimpses of which appeared when the improvised piano solo would suddenly become agitated and scramble into action with its introspective melody of sadness.

All along, the orchestra kept its gentle pulse, the pulse of life that continued to beat whatever happened: the wind that would always blow, the trees that would always sway in it, the waves that swept up and down the beaches. The harmony of life always existed whatever people were going through.

It just wasn't fair. The Fires had got there first. Vladimir had the Akasa Stone in his very hands before Duffy snatched it from him.

He knew all about that Dim Reaper bastard, but surely the boys could have put up *some* resistance. Since when did the Fires become walkovers? And Henry had sent the cream of the organisation. Not that he would have wanted any of them to get harmed.

He didn't expect them to appreciate the stone's real importance, though. Vladimir may be sharp and he may be perceptive, but he was still young. He wouldn't understand what it was about this stone that made Henry want it so badly.

Where he went from here, he did not know. The stars filled his eyes, the piano concerto filled his ears, and the brandy settled his stomach, but Henry realised he wouldn't find answers in any of these things. Only comfort.

As the Andante moved on to the Allegro, Henry retired to his bedroom. When he got into bed, the stars would eventually fade from the sky as the April sun would slowly rise to burn off the morning dew. He would wake the next day and life would go on.

Somehow Henry would have to get his head around the fact that he had lost. Years of search and they had beaten him to it, pipped him to the post, and now someone out there suddenly found themselves with new powers at their fingertips. Undoubtedly they were the wrong hands.

Whilst he hoped that Floyd was not the one to have hired the Dim Reaper to obtain the stone, he knew the only other suspect his mind could muster was an even worse prospect.

Henry drifted off to sleep with a nauseous feeling provoked by the sense that there would be dark days ahead.

Chapter 5.1

Danny was sitting in the cafe when the thought struck him. *The universe is conspiring against me.* He'd done everything he could think of recently, distracting his mind with college work, hanging out with his friends more. He'd even stopped catching that damned 1906 bus.

But still there was no escaping her. In a town the size of this one, it must have been a mathematical miracle the number of times their paths would cross. At least this was a safe place. Close to the college, students frequented between lectures as they topped up their caffeine levels and tried to recall their drunken rollicks from the night before.

Danny knew the best thing was to avoid her. Out of sight, out of mind. Not that it worked as simply as that, but what else was he to do?

Just what would someone think if they were to open up his head and look inside? He was obsessed. Delusional. What kind of idiot spent that much time thinking about one person?

There was no way he could talk to anyone about this cacoethes. They'd tell him he was insane for wanting her, crazy for imagining him and her together. It was an impossibility. She was engaged to someone else. Her heart belonged to Samuel's so there was no room in it for Danny. He was certain a much simpler mathematical equation could be applied to that, too.

Danny took a sip of his tea as he opened up his book. *Great Expectations* was the subject of his latest essay and he'd set the goal of getting through it by the end of next week. Today he'd finished just two more pages.

Inside the book was a piece of paper on which he'd made some scribbling, another composition he'd started.

It was another poem about her. Writing was better than

reading, anyway.

After he'd completed the first poem, things had become choppy again inside. Without a way to release those ever-churning feelings, Danny had decided he would carry on writing verses for as long as he had to, for as long as the Stella hurricane would twist and taunt his inner ocean.

It helped to calm him, helped to sedate his so stubborn emotions. They. Just. Would. Not. Go. Away.

It was like some evil goblin was inside him, stabbing all the time at the keys of a grand cathedral organ, playing the disturbing tune of obsession that jangled throughout his every cell, and at every moment of the day.

He longed to be free of it all. If only they did emotion-ectomies on the NHS. Or maybe he just needed to nullify it all with some hard drug.

As he stared into his mug like he was trying to find the hints of a better fortune in the tea leaves, Danny chewed on his pencil. He couldn't quite grasp the word, the one that would most effectively transfer the emotion onto the page.

And then it was gone, his focus distracted by movement in the corner of his eye. He glanced towards the door to see yet another of those mathematical improbabilities occurring.

Why? Why did she have to be here? *Why can't the universe just give me a break?*

The pencil in Danny's hand snapped in half as he watched her walk across the room. She was wearing a broomstick-shaped gypsy dress, lavender in colour. Her silk top was ocean blue, ruffled at the sleeves like the waves. Delicate silver bracelets hid beneath her cuffs and resting around her neck were about three necklaces, weaving between the strands of her honey-flowing hair.

And as she glided past, the scent of her perfume breezed along as though he'd just smelt the wild flowers of an angelic paradise.

Danny knew he would never see anything more beautiful than her ever again. She must be the most beautiful that she would ever be. The precision of her curves, the shine of her hair, the radiance of her buttery skin, all of it had come together to this apex of perfection in this very moment.

She sat down at an empty table and her eyes searched the room. Searching, it seemed, for the one who fixed their sight on her.

Danny.

That same electrifying spasm surged through his body as her eyes met his. But this time he was not about to break the ocular connection. This time he no longer cared what he gave away. She could see it all. Let the dam burst and the waters gush free.

Time froze, two pairs of eyes brought together like metal to a magnet, the white hole joined to the black hole, Danny on the event horizon as her amaranthine orbs swallowed him.

A waitress terminated the moment, approaching her table and blocking Danny's view. He gathered himself and closed his book with a snap. He gulped down the rest of his tea, threw away his broken pencil that had failed him yet again, tucked the story of Philip Pirrip under his arm, and then got up to leave.

He didn't bother with any parting glances. It was best to just leave.

**

Danny noticed his hand shaking as he raised it. Clutched between his finger and thumb was a coin that he brought to the slot of the ten-penny falls. He watched it bounce down the panel and crash onto the ever-growing pile inside.

One after the other he robotically fed the greedy machine that spewed back nothing in return, not even any of the plastic key rings and tacky jewellery on top of the loot. He could have done with the cheap thrill of winning such a piece of junk. But surrounded by the merry cacophony of electronic tunes and flashing lights, the arcades were a handy distraction to gather his thoughts.

Just what had he done back there in the café? Why had he carried on looking at her for so long like some crazy creep?

He sensed his world had suddenly changed, that his

actions had shifted the entire dynamics of the universe, releasing something into the cosmos.

Danny reached his final coin. Almost a pound's worth he'd put in, but his tray was empty. What a surprise.

A spark of frustration welled within, another discordant arrangement from that infernal goblin, and he hammered the coin into the machine. It dislodged a few onto the next level, but those just bunched up even more, defying the laws of physics as they teetered over the edge.

His empty hand fell to his side and he stood there staring vacantly at those shiny moon-shaped disks of silver, the random mosaic of heads and tails that had come to this unique arrangement in this moment in time. All of a sudden he saw something beautiful in it. Something so beautiful in the fragile yet fateful way things come together.

He felt something touch his hand. Calmness came over him, as though he'd reached the eye of the hurricane. All the ragged fragments of his mind fell together and there was quiet, the goblin having finished his interminable performance.

It was the touch of another person. That person was her.

Danny turned round as her soft hand slid from his fingers.

'Hello there,' she said in that sweet voice of hers.

He opened his mouth, but no words came out. There appeared to be an infinite chasm between his brain and his tongue.

Was he dreaming? Had he become so delusional he was now imagining her talking to him? It was all so unreal. Time had stopped as the workings of the universe had ground to a halt.

He heard the abrupt clank of coins crashing onto metal, and it returned him to reality. His tray had filled with treasure as the mechanics of the ten-penny falls continued with their motions at least.

'Come with me,' she whispered. Nope. This was real. She was still there.

She glided away, a glint in her eyes.

All this time he'd thought her eyes were blue, but being this close to her he saw an orchid-coloured hue within them.

He cleared his throat and ran a hand over his face, rebooting himself. Eventually he was able to put one foot in front of the other and walk after her. It was time to enter her world.

The sea air sobered his senses as he stepped outside. In the hazy brilliance of the evening sun, the seafront amusements were in full swing as the dodgems battered around and the teacups span. Everything seemed more alive, more colourful.

There was one colour that stood out even more within this illuminating new world, and that was the pellucid radiance of Stella's violaceous eyes. There she was at the edge of the park. Once she'd spotted him in tow, she walked on through a break in the sea wall, and like a helpless child of Hamelin following the melody of temptation, Danny strode after her.

Beyond the wall ran the promenade, sets of steps interspersed along its course inviting people to explore Dark Harbour's beach. Danny saw her walking across the sands towards the shoreline. The sky was teasing the first signs of a glorious sunset.

The nearest steps looked too far away, so Danny jumped straight off the promenade, landing clumsily, and almost stumbling into a rock pool. With a little more grace returning, he hopped his way around the water and then coolly walked over to her in his best Brad Pitt walk.

Talking to her was something the lovestruck poet could only fantasise about before, but perhaps all that dreaming had finally manifested his desire, for here he was about to say his first ever word to the one who had held him under such enchantment for so long.

'Hello,' was the word that came from Danny's now functioning lips.

'I like to stand here and watch the sun go down,' she mused. 'So many times I've stood on these shores and watched it.'

He didn't follow her gaze, instead observing the strands of her honey hair dancing freely around her face as though they'd been inhibited for a very long time. Feeling his stare, she turned to him. Again she smiled.

'Will you sit with me?' Stella asked as she knelt down on the pebbly sand.

He positioned himself next to her, as close as would seem appropriate.

'What's your name?'

'Daniel. Danny.'

'And do you know my name, Danny?'

'Yeah.'

Stella clutched her knees. 'I thought you might. Know anything else about me?'

'I do,' he replied, not really wanting to expand upon it.

'So, you're a reader,' she then said on seeing the book tucked firmly under his arm.

'Yeah, I'm a... I study English Literature.' He placed the book the other side of himself, suddenly remembering the scrap of paper enclosed within it.

Stella stared back towards the swirling waves as though hypnotised by their sibilance. 'Do you ever look at someone and feel a familiarity?' she whispered softly. 'Like you've just seen some part of yourself in somebody else? Or something long forgotten.'

Danny took a moment to ponder her question. He could have carried on listening to her sweet voice all day. 'I think so.'

'You looked like you were drowning, Danny. A lost soul. Sinking into the waters. It... it's haunting.'

'Is that what made you speak to me?'

'Because one lost soul may understand another lost soul?' She turned to face him. 'It was your eyes that gave it all away. It's always the eyes.'

She was such an enigma, but her expressions resonated with him on some level, as if he understood what she meant but couldn't find the words to explain. It was so typical of Danny to be without words these days.

'Will you stay with me and watch the sunset?'

'Sure. I'd like that.'

And so for the next half hour, there they both sat in silence on the sands of Dark Harbour, watching the sinking sun flood the sky with its sanguine tones. He could feel the tingle of her zephyr presence, her aura against his as though it flowed inside him. In this moment he no longer saw himself as an average nobody student. Here the universe had reserved a special seat for him, among clouds that floated high above all others. Danny was soaring, an eagle flying within her airy heights.

Stella broke the silence. 'What time is it?'

He looked at his watch. 'Just gone eight.'

'My goodness,' she said, getting to her feet. 'I must get going. Sam will be wondering where I've got to.'

The skies may just as well have clouded over and spewed cold rain over him. Hearing that name brought Danny back down to the normal world, a reminder of the man to whom her heart belonged. He got up.

'Thanks for sitting here with me.'

'I enjoyed it.'

'You're so sweet,' she said with that ever-captivating smile.

As usual, Danny bashfully lowered his eyes to the ground and at this point Stella stepped closer to him. Leaning in, she pressed her lips to his cheek and kissed him.

Anyone looking on could have easily assumed that they were two young people consumed by romance and completely in love with each other. The way they'd sat on the beach like that watching the sunset, and the tender way she'd kissed him goodbye, it all seemed so obvious what this picture conveyed.

Unfortunately for Danny, someone was looking on.

Chapter 5.2

Larry was in bed snoring. The air in his bedroom was musky, clothes and magazines scattered like debris from an explosion. Every time his alarm sounded he hit snooze and promptly fell into another nine minute increment of sleep.

Getting out of bed was always a struggle, like giving birth to himself.

During the twelfth snooze, at almost two o'clock, Larry heard a scuffing sound at the door.

'Go away,' Larry groaned in his semi-sleep.

Still the disturbance continued, followed by the door hinge creating a grating creak that couldn't possibly be any more annoying. Heavy breathing came next, and he could have assumed some demented pervert had trotted into his room, especially when he felt the intruder licking him. But Larry knew it was only the new resident at their flat, Eddie's dog.

Having a pasting of slobber was finally enough to wake him, and he sat up and wiped a pillow over his soggy face.

'Thanks. Just how I like to start the day.'

The wide-eyed mutt sat on its hind legs as it panted cheerfully, proud of himself for having been so friendly to one of his new pack members. He cocked his head at Larry as if to say, 'As I was so kind to you, can we play?'

'Go find your master. Eddie will take you for a walk,' he told him as he lay back down again, resting an arm over his face to shield himself from the stinging daylight.

'Get lost. I'm not walking him again.'

Larry opened his eyes to see Eddie standing in the doorway.

'All right, mucker?'

'You want an old mutt?' his roommate asked.

'You know, when you told me you'd brought a dog home I didn't think that you'd brought home an actual *dog*.'

'And still he's prettier than anything you ever brought back.'

'Touché. So what are you doing here? I thought you had a seminar on Friday afternoons.'

Eddie looked at his watch. 'Yeah?' he said blankly, almost as if he didn't understand what Larry was getting at.

'You're not going?'

'You not getting up?'

'It's still early yet.'

'It's early afternoon.'

'That's what I said. It's still *early*.'

He noticed Eddie smile momentarily before the usual glower returned to his face.

'Anyway, is being a student really about studying these days, eh?' Larry pondered.

'Studying to be an unemployed bum maybe,' Eddie added. 'Next year all we'll be doing is collecting our jobseeker's allowance and pissing it up the wall. It's all a waste of time, you ask me.'

'You heard about Michael?'

'No. What now?'

'He's going to be doing an internship at the *Gazette* this summer.'

Eddie shook his head. 'And no doubt your mate Danny will have his bestseller on the shelves soon. Writing about his student days in the famous frigging five.'

'Do you know what you're going to do when you leave college?' Larry asked.

'Do I bollocks. There's no jobs, anyway. We're living in a no-man's-land, and the last suckers that anyone looks at these days are single males. Hell, if I was a woman I could get knocked up and there's my bloody career. A child benefit collector with my own house thrown in to the deal. But you're British, and you have a dick? You're not an immigrant? You don't have daddy's corporation to inherit? Then you got no cards to play at all. We're on our own. Our very existence is a political incorrectness.'

Larry was speechless for a moment, allowing the angry dust from his diatribe to settle. 'I thought you were foreign,' he eventually responded.

'Not that I care.'

'Come on, you got the black card.'

'No, I don't. My mother's white.'

'Then... wow. You really are screwed then.'

'And you were screwed to begin with because you can't even get out of bed.'

'Well, who wants to get out of bed when they're being screwed?'

Eddie laughed, clearly that time.

Larry propped himself up. 'Oh well. I guess I should get some work done.'

Instead of taking the cue to leave, Eddie went over to the chair and started removing the things piled on top of it: a dinner plate with stale crusts, clothes, an empty DVD case for a program about extreme impact car crashes. Eventually he was able to sit down.

It was most unusual for Eddie to do this. Perhaps he was trying to be friendly for a change. Larry didn't know what to say though. The conversation they'd just had was about as long and involved as they came.

He looked back at the dog who was now lying down on the floor with its paws outstretched.

'What's he called?' Larry asked.

'What?'

'The dog. What have you named him?'

'I don't know. I'm not keeping the bastard thing.'

'So what are you going to do with him?'

'Hopefully his dumbass owner will get in touch.'

'And how will they know you've got him?'

'Oh Michael, he put on his saviour cape and Facebooked it, even made some posters.'

'We can still give him a name.'

'Like what?'

Larry glanced up at his wall. In amongst the pictures of scantily clad women was a film poster of *The Return of the King*.

'How about Frodo?'

Eddie looked at the poster too. 'That's, like, the first name you thought of.'

'Yeah?' Larry replied defensively. 'Okay, how about Meriadoc then? That's an awesome name.'

Eddie rubbed his eyes. 'Okay, sure. Sod it. We'll call him Meriadoc. I'll get Michael to put on his robes and we'll Christen him later. Happy now?'

'Can I be the godfather?'

Eddie couldn't help but smile again until another thought quickly dissolved it.

'Hey, do you want to...?'

'What?'

'Doesn't matter.'

'What?' Larry persisted.

From under his baseball cap he asked, 'Do you want to go kick the football around or something? I'm bored.'

Larry looked at his bedside clock. 'I don't know. I got this essay to do today. Supposed to be in on Monday.'

'What, you've not started it?'

'Dude, I've not even read the brief.'

'What were we saying two seconds ago, Larry? None of this academia crap is going to get us anywhere. Come on, are you coming?'

It may have seemed a trivial decision in the grand scheme of things, but Larry sometimes noticed how the universe threw up out-of-proportion consequences to small decisions. But what would it really matter if he spent an hour playing football? Perhaps Meriadoc would like to come with them too. He was sure Eddie hadn't taken him for any walks.

'Okay. 'We could go to the common. They have goal posts up.'

'Cool. Yeah, that's the other side of town. We can get the bus and it'll...'

'No,' Larry quickly cut in. There was a silence. 'Not the bus. I don't take buses.'

'Okay... so we'll walk.'

He stood up and left the room, the newly named dog trotting after him, sensing already there was fun about to go down.

After a fifteen minute stroll, they reached Westfield Common. Backing onto an estate of council houses, it was a popular area for people to walk their dogs or for youngsters to smoke cigarettes and drink cider, there being plenty of evidence for these activities. The field was also the training ground for the local football team, Dark Harbour United, and with fixed goal posts up all the time, it was the ideal place to practice penalties.

As they kicked the ball around, Larry soon forgot about his earlier concerns of finishing his essay. Eddie didn't seem so much of a troubled wrist-slitter either. He was often privy to his lighter moments. At college he'd always seemed like a growling dog nobody would dare go near. Nobody except Larry, that was.

The football in his hands, Larry paused, wondering again if he'd made the wrong decision in coming here; in the distance the grey clouds had collected and the first rumblings of thunder crackled in his ears. The air had become incredibly still as though an angry universe had been watching the unforeseen events and now had to stop everything and re-plot the course of destiny, all because Lawrence Stewart, 20 years old, of Dark Harbour, hadn't stayed in and done his college assignment.

'Let's go. It's going to rain,' he said.

'Well, let's finish the penalties quickly,' Eddie replied as he stood in the goalmouth. 'Who's taking this one?'

'This time it's Beckham.'

Meriadoc looked on eagerly, very much enjoying being the ball boy.

After placing the ball carefully on the spot, Larry ran at it and tried to cleverly 'bend it' into the top corner. But, lacking the England superstar's finesse, Eddie easily saved it as the German goalkeeper. Meriadoc chased after the tatty white sphere as it rebounded away.

'And Germany keep their lead,' Larry commentated. They swapped positions. 'Who's up next?'

'Klinsman.'

'He took the last one.'

'I can't think of any more Kraut players.'

'Told you you should have been Holland.'

'Sod that.'

'Okay... Ballack, Schweinsteiger, Ozil...'

'Kahn,' Eddie eventually decided.

'He was the goalkeeper.'

'So?'

The frenzy of the Wembley crowd rose as Kahn prepared for his spot kick. The German fired the ball at the right-hand corner, but Larry, or David Seaman as he now was, somehow got a hand to it and kept it out. The delighted goalkeeper punched both his fists into the air.

'And Oliver *can't* yet again,' Larry shouted.

'Not over yet. Not until the fat frau sings.'

Larry picked up the ball as he transformed into his next player.

'Right,' he said in a Liverpudlian accent, 'let's put some scouse into this shootout.'

'Either that's Gerrard or it's Cilla Black.'

Once Kahn returned to the goalmouth, Gerrard looked at the ball with that twinkle of determination in his eye. He struck the ball beautifully and whilst Kahn guessed the correct way and got a touch to it, the ball squeezed past him into the goal.

This sent the crowd over the edge as Gerrard ran around pulling on his shirt.

'England take the lead. A German miss and the Three Lions win the World Cup!'

'Time for Hamann to step up. And you know how he likes to score at Wembley,' Eddie said in the face of England's impending victory.

Once Hamann had placed the ball on the spot, he took a few careful steps backwards. Silence descended on the stadium as Seaman studied the minutiae of his body language.

The German began his run. When he reached the ball, he paused as though employing some crafty gamesmanship, then back-heeled it, kicking it harmlessly across the field. Eddie punched his arms into the air and looked skywards as he roared in celebration, 'England! En-ger-land!'

An ecstatic Larry ran out of his goal and embraced him in the wild celebrations of England winning the World Cup. To Meriadoc they might have seemed like two dancing idiots, but the dog wanted in on the fun as well and began circling them with his tongue flapping around.

The imaginary sounds of a roaring Wembley crowd gradually faded from their ears, their excitement soon dying down as they realised there was nothing to be excited about. A chocolate bar wrapper danced its way across the penalty area, the breeze stiffening in the dull reality of a shabby playing field. Back to their mundane lives. Two struggling students, not superstar footballers.

'You can go fetch the ball though,' Eddie said, dryness returning to his voice. It was at that very moment that Meriadoc started barking.

They looked across the common. Near where the football

had come to a stop was a man in a red tracksuit running in their direction. He was skinny, his top zipped right up to his chin. The way he pumped his arms and legs reminded Larry of one of those nature documentaries where the gazelle was fleeing from the cheetah; the guy was frantic.

The two students exchanged a mystified glance while Meriadoc continued barking. That was the strangest thing about it. In all the weeks they'd been looking after him, they'd never heard him bark until now.

'What's...?' Larry muttered.

The sprinter stopped about ten feet away, bending his body over to catch his breath, or maybe it was so he could throw up. He didn't register the two students, or the inquisitive dog who was now at his feet sniffing him.

'You all right, mate?' Larry shouted over to him.

The man fell to one knee in exhaustion. He looked up at Larry, but he was panting too much to get any words out, except for a high pitched, half syllable. His scrawny face peered back across the common. Confused, Larry followed his gaze. He couldn't see anything.

His composure returning, the man clambered to his feet. He trotted towards the housing estate, constantly jittering his head round to check if his mystery predator was in pursuit.

'What the hell was all that about?' Eddie asked.

'Look!' Larry replied.

Running straight towards them there now came two more men, the angry hunters from which the slippery weasel had escaped. One was built like Vinnie Jones, the other dressed completely in black with a long coat that flapped behind him like a cape.

Larry noticed Meriadoc had now started whining. It seemed the dog had a better idea what was going on than they did.

The two men stopped running. They watched the Vinnie Jones one pointing towards the houses, the other man nodding, Vinnie sprinting over there. The man in black then approached Larry and Eddie.

'Did you see that guy? See where he ran?'

'Uh huh,' Eddie replied.

'Yeah, that way,' Larry added, pointing. 'Where your friend went.'

Meriadoc's whining was so loud it almost muffled their voices. The dog kept shifting about on his paws as though it was dinner time and hadn't been fed in days.

'Not missing a dog are you by any chance?' Eddie asked him.

'I don't seem to remember ever owning a dog,' he replied as he approached Meriadoc, strangely more interested in him now than anything else.

'Sure? He likes you.'

As the man crouched down in front of him, Meriadoc calmed down, stopping his wailing. The two of them just stared at each other silently, as if the stranger had some psychic ability to communicate with animals, secret thoughts exchanged between them. Larry felt the wind gusting around him, the storm getting closer.

The man stood up, his head bowed as he continued to look down on the dog. He looked like a mourner weeping beside a grave.

'Where did you find him?'

'He was a stray. Followed me home. Can't get rid of him. You can have him if you want.'

The man walked up to Eddie who now became the subject of his heavy glare. It was like his sharp eyes were peering into a kaleidoscope, and Eddie was the shattered, random crystals he was trying to twist into a meaningful pattern. Eddie angled his head down so the brim of his cap blocked the connection.

'We're looking after him though,' Larry said. 'We even got a name for him.'

The man now turned to Larry, who flipped his sunglasses over his eyes.

'What's he called?'

'Meriadoc.'

'Yeah?' the man replied as he turned to look at the dog once more. 'Nice name.'

'See,' Larry cried, nudging his friend who rolled his eyes.

'Anyway, I need to...' The words were lost in the man's throat as he gazed at Meriadoc.

'What do you want with that guy you were chasing?' Eddie asked.

'He's a thief. Did you see him? Looks like he's dying of cancer, doesn't he? But no, he's a worthless junkie, that's what he is.'

'I don't think you're the police though, are you?'

'No.'

'Oh shit,' Larry interrupted. 'You're those Halo of Fires people.'

'You've heard of us,' the man, Vladimir, replied.

Larry brought out his wallet and quickly searched for the business card he'd taken from Michael. He showed it to him.

'That's an old one. Yes. That's us.'

'So who hired you for this job?' Larry inquired.

Vladimir ignored the question. 'What's your names?'

'My name's Eddie. That's my friend Larry.'

'Are you guys students?'

'Yeah.'

'I guessed you weren't professional footballers.'

'Hey, you want us to help you find that guy?' Larry suggested. 'Maybe Meriadoc can follow his scent.'

Eddie shook his head. 'Don't be an idiot.'

'He might. Find that man, Meriadoc. Go on, get him.'

Whether Meriadoc understood Larry's instruction, or whether Vladimir had used his telepathic ability to communicate it to him, the creature appeared to get the message, putting his snout to the ground as he retraced the weasel man's steps.

'Strange mutt,' Eddie said, shaking his head.

Vladimir jogged after Meriadoc. After shrugging his shoulders, Larry did the same, his friend following in his wake.

***

Westfield estate comprised many boarded up houses no longer fit for human residence. The area was a rancid wasteland of humanity, a place that used to exist only in the city but had now spread into the towns like a venereal disease. Gangs in hoodies would congregate at night with their knives, and in the day they cooked up heroin on the bottom of rusty lager cans.

Meriadoc paused outside a house so Vladimir tried the front door. It was open. The blackened room inside was lit only by a small candle, dotted around which were spoons and needles. Some skank in fake designer clothing, the sort of girl found on *The Jeremy Kyle Show*, was curled up in a ball on the grime-caked carpet. A grubby young man was opposite, slumped against the wall like he'd been swallowed up and spat out again.

As Larry and Eddie entered the house they saw Vladimir crouching in front of the pallid girl, in curious, yet regretful, fascination. He put his hand to her face and in her self-induced oblivion, the girl looked up at him and smiled thinly.

Vladimir stood and shook his head, wiping his hand against his trousers as he tried to put yet another distraction out of his mind. They couldn't see the weasel anywhere, but then Meriadoc began sniffing at the crack of a door. Eddie stepped over to investigate, and when he pushed the door open he saw the man in the red tracksuit standing there.

'Here he is.'

As soon as he saw Vladimir appear in the doorway, the weasel man freaked out, squealing like a cornered rat, furiously tugging the handle to the back door. It was locked.

'Stay back,' Vladimir commanded. To his mobile phone he said, 'Jake, number twenty-two. Go get the car.'

'No. No...' the weasel whimpered.

But then, after rattling the ramshackle door so much, it suddenly gave way and opened. The weasel ran out into the back garden and Meriadoc chased after him, followed by his human companions.

Out in the overgrown garden, the man turned as he realised a canine was on his trail. He paused and kicked Meriadoc in the head.

At that point, Eddie charged at their quarry, grabbed him by the throat and punched him hard in the face. The weasel recoiled, then swiped at him too, catching him cleanly on the chin. Eddie stumbled backwards, startled by the weight of the scrawny man's punch.

Larry stepped in. The weasel threw another jab, but Larry caught his fist and in a fluid motion he twisted the guy's arm round and threw him onto the grass.

Eddie marvelled at Larry's masterful move in his daze, and on seeing the weasel on the ground, he darted over and kicked him hard in the guts.

'Bastard.'

He booted him again and again, but somehow the weasel managed to get to his feet. Just as he was about to give Eddie another punch, he froze, eyes wide as he stared beyond him, his face about to wring with tears.

Jake smashed his fist into the weasel's head like a meteor hitting the ground. The guy was instantly unconscious.

'Thanks,' the muscleman said to them before picking the guy up like he was a sack of rubbish to be taken to the tip. He carried him along the side of the house to where he'd parked his car.

'Dog okay?' Vladimir asked, doing up the buttons on his coat.

'I think so,' Eddie said as he crouched down to the sheepish Meriadoc.

The rain was falling now. Vladimir smiled appreciatively at them, nodded. He glanced round to see Jake closing the boot of the black Mercedes.

'Let's get out of here,' Jake called over to him.

But his colleague was hesitant. He looked back at Larry and Eddie standing there in the pattering rain. And the poor dog.

'Do you guys need a lift?' Vladimir asked them.

'Sure. If that's okay,' Larry replied.

'Come on.'

***

Driving away from the cesspit estate, they soon became

snarled up in the evening rush hour traffic. As he clutched onto Meriadoc, Eddie looked out of the side window, trying to see the drowned world outside as the rainwater streamed down the steamed up glass. It was like he'd suddenly been given a new angle on his hometown as he watched the cars trundling by on the other side of the road, miserable metal beasts crawling through the tempest like soldiers on a slow march to combat.

Eddie wasn't in a rush. Even though he was sitting in a car with two vigilantes, a junkie thief bundled into the boot, he felt strangely at ease. He'd heard of their organisation before, one of the many things the kids at the caravan parks used to talk about on his holidays. Not that Eddie had believed these kids, however intriguing their stories were. But meeting these Halo of Fires agents was like meeting a fat man with a white beard and discovering Father Christmas actually existed.

He turned to his friend and said, 'Didn't know you were a ninja.'

'I used to take judo lessons.'

'Oh.'

'How's the chin?'

'I'll survive.'

'Where do you guys live?' Jake interrupted.

'Oh yeah. Uh, it's Toledo Road,' Larry projected over the sound of the rain that thumped against the roof of the car like machine gun fire.

'Of course. The student end,' Vladimir added.

The vigilantes didn't appear to want to say anything more. It seemed an unusual situation for them all to be in, but then what would they have in common with two students?

Jake crept up to the red taillights of the vehicle in front that blurred through their rain-drenched windscreen like simmering hellfire. Traffic was an absolute crawl. Suddenly Larry breathed in, eager to spark up some conversation.

'Could I get you guys to go beat someone up for me? If I wanted to.'

Both the agents remained silent, probably waiting for each other to deal with the question.

'You got someone in mind?' Vladimir eventually asked.

'No, I mean hypothetically. How much would that cost, just out of interest?'

'I thought students were poor.'

'Yeah. I just wondered.'

'Who says our service costs anything?'

'Do you ever go and kill people?'

Vladimir paused, looking Larry over. He then turned to Eddie. 'Is your friend trying to tell us something here? Did his professor give him a bad grade?'

'Most likely.'

Vladimir's phone started ringing, killing the conversation. 'Excuse me.'

Both Eddie and Larry peered out of the side windows, pretending they weren't compelled to listen in.

'Hello... Yeah all sorted... No, no we're not there yet... Because we got held up... What?... That's a new one... You want all that *tonight*?... We can't do that, we're already tied up... Who?... Junior?... Yes, I appreciate that but there's no way I can get to the beach and sort that out beforehand. You can't get anyone else to do that for us?... I know it's short notice... Yeah I know, I don't have time, I... Can you hold on a second?'

Vladimir pulled the phone away from his ear. His jaw tightened and he made an idle clicking sound against the roof of his mouth with his tongue, as though giving an indication of the ticking cogs in his mind. He shared a quick glance with Jake but no words passed between them.

'Okay, Henry,' he said as he put the phone back to his ear. 'Leave me the details out... Catch you later.' He hung up.

'You think that's a good idea?' Jake whispered to him.

Vladimir didn't answer. He just cleared his throat.

Chapter 5.3

The storm disappeared as swiftly as it arrived. Like an angry snake that had spent its sticky venom all too quickly, the clouds were soon exhausted so that there was no more rain to squeeze out of them. Other than a drenched town, the legacy of this outburst was a cool breeze and lethargic clouds that refused to release the late evening sun.

Michael and Danny gave up waiting for their two friends and carried on to *The Mermaid's Cape* without them. Instead of having their usual Friday night doubles contest, they just played a few relaxed frames on their own. Larry and Eddie would most probably turn up later.

'How's Faridah these days?' Danny asked as he chalked his pool cue. 'Heard from her recently?'

He attempted a ball on a tight angle and smacked it firmly into the pocket. Danny was on fire tonight, playing like a professional.

'She's good. She called this week.'

'You guys going to meet up again this summer?'

'I'm hoping so. Depends if she can fit it in with her work.'

'That's good.'

Danny arched over the table again and pocketed another one of his reds.

'And how's your assignment going?' he asked next.

'Slowly. Wish I'd picked a different story. It's been difficult to research.'

'You still got a while left though, yeah?' Danny played his next shot. Finally he missed one.

'Yup,' Michael replied, watching the balls clinking around the table and slowly coming to a stop. Instead of getting up for his go, he stared at the pool table as though he might divine something in the arrangement of those yellow and red spheres.

'Your turn,' Danny prompted him.

'What happened to you, bud? Seriously, you've been like a different person since yesterday.'

He could clearly see the newfound excitement in his friend. Things that would have been an irritation to him before were now like a special gift from the universe, everything a sparkling moment of magic.

'Something happened actually,' Danny said.

'So I understand,' came the reply. But the voice did not belong to Michael. Their heads simultaneously turned.

Behind them stood a stranger dressed completely in black, an ominous blaze in his eyes. He was darkness and radiance in one.

'Just what have you been up to, young Daniel?'

'Who the heck are you?' Michael asked, gripping his pool cue tighter.

He walked around them with a lordly demeanour, whether he was just about to ignite a red laser sword or hop away into a police box. The man was multifaceted yet menacing mystery, as Vladimir was to everyone.

'Santa Claus visits the good boys; I visit the ones on the naughty list,' he replied.

The Angel of Karma took a pace towards the retreating Danny, both of his hands clutching the lapels of his coat as though he was revealing an insignia on his chest before springing into action. 'And this little one here has been a very naughty boy.'

Michael suddenly understood. 'You're Halo of...'

'Indeed, we are.'

Two hulking brutes appeared out of nowhere, towering either side of Danny as they each gripped an arm.

This had to be a case of mistaken identity. What misdeed would Danny have done? Michael threw his arms up in the air and yelled, 'Hold it!'

Strangely, both of the thugs paused and turned towards him with their steely eyes. Michael's mouth was dry. They were absolute giants and seemed to radiate an unnatural force from every one of their bulging muscles.

'Yes?' Vladimir asked.

'You can't do this. What did he do?'

'Your good friend here has been messing around with someone else's girl,' Vladimir told him. 'Someone else's fiancée, actually. And this someone else is rather upset right now.'

With that he gave a pointed nod to the two powerhouses who immediately resumed their operation. Clint held Danny in place while Jake slammed his fist into his nose. Lines of blood streamed down his mouth as he slumped to the floor.

'Stop it! You can't do this!' Michael shouted.

'Dangerous game kid, moving in on someone else's woman,' Jake said to Danny as he effortlessly hoisted him to his feet.

Clint chuckled. 'Yeah, Jake can tell you a thing or two about fast women.'

'Okay guys, let's get him outside,' Vladimir cut in.

'You're not taking him anywhere,' Michael said, raising his voice to draw attention to the scene taking place in this normally easygoing pub.

No one got up to help, though. Faces peered their way like frightened little rabbits, staring at the two wolves and the one raven, grateful they weren't the ones being torn apart by them.

'Are you going to stop us?' Vladimir asked.

'Even if I wasn't a pacifist, I'm really not that dumb,' Michael said as he could only watch the giant vigilantes dragging away his semi-conscious friend.

'Sounds a bit of a contradiction,' Vladimir replied, turning away, eager now to leave.

But Michael wasn't done yet. He had his own way to fight them.

'What are you going to do with him then, you cold-blooded child killers?'

Vladimir paused in his tracks. By now Jake and Clint were disappearing out the door.

'Nothing too permanent. Okay? Your friend didn't plant a bomb or anything.' He tried again to leave.

'You're not going to kill him then? Not like those two school kids you murdered?'

That stopped him dead. Slowly he turned, his eyes so stern it was like he was trying to project a magical flame from them. 'What did you say?'

'You murdered a teenage boy and his little brother.'

It was like standing on the tracks of the roller coaster, Vladimir hurtling towards him, out of control. Something savage was exploding inside him, as though Michael had just flipped a very dangerous switch. The vigilante reached forward and grabbed him by his throat, pushing him down

144

onto the pool table, leaning over him, squeezing his neck to stop the words coming out.

'You... killed them,' Michael spluttered. 'He was just a six-year-old boy... and you killed him!'

The vigilante's black eyes hovered above him, open as wide as they would go. They were like looking into a mirror and all Michael could see in them was a distorted version of himself, someone possessed by a demon. He closed his eyes as he searched for more stinging words to use against the nerve he was hitting.

'My brother told me. He knew that boy. Simon Helliwell was his name. He was friends with him at school before you went and murdered him.'

Hot breath snorted on his face, Michael fearing the man had combusted in his rage and now threatened to burn him away too.

As he dared to open his eyes, he perceived a self-conscious realisation creeping into the vigilante's features. The grip on his neck released, his attacker looking at his fist as though he hadn't realised it had been clamped to someone's throat. Vladimir straightened his coat.

'How old are you, pacifist?'

'Twenty.'

'A little too old to be telling playground stories, isn't it? Halo of Fires didn't kill Simon Helliwell. That may have been the story going around, but it's not the truth.'

'Why should I believe you?' Michael shot back, standing up straight again. 'One day they'll dig up his little brother's skeleton and discover your calling card on it.'

'What has this got to do with you?'

'Too bad you guys hid the body so well,' Michael said, goading him into keeping this conversation going longer.

'The police searched. No one ever found a body because there was no body to find. The Fires came and helped the kid, hiding him away so the killers would never find him.'

'So Jeremy's alive somewhere?'

Vladimir's mouth remained shut and he swallowed hard.

'But what about Simon?' Michael persisted. 'Who killed him if it wasn't you?'

'It's nothing to do with you.'

'There's two, *possibly three*, unsolved murders. The killer needs to be found and brought to justice.'

Vladimir took a step backwards. The guy was seriously clamming up now. Good job Michael hadn't mentioned from the outset that he was a student journalist.

'Possibly three,' the vigilante muttered.

He centred himself once more as he recomposed his magnificent aura, and then glided out of the building like a bird that had just straightened its ruffled plume.

***

Danny felt smothered by the enveloping blackness, his mind flailing around as it frantically tried to grasp onto whatever it could, to break out of the nightmare that was impossible to break out of. The stuffy air was thick and bitter, filling his lungs like molten rock.

Where was he? Where was his world? He was now in a realm of nothingness, a purgatorial stasis. Danny could not even die in his death. He reached around himself in his juddering tomb, which rocked and swayed him about. He could see nothing.

The vibration stopped. Silence, then clicks and thuds. Footsteps. That angel of darkness again, lifting the lid, dull light sluggishly creeping inside. As if there to administer his last rites, the three faces looked down on him, tinted by the sickly orange hue of street lamps. There was no escaping that raven-like angel and his two demons. His fiery eyes kept peering down on him, and it felt like they were piercing into his soul. He knew what this meant. Nevermore. It was the answer to everything.

Here on the shores of his underground world, the raven controlled all. Danny heard the churning of the waves. Hissing and roaring. Hissing and roaring. It teased from him a memory of the day before, of sitting by the shore with that enchantress. Gone was the beauty that he'd looked upon yesterday, replaced by this trio of fiends, and even the waves had turned wicked and would wash him into their black beyond.

Why, oh why, had he succumbed to her temptation?

Why had he risked incurring this wrathful consequence by venturing into her world? Danny was being delivered the ultimate punishment, for treading where he shouldn't, for roaming into the forbidden heights. They weren't for someone who'd been assigned a safe life of normality. Ordinary people weren't supposed to fly with the angels.

They shoved him into a grave. The two demons piled in the dirt as the raven, dressed in his deathly black plumage, stood watching like a servant of the netherworld.

They spared him his sight. His bleary eyes would forever face those roaring waves, a twisted reminder of his sin and her world.

A world that he should never visit again.

***

Michael had darted after them. As soon as that fiery vigilante had walked out of *The Mermaid's Cape*, he followed stealthily, doing his best to channel the spirit of every James Bond movie. Up the road he witnessed Vladimir approaching a black saloon as the two thugs stuffed Danny into the boot. They then trundled away like a hearse on its way to a funeral.

With his sight fixed on that Mercedes, Michael had run after them as fast as his legs would allow. He wasn't used to running, but he wasn't unfit either, so he kept a reasonable pace. The adrenaline was really helping. At the end of the road the car had disappeared out of view as it made a right turn towards the seafront. Michael kept up his pursuit.

He soon found them again, the only vehicle in an empty car park by the seafront. He hovered behind an ice cream stand as he caught his breath. He could feel his limbs shaking with all the excitement, but right now he had to hold himself together somehow. He'd never make a secret agent.

Through the gloom he saw the three vigilantes emerging from the beach, heading back to their car. Where was Danny? He scanned the area, but there was no one else around. Had he escaped? Was he still in the boot?

The two big thugs sat on the bonnet of the Mercedes and

folded their arms. The one in black looked around as though someone had just called his name. With a seemingly preternatural sense, he picked out the person who was spying on him: Michael.

A chill emerged from his warmed blood. How did he know he was there? He stepped out from the stand; it seemed pointless hiding any longer. The vigilante just nodded his head to him, as though answering a question Michael hadn't realised he'd asked. Two opposing forces on each end of the spectrum, sizing each other up before the battle. Tonight was only the beginning.

Vladimir ordered his cohorts to get in the car and start it up. Michael approached him, but doing so felt like forcing two magnets together.

'What have you done with him?' he called out.

'You're a persistent fellow.'

'Where is he?'

'He's dead, obviously. That's all we ever do. Just go round killing people. Go dig up his bones if you want,' Vladimir said as he pointed towards the beach.

Michael looked over there. He spotted what appeared to be a football just a few yards up from the drift line. Or perhaps it was a rock, or maybe some kid had left his bucket there.

'Why do you do this?' he asked him.

'Take a look at the world, my friend. Nobody knows what right is any more. I bet you're religious, aren't you?'

Michael was a little surprised at the man's observation. He didn't reply.

'See, people needed that moral compass before. But now they're throwing them out and using the ones they were born with. Trouble is, people don't know how to use them.'

'Danny's a good lad. He doesn't deserve this. He wouldn't intend to ever hurt anyone.'

'The road to hell.'

Michael shook his head as he looked again beyond the dunes, now realising what he'd spotted was Danny, buried to his neck in the sand.

Vladimir caught his gaze. 'I guess I can go now.'

He got into the car and the vigilantes sped off into the

night in a plume of dust.

Michael ran down to the sands. Poor Danny's head lolled to one side, but as he kneeled down in front of him, he realised he was okay. Or rather, he was *going* to be okay. Dried blood covered his mouth, speckled with sand, and his nose didn't look too good. And he was still punch-drunk, murmuring nonsense to himself.

The tide was edging its way up the beach, so Danny would have had an hour or so to escape. In the back of his mind, he tried to recall the film where this same thing had happened. Some cheesy horror movie. Leslie Nielsen had buried Ted Danson in the sand and watched him drown via a television monitor. But then Ted had returned as a seaweed-covered zombie. Revenge always had its own consequences!

The Halo of Fires thugs hadn't intended to kill Danny, it seemed. Their target hadn't committed murder, so there was no eye for an eye to be had. They were just scaring Danny into *thinking* they would kill him, standing by at the car until a watery death licked at his neck. Or until some good Samaritan came along and dug him out.

Whatever their silly intentions, though, he saw how despicable this was. Who appointed them judge, jury and *pretend* executioners? That's what he despised about Halo of Fires; they brought this service of gangsterism to regular folk, placing a fiery power at their disposal. And not to mention that they did the work that should be left to God. But this was a time of making people pay.

Danny seemed to recognise him as he scooped the sand away from him. He mumbled something, but Michael couldn't tell what he was saying.

'It's okay, Danny. We'll have you out of here and home in no time.'

'I'm... I'm sorry.'

'What for?'

'I shouldn't... I shouldn't have talked to her.'

Michael soon felt something solid. It was Danny's arm. They hadn't buried him that deep at all.

'Let's look on the bright side. You've done me a big favour, you know. You helped me get the perfect interview for my assignment.'

Danny managed a smile. 'You'd better get a good mark now.'

There was still a question he wanted to ask him though, something still playing on his mind. 'Who was she?'

Danny looked up at him and Michael noticed his eyes regaining their clarity.

'Stella Connoly.'

'I see.' It was the name he suspected he would hear. He was sure Samuel Allington was the type who could click his fingers to manifest such swift retribution.

'I didn't do anything though. All I did was talk to her, and... okay, maybe she kissed me goodbye.'

'Well, be careful, mate.'

Danny leaned his head back and gazed up towards the heavens. The clouds had now rolled away, a glittering blaze of stars sprayed over the sky. Despite the drama they'd just endured, he seemed rather mellow.

'You're lucky, Michael. You know exactly what you have with Faridah.'

'It's far from straightforward. The distance thing, I mean.'

'But you'll work it out. You'll be together one day.'

'One day, yes.'

'Do you think that people are meant for each other? That it's written in the stars?'

'It's an interesting thought, isn't it?'

Danny didn't answer, but Michael could see his head softly nodding.

***

'Holy hell, Michael, you're seriously not going to believe what happened to us today,' Larry blurted as soon as Michael stepped into the living room.

Normally Larry's froth-mouthed excitement would have piqued his interest, but instead, Michael sniffed before coolly taking a seat opposite Eddie. At his feet, a sleepy Meriadoc raised his head to see who'd just walked in.

'Larry, I guarantee you, whatever happened to you, me

and Danny got that beat.'

'No way, not this one. Where is Danny? He'll want to hear this too,' Larry persisted.

'He's in the bathroom. Cleaning up.'

Larry skipped a beat. 'Why, what happened to him?'

Michael leant forward for his own big reveal. 'You know those Halo of Fires people I told you about? Tonight they came and got Danny.'

Larry swallowed hard. 'What... What did they do to him?'

'We were in the pub when suddenly they appear. These two meatheads the size of Geoff bleeding Capes grab him and one of them leathers him on the nose.'

'Shit, is he okay?'

'Then they drag him away, bundle him into the boot of their car and take off.'

'To the beach?' Larry asked.

'Yeah! I chased after them, so I'm running down...' Michael's narration suddenly clogged up. 'Why...? How did you know they took him to the beach?'

Larry was now by the window, looking like a naughty pupil sent to the back of class. His folded arms rested on the windowsill, his eyes far away from the room.

'Diamond?'

His back still to him, Larry asked, 'What did they do to him?'

'They buried him in a hole. I managed to find him again so I was able to dig him out.'

An anticlimactic silence hung in the air.

'So, your story was...?'

Larry took a deep breath. 'Doesn't matter.' He left the room.

Michael turned to Eddie. 'What's up with him?'

'We met them Halo of Fires people as well today.'

'Really?'

'We ended up helping them out with something, then later they offered us a little bit of work.'

'Doing...?'

'They asked us to dig a big hole at the beach.'

Michael put his head in his hands, staring through his

fingers. 'How could you?'

'We didn't know it was for Danny, like. And hey, it's not our fault he's been a knobhead.'

'But he's your friend. You don't care, do you?'

Eddie sneered as he stared at nothing on the floor. 'Why should I?'

'You selfish bastard.'

'Language, mate. That must be ten Hail Marys.'

'Get lost. Why do we even bother with you? You're a total waste of time.'

'Oh well, nice to know how you feel, Michael. Yeah, that's really Christian of you. You're all the same, you bunch of hypocrites.'

Michael held his breath a moment. The words seemed to be slipping off his tongue on their own, and hearing the profanities he was spewing just made him even more angry. He knew he had to detach from this emotion. Had to rise above. Rise above.

Eddie got up. 'And you know what? I didn't ask to be friends with any of you or to play your loser pool games.'

As he stormed off, Michael shook his head. It was strange how one's whole world could turn upside down in the space of an evening.

Part 6: The Harbour Master

Chapter 6.1

The cigarette protruding from Floyd's mouth was about to burn out. He'd initially taken a few drags to help settle his nerves but those heavy thoughts were swarming through his mind like an infestation of cockroaches and not even the fading wisps of smoke could distract from them.

A gust of wind swept the fragile line of ash into his eyes. He brushed the back of his hand over his face as he spat the butt onto the ground. As was his habit, he then snorted up a gulp of mucus from his throat. Instead of scuffing his foot over the discarded cigarette to make sure it was out like most people did, Floyd liked to gob over his fag ends. It was just a Floyd thing. He was an excellent aim when it came to spitting, and the brown wad of slime fell precisely on it.

It was a glorious sunny day at *Floyd's Amusements* and the screaming children were out in force on the dragon roller coaster, the waltzers, and all the other exciting rides at his world of fun. They munched on toffee apples and clouds of candy floss the size of their heads, no unhappy faces anywhere. Nowhere except for the face of the mucus-spewing Floyd, that was.

Floyd hated children, absolutely despised the little shits. They didn't contribute anything to society, yet these days everything was about them coming first. Adults lived in a child-friendly world, when it should be the other way round. Television, Christmas, speed limits everywhere on the town roads, it was all geared towards kids. All the useless crotch droppings wanted to do was play all the time, and they'd cry if they didn't get their way. They didn't have the mental faculties to behave differently. Floyd had been told how the human brain only finishes developing at nineteen years of age, and that children only stop thinking *animalistically* when they're around thirteen. Put simply, children shouldn't be considered normal human beings.

He could live with the fact his amusements were a source of enjoyment for them. Every scream of excitement he heard was another quid in his hand. Every shoot-'em-up game that rotted their minds and every sweet that rotted their teeth just improved his bank balance. He took pleasure when the kids gorged themselves on junk food and then threw it all up on the rides. Let them suffer in their selfish overindulgence. That's what all the brats deserved, and, for that reason, the proprietor of the amusements had purposely modified every one of his rides so they would go that bit faster.

Floyd was in a strangely contemplative mood this afternoon. After receiving the letter, he'd come outside for some fresh air and a smoke. All of a sudden he had so much to think about.

In the periphery of his vision, he noticed one of the horrible brats lurking beneath him. How long had he been there?

'Excuse me, mister,' the sniffling little boy said, swamped in Floyd's tall shadow.

He crouched down so he could hear him properly, beaming a friendly smile. 'What's the matter there, soldier?' He adopted a bright tone of voice as he'd learnt early on in this business it was profitable to be pleasant to the customers.

'I can't find my mum anywhere.'

The kid had a raspberry ice cream in his hand, sticky crimson lines dribbling down his fingers. He wore a navy-blue T-shirt that said something about it being US Army property. Some heroic trooper this little ragamuffin was.

'Don't cry, soldier. What does she look like?'

'Her hair is black and red. She's wearing her pink hoodie.'

Floyd put on a thoughtful face even though she sounded like every other moronic slob that came to his amusements.

'You know what? I saw your mother. I just spoke to her a minute ago.'

'Where is she?' the boy asked.

'Well, she's gone.'

'Where to?'

'Oh, you won't find her. No, she's left. She told me she didn't want to see you any more because she hates you.'

'She did?'

The boy's bottom lip quavered. Raspberry slush trickled down his arm onto his bright trainers as tears dripped from his cheeks.

'That's right. She said you were a worthless piece of shit and she wishes she'd had you aborted because one lousy shag wasn't worth all the years of misery you brought her.'

Floyd stood up again, the same pleasant smile still on his face.

'What... What should I do?' the boy whined.

'I don't know. I've got my own problems. Looks like you're on your own, kiddo.'

Only mumbling followed from the waif as he surveyed the park, the enormity of his apparent situation starting to hit him.

Floyd looked on as the kid disappeared into the crowds, wondering why he'd come to him, of all people. If God or his heavenly messengers genuinely cared about the wellbeing of their children, why not guide them to someone who would actually give a crap about their predicament? Floyd was proud he was an absolute bastard. It was important to have shits like him in God's world. They were, in fact, just as important as the saints and the Mother Teresas.

From the very beginning, Floyd had been groomed to hate. It had been his purpose ever since he'd been born. Even as a mentally undeveloped child, he'd started *his* teaching, learning what the world was really about. When he'd reached adulthood, become a proper human being, that's when he'd understood it all properly. Evil didn't really exist, it was not a force of nature found within the heart of any man that walked the earth. But if someone *did* want to become evil (without any lunacy side effects, that was) the only way to do this was to apply one's mind to a *doctrine* of evil. Floyd had spent many years studying this.

One thing he'd been taught under this doctrine was that extinguishing someone's life was no worse than extinguishing a cigarette. And so, when *he* had called his disciple to extinguish, Floyd had developed his own way of doing it. It was just another Floyd thing. Instead of putting a bullet in the head of that dealer who miss-sold them, Floyd had extinguished his life in a much more elaborate fashion. Having severed all the guy's limbs with power tools and observing he *still* hadn't died, he'd thought it would be exceptionally evil to next use his circular saw. The man's screams had certainly sounded funny with half of his face sliced off. He continued screaming for a few seconds more when Floyd cut open his midriff and made his intestines slop onto the floor. He had told him he was going to make him spill his guts, after all.

Extracting as much suffering from this man as possible, and not feeling an ounce of remorse in doing so, was a sign that Floyd had become a masterpiece of evil. But all went to hell after Henry Maristow started tagging along with him.

They got on okay at first. For a couple of months there was even a semblance of friendship, as he introduced the beancounter to the workings of the Network. It was during that Forseti business when Henry could not break free from his conscience and took matters into his own hands.

What a screw up that was. It was so embarrassing for Floyd, for everyone. No wonder everything disappeared down the pan after that. He left him to do all the explaining to the boss, of course. Not that he had to do it face-to-face, for it was rare for people to be an audience to *him*. He could count on one hand the number of times he'd actually met *him*.

Usually contact would be by letter, like the one he had in his trench coat pocket at that moment. He'd immediately recognised its characteristics. That same meticulous handwriting. The same way *he* signed them. Three initials, indicating the only name that people knew *him* by, and the name that no one ever liked to hear: The Harbour Master.

There in the middle of his mechanical playground, as the giant teacups continued their tedious spinning and the mindless children scampered around him like rats in a laboratory cage, Floyd read through the letter again. It was a call for reconciliation, a call for the two of them to bring their forces together again.

Somehow he'd earned *his* redemption, and once more, after all these years, The Harbour Master wanted to set him to work.

Chapter 6.2

'I think it be wonderful you come out here with us, Mr Floyd,' Harp shouted over the laboured chugging of the *Alchemist* engines. 'Great to meet the project executive at long last.'

'Well, it was time I met this brilliant bunch of explorers,' Floyd called back to him, his hands stuffed inside his pockets, all the buttons on his trench coat done up.

Devlan had been peering at him through his shades all morning. He could smell something was off, just as he could smell that Floyd desperately needed a shower. The guy had been sweating more than usual, and there was a strange colour in his ever-blinking eyes. It was like he was looking at those eyes for the first time, a disorientating mist crawling over the swamp.

'Why are you here?' he asked. It was the third time he'd asked him that question.

Waking up in the cabin earlier, Devlan had gone about his usual routine of cooking some porridge when the sound of elephantine footsteps stomping along the quay filled his ears. It appeared the uninvited guest would not only be joining him for breakfast but also fancied a boat trip.

Before Devlan could get out of him what he was doing there, Captain Harp had arrived at the harbour and instantly seized on the fresh blood, a new person to recount his seafaring tales to. Devlan and the divers had heard them all by now, often more than once, so Harp was clearly very enthusiastic about having the project chief aboard the *Alchemist*.

'Well?' Devlan persisted, his impatience building.

Floyd's cracked lips gradually formed a crooked smile,

157

but his jittering eyes wouldn't connect with his.

'You'll see. When we get there, I have a very important announcement to make.'

Devlan opened his mouth to ask another question, but he didn't know what else to say.

'Now then,' Harp began again, interrupting their uneasy silence, 'just because that wreck has been down there all this time, it doesn't mean it has gone unseen ever since.'

Floyd turned his attention towards the talkative captain, shrugging the focus from himself. 'Seen what?' he asked.

'I've been on these waters a good many years, you know. Strange things are to be found out here. It can be like a whole other world at times.'

Floyd stepped closer to the storyteller. Devlan angled his ears, sensing a story he hadn't heard before. Somehow Harp had dug up a new one at long last.

'I should think it were nigh on forty years ago now. Young pup I was in those days. More interested in my sweethearts that time than I was with fishing. I remember one young lass, broke off with me one Valentine's, she did. Boy, was I all broken up about that. Beautiful girl, she was. But outs I came here. Just me and the faithful vessel for an entire week. You learn some things about yourself when you're on your own, I tell you.'

Harp gazed across the sea as the *Alchemist* skimmed along the blue expanse. Nothing but limitless water and limitless sky was before him, a stark but pure natural wilderness, with a force that man could never harness, and a depth of mystery he could never fully unveil. The spirited captain took on a new tone of voice, one that Devlan was not familiar with.

'For a whole week I never spoke to a soul. And you know what? I never felt so peaceful, out here on these waters. All day I would ponder the universe as I swayed about on the waves.

'It started to feel like I was in a dream world, likes I had been hypnotised. That's my only explanation as to the strange sight I saw one night. Coming out of the evening mist she appeared, gliding along so silently, but solid like this here deck I'm standing on now. She sailed right on past and as I looked at her stern I caught her name before the mist swallowed her up again.

'But all night I was kept wide awake. There I lay in my cabin, praying those noises would go away. All that screaming. I'll never forget that. Poor souls. I heard them all drowning.'

Harp fell silent. Devlan took in a big breath of spicy sea air, and then released.

Realising the tale was over, Floyd arched his head down to him and muttered, 'You know, I'm really going to have to shut him up in a minute.'

***

There was nothing in sight when Captain Harp killed the *Alchemist* engines, nothing except a glimmering blue landscape and a serrated line on the horizon that was the now distant town of Dark Harbour. It was a naked patch of sea, free from fishing vessels or pleasure boats out spotting seals. Perhaps the spot on the sea's blanket was like a Devil's Triangle and the vortex would swallow anything that sailed over it. But, right now, if someone was to scream in calamitous panic at the top of their voice, not a soul would hear them.

With both his hands still stuffed inside his pockets, Floyd glanced over the three divers with more scrutiny as they waited for Harp to clamber down from the bridge. Devlan had informed him of their names, but he'd immediately forgotten them all. Drip One, Drip Two, and Drip Three were the names he'd mentally assigned the nonentities.

What a bunch of tossers. And as for Captain 'Harp-oon Me Quick, Someone', he was just an annoying twat.

Floyd couldn't deny how well they'd done in finding the *Tatterdemalion*, though. They'd achieved what no one else had before, so there had to be something to this unlikely band of explorers Devlan had dug up. They were still twats though.

'Okay, tw... guys,' Floyd began, 'I wanted a little word

with you before I send you off down there. We've done something fantastic here. I was told only yesterday that we weren't the only ones to go searching for this *Tatterdemalion* ship. There's one or two chaps that'll be really envious of us. The thing is, I've only just realised how important this discovery is. It's a lot more significant than we would have known.'

At that point, Floyd turned to Devlan. 'Can you get the GPS co-ordinates for me?'

'Why?' Devlan replied.

'Just do it.'

'Sure, Mr Floyd,' Harp interjected as he walked towards the cabin. 'We'll go get that for you.'

His eyes over his shoulder, Devlan followed him.

'Now, my friends,' Floyd went on as he faced the Three Drips. 'It's essential that no one else learns this information. And, I'm afraid, there's only one way I can make certain of that.'

Floyd's hands flew out of his pockets. In each one he held a .45 calibre Glock 21. He pointed them at the heads of Drip One and Drip Two. A head shot at this close a range was more than sufficient, and as Floyd pulled the trigger, and fragments of brain and skull shattered across the deck, the two drips dropped dead.

Anticipating that Drip Three would frantically flip out on him, Floyd immediately re-aimed his left Glock at him in a continuous movement. He fired once but uncharacteristically missed his target.

The surviving frogman scrambled over the side, into the water, flapping around for his mouthpiece.

At that moment, Floyd suddenly remembered a scene from a film. Recalling how the killer shark met his doom in the waters of Amity Island, he pointed his gun at the aluminium oxygen pack on Drip Three's back. What a great myth-busting opportunity to see if fiction lived up to reality.

Upon saying, 'Smile, you son of a bitch,' Floyd pulled the trigger, precisely on the word 'bitch' in shameless emulation of Chief Brody. To emphasise his drama further, he lamely attempted the line in an American accent.

Rather disappointingly, Drip Three didn't explode in a

mass of blood and flesh and rain back down again on the sea. As the diver screamed and flailed around, Floyd fired a bullet at his head and promptly ended his fussing. Silence.

He turned towards the cabin. There stood Captain Harp, his face as white as the collecting clouds in the sky.

'Please, Mr Floyd, I...'

There was no point listening to any pleas, so with both Glocks he fired them repetitively at Harp's head. One bullet would have been enough to extinguish his life, but the agent of destruction shot half a dozen. Harp's body hit the cabin door and flopped to the deck.

'That shut you up, didn't it?'

He looked down to see what a glorious mess he'd made. A section of Harp's face hung off his neck like a torn Halloween mask, thick crimson blood soaking his woollen sweater. Floyd had to contain himself and resist the urge to fire more bullets and destroy him further, even though Harp was as dead as the *Tatterdemalion* pirates who'd haunted him in his youth.

Next he had to find Devlan. Where was he? Floyd peered through the cabin window. No sign of him.

'Looking for me?'

Floyd whipped round so quickly he lost his balance and toppled over. How did that freak move about so swiftly? He kicked his legs against the deck to put some distance between him and that animal, holding out both his quivering arms. Why the hell did he have to remove his shades? Despite having a loaded weapon in each hand, looking at those fiery eyes wasn't any easier.

'Floyd, what in God's name was all that about?' Devlan asked him. His voice was strangely measured, as though he were a psychiatrist and Floyd was lying on the couch.

'Stay back!'

'Or what? You're going to shoot me?'

'Where are those co-ordinates?'

'Sorry, couldn't get them. The machine's not working.'

The guns still aimed, Floyd steadily got up, not taking his eyes off him for one second.

'Now, are you going to tell me what the hell's going on? Either that or just get on and shoot me.'

'You think I would do that?' Floyd protested.

He risked lowering his arms. When it appeared no countermove was about to spring at his face, he returned the guns to his trench coat pockets.

'The situation's changed.'

'You don't say. I take it from this gesture you no longer want me to search for the Akasa Stone.'

'No.'

Devlan's eyes suddenly swelled blazingly wide like supernovae and with extraordinary swiftness he leapt at Floyd, pinning him to the deck with his claws.

'Then why the hell did you kill all my friends?' he roared, his forehead pressed firmly against his.

Floyd couldn't find any words to reply, only whimpering groans. Locked beneath this creature, he feared he was about to black out.

'Why, you bastard?' Devlan continued to growl, spittle splashing against Floyd's face.

He felt a searing pain in his shoulders, like razor blades were slicing apart his flesh. Grimacing at the sight of Devlan's eyes, Floyd noticed a detail he'd never noticed before, how the pupils were elliptical, like the eyes of a panther. It made his stomach lurch even more.

'It's not down there,' Floyd somehow panted.

'So what the hell are you trying to protect?' the creature shouted, his hot breath billowing against his face.

'More than you would know.'

'Tell me.'

'That ship was cursed. There's bad things down there, and they need to be left where they are.'

'Who told you this shit?'

'The Harbour Master.'

Devlan sighed as he released his claws and stood up. 'Cursed? Why on earth would you think…?' He didn't finish his question.

'Had to be done. Had to protect the town,' Floyd said, remaining flat on his back. He summoned the courage to open his eyes again. His shoulders throbbed with each thud of his heart.

'You're a superhero now?'

'I do what I'm told. The Harbour Master knows.'

'*He* tell you to kill me as well?'

'Have the legendary Devlan killed? I think The Harbour Master would rather have you working for *him*.'

'No matter how long I'm here for, that'll never happen.'

'You work for me, you're working for *him*,' Floyd said as he dragged himself up.

'So what happens now?'

Floyd straightened his coat. 'This heap of shit have a lifeboat?'

'There's one somewhere.'

'Go sort it.'

As Devlan searched out the inflatable dinghy, Floyd went below deck and saw to the scuttling of the *Alchemist* by firing some bullets into the hull. While there was still time, he then took a brief look at the GPS machine but found it was indeed kaput. Devlan must have killed it. The co-ordinates weren't important, anyway. All that mattered was that the resting place of the *Tatterdemalion* was no longer known to anyone. That's what The Harbour Master wanted.

Floyd realised that there was still something of a loose end in Devlan, who possibly hadn't memorised the co-ordinates, but who'd been trailing out to this spot each day and might be able to find it again by memory. He couldn't worry about that now, though. With this operation over it was time to be getting on with the next one.

***

'Don't look on this as a failure, my friend,' Floyd said as Devlan struck up the zodiac's engine. 'I've achieved exactly what I wanted.'

'Where is it? Who's got it?' he asked. The zodiac sparked into life and they stuttered away from the listing *Alchemist* as it made its way towards the ancient graveyard for doomed vessels. It wasn't any pirate ship that was cursed, it was Devlan himself. Everything he did in life had darkness and tragedy written all over it.

'The Harbour Master has it.'

'I see.'

'We'll get our hands on it. We just have more work to do.'

Devlan nodded as though he was agreeing with him, but really he was thinking of his next step once they reached the shore. He had no choice but to wash his hands of Floyd and slink away once more, back to the abandoned factory and his rodent friends.

When it came to matters concerning The Harbour Master, he knew to stay out of them. *He* was an individual so shrouded in mystery, danger lurking underneath *his* cloak. Too many had dabbled with the nefarious forces of that man and paid the price. There was only one winner with that slanderer.

They'd come looking for him. *He* would know about Devlan's shrewdness, and *he* would be right for thinking he would commit to memory the *Tatterdemalion's* co-ordinates.

Perhaps it was best if he stayed with Floyd, though. He just couldn't believe he might have to look towards this animal for protection. Whichever route his thoughts took him, Devlan knew that misfortune lay in wait down every route. It was always the way with him.

He gazed into the sky and saw a small ruffling of white clouds, imagining Harp's spirit being guided by an honour guard of angels into those eternal heights above. All of a sudden he felt so lonely. He'd read how everyone was supposed to have their own angel, a guardian spirit to look over them. Theoretically even the monster next to him with the piss-stained pants had one. But being a different type to everyone else in this world, Devlan accepted he wouldn't have any angels assigned to his soul. Of that, he was now certain.

Across the zodiac, Floyd began whistling to himself. He was clearly pleased with how much destruction he'd caused in one morning.

Chapter 6.3

'Not eaten yet, have you?' Aurelia asked as she walked through the grand mahogany door.

'No time,' Henry replied as he lifted his eyes from the stack of papers on his desk.

'Okay, stop what you're doing. I got you a sandwich from *Bon Appétit*. Bacon and brie.'

'You're an angel.' Aurelia was often something of a mother hen to him, nagging him whenever he skipped lunch.

She smiled as she placed the paper bag down in front of him. 'Oh yes, and one other thing. I found this just now when I arrived back.'

Henry squinted as she handed him an envelope. His first name was handwritten on it.

'You look confused. Perhaps someone has written you a love letter.'

He smiled. 'I don't think anyone would want to write one to me.'

'You never know,' she replied as she turned for her desk.

'Thanks, Aurelia,' Henry said. 'For the sandwich.'

'You're welcome.'

As the door closed, Henry's smile instantly faded.

He knew straight away whom the letter was from. He knew that for the first time in eighteen years he'd heard from The Harbour Master.

A dozen thought processes ignited in his brain like electric shocks, all speculation on the reasons why *he* might have written to him, and as he held the envelope, he noticed his hands were unable to hold it still. Instead of just staring at it, Henry picked up his letter opener and sliced it open.

He read it once, and then immediately raided his cabinet for a drink of brandy. There were no threats in the letter. Henry's old boss made no declaration of war on the Fires or wished any plague on their house. There was no seething resentment about his past actions behind any of the words. It would not appear to be a letter authored by someone whom Henry had let down royally. All that was a long time ago, anyway. Perhaps The Harbour Master had moved on now.

What *he* did talk about was, to no surprise, the Akasa Stone. On that matter *he* didn't go into significant detail, however. As they'd thought, it was The Harbour Master who'd employed The Reaper, the man who'd grabbed the stone from Vladimir's very clutches. *He* made no apologies for what had happened, nor offered Henry any condolences, sincere or sarcastic.

All it said was that Henry needed to meet with *him* soon to talk about 'the stone they'd taken from the heathen David Tovar'. What that actually meant was that he would meet with The Harbour Master's representative, most probably Seleven Vear, for the big guy rarely spoke face-to-face with anyone other than his closest cohorts.

As for why *he* needed to talk to him, Henry couldn't quite tell. Perhaps *he* would allow him to view the stone, or even let him hold it for a few moments. Would a rival Akasa Stone searcher appreciate how soul-destroying it must have been for Henry to have been so close to obtaining it?

It would be out of character for *him,* though. *He* wasn't a man who cared for the emotional needs of his fellow humans, especially those who were once *his* enemy. But maybe *he* had changed since owning the Akasa Stone, or more specifically the stone had changed *him.* Isn't that what it was supposed to do?

Chasing that rainbow again, Henry. As always, you're trailing down that street called No Hope!

Impossible. Not after what Henry did all those years ago, how his actions triggered the chain reaction.

He poured more brandy into his glass. A meeting loomed in half an hour, but right now his focus was obliterated, his head unsettled by the bad memories. They were like a pack of wild jackals released from a cage running riot in his mind.

What could he have done? If he'd had any idea that Floyd was a complete psychopath, he wouldn't have been there in the first place. It was The Harbour Master's fault for not telling him what Floyd was all about.

Henry was only supposed to be an accountant, anyway. They'd employed him to balance the books, not collecting the debt to make sure they balanced. That was Floyd's job.

Why didn't you just stick to your boring office job?

Being cooped up in an an office all day looking at numbers was no fun, not for a young man. He wanted to explore, find out exactly what this Network was all about. Or maybe it was in later years that he would justify his actions, kid himself into believing his eyes didn't want to be blind.

With youthful arrogance, he'd peeled off the lid and looked inside, but Henry had not run away from what he'd seen. It wasn't long after that when The Harbour Master summoned him, that meeting where *he* talked to him about Nephilim and the son of Jared and lots of other things that Henry hadn't followed. He soon found his role expanding, and it felt like there were no limits, as though young Maristow was a man with fire in his hands for the first time, feeling the seduction of power.

He hadn't been ready though, not to see Floyd's true colours. It was that damned Forseti affair, that strange man who'd taken the city associates for a long and merry ride and run up a tremendous debt along the way. They'd underestimated him severely, but The Harbour Master would take care of him.

Floyd, with the young Maristow in tow, had gone to the guy's house to sort it out. One way or the other, the case would be closed by them. Why it hadn't occurred to Henry that Forseti's family might also be there, he just didn't know. Even so, he would never have imagined that Floyd would have 'used' them to settle the matter. Worse, though, Henry never would have imagined he'd stand back while Floyd got on with it.

He did break in the end, though. Witnessing Floyd slice open the wife's face with razor blades, and then watching him remove all the fingernails on the young daughter's right hand went a long way, but it was Floyd's next action that pushed Henry over the edge. Those were the visions that felt like they'd been etched onto his mind by a blunt chisel.

So Henry intervened, and from that moment on things

changed forever. They botched the job, the associates were livid, Forseti slipped away, and Henry was no longer employee of the month at the Network.

Instead of running away, which is what he should have done, Henry sat it out as he waited for *his* men to come and douse him in nitric acid or plant a bomb in his car. As the weeks turned into months, he realised that none of those things would apparently happen.

Realising that he still had a life, he eventually got back on with living it. He returned to his blissfully boring accountancy and chased up some of his original clients whom he'd abandoned when taking the full-time position in the Network.

One of those clients was a certain Alan Hammond, a city barrister from Dark Harbour with his hands in various local enterprises. Alan was pleased to hear from his old friend, but along with wanting Henry to do his books once more, he presented him with another opportunity.

More than that, Alan asked Henry for some help on something. He would eventually let him in on a secret that Henry would promise to keep for the rest of his life. Such was the path he'd had to take with Halo of Fires. It was necessary, though. He'd needed to make up for his waywardness under the Network, to redress his karma.

As the jackals prowled away into the hazier nooks of his mind, he opened the paper bag and brought out the sandwich. He took one bite but swallowed it awkwardly. He knew it wasn't going to go down well, and so he bagged it back up and sipped the brandy instead.

The phone rang, and Henry jumped as though that bomb had finally gone off. After clearing his throat, he picked up.

'Henry Maristow.'

He heard busy traffic on the other end of the line and then, 'Henry, it's Devlan.'

'It's who?'

'It's Devlan,' the voice replied, thicker and huskier.

'So it is.'

A truck roared past, and the proceeding silence soon became tense.

'How can I help you, Devlan?'

'Floyd... he's lost it.'

'He's lost it?'

The roar of traffic swelled just as Devlan was answering the question, and Henry didn't hear a word.

'Devlan, why are you phoning me?'

More silence. 'I need to talk to you.'

'Then talk.'

'I think... I think we could both do with each other's help right now.'

'Why would I need your help?'

'Because... Floyd... You don't realise what...'

The phone went dead. Henry dialled 1-4-7-1 but there was no number listed.

His mouth was completely dry.

Part 7: Seductions

Chapter 7.1

The evil goblin was not being so malignant. He still sat at the cathedral organ with his creeping fingers as they hovered above the black and white keys, but it seemed he didn't know which ones to press, didn't know how to attack the notes to create the noise that needed to be echoing throughout the corridors of Danny's mindscape.

The young poet's emotions had reached a stasis, caught in some sort of suspended animation. Or perhaps recent events had just masked them, like stony clouds blocking the sun.

He hadn't seen Stella since that day on the sands. From being everywhere she'd gone to being nowhere. Wherever Danny looked he found only unfamiliar faces with cold, dead end eyes.

Had life stopped? He wondered whether Michael hadn't rescued him in time and the surf had inched up the beach and smothered him. It had been nearly a week since that day and Danny was still wearing the same clothes. Carrying his Dickens around everywhere, he felt like Bruce Willis in *The Sixth Sense*, but unless the bartender at *The Mermaid's Cape* was secretly another Cole who could see more than merely the liquid spirits that hung from his bar, Danny had to conclude that he was indeed still alive.

As he sat on a stool with a line of empty glasses in front of him, he fulfilled the cliché of every forlorn movie character who was down on his luck. His shoulders sagged, his head drooped, the beer towel with the reassuringly expensive brand name staring back at him in big red writing. The universe would hide her from him, but it wouldn't stop taunting him.

He'd made no advancement on his poem, still tucked within the same pages of *Great Expectations*. That roadblock of inspiration was impenetrable, the word he'd been looking for that day forever lost.

'There is no word,' he mumbled to himself, catching the bartender's attention as he wondered if it was time to pour drink number six.

At least Danny had control over this poison. It was a change from drowning in a whirlwind of frustration, as it was only fate's cruel hand that controlled those strings, pulling Danny's yearning into all sorts of hopeless and sadistically twisted contortions.

Someone sat down next to him, and Danny instantly felt the prickly vibe. He peered round to see a stubble-faced Samuel Allington sneering at him. He looked like a completely different person to the one who'd waltzed into the pub and bought them all drinks that evening. This Samuel Allington had lost his glow.

'Found you.'

Danny sighed. 'What do you want with me now?'

'They told you why they came for you, didn't they? You know the mistake you made, don't you?'

'What do you think I did?'

'Please. Don't play the innocent card. I saw you. I saw her kiss you.'

'Yeah, exactly. *She* kissed *me*. I didn't do anything.'

Samuel fell silent for a moment as the two of them stared at each other like wild stags about to attack the other with their verbal antlers.

'What the hell are you, Daniel? You work in a chip shop or something? Still a teenager. What would she see in someone like you? Just keep away from her, man.'

'I think I got the message.'

'You know, everyone's in love with her, someone like her. Hard not to adore someone like her, isn't it?'

'Look, mate...'

'But I don't want no complications,' Samuel interrupted. 'She's engaged to me. She's mine.'

'Yeah, because *I'm* the complicated one,' Danny muttered.

Samuel broke his stare and looked at the half-empty bottles hanging above the bar.

'There were two places I could have gone after I saw what you and her got up to. It had to be one or the other, but in the end I chose to go to the less severe of my options. Did they... did they really break your nose?'

'Yeah,' Danny replied.

'They were just supposed to scare you.'

They did that too, Danny thought to himself.

'So, the other person I could have turned to was for something a little more drastic. There's this guy in town called The Reaper. You heard of him?'

Danny shook his head.

'He kills people. If I'd wanted to go that way. He's going to be my next option, in case you didn't get the message the first time round. I just wanted to leave that on your mind.'

Samuel stood up. A numbing chill juddered through Danny's body. His mouth was too dry to respond, even after taking another comforting swig of Jack Daniel's.

Before Samuel disappeared, it appeared there was more he wanted to say, more he wanted to unburden.

'People think they know me,' he breathed, his voice low and bleak. 'They think I'm this cheerful, friendly mister ray of sunshine. They're all wrong. I got this nasty black dog syndrome. He bites pretty bad sometimes. A lot of times. Nothing I can do about it.'

The murky shape of Samuel Allington evaporated from the corner of his eye and Danny scrunched up the beer mat. All of a sudden he was grateful for his emotions being in suspended animation, and that Stella was no longer lurking on the fringes of his world.

He now hoped for a different mathematical probability, that he would never see her again for the rest of his life, for now his life depended on it. It was the best way. He just didn't want to put his self-control to the test. With her... it was impossible.

With a deep sense of mourning, but not knowing exactly what he was mourning, Danny took the final swig from his glass.

He decided he would go home. It was safer there. She wouldn't be there.

Chapter 7.2

Eddie didn't know why he was wasting his time staring at the empty page. The deadline for the essay was eight days away and there was no way he was going to complete it in time. He couldn't even *start* the damned thing by then. Besides, the assignment brief was about as inspiring and inviting as a cold, steel wall.

On his desk were three textbooks he'd taken from the library weeks ago. He knew how these assignments worked: you scanned through the books to find relevant quotes to make it *look* like you'd been studious, and then you slapped them in wherever you could. Eddie had flipped through one of them, but his search was fruitless.

There was his entire failure in one blank piece of A4 paper. By now he should have found something to inspire him, a career he would commit his life to. It's how it seemed to work with everyone else his age, like they'd tapped into their genetic code and cracked their soul purpose.

Yeah, I'm going to Luton University to study Drama and then I want to be a drama teacher... I'm going to take my NVQs and then I'm going to be a mechanic...

Everyone else had it all worked out so elegantly. Why couldn't Eddie? It sometimes felt that he brought nothing to the world. The page was as empty as himself. Devoid. Barren. Doing nothing. Bringing nothing.

But worse still, Eddie didn't *even care*.

How was he going to pass this year and make it through to the third year? The more time he spent on his Sports Studies degree, the more of his life he was wasting. He may as well just jack it all in right now. But the thought of doing that worried him. What would he do *then*? There was absolutely nothing in this world to do!

Eddie looked to his bedroom window where a film of condensation veiled the nocturnal landscape. He got up and tried wiping his sleeve over it, but much to his frustration it had no effect at all. The moisture had probably got in between the panes of double-glazing on these shabby windows.

A sound distracted him, the scuff of claws against carpet. At his feet, Meriadoc twitched in his sleep, immersed in a dream of running through fields, searching out endless smells and sounds.

He noticed his mouth twitching too. Maybe he was now barking at a cat or the rabbits that ran from him. Perhaps he'd even caught one of them. In which case he wouldn't be barking at all, he'd be chewing.

Chewing dream rabbits because he wants to eat a real rabbit.

Eddie crouched before him and stroked his head, at which point Meriadoc jolted awake. The realisation melted into his eyes that he was no longer running around in a dream field chasing dream rabbits, but was now in the real bedroom of his real, directionless master. The dog nuzzled into Eddie's hand.

'You're a funny old mutt.'

He should have been rid of him by now, especially as he couldn't afford to feed him. Not that Meriadoc had sensed any of these thoughts. The dog seemed intrinsically attached to him whatever Eddie did or said.

'You're a worthless piece of shit, you know that?'

Meriadoc cocked his head as if those silly words had meant something, or as though shifting his gaze enabled him to perceive the real meaning behind them. Eddie stared back at the dog's large syrupy eyes. For a moment he imagined he was looking into the eyes of an enlightened human being, depth and knowledge in that prism of photoreceptors, like two crystal balls of mystery that held the answers to Eddie's destiny. It was as though Meriadoc had swapped bodies with someone, like in some cheesy eighties movie, and now it was Eddie's mission to bring him back to whatever had caused the soul transmigration so he could restore the mystic mayhem.

Eddie broke his gaze and blinked, as though trying to pinch the stupid thoughts from out of his head. What a load of crap. The only thing he had to do was get him a tin of Pedigree bloody Chum.

'Hey,' came a voice. It was Larry, standing in the

doorway, chewing on one of the temples of his sunglasses.

'All right, dude?'

'Michael's asking for the rent.'

Eddie rolled his eyes. 'He can get lost.'

'No point in asking if you can lend me some money then.'

'Don't worry, mate. Wouldn't be very Christian if he threw us out on the street, would it?'

Larry went quiet. He stepped inside and sat down on the bed.

'I'm completely broke,' he said.

'I wonder if those Halo of Fires geezers have anything else for us to do.'

'That'll go down well with our flatmates.'

'He wants his rent money, don't he?'

'I was thinking of going back to them anyway, just to... talk to them.' His words trailed off as he placed the sunglasses over his eyes. It was amazing he could ever see anything wearing those things all the time.

'About what?' Eddie asked. Larry crouched as he now began fussing over the dog.

'Stuff. You know... about doing some work for them. Who's a good boy, then?' he cooed to Meriadoc.

That's what I just said, Eddie thought.

'Cool. Well, I think randomly bumping into them for the second time in as many weeks would be a bit of a coincidence.'

'Too much of a coincidence. Good job I have this.'

Eddie didn't have to look at what Larry was referring to, the tatty black business card he clutched in his hand.

'So?' Larry asked. 'What do you reckon?'

Chapter 7.3

Dressed in his black coat, pointed swallow tails fluttering from the quickstep of his suede winkle pickers, it was easy to mistake Vladimir for a vampire. But unlike regular preternatural bloodsuckers, Vladimir didn't take the blood of just any living person, only the ones that deserved to have their blood taken from them. Seeing the suffering in their eyes was what he fed on.

The undead giveaway, however, was that he had a reflection. Indeed, the young vigilante relished checking his image, making sure it was perfect. But he didn't look past the surface, beyond the gelled locks of his sculpted hair or the alignment of his lint-free collar. Vladimir was a deep searcher when it came to other people, but not of himself. He knew he was already faultless, sublime, and so there was no point in putting himself under the spotlight.

In fact, he *was* the spotlight, hovering above the world he lived in. He was the watchful bird of prey swooping on the vermin that polluted the land.

This was the role the universe intended for his soul, and to fulfil it he had to be separate from everyone else. Sure, he appreciated the good in people. That's what it was all about really, the hope that his fellow citizens would choose kindness over causing harm.

But Vladimir was no redeemer. As Throne of the Fires, he was the punisher. Whilst he acknowledged the love between humans, he could never give any nor, for that matter, receive any.

Besides, angels didn't concern themselves with human desires and physical relationships. Vladimir was no different in that respect. He focussed all of his drive into a purity of intention, and any give or take of love on his part would bring him down onto the same level as everyone else. There was no time for that kind of weakness.

He certainly had no love for the person tied to the chair in front of him. Looking at him disgusted him, as the harrowing thoughts of the suffering he'd brought on people grated in his mind like barbed wire dragged over skin. Wayne Ticehurst was evidently incapable of love, proper love, that was, not a perverted deed that may masquerade as it.

Tonight was a special assignment for Halo of Fires, one that Vladimir and his Virtues had delicately investigated. After learning the cold facts, the karmic angel was psyched.

He'd spoken to his victims; he'd felt their suffering.

'Prison didn't change you then, Wayne,' he delivered. 'Why would it? Too busy playing video games or watching TV to think about what you'd done. Isn't that so?'

The recipient of his lecture shook his head as he snorted deep breaths. He couldn't make a proper verbal response other than whimpering because Clint had just finished taping his mouth up with duct tape. There were tears in the brute's eyes. He was a hulk, bigger than both the Powers, a belly drooping onto his lap, walrus blubber around his neck. He must have been an absolute horror to the people in his clutches.

He generated no fear in Vladimir, though. These days he felt indestructible. Faster than a speeding bullet? He didn't even have to move to get out of the way of them.

'Why would it stop you? Maybe you were just thinking of the day you'd be let out so you could go do it again.'

'Once a rapist, always a rapist,' Jake added, disrupting Vladimir's rehearsed flow.

Instead of picking up where he'd left off, the interruption shook off his composure and he darted over to the defiler, pouncing, unleashing the fury. His searchlight eyes pierced into his as though they were reaching inside and strangling the light out of his soul.

'Everyone pays the price in time, you worthless piece of scum. And for you, Wayne, it's going to be now.'

Until that point, he'd kept the machete concealed. The rapist's fatty, bloodshot eyes tried to focus on it as he slid the blade against his stubble.

'We'll make it impossible for you to destroy anyone else's life.'

He straightened up and handed the weapon to Jake. Clint leaned towards Vladimir's ear and whispered, 'You really want us to...?'

'Yes.'

Jake then stepped the other side of him and asked, 'Are we checking his back? Guy's covered in tats.'

The possibility that Wayne Ticehurst was more than a rapist was the first thought that had gone through his head when the case had been presented to the Fires. It was always the first thought. But seeing Wayne in the flesh had confirmed his doubt, that this would not be a night of finding longstanding vengeance.

He shook his head. 'He's too young.'

After spitting in the Kolley's face, he left the apartment. Jake and Clint would finish the work. He didn't need to see that particular bit, didn't want to tarnish his feathers.

Standing out in the hallway on the top floor of the Altham Court flats, Vladimir could hear the demon's duct tape-muffled cries filling the building. The screams echoed all the way down the barren stairways, the sound of the sinner consumed by the flames that his actions had created.

Wayne's excruciating suffering disturbed the ether. Like a rock thrown into a pool of water, the waves would be a message to those who may be tempted to stray from the light, that consequence awaited, as it did for that man with the black widow spider tattoo.

When the howling died down, Clint and Jake appeared from the flat, their hands scrubbed.

Vladimir felt a vibration against his leg and reached into his pocket.

'What's next?' Clint asked, dabbing his palms against his jeans.

'Another spark, another flame,' Vladimir replied, putting his phone away again.

'Got some wheels to burn,' Jake added.

Vladimir set off down the stairway, the two Powers falling into step behind. He wasn't going to tell them that the car in question, the one they were supposed to break into and steal, was already in flames. By the time he navigated Jake out of town to a secluded farm track leading to Barrow Hill Thorns, Clint was growing frustrated with Vladimir's tightlippedness.

'So, someone's already done it?' Clint asked as the car came to a stop by the edge of the woodland. 'And you're bringing us out here because...? Who did it? Was it Cassidy?'

Vladimir peered out the side window, his eyes adjusting as the headlights went out. He soon spotted the beacon he was searching for.

'How can it be Cassidy?' Jake contributed as he whipped the keys out of the ignition. 'He can't even drive.'

'Well, I don't know. Tell me then.'

'You think I know what's going on here?' Jake grumbled.

Vladimir undid his seatbelt and said, 'Come on, I want your opinion on something.'

He got out of the car and approached the glowing flames that flickered within the gnarly boscage of twisting trees. Clint and Jake exchanged a glance, then did the same.

The trail revealed the silhouettes of two figures who looked like a pair of homeless guys standing around a fire to keep warm. Smothered in the blaze was the skeleton of a Porsche Carrera GT. The scent of petrol perfumed the air.

'*These* two?' Jake asked.

One of the young arsonists wore a baseball cap, the other had a pair of sunglasses tucked into the neck of his shirt.

'I don't get it,' Clint said. 'Who the hell are they?'

'Why would you let them do it?' Jake went on.

'I did give you a crack at this car last week, if you remember, Jake.'

'Told you I could get into it,' Eddie said.

'He cracked the Kintner Immobiliser,' Clint observed.

'How did you manage that?' Jake asked.

'Piece of cake, mate.'

'Yeah, Buicks, buses, cop cars, we do them every day in Vice City,' Larry added.

'Is life one big computer game for you, Larry?' Eddie asked.

'So, what, Vlad?' Jake continued, 'We're doing a work experience program with the college now? Does Henry know about these two? What are you thinking?'

'Not sure yet,' Vladimir replied. 'What do you two think?'

Clint looked them up and down, and with one eyebrow raised said, 'You ask me, these couple of punks look like our typical Kolley trash.'

'Fuck you,' Eddie shot back.

'That one's a volatile one,' Vladimir said, pointing at Eddie as though he were at a pet shop picking out a puppy Rottweiler. 'Large bomb on a short fuse. Waiting to blow everyone to kingdom come.' Vladimir now looked at Larry.

'But this one, who knows? Usually wearing his glasses, so it's difficult to tell.'

'Like a young Peter Griffin,' Jake spat.

'Hey, we helped you out,' Eddie said.

'No, I stopped that guy owning both your arses.'

'Right, coz you're such a fucking He-Man, aren't you?'

'Eddie, dude, shut the hell up,' Larry said.

Jake turned to Vladimir, the blank expression on his face enough to suggest that he didn't really need to say any more.

Vladimir sighed. 'That went well.'

There was silence except for the hiss and crackle of fire, everyone waiting for Vladimir to continue. Instead, he just stood watching the flames inside the Porsche as they built in ferocity. Everyone else felt the pull of the blaze, as though they'd all been hypnotised by the explosion of repressed primal passions.

'Who did this car belong to?' Larry asked.

'Some charity worker,' Vladimir answered.

'Really?'

'Yup.'

'We stole a charity worker's car?'

'That a problem for you?'

'I thought you dealt with, you know, wrongdoers.'

'We deal with anyone we have to,' Jake informed him.

'Eddie?' Vladimir asked.

'I don't care. Don't care whose car it is. Fuck 'em.'

'You don't believe in charity?'

'Only the Eddie Jansz charity.'

'He's a worthy cause, is he? Disadvantaged individual? In need of others' help?'

'You gotta look out for number one. Screw everyone else.'

'Why didn't you tell us this was a charity worker's car?' Larry whittled on.

'Why didn't you ask?'

'I just assumed whoever's car it was they deserved this to happen to them.'

'They did.'

'They did? How?'

'The charity was a sham. Supposed to be for homeless people, but the only person it went to was our Kolley who could somehow afford a Porsche.'

Eddie regarded the devastated car, its broken windows and melted upholstery that bubbled in the immense heat. 'I dunno. They might be able to afford *this* one now.'

There was silence, and then Clint started chuckling, a laugh that soon swelled into a hearty roar.

Jake looked at him as if he'd been breathing in too much smoke. 'Well, we better not let this turn into a merry camp fire,' he said. 'Come on, let's get out of here.'

'I changed my mind, Vlad. I like this clown,' Clint added before he and Jake trailed back to the Mercedes.

Eddie turned to Vladimir. 'So?'

'So what?'

'So obviously we didn't get the seal of approval from the Masters of the Universe contingent. That's it now? We're not going to hear from you any more? Man, what a bunch of tossers.'

'How's your dog doing?'

'What?' Eddie replied, as if it was the last question he expected to be asked right now.

Meeting people was like seeing road signs go by on a car journey. Every sign meant something, told you that you were twenty miles from Timbuktu, or warned you what hazards might be ahead. But some road signs were more significant than others. Some signs informed you how far you were from your own particular destination, which way to go, which exit to take. These were the ones you paid most attention to.

The two students before Vladimir were like weathered signs too close to the side of the road, battered by the relentless winds and broken by bulging lorries, or defaced by aerosol-spraying vandals so that their original message had become lost.

Vladimir's extraordinary perceptions told him that there was something to be read within these two, something beyond their cockiness and cold, uncaring scowls.

No one would understand how he knew this, what had made him look at these signs in the first place, and besides, there was no way he could explain.

The heat from the flames prickled Vladimir's face, but he could feel a much more powerful fire burning somewhere. Pain. It pulsed beneath their auras, and it chimed with his own.

'I'll be in touch. There's another job we have for you,' Vladimir said before heading back out of the trees.

Chapter 7.4

Danny had successfully avoided her. The distraction of computer games and cheap whisky had helped with his social distancing, holing himself up at the flat whenever he wasn't at work or college. Mortal fear was a powerful motivator.

There didn't seem any point in going out into the world now, anyway. There was no meaning to anything without her. Danny felt like that little boy in *Northern Lights* who'd had his demon cut from him. Like a ghost. But not dead. The experience had corrupted his soul, the missing piece slotted perfectly within and then taken away again. He'd never be able to feel for another what he felt for her. He'd only be aware of his incompleteness for the rest of time.

No book he read could ever inspire him again, no desire to make something of his life would find a place in his mind. That's how it seemed, until he received the letter.

It was on the doormat when he returned home from college. He knew immediately whom it was from. Not that he'd ever seen her handwriting before but somehow her energy emanated from the white envelope, from the five letters that spelled out D-a-n-n-y along with the dainty little squiggle beneath. As he gazed down at it, he breathed in deeply, filling every corner of his lungs like they'd never been filled before, as though the moment had given him the kiss of life.

He quickly scooped it up, a twinge of paranoiac guilt soon jabbing him in the guts. He peered back towards the street to see if anyone had noticed him. What scandal! Someone may have seen him pick up an *envelope*!

It wasn't just any random letter, though. It was a letter from the fiancée of Samuel Allington, the man who would kill off any love rival.

Danny tore off his scarf, kicked off his shoes and rushed up to his room, shutting his door behind him. With a shaking hand he ripped open the envelope and released the note.

Dear Danny,
I've been looking all over for you! Where have you been, my lost one? Sam has been acting weird recently. I need to speak to you. Can you meet me tonight? Please. I'll be at The Cape *waiting for you. I just want a little chat. Sam's out of town, so there're no worries about getting caught this time.*
Yours
Stella x

Weeks of repressed emotion erupted, that bastard goblin going berserk on some concupiscent inspired conniption fit; she'd taken control of him once more. He could have ignored the letter, could have thrown it into a fire but no. He'd opened it, had read the words which were really an incantation, and now they'd trapped him in her spell. There was no way he would resist acquiescing to her request.

He hoped to hell that Samuel really was away. Either way, he realised this was a step onto a trapdoor and he'd soon be tumbling back into that world of revenge-seeking angels. In his hands he held his death warrant.

He took a shower, brushed his teeth, and put on his best shirt, a grey and black chequered Ben Sherman, one of the few things he hadn't bought from a charity shop. After standing in front of the mirror for ten minutes making sure his hair was immaculate, Danny sprayed some aftershave on his neck. It seemed at this point the evil goblin had now found a voice:

Not just going for a little chat, are you? Making all the efforts you would for a date, *aren't you?*

The goblin was right. This was all to make an impression on her. He couldn't help but wonder if she'd meant to imply anything more when she'd said about not getting *caught* this time. Just how far would she go behind his back?

You're not going on the pull here!

Why would she be marrying Samuel if she was having adulterous thoughts about Danny, some nobody student who worked in a chip shop? Even so, as he set off for the pub, it felt like walking to his own funeral. Step by step his feet splashed through the puddles, mechanically making his way to that temptress like a ship drawn to the call of the destructive siren.

With his head to the ground, he saw his legs moving, but it was as though he was watching someone else's legs. He wasn't aware of his brain generating that thought process to lift his feet and arch his knees. Something else was in control, a mischievous spirit that had attached strings to his limbs like he was a puppet, cackling to itself as he manipulated the helpless romantic to his doom.

He ran the back of his hand over his forehead as he stepped into *The Mermaid's Cape*. The rain had mixed with the hair gel and trickled into his eyes, making them sting. Despite blurred vision, he made it to the bar and ordered a drink.

He knew she was already there. He could *feel* her.

Few other punters were present, the weather keeping many at home. Rainy days were a way of finding the true alcoholics. At least there was less chance of anyone seeing him, yet Danny felt exposed without a crowd to hide in.

After paying for his drink, he turned around. He could swear her eyes weren't real. Eyes just weren't that colour, like hers had been replaced by two gleaming amethyst gemstones. She sat on a beige leather settee in the corner, a fire roaring away nicely in the nearby hearth.

Hoping the elements hadn't disturbed his delicately arranged hair too much, Danny approached her. There was a space on her settee, or there was a stool on the other side of her table. Which one should he take? Which seat would she expect him to sit on? He could cozy up next to her, but then that really would look like they were on a date. As the goblin had made it clear to him, that wasn't the nature of this meeting. Yet, he'd sat right next to her on the beach that day. And sitting beside her would increase the chances of their bodies accidentally, or not so accidentally, coming into contact...

He perched on the stool opposite. There he had his back to the rest of the pub. Taking that sensible option gave him some reassurance that he still had some self-control. Besides, the view from there was great on the eye.

Her damp and tasselled hair clung to the side of her face, her cheeks still glowing from the whip of the wild weather. She wore a black velvet coat with a puce-coloured vest underneath. It was tightly fitting and low cut against her ripely shaped breasts, as Danny could not help but notice.

Her ruffled appearance gave her an unusual edge this evening. She didn't seem as soft and buttery as during their previous liaison. Tonight she was more spice and zing, the wind and the rain having stirred up her senses as she seemingly oozed a celestial pheromone. She was a post-coitus vision, passion tangibly simmering on the surface of her skin. Danny envied that to Samuel it wasn't an unfamiliar sight.

All her wild orchid beauty was there, but this evening she was more like nightshade, dangerously tempting and ready to destroy.

'Lovely weather,' she said to him, her sweet voice infused with a slight huskiness.

'We're supposed to be getting a lot more rain this week. There's some low pressure sitting over us,' Danny replied.

He internally cursed himself for sounding like an old woman on a bus.

Ben Sherman, Danny? Might as well have come in cardigan and slippers.

When he was nervous, he often struggled to find stimulating topics of conversation. Repeating weather forecasts was a crutch he over-relied on.

Stella nodded in reply.

Nice. She's loving this, lover boy. You got her really turned on.

'I got us a seat by the fire so we can dry off, as much as I would like to get out of these wet clothes.' As she spoke she pulled apart her coat slightly as if it needed demonstrating.

The action pulled Danny's eyes to her body, excitement fluttering in his stomach as he studied her cleavage.

She wrapped her coat round her once more as a tepid trickle of rain-gel ran down his cheek. He looked to the fire for warmth.

'Where have you been, Danny? Busy reading your Dickens? I missed you.'

He sat up.

She missed me? What exactly does she want me here for?

'Yes, I've been busy. Exams coming up and stuff,' he replied. He realised his answer was as cold as the rain that continued to pound against the window. It fell so violently as though it might soon break the glass. 'Would have liked to... you know, sit on the beach again. If we had the weather for it.'

'That would have been lovely. I've wanted to talk to you again.'

He so wished that flash-boy Samuel Allington didn't exist. If only they weren't together, if only he was free to tell her he'd missed her like hell.

'Why?' he asked her. 'Why did you want to talk?'

She lowered her eyes, running a fingertip round the rim of her glass.

'Sam's been troubled recently. I know he saw us and I know what he did to you. I tried to explain there was nothing going on, but he just wasn't having any of it.'

There it was spelt out for him.

She said it. There's nothing going on because she's not interested in you!

Danny replayed her words in her head. Nothing *was* going on? She didn't say that nothing *is* going on. Of course there was nothing going on *that* day. They'd only talked. She'd only pecked him on the cheek. What relation does that have to what was happening right now, to what was developing?

'I'm so sorry about that,' she went on. 'So sorry I brought you trouble. I missed you, Danny, because I know you're someone who would understand me. I know that, because when I look into your eyes, I know what you are.'

She fell silent, lost in thought. Danny needed her to keep talking. 'What do you...'

'I'm thinking of leaving him,' she said, before he could get out the rest of his sentence. 'He's like a weight that I'm carrying around. All the time.'

'But don't you... Aren't you in love with him?'

She sat back, her gaze fixed on the rainwater that streamed down the window. Through a gap in the seafront hotels could be seen an ebullition of waves flurrying along the beach.

'It's easy to say you love someone. But some you love more than others. Some you love as though they were the missing part of yourself. And when you find them you know it isn't possible to love anyone else as much.'

She brought her attention away from the storm outside and met Danny's eyes.

'I realise that leaving him will destroy him,' she said.

'You have to do what you think is right.' He could hear the hint of disappointment in his voice.

'I know you know what it's like. To be lost. Not being able to touch the one you desire. It consumes you, takes you over. But that frustration burns so much because there's nothing you can do about it.'

'You... know that, huh?'

'I can see you've been searching. What can we do?'

'Maybe there's something.'

'You name it, Danny. Tell me what you want me to do. Anything you want. Anything to help you.'

'Anything?'

'Yes, my lost one. What would help? What do you want?'

'I would like...'

'Yes?'

'I would like... to know what it feels...'

'Yes?'

'To kiss you.'

It had slipped helplessly from his tongue like a tear would fall from the eye of a bereaver.

'I see. So that's what you're thinking, is it?'

'Sorry.'

'Shall I describe it to you? Not that I would know what it's like to kiss me, exactly. Something like that you'd have to experience for yourself, I'm afraid. And I don't think that would be a great idea.'

'No. Sorry, I shouldn't have said that.'

'Why? I asked you what you wanted.'

'Yeah...'

'So if that's what you want...' Stella stood up. 'We'd better go somewhere where no one can see us.'

She stepped away from the table and floated across the room towards the beer garden.

Danny was numb. Had that conversation really happened? It was like he was in a dream, as though he'd been breathing in too much oxygen.

She was waiting for him, ready for him to satiate this obsession that had haunted him for so long. This could be the greatest moment of his life, but one that would also signal the end of it. Samuel Allington had told him to stay away from her, that he would kill him if he didn't.

But he'd already betrayed his warning by seeing her. If he was to kiss her right now, it wouldn't make his sentence any worse. It was better to die having kissed Stella Connoly than to go out without having done so.

He made his way over to the door, a furtive glance to see if anyone happened to be looking at him. The small scattering of strangers were all caught up in their own conversations, oblivious to the scandal taking place under their noses. Danny stepped outside.

There was no one out there, all the smokers waiting for a break in the rain. He saw her standing in the corner underneath a parasol, a soft smile on her lips.

'Hey,' she said to him.

Danny walked over. For a few moments he stood watching her, waiting for the sting, the punch line, the candid camera, the alarm clock.

The Uzi 9mm to pepper holes in your skull. Hasta la vista, baby!

'So... you said you wanted to do something to me.'

His body edged closer to her with every breath and she

swallowed in anticipation. His eyes wandered down her face, taking in the finest details of her velvet skin, every freckle, every mole, and every shimmer of light that bounced off her like moonlight on the paradise sands. He gazed into her perfection closely, as though he wanted to merge his body with hers and be within her very molecules.

The gentle rise and fall of her breasts against his chest took his attention. They moved into him like mounds of warm dough. Oh how he would love to grab hold of those.

So he did. With both hands. Grabbing, squeezing. Stella caught her breath and closed her eyes. Rubbing them in his palms, gently caressing, pushing them together. He felt them respond.

'Now then, young Danny. I don't remember that being what you asked for.'

He smiled. His head was so close to hers he could feel her sweet breath on his lips. Her mouth was open, in a silent Om, waiting for his connection.

And so he kissed her. In that moment he felt complete, like all that longing had been the deepest trough before the greatest peak. All those months of yearning were a necessary journey for this one kiss.

There was no torturous past, no foreboding future. Time had stopped, locking Danny within this moment of bliss. It seemed Stella would let him wallow in it for however long he wanted.

He pressed his chest harder into hers. His hand slid over her hip and pulled up her thigh. His other hand drove through her silky hair. He needed to be closer. Within her. He thrust his tongue into her mouth and she took it in, swirling her soft muscle around his. He wanted her to know exactly what she was doing to him so brushed his groin against her.

He heard a soft moan, but it seemed like it had come from deep within her, an ache of sadness, the trembling of the earth as it shivered with the escape of cosmic energies, the release of tension as the fabric of the universe suddenly slipped into balance.

Danny rested his forehead against hers and panted. Her eyes remained closed, her breathing heavy.

'So,' Stella eventually said. 'That's what it's like to kiss me.'

'Yes.'

'Danny, please know that I'm not going to tell Sam anything about any of this. But I need you to be careful. I can't control him.'

'I understand.'

'Just as I can't stop myself.' She kissed him again, just on the neck this time. 'And that brings me to my next question. What else can I do to help you? What else do you want?'

'I want...'

'I hope you've learnt now that you can come straight out with it.'

'I want you.'

'How? Want me to help you more? Want me to take that loneliness away?'

'Yes.'

'It might not seem it, Danny, but I'm lonely too.'

'You are?'

'Tell me,' she breathed in his ear. 'What is it you want?'

It was one thing saying he wanted to kiss her, but his other desires were a little harder to deliver the words for.

'I'll say it for you,' she whispered. 'I think you'd really love to know what it feels like to be inside me. I mean, it's not like there isn't a big giveaway right now.'

'Well, there you go.'

'I would suggest you don't carry on being so reclusive,' she said as she released herself from him.

Coarse, jarring voices suddenly flooded the area as a gaggle of young women came outside to smoke on fags.

It was her cue to leave. As she beamed a smile of goodbye, Danny sat down and casually wiped the lipstick from his mouth and waited for his blood levels to restore. For the next couple of minutes he endured listening to the gossiping Vicky Pollards talking utter dross.

What did it matter that Samuel Allington was going to have Danny killed? Being stuck out here with these three plebs for too long and Danny's head would soon be in a noose anyway.

By the time he returned inside, Stella, as expected, was

nowhere to be seen.

He'd search her out again. Now he was already on the way to Davy Jones's locker, he was going to make damned sure he went out in style.

Part 8: Darkness Descends

Chapter 8.1

'I feel like I'm becoming a mobster,' Larry said with surprising nonchalance, as though he'd just been given their Sunday league team sheet and seen he was to play left wing instead of central defence.

'So what?' Eddie replied as he stared at the yellow lights above the lift doors, lighting up each floor as they moved upwards.

'Did you ever think that this is where you would end up? When you sat down with the careers advisor at school, was this something he happened to suggest?'

'You want to be normal, Larry? Want to let mediocrity win out? Do all that nine-to-five crap, fitting into a system that's only going to screw you over, that'll give you a mortgage you can't afford and a pension that won't support you until you're eighty-five? This is an opportunity, something that don't come along for everyone. We gotta take this, dude. This is what we wanted, right?'

'Right.'

'I'm just tired. Tired of life passing me by. Looking me over. Don't you always wonder when your life is going to begin?'

The lift came to a stop as the light pinged on floor three. The doors opened.

'Maybe it's here.'

The top level of the multi-storey car park was empty of vehicles, but not devoid of people, for at the far end stood a figure. He perched at the edge like an eagle, peering down on the tainted world below.

It was Vladimir, the agent of karma, and Larry and Eddie were drawn to him like cats sidling up beside a fire. The way he was standing there in his long, dark coat reminded Eddie of something. He could have passed for one of the heavenly beings in that film *City of Angels*, silently watching everything, looking for anything that would call for him to intervene. Dark Harbour definitely wasn't a place of heavenly beings, though.

Despite the approaching footsteps, Vladimir did not turn to face them. As the two youngsters took their places either side of him he asked, 'What do you see down there?'

'One or two drunks,' Larry replied. 'Some chavs. And look at that; some guy's taking a piss.'

'And you, Eddie?'

'Asbo punks wanting to stab everyone, pissheads looking for fights, scummers dropping pills into drinks, kids getting shot, little girls getting raped. That sound about right?'

'Decadent Dark Harbour. Stronghold of hopelessness.'

Drunken revellers stumbled by on the littered streets below, swallowed by the whirlpool of disillusionment and apathy. Eddie spotted an adolescent lying on a bench, an arm draped across his head, his skin pallid and yellow like candle wax. He wore a baseball cap much like the one Eddie wore. The youngster wasn't moving at all, didn't even appear to be breathing. For all Eddie knew, the lad was dead, but everyone just walked by him as though they hadn't noticed him. Up here he had a new perspective on it all.

'Where did it all go wrong?' Eddie pondered.

'Where's the dream?' Vladimir went on. 'Decay, authority, and the pursuit of hedonism. We ruled the world, held it tightly in our hands, but it crumbled from us. Now we know the ship is going down we're just partying our way out.'

Eddie folded his arms and looked to Vladimir. 'So, you said you have another job for us.'

'I did.'

'And you thought that two random losers you met at the park one day would be the perfect ones for it.'

'Nothing's random. I think we were meant to run into you two lads that day... and your dog.'

Why was this guy so fixated about Meriadoc? He was just an animal!

'You know what?' Eddie said. 'Your muscleman buddy

was right. We would have been your work one night, coz one day I'd hurt someone, and it wouldn't be pretty.'

'I'd like everyone to see your true colours.'

Confused by this, Eddie just shook his head, his mind stalling. This was unfamiliar territory to him. No one had ever given him a break. No one had ever given him anything.

Vladimir turned to the other student. 'And you, Larry. Maybe one day we'd have met you, too.'

'Yeah. Yeah, maybe so.'

'You carry the damage. It's always lurking behind you.'

Eddie frowned as he looked over to his friend, but Larry faced away. The mysterious vigilante seemed to know them so well, seemed to be able to cut to their cores with crystal-edged sharpness.

'Why the hell are you going to trust us with this job of yours?'

'Because I don't think you're dumb enough to cross an organisation of vigilantes.'

'Yes, but how do you know we're cut out for working for Halo of Fires?'

Vladimir nodded, his head tilting. 'I tell you what, think of it less as a job and more as a test.'

'A test? And if we pass?'

'You'll discover what you're looking for.'

'What if we fail?'

'You'll still be a lost soul, just floating in the wind, not knowing why you're here, not knowing your purpose.'

The two of them fell silent listening to his words, listening as they would to the angel of death taking them through their lives after their final chapter when the plot had been well and truly lost.

'What do you say?' Vladimir asked them.

Eddie glanced over to Larry. He looked like an actor waiting for Eddie's next line so the play could continue.

'We're in. We'll do this test of yours.'

Vladimir gazed up into the heavens for a moment, as though tired of looking down on his own world. With a deep breath he then turned around. 'Follow me.'

They did so. Eddie glanced once more at the recumbent

youngster down below. Whether he was paralysed by drugs or whether he was dead, Eddie would never know.

Chapter 8.2

Rooms are like mirrors; they reflect back to you everything about yourself. The room on the first floor of 38 Toledo Road said a lot about the four individuals that lived there. It said a lot about them based on what *wasn't* there.

Michael snapped on the light as he entered the lounge. Two empty crisp packets sat on the arm of the chair, both the flavour that Larry liked so much. One stained tea mug and two pint glasses were on the floor next to the settee, laying on their side with a stale froth of beer oozing inside.

Getting another drink was evidently not an ordeal for Larry. Going to get a glass and *taking an empty glass back to the kitchen at the same time* was apparently an unreasonable expectation. Too much real-life logic for him to process. Didn't the bad guys just disappear into thin air after you'd shot them? Ridiculous to assume that anything you were finished with should continue to exist. Besides, how did those dirty glasses eventually get washed up if Larry never bothered to take them away?

Michael disliked living in the remotest sign of squalor, yet he tried not to judge his friends on their lower standards. Crouching down to pick up the vessels, he noticed there was also a plate with a piece of toast on it. He sighed and sat down on the settee.

Where were all his flatmates? It was a Friday night and yet none of them, the three other corners of the square, was anywhere to be seen. Michael couldn't help but notice how things had changed in the past few months. The square had now crumbled and left behind an unknown, distorted shape. It was more like a doodle drawn by a four-year-old.

What could he do about it? He'd sometimes talked to them about his religion. He was careful not to sound like he was preaching, but when the situation called for it, he wasn't afraid to tell them what God brought to his life. It was so sad that Michael could see exactly what they were lacking, yet when he tried to offer it to them, he usually had it thrown back in his face.

He wasn't one of those Catholics that arbitrarily called himself one just because he'd been born into the religion. Michael truly believed in it. He saw himself as a creature of sin and had accepted Christ as his saviour. There was no point *being* a Catholic if he wasn't going to *act* one.

At times like this he saw how religion had strengthened him, how it had made him avoid becoming a person who would lust after someone else's fiancée or associate with criminals. For those were the trails of temptation that his non-believing friends were now lost down.

They frustrated him, but Michael didn't want to become resentful. What hope would there be then? He had to be better than that, had to keep in his heart what once their friendship square was, that he still loved his friends. He had to stay true to those feelings, for they were the feelings that were true to him. That's what Jesus would do now.

So perhaps the three lost lambs would come running back in time, wherever they were. Danny going after Stella, chasing after the wrong girl. Samuel Allington's threat to him if he should carry on seeing her. Michael was aware of it. So where was Danny tonight? Why had he gone out alone without telling anyone where he was going?

And Larry and Eddie, joining up with that dreadful vigilante organisation. How could they do that, especially after seeing what had happened to Danny? They hadn't displayed even a modicum of remorse.

The slugs of worry crawled around in Michael's stomach as his eyes rested on the piece of toast on the plate beside him. Slathered in lime marmalade, Larry had eaten only half of it, the remaining triangle curled up and stale.

An ominous thought suddenly crept into his head, as though one of those slugs had slithered its way up there and whispered a diabolical idea. A triangle.

Having been thinking about his square of friends for the past few moments, he couldn't ignore the synchronicity in now seeing an object that was once a square, now existing only as a triangle.

One of the corners is missing.

Michael felt sick and swallowed awkwardly as a drought of saliva hit his mouth. Where had this thought come from and why was he unable to shrug it off?

Missing, or no longer in existence? It was an odd intuition to have, but he had to be careful about it. Certainly it was affirming to think that God had inspired him with an echo of the future, or an angel had whispered it to him, but what if it was the Devil putting insidious thoughts in his head?

Still the thought throbbed in his mind. One member of the square would no longer be with them at some point soon. That member would no longer be in existence. He would be dead.

Which one? There were so many dangers now threatening their lives. Least likely was that it might be Michael himself, but a possibility nonetheless. That's if he were to give this idea any credence. That's if he were to believe that looking at a half-eaten piece of toast was a sign that someone was about to die. *Obviously!*

He stood up again with the collection of dirty glasses. As he walked downstairs, he saw Meriadoc sitting by the front door, hoping that if he whined loud enough it would make his lost master appear at it.

It seemed that the dog was worried too. Or maybe not. Maybe he just wanted to be out there with them.

Chapter 8.3

Danny fought the urge to touch her again. It had been over a week since he'd done that, waiting for her to slip out of the ether once more. Their eyes aligned, but he kept his hands in his pockets. There were better places to display affection than on the street outside *The Mermaid's Cape*.

'Fancy seeing you in here again,' she said.

'Someone told me not to be a recluse.'

She leant towards him, smelling the whisky on his breath. 'I didn't say become an alcoholic.'

'I can think of other things I'd rather be doing,' he replied.

'Yes,' she said in that delicately airy voice of hers. 'Yes, I'm sure you could.'

Since the last encounter, Danny had puzzled at how to get in touch with her again. It wasn't like he had a phone number to dial, no known address to knock at the door (not that that would have been the brightest of ideas). He didn't even have an email address for her. All he could do was wait. Nine days had floated by listlessly, Danny like a sailboat in a vacuum.

All he had to go on was the pattern of their past encounters, waiting for the flap of the letterbox at the flat, lurking around those places he'd seen her before, all on the outside chance she might be there. He realised he was desperate, like an addict trying to find his dealer, but he didn't care. He wanted her.

'You know, Danny. Lost little Danny. I know that...' Her words trailed off, as though they were pinned in her throat.

He looked up and down the late night high street. 'Let's go somewhere else, shall we?'

'Good idea.'

The sense he was being watched constantly nagged at him. The suspicious eyes of a jealous boyfriend would surely be checking if Danny was heeding the warning he'd been given. *This* was exactly what he'd been told not to do, treading within the flowers of the forbidden garden.

They headed across the road and down onto the beach. The tide was out as far as it could be tonight, and the stroll to the shoreline was long, the comforting darkness enveloping them gradually, lowering a shroud over their illicit meeting. However wrong it might be for Danny to be in her presence again, he accepted he could not resist being with her any more than the moon could resist being pulled towards the Earth.

It was muggy, the air congested and thick like treacle as though the universe had turned up the level of gravity a notch or two. Walking seemed that little more onerous.

'The thing is this, sweetie: have you thought how Sam would react if I said I was leaving? Especially after the idea we put in his head. The idea about...'

'Us?'

'Yes.

'So what are you saying?' Danny pressed.

She sighed, brushing back a stray lock of hair behind her ear. 'Sometimes I wish I could just jump into the sea and swim far away from everything. It seems all I cause is trouble. Everyone I put my hand to falls apart.'

Her words were jarring. She'd always been a bright soul radiating inspiration wherever she went, not the type for this kind of melancholy. Danny put his arm around her, his fingertips rubbing her shoulder.

'That's not true,' he said.

'Yes it is, Danny. Look at you. Look what I've done to you, distracting you like this, corrupting your heart.'

'You've not... you've not corrupted me. What are you talking about? You've lit everything up.'

'*Blinded* you, I think.'

'Stella, this is nonsense. It's not your fault I want you. To feel the things I feel. It's human.'

'Why do you desire *me* so?'

'Because you're perfect.'

'And is happiness found through yourself, or through another person?'

'What does it matter?'

Having reached the shoreline, Stella kicked off her sandals and sat down on the damp sand that glistened in the dull moonlight. Patchy clouds hung in the air like phantoms, the delighted overseers of this meeting of uncontrollable lust. The dark waves rustled nearby, gently sweeping up to her toes, a tempting invitation.

'Do you love him?' Danny asked.

'There's love for Samuel, yes. But what exactly are those feelings? Now that's the question to ask. Do I love him more than I could any other? The answer, Danny, the crucial fact is that no, I do not.'

'Then why are you with him?'

'He needed me. I know how it seems to everyone else.

They see perfection. But it's not. It's just so... smothering. A weight on my soul.'

She turned away and laid herself down, her cheek pressing against the fine crystals of the sand. Danny sat down beside her and watched over her like a would-be angel looking over a bedridden hospital patient diseased by demanding and conflicting affections.

'I don't know how to tell him I don't want to be with him. How can I do that to him?'

He placed his hand on her arm. She wore a deep indigo sleeveless top that fell perfectly above her hips. On the front of it there was a silver V that contained a glittering array of dazzling sequins, a garment that appropriately represented her celestial name and her mysterious nature. Her skirt was a rain cloud grey emblazoned with delicate swirls and frills. She was timeless, her sophistication not needing to be accentuated by any vogue.

'It's okay, Stella. I understand.'

'I don't want to bring any trouble upon you.'

'You should do what's right for you.'

She sat up and gazed into his eyes. 'You'll understand the truth about us soon. I want to show you.'

Danny smiled to her. 'So thrive my soul,' he whispered.

He already knew the truth, for there was no other explanation he had for the depth of his feelings. He didn't need to search within his soul to understand how its aching had guided both of them together like this. There was only one thing that could mean. But yet, he longed for her to say it.

'You've got sand on your cheek,' he said, brushing his fingers against her face.

She took his hand and pulled him over. Danny fell into her, pushing her back against the sand as he glided his body over hers. He peered down into her violet eyes. Pinned beneath him, within his very clutches, and with a knowing smile that beamed back at him, he felt he'd finally harnessed his emotions. At last they were under his control.

That infernal goblin was now dressed like a concert pianist, ready to deliver the performance of his lifetime, an arrangement reserved for the ears of angelic beings within their heavenly realm.

Danny ran his hand over her waist, feeling the edge of her top. Sliding his fingers underneath the fabric, he pressed his palm against her warm flesh as her chest slowly rose and fell. Her skin was so smooth, as though he had in his hand a fallen peach from a paradisiacal tree.

'So then, lost one, are you going to tell me?' she asked him.

'Tell you what, my found one?'

'What you want to do to me.'

'Why don't I just do it?'

'Yes. I'd really like you to do all the things you've ever thought about doing to me. Because when I look in your eyes right now, I don't see you drowning anymore, Danny. I'd like to be an island for you to run wild on.'

'I want to be on the island. Forever.'

'Forever is a long time,' she replied. 'And waiting for what you want is something, it seems, that never comes.'

The sadness was back in her voice. It was a powerful sentiment that overrode Danny's lustful energy. He paused for a moment, then rested down beside her, his arm draped over her hips.

'Ever thought what it all means, Danny? Ever wondered what the meaning of all this desire is? Imagine if you could see beyond it, to understand perfectly what it is your soul wants, and you know that you actually have everything you need, but still... still you're forever haunted. One taste of that bliss and you'd know that to taste it again is worth waiting forever. You just can't let it go.'

Her voice was low and crystal clear, delivered from a perfect centring of herself, as though she'd been privy to some pure, universal wisdom. Her words carried Danny away from the moment, like a waft of temple incense. Suddenly it was like he didn't know where he was.

'I'll need to sort things out with Sam first. And then...'

'Yeah. You seem to know best with everything,' he said, propping himself up.

He really hated hearing that name. Why did this perfection have to have this imperfection? He wished Samuel would just disappear gracefully and allow their romance to blossom, for there was no doubt to him whom he would love like he could no other, for whom his commitment would be as boundless as the sea before him, and his love as deep.

'I'll be in touch. You'll find me again soon.'

With that, her light sank into the night, the moon disappearing beyond the horizon, the enamoured student lying by the shoreline as the venomous waves slithered towards his feet.

'A thousand times the worse to want thy light,' he quoted to no one.

It felt like it wouldn't be much longer before he would be back here. Except, the next time he would be as a bloated corpse with his brains leaking out of his head and his flesh in tatters from having been nibbled at by the fishes.

Chapter 8.4

Trailing after the fast-footed Vladimir through the back streets of Dark Harbour like two lost sheep following a shepherd, Eddie imagined how their meeting with the Halo of Fires Seraph, Henry Maristow, would go. Presumably, he was the one setting this test for them.

Would this master of darkness put them through some sort of strange initiation process? Maybe they would give them blood to drink, etch a symbolic tattoo on their arms, or maybe they'd burn their hands in a fire so they'd carry a scar as their 'badge' for the rest of their days. What actually happened was an anti-climax in comparison: they sat down with Henry and had a cup of tea.

It seemed apt considering where Vladimir had led them. *Clarence Hotel* had always stood on the seafront road like a prince's palace, harp music piping from the front doors whenever Eddie had walked past.

They didn't enter that way, didn't tread over the shimmering marble floor of the reception foyer that was like a solid layer of clouds. Instead they took the tradesman's entrance, up a fire escape stairwell round the back.

Aware of the majesty of this building, Eddie wouldn't have been surprised to find another angel up there, ready to give an inside opinion on what the clueless student was doing wrong with his life and why he was a screw-up. He would surely tell him that with no direction he was just a useless scrote, not even capable of taking care of a stray dog.

But Eddie had finally come somewhere. He'd taken some small steps with Halo of Fires, so already he was a vigilante, already *something*.

Inside the building they followed Vladimir through a grand mahogany door with an ornate chambranle. Eddie could only glimpse its detailing, whisking leaves in the breeze or perhaps they were feathers floating from the sky. It was less a door and more a gate. Beyond it was Henry Maristow's office, a pristine and airy room with lines and lines of filing cabinets. The leader of the Halo of Fires organisation was standing by the window. He turned and greeted them with surprising warmth, but his face didn't seem used to smiling.

As they sat down at the desk, Eddie felt himself holding his body precisely, crossing his hands neatly on his lap, his eyes wide open. He'd even taken off his baseball cap.

'Let's have a brew then,' Henry said. 'How many sugars do you have?'

'None,' Eddie said.

'Three. Please,' Larry replied.

'Very well,' Henry said as he walked out of the room.

The man seemed more a kindly old uncle, or Ebenezer Scrooge after he'd been visited by the Ghost of Christmas Yet to Come, than the boss of a vigilante organisation.

After shuffling back into the room with a tray of teas, Henry orchestrated light conversation about their college studies, what their hometowns were like, what football teams they supported. He listened keenly to all their responses, contrasting comfortably with Vladimir's dark intensity.

The vigilante master dressed exquisitely, as though he was about to leave for an evening at the opera. He wore a perfectly fitting grey pinstriped suit, with a white handkerchief in the breast pocket, a burgundy tie around his neck.

Although not very tall, Henry had quite a bullish frame. His broad shoulders and large hands were in contrast to his narrow feet. He could have been a boxer when he was younger, dancing around on his tiptoes one moment and then socking his opponents out cold the next. Not that he could do that now though, for Henry's movements were slow and steady, as if he had to summon the energy from deep within in everything he did.

His hands, however, seemed to belie his inertia, for they portrayed a restlessness as he used them continuously to emphasise his words, waving them gently in front of his face then clasping his fingers together, as he did now, like a priest leading the congregation to prayer.

'So then, Lawrence and Eduwart, let's talk about why we are all here tonight,' he began, leaning forward in his tall, black leather chair.

Vladimir hovered in the background, pacing up and down the room with his pent-up energies.

'Let's go over your reports,' he went on. Henry put on his reading glasses before picking up a Manila folder in front of him. He pulled out a printed sheet.

Eddie hadn't imagined they'd look into him to this extent. Where had they got this information from? Did these filing cabinet house the reports on everyone in this town, the eternal observations of angels as they recorded every thought and action?

'Young Lawrence Stewart, six foot two. Played football and rugby at secondary school. Reasonable GCSEs, a couple of A Levels. Student of Sports Studies at Dark Harbour College. You have two older brothers. Your parents died when you were four months old. You and your brothers were looked after by an aunt for most of your childhood. When you were fourteen you were absent from school for several months. The official reason was that you were ill in hospital.'

Henry looked up from his prompt for a moment before then turning to Eddie.

'And young Eduwart Jansz the Dutchman. Six foot one, one older brother, one younger sister. Your father lives on the continent, your mother is an invalid. Your school report says you were a disruptive pupil who wouldn't apply himself. Academic achievements were therefore damp, but, like Lawrence, you have a flair for sports.'

'Sounds about right.'

Henry placed the piece of paper down on his desk and then pressed his fingertips together in front of his chest.

'So, by whatever mystery the universe has in play here, the point is you've made acquaintance with my boys and assisted them in their work.'

'We have,' Eddie said.

'What do you make of us?'

'Some of your other guys are like Rainier Wolfcastle, but I like your style,' Eddie replied.

'Why?'

'Because there's so many knobheads out there and they're spreading. Everyone else just fits in with them. Nobody cares any more.'

'But you care?'

Eddie was quiet for a moment. 'Look, I get it. The world is going to hell. Might as well help everyone on their way.'

Henry looked to Vladimir, an unspoken thought passing between them.

'And you, Lawrence?' Henry asked.

'There's a lot of victims out there. Too many.'

Henry nodded, then looked down at the folder once more. Eddie expected him to carry on divulging more of its contents but it seemed he'd said enough.

'Vladimir said you have another job for us. A test,' Eddie said.

'Yes. We have a task for you.'

'What is it?' Larry asked.

Henry picked up his mug of tea and took a sip. 'Yuck. I didn't brew it long enough.'

Their gaze remained fixed on Henry. In the pregnant pause that followed, the ageing man's eyes seemed to focus on something behind them, or perhaps on something far beyond them all. He gently eased himself out of his chair and walked over to a wall that looked like some murder detective's display of evidence. Maps and photographs hung from it, some with curling edges as they'd faded and frayed through the years of sunlight streaming onto them. This must have been an old case. Henry came to a stop as his eyes focussed on a Polaroid photograph right in front of him.

'I would like you to find someone for me,' he resumed. 'An old acquaintance has suddenly gone missing, blipped off our radar screens, and his disappearance is worrying me somewhat. Unfortunately, I don't quite have the resources to comb every inch of this town.'

'What would you like us to do to him?' Larry asked.

Henry suddenly turned around as if Larry had cracked a good joke. He chuckled with laughter.

'There's no questioning your eagerness, is there, Lawrence?' The smile switched off in a half-moment. 'I don't want you to *do* anything to him, my boy. I want you to *give* him something.'

Henry walked back to his desk where he slid open the top drawer. He pulled out an envelope sealed with a red wax blob.

'Deliver him this letter. That's all you need to do.'

'Why don't you just put it in the post?' Larry asked.

Eddie noticed that Henry was already looking across at Vladimir, as if waiting for him to take to the stage.

'This... person doesn't have a fixed abode,' Vladimir delivered. 'He's a recluse, but he has a very good reason why he keeps himself hidden from the world. He's no ordinary person, you see. Those who set eyes on him are scared numb because they think he's a demon.'

Eddie could no longer keep his hands restrained in his lap and began twisting the piercing in his eyebrow. Larry tried to take another sip of tea even though he'd already finished it.

'But we hope he's not, of course,' Henry added, talking like a parent trying to reassure a child who'd just been told a bedtime ghost story. Or perhaps he was trying to reassure himself. Suddenly he seemed a little antsy.

'I don't think he'll harm you,' Vladimir went on. 'We've

both met him plenty of times before and not once did he ever try to eat our souls or anything.'

'Explain to them how he gets his name,' Henry added.

'Nobody knows his name. His real one, that is. He probably doesn't even have one. But he does go by a name which has steadily formed over time. The Devil One, frightened folk would call him. Years and years of lazy, slurred speech eventually simplified it to Devlan.'

'Why are people so scared of him?' Eddie asked.

'You're best seeing for yourself,' Henry replied. 'If you can find him.'

'What exactly is he?' Larry asked. 'Some sort of freak?'

Neither Henry nor Vladimir appeared willing to answer this particular question.

'We have a list of areas for you to look,' Henry said. 'The more insalubrious corners of this town. That's if you want this task. I can understand if you don't. It's up to you.'

Like a soldier about to be sent off to a foreign land to fight, Eddie sensed that a large journey was ahead of them. Although it came with a sinister edge, it was exciting at the same time. He just wished he knew what was in store for them if they were to pass this test. Or if they were to fail. That's what worried him most of all.

He looked to his friend. Again, the look on his face suggested that the next line was not Larry's.

Eddie nodded. 'We'll do it.'

'Good,' Henry replied. 'Now let me have another go at fixing myself a decent cuppa.'

He picked up his mug and carried it from the silence of the room.

***

'So, now we're devil hunters,' Eddie said to Larry as they walked down the fire escape steps.

'Feels like we've become the Winchester brothers,' Larry replied. 'Maybe there's more to this town than I thought.'

They made their way back to the flat. It had gone midnight, but the pubs were still bulging with rambunctious revellers. Soon they'd all be queuing to get into the

207

nightclubs. Perhaps within the shadows of one of these hives this devil person was to be found, lost in the maelstrom of nocturnal indulgence.

Larry looked at the envelope sealed by the wax blob. In the dim light he could make out the imprint on the wax. It was the same symbol on their calling card, two ever-searching eyes peering through a flame.

'We should open this. See what it says,' Larry suggested.

Eddie shook his head. This was a *test*. Maybe that was the point of it, to see if they could trust them, not find some devil freak that they'd probably pulled out of their arses.

'No. Leave it.'

'What do you think it says?'

'This letter will self-destruct in five seconds. Bad luck, you failed, guys. Kaboom!'

'Or maybe it's blank. Maybe they just gave us this to get rid of us.'

'And like two gullible rookies, we took it.'

'We should just throw this away and go back to them and say "Yeah, we found him. We gave him it."'

Their banter soon ran dry. Neither of them was actually in the mood for being witty. They were still digesting the conversation they'd had back on the top floor of the hotel.

After Henry had made himself an acceptable cup of tea, he then talked about the organisation. The vigilante master explained the ranks that Halo of Fires was built on. The top guys were called the Seraphs. Next in rank was the Throne, a position held solely by Vladimir, whose job was to lead the rest of the recruits: the Powers, who, as their name suggested, were the powerhouses, the men with the muscle. Those were the two guys they'd met in Barrow Hill Thorns by the burning car. Beneath them were Dominions and Virtues and various others, but Henry didn't talk too much about those.

As for Larry and Eddie, they were would be Guardians, for now. Larry figured it was the same as being a private in the army and that the name was equally as nonsensical. Guardians to what, exactly? At least it sounded cool, he supposed.

'You reckon we're getting a foot on their ladder?' Larry

asked.

'Hopefully.'

'You really want a career in a professional vigilante organisation? What if you decide on a more mainstream job one day and you have to explain to your new boss about this little section of your C.V.?'

Eddie shrugged. 'Don't think I'll get to that bridge.'

'Hmm. We'll stick with these guys then,' Larry agreed.

'It's an easy decision for you, isn't it?'

'What do you mean?'

'You believe in revenge. It's something you think about.'

A certain day when Larry was fourteen years old had been on his mind quite a lot since they'd met Halo of Fires, and he wondered if it was a detail that Henry had in his report but had chosen not to mention.

Were the Fires aware of what had happened to him on that double-decker bus? Perhaps there was a criminal report of it somewhere. Larry didn't actually know. He didn't like thinking too much about that incident, let alone talking about it.

'Don't know how I can't not believe in it,' he muttered.

'What happened?' Eddie asked. 'Wanna compare scars, like?'

He did not get a reply, but neither did his friend push it.

They'd sent Larry to a string of counsellors and psychiatrists for the rest of his teenage years, and they'd all poked and probed him with questions which he'd stubbornly repelled. How would they be able to understand his trauma when they'd never experienced anything like it themselves?

Someone like Eddie though... who didn't care about anything... who probably wouldn't even care about *this*, perhaps, in some strange way, talking to him might be the psychological antidote he needed.

It always seemed safer to keep his mouth shut, though.

'You know what I reckon?' Eddie began. 'I reckon we're on our way to facing our demons now.'

Part 9: Floyd's Chamber of Fun

Chapter 9.1

The old bitch hadn't stopped prattling since he'd wheeled it outside. Of all the crips he could have picked and Floyd had gone and got motormouth of the millennium. It could barely move its arms or legs, but as far as verbal capabilities went, it would earn a place representing England if Talking Shite was an Olympic event.

With complete nonchalance, Floyd walked in as though he'd been routinely visiting the retirement home for years. He followed the deafening boom of the heart-beating music and Chris Tarrant's giggling voice reading the possible answers to a question about New York's nickname: '*The Big Potato, the Big Apple, the Big Orange, or the Big Traffic Jam...*'

One or two of the people in the sitting room may have known what television show they were watching; the rest probably didn't even know what year it was, let alone what planet they were on. Here was a collection of living dead, all hunched, mangled and decrepit like vehicles in a scrap yard, written off by the car crash called life. They were all waiting for bedtime or waiting to die, whichever came first.

Positively ignoring the demented fruitcake who insisted the correct answer to the three hundred pound question was A, Floyd scanned the room for one that seemed reasonably docile. One of them sat in the corner of the room, a purple knitted blanket wrapped around its lap, a line of drool slopping from its mouth. It looked at least two hundred years old.

No one said anything to him as he released the brakes on its wheelchair and quietly pushed it away. Apart from the fairy-seeing residents, no one saw him do it, for the wardens were most probably occupied with the other worthless geriatrics. And so, as though he'd dutifully gone in there to take his elderly mother out for an evening stroll, Floyd left with a random resident.

He was really warming up now. *Where's the Floyd I used to know?* That was the question in the letter that had stuck out in his mind. Tonight would prove to The Harbour Master that his old apprentice had come back to himself, that the plan was on course. This new dawn had been a long time coming. Soon they would both be back where they belonged.

'Can you take me to bed now?' the old cripple asked for the six hundredth time.

'I'll take you later,' Floyd replied as they neared the edge of town, the row of streetlights coming to an end.

'Why can't you take me now?'

'There's something I want to show you first.'

He knew no one would care that this useless bag of shit would suddenly have gone missing. If it had any children anywhere, then Floyd knew they'd be relieved. They'd no longer have the burden of handling its finances, or have to visit each Sunday to listen to medicine-induced babbling. No longer would they have to keep up the lark of *pretending* they cared about it.

'Where are we going then? Are we off to see Betty?' the cripple asked.

'Who's she?'

'My daughter. Do you know her? She's a teacher at Ashtree Primary School. Wonderful baker too. Makes lovely scones.'

'I'm taking you on a little excursion,' Floyd said in that apparently sincere tone of his. 'You enjoy the fair, don't you?'

Annoyingly, the cripple was finding it too difficult to articulate the one word response that the question required and so he carried on. 'I run the seaside amusements, and I have a new ride that I thought you might like to try.'

'I 'spect she'll make you a mug of hot chocolate if you ask nicely. Warm you up. Still, it's quite a nice night tonight, isn't it?' the cripple said.

Floyd shook his head. It was rather cool and murky this evening, a fine drizzle of sea mist slowly creeping over the town. He could feel a continuous cold spray against his craggy face, as though his skin was infested with tiny crawling insects. The cripple was so wrapped up in cardigans and blankets that it couldn't feel anything.

'Beautiful,' he said as he wiped his trench coat sleeve over his itchy forehead.

'Are you going to take me to bed soon?'

'Nearly there.'

They weren't heading to the regular amusement park. Tonight Floyd was taking this cripple to his *other* park.

Floyd's Chamber of Fun was initially a storage area, a dumping ground for his old rides from the seafront. Here he brought the failing roller coasters, ghost trains, and gallopers that were no longer safe for children to ride. But like old people in a retirement home, Floyd could still see a use for them.

At first he'd employed Devlan to fix them. Knowing him to be a mechanical genius, the Chamber had become his home as he reconditioned the rides or salvaged them for parts.

After a while, Devlan was reassigned. Floyd continued to tinker with the rides on his own and kept other people out of there. Most people.

Working for The Harbour Master had given the agent of destruction such imaginative ideas, and he couldn't help but manifest them in his own world of obliqueness. According to a magazine he'd read last month, there was only a one in one-and-a-half billion chance of someone being fatally injured on an amusement ride. Not surprising when all they did was jolt people around a bit.

The Chamber was different. Floyd had geared everything in it towards his own idea of fun, something that was at odds to everyone else's. He just had his own tastes.

The first subjects to experience the enjoyment within his Chamber of Fun occurred when one of his associates discovered a family of Chinese stowaways onboard a vessel at the harbour. Floyd had offered a place for the young mother with the long black hair and her three famished children to stay. One by one, he used each of them to test his specially modified rides and it had been a most enjoyable experience indeed. Floyd also gained much satisfaction from knowing he'd saved the local taxpayers from having to house even more needy refugees.

There were so many worthless people in this world who drained society of all its valuable resources and gave nothing in return, a fine example of which was the useless geriatric he was wheeling farther into a cold murkiness of concrete and iron.

Chapter 9.2

Frawley Holt Industrial Park seemed a contradiction in terms, for the landscape of that area of town was bleak, almost like some futuristic waste ground where T101s would battle against a resistance on the broken flints and sparse shrubs that dared to grow where once a wood had been sacrificed in the name of industry.

Within the warehouse in the far corner of the park was a more cheerful sight. At a glance, Floyd's Chamber seemed like a tenderly constructed monument rather than a graveyard for fairground apparatus. Most of the lights on the rides would still illuminate. The Orton and Spooner merry-go-round of horses and carts would still bellow its hauntingly nostalgic melodies, evoking bygone Victorian summers.

After three years of desertion, the dust had thickened and the paint had flaked, as Floyd discovered when he walked inside and switched on the straining floodlights.

'Oh this is very nice,' the cripple said.

Floyd darted in front of the wheelchair and proudly threw his arms open wide as though he were trying to embrace his secret world. 'Welcome! Which of my magical rides would you like to experience?' he boomed. 'There's the Chair-O-Planes Planer, the Road to Hell Ghost Train, the Hard Impact Orbiter, the Bone Breaker Waltzer, or maybe you would prefer the Crazy Catterkiller!'

As he announced them, he darted from each of his

twisted rides to the other, making grand gestures with his arms like a ringmaster performing to a sell-out audience of rowdy pucks and demons all baying for destruction. He imagined their cheers and was keen to satisfy their desires. In a hammy motion, he rested his elbow in a hand as he stroked his jutting chin in exaggerated contemplation.

The Road to Hell Ghost Train was very tempting. Atop the entrance was a giant skull with glowing orange eyes, beckoning hopeless souls to come inside. That was the very first one he'd tested. He remembered so vividly standing with the Chinese woman as one of her kids got on. He was the eldest and bravely insisted he rode it on his own.

The ride had squealed into motion as the crash doors opened, the gaping mouth of a giant zombie head swallowing the cart. Once inside, the kid encountered a pair of severed hands playing a deathly tune on a pipe organ before gliding on to the hall of ghouls. There a gallery of ghastly paintings adorned the wall, their eyes eerily following the path of the cart as it continued towards even more horrors.

Outside they could hear the boy screaming in excited fear at all the spooky sights and sounds within the train. That was until he entered the final stretch where pitch-black darkness fell over him. They weren't hearing screams of fear then.

'I think, my dear, we shall go for my favourite, the Head Over Wheels.'

'I ought to be going to bed now. Can you take me?' it asked for the last time.

The Head Over Wheels was a rickety old roller coaster in the shape of a snake. Devlan had initially done a fine job in restoring it to basic operation. It sure wouldn't pass any health and safety test though.

Floyd pushed the cripple over to the cart and lifted it into the back seat. It was surprisingly heavy and stank of piss. He yanked the bar down to keep it securely locked in, then crouched down to play one of his favourite games before sending it on the ride of a lifetime.

'I spoke to Betty earlier,' Floyd projected, saying each word slowly to make sure it heard him. 'She told me how much of a nasty piece of work you are. Said she's hated you her whole life.'

There was confusion in the cripple's glazed eyes. 'My Betty said that?'

'Oh yes. Your little Betty. She hasn't been visiting you much recently, has she?' Floyd hazarded.

'No. She hasn't.'

'I'm sorry to have to tell you, but it's because she hates you. You know what she called you? A good-for-nothing whore. How about that? Your own daughter called you a whore.'

With a grin, Floyd merrily skipped over to the control box and cranked the lever. The snake set off and entered the lift hill where it was yanked up a steep slope. By then the cripple started wailing.

'Oh, I don't like this. Can you take me off? Please, I want to get off.'

The modification on this ride was the tunnel at the bottom of the drop. Floyd had lowered it so that the snake-cart would only just fit through.

The cart reached the summit and teetered teasingly over the edge. Suddenly it made its free fall, the roar of steel against steel echoing throughout the concrete chamber like the sound of the earth's crust being torn open. Swooping towards the tunnel with unrelenting, uncaring speed, the cart's passenger started screaming. It could see the snake disappearing into the giant apple, and although the old woman tried to slink into the seat, its head still protruded.

A blade ran along the edge of the tunnel and it sliced off everything above the mouth. The severed crown flopped between the tracks as the rest of the corpse appeared from the other end of the tunnel, its hands still clutching the bar, its lips still peeled back in silent terror as though willing to ride the circuit for the rest of eternity. Floyd smiled like a hound as he continued to watch it hurtling round like a torn rag doll on a child's train track. Things didn't get any more fun than this.

He again thought back to that Chinese kid when the ghost train had returned him to the start. Not that there was much left of him. The two chainsaws had swooped down on him in the darkness of the ride and mangled him beautifully. How his mother had cried!

But that was only the beginning for her. She'd then had to watch as her other two kids were used to test rides. The middle child went on the Chair-O-Planes Planer where the chairs had swung ever-higher towards a blade attached to the wall. Eventually his legs were 'planed' off and Floyd had left him dangling up there while his blood rained down on the ground. His pathetic calls soon became fainter and fainter until they stopped completely.

Then there was the youngest one, her quiet little daughter whom he'd had to wrestle from the mother's frenzied clutches. She'd been put on the 1001 Frights Flying Carpet ride, from which he'd removed the lap bars. Floyd had also altered the ride to make the carpet arch up higher, flaunting the force of gravity so the girl would fall to the spikes waiting below. She'd landed with an almighty squelch. Floyd had crouched down to have a look at the mess and miraculously, for about a whole minute, the little girl was still breathing.

As he terminated the Head Over Wheels ride, he reflected on why he'd built this twisted world of horrors. He always felt such fascination watching people die in the most painfully bloody of ways. Causing that torture created a tangible vibration that soured the air and excited every cell in his brain.

He'd often wondered what the maximum amount of suffering was that you could squeeze out of someone before they died. That involved emotional pain as well as physical pain, which is why he'd made that mother watch all her kids die. He was intrigued to see whether that experience itself would kill her. It hadn't, not exactly. She'd ceased shrieking by the time her daughter stopped breathing, and when Floyd dragged her to another ride, she complied willingly.

None of it mattered. He didn't see that there was any difference between killing an entire Chinese family and stamping over a nest of ants. Humans weren't any more *living* than ants, and so their lives didn't *mean* anything more. People just died, just ended their meaningless existence, and that was it. He didn't believe he would go to hell or anything like that; that was just fabricated nonsense to keep people in line. Whatever waited for everyone on the other side was the same, whether he was the Pope or a cold-blooded son of a bitch.

Floyd didn't believe in a world of consequence, or a world of compassion. He'd been doing what he'd been doing for years, and nothing had stopped him yet. Nothing would ever catch up with him here, just as nothing would in an afterlife. He could be as sadistic as possible, and it didn't matter at all. That's what *he* had taught him.

Floyd wasn't any less human than anyone. He knew he wasn't deranged or anything, that he could function properly in society by paying his taxes and not dropping litter anywhere. And he knew that God was within him just as much as in a Sunday church-goer. God was in his Chamber of Fun just as much as he was on that mountain where Moses had received the Commandments.

He'd learnt all about that under The Harbour Master and *his* cronies. God *loved* everyone. God was *inside* everyone. God loved *whatever* Floyd did, and so life was a game he could not lose. But more importantly, Floyd knew that if his former boss could see him at this moment, *he* would be so proud of him. Floyd was now just one step away from fulfilling a longstanding and delicious act of supreme revenge.

He was feeling so pleased this evening. It was likely he'd test the other rides before too long, to make sure they were all working. He wanted a fully functioning Chamber of Fun before he brought Henry down to choose his ride.

Part 10: Back to the Cove

Chapter 10.1

Whether it was a gun, a knife, or just your own blood-scuffed knuckles, such weapons were necessary to help you get by in this town.

Michael was a weapon carrier too. He took it wherever he went and had to use it every day: his silver ballpoint pen. The only problem was he'd lost it earlier in the week. Larry had probably nabbed it, picked it up to do some stupid word search in a television guide.

Since its disappearance, Michael had bought a pack of ten biros from one of those knickknack shops on the high street: *Everything is a pound... but everything is complete crap!* He'd scattered them around: a couple on the desk in his room, a couple in his bag, a few in the lounge. Hopefully his flatmates would leave his silver pen alone from now on. Assuming it would ever show up again.

As Horace Goldby, the retired entertainer with the bronzed skin and pearly eyes, continued his diatribe of the Halo of Fires organisation, Michael used one of those biros to jot down his words on a notepad.

Michael's assignment was alive and dancing like the cancan now, ever since that kick-start interview with the man in black. 'Halo of Liars' was the headline. He already knew it would get a first. It was just a shame it was only a student article. The stuff he was writing surely deserved to be printed in the local newspaper, shining the spotlight on the flies and bugs that crawled in the darkness, uncovering the rot and toxic rage that smouldered beneath the floorboards of the crumbling shack that was Dark Harbour society.

Right now it seemed Michael had a kindred spirit before him in Horace Goldby.

'See, I knew Ulric was in with them,' the old man said. 'I

told him they were nothing but trouble but you could never tell him anything.'

What a gem. Although he was in his nineties, Horace had that Cliff Richard glow of undying youth. In five years' time, he would probably look only one year older. Decades ago he'd been the resident compère at the Paragon Theatre on the seafront. Judging by his burgundy dinner jacket, his green shirt, and the passionate way he recounted his memories, Horace still felt a pull to entertain, was still ready to take to the stage. If Michael were to hand him a microphone, he was sure he wouldn't need any encouragement to croon off his *Oh I Do Like to Be Beside the Seaside* routine.

Within the living-room of his seaside chalet was an array of black and white photographs of his erstwhile theatre days. He'd explained the story behind just about every one of them before the student journalist had managed to get in any of his questions.

Lex McLean and Tommy Morgan were two 'stars' that Horace appeared in photographs with. Michael hadn't heard of either of them. In a monochrome poster, he was the star billing himself in 'An Evening of Giggles and Gaggles With Horace Goldby'. Michael was sure it was a sell-out in its time.

The chalet was on Tennyson Avenue, a short way down the road from the flat that Ulric Helliwell and his grandsons lived in. With a growing population of pensioners, the north end of the town was considered one giant old folks' village. As with Horace's chalet, many of the homes overlooked the expanse of Dark Harbour's waters, as though their inhabitants could peacefully see out their days awaiting the ship that would take them from their Grey Havens.

Before then he'd lived in the same block as Ulric Helliwell. He was, as Michael had discovered, about the last resident from that era who was still alive, and fortunately his mind hadn't clouded with age.

'But apparently Alan Hammond was going to sort things out for him, going to help get him out of the hole poor Ulric had dug for himself,' Horace spoke in a loud, gossipy whisper. On certain syllables he made a whistling sound, but it was probably way out of range for him to notice.

'What exactly had he done?'

'Ulric? From what I gathered, he'd blown the whistle on a ring of city crooks. They put him over the rocks. Caused a calamity. That's why he came running to Dark Harbour.'

'So he was friends with the Halo of Fires leader? They didn't kill him?'

'Oh, no. The Fires were *protecting* him. What do you think? They did a good job of that? As a matter of fact, I don't know who killed him. Don't think anyone does.'

'But... Jeremy. The youngest grandson. Didn't he escape?'

An ice cold silence came over Horace as if he was listening for something in the distance, perhaps the clap of thunder that would signal it was time to close the chalet windows that were wide open to let in the sustaining sea breeze.

'Little Jeremy, yes. He escaped. Do you know much about him?'

'A bit.' He could have said more, but he wasn't the one being interviewed.

'The poor lad, he ran away. They found some things of his at Moonlight Cove, strewn over the beach.'

'Were these items dumped there?'

'Who knows? All I know is there's something they don't want people to know. You know when someone's got a really dark secret, how they'll hold on to it so tightly, but it's the way they're acting, you just know it's something terrible.'

'What do you think happened to him?'

Horace sat back in his armchair and breathed in deeply the half fresh, half stale, air.

'I often passed by Jeremy in the corridor. Lovely little boy he was. Never met a boy quite like him before. And not since. He had these eyes, such absorbing eyes. So clear you could see yourself in them. But you'd wish you could see inside and know what was going on up there in his head. Why such a terrible thing would happen to a lovely boy as him, I'll never know.'

Michael circled some of his words. 'A *terrible thing*?'

Horace snorted up some air and grimaced. 'It appeared Ulric told him to go looking for Alan Hammond. Thought that Hammond would look after him, as he was supposed to have looked after Ulric. That's where the boy went.'

'Jeremy found Hammond?'

'Yes.'

'And where is he now?'

He paused for dramatic effect like a talented actor. 'I can only tell you what I think, but of this I'm ninety-nine percent certain.'

'What?'

'He's dead, the poor lad. Bless his soul.'

'The Fires killed him?'

Horace shifted in his armchair and leaned forward. 'Now from what I heard it goes like this: Hammond realised it was too dangerous keeping hold of the boy, a witness to two murders. Specially when there's such a bloodthirsty murderer out there. It was too risky having him on his hands. They knew his killers, and so they handed him over to them. What did it matter? Ulric was already gone. Hammond had no more favours to keep. Not to a dead man. And especially not to some innocent youngster who didn't have any more family out there. They realised no one would miss him, and they didn't care. Didn't care if he would live or die.'

Michael finished scribbling his words, then paused. His eyes lost focus as he stared into the ink and the grain of the paper.

'I challenge you to find that boy anywhere. He's gone. He's no longer of this world. You got more chance of walking past Elvis in the street than you have of finding poor Jeremy.'

Michael looked up again. 'What about Hammond? He's dead too, right?'

'Yes, he's a gonner. And good riddance, I say. Him's another mystery. You'd have to talk to someone in the organisation to find out what happened to that slimeball.'

'I'd sure like to,' Michael said with a slow nodding of his head. He looked down on his notes again. There was some more great stuff there.

The old man eased himself out of his chair and shuffled across the room to close the window. Michael guessed he'd had enough talking for one day and was now retreating into his mind's dressing room.

'Thank you for your time, Mr Goldby. It's been a big help.' He replaced the lid on his ballpoint pen and folded over the cover of his notepad.

'My pleasure. Good luck with this, young Mister Foxbury. If you ever work for the *Harbour Gazette*, make sure you remember to do a feature on me. Plenty of happier stories I can tell you.'

'I'll keep that in mind.'

Michael stood and zipped up his white jacket. Standing by the curtains, Horace was staring down at another silver-framed vintage photo of his theatre days. Time to get going before the old guy continued talking his ear off.

Horace cleared his throat and gazed through the window down Tennyson Avenue. 'I was in the flat that evening. We actually used to live directly above Ulric over there. I heard a scream. Must have been Jeremy. Can hear him like it was yesterday. Still makes the hairs in my ear holes bristle. I was about to go downstairs to investigate, but we could sense there was some serious trouble. And, Alice, rest her soul, she insisted that I didn't go. So, I waited, and by then he'd gone.'

Michael was silent for a few moments as he replayed Horace's words in his head, making sure he'd mentally recorded it. Why did he always put his pen away ten seconds too early? He held his breath for fear of the words escaping his head.

'I see,' said Michael as he sat back down again and removed the lid off his pen. 'And do you remember anything else about that day?'

Chapter 10.2

After another half hour talking to Horace Goldby about the

mysterious case of Jeremy Helliwell and only fifteen minutes listening to hilarious Paragon anecdotes, Michael began his walk back home.

His mind was stacked full of information, like someone had scattered all the pages of the mystery in front of him, and on one page there was the answer. He just needed to wait for God to direct his eyes to the right one.

Not that this was what he'd initially set out to do. He'd only wanted to write a general exposé on the reprehensible entity known as Halo of Fires and gripe about vengeance, enlighten the town about another one of man's futile attempts to play God. But then this subplot had bubbled to the surface, the case of a disappearing young boy.

Although Michael hadn't even been born when the Helliwells were murdered, he knew the story of their misfortune well. It came from having so many older brothers, Michael being the youngest of five. Between him and his eldest brother there had been a seventeen year gap. Oliver had been something of a father figure to his siblings, the one who'd been through school and the adventures of growing up before them.

He arrived every week on time for their Sunday afternoon dinners, a motorbike helmet under his arm, a shaggy mane of hair on his head. Oliver was so old that he was an adult now, and was allowed to grow his hair as long as he wanted.

While they ate, he would give a commentary on everything like he was at a football match. He was always the last one to finish eating.

He told Michael all the lurid stories about their hometown, but the most fascinating one was the story of the murdered new kid. Oliver had actually known Simon Helliwell, the only one to make friends with him. They had many things in common, mainly karate and comic books.

'We were going to go fishing the next day, Mikey. I was there at the beach wondering why he hadn't turned up. Never imagined he was dead. Never caught a thing that day either.'

Michael remembered during his own time at school how the rougher kids would sometimes crudely speculate on the bloody details of Simon's murder. No one really mentioned Jeremy Helliwell though.

But Oliver Foxbury did.

'One time me and Simon biked to the abbey and he was in a really strange mood. Told me things I thought he was just making up. He said his little brother was born without a face.'

Apparently, these were details Simon never even told Jeremy himself, things that had been relayed from one brother to another brother, orphaned stories that ended up in the sanctuary of Michael's mind.

'Simon told me he'd delivered his own brother. When he handed the baby to his mother, she took off this shimmering membrane. He'd been born with a caul, you see. She said he was a special child. He never cried when he came out. Simon thought he saw wisps of light around his mother's head, like fireflies. And the strangest thing is he never knew who the father was, said he didn't know his mother had a boyfriend or anything.'

The impressionable young Michael had instantly felt his brother had given him some important knowledge, and that the missing Jeremy needed to be found again. It had been Simon's role to look after this light bringer, to be his guardian, but without him the boy was lost. Or dead, according to Horace Goldby.

As Michael walked along the pavement with this mystery being twisted and turned in his mind like a Rubik's Cube, he eventually realised he wasn't walking back home at all. He was edging towards Moonlight Cove, the last known location of Jeremy Helliwell.

Michael had not been there in a long time, not since his birdwatching phase when he was in primary school. Other than being a good place for spotting little egrets and black-headed gulls, Michael also vaguely remembered being told about the beauty spot's mystical reputation. The place was supposed to be haunted. Perhaps it wasn't famous enough for Derek Acorah and Yvette Fielding to have traipsed down there, but the odd story of the ghostly spirits within the cove had surfaced throughout the years. Michael also seemed to remember that people communed with the spirits there. Or something. He'd never really paid much attention to this superstitious hokum.

The sky was full of activity this afternoon as layers of clouds bustled over one another. Their ever-continuing movement created a panorama of drama: wizards with long beards blending into galloping horses blending into snow-covered mountains from a fantasy wilderness.

After walking along the meadowland, Michael set eyes upon the magic of the real world beneath the celestial theatre: Moonlight Cove. Descending the cliff face where once the boy's satchel and torch had been tossed, Michael clambered down to the sodden sands.

Where would the young child have gone next? Why did he even come here in the first place? Why would he go to a place that was haunted? To find the spirit of his murdered brother, perhaps?

The crescent of looming cliffs flanked the cove like the wall of a fortress. A lone tree at the top of the escarpment stood watching like a sentinel. It swayed back and forth in the wind, pointing its branches towards the sands as if to encourage people to remain within this retreat rather than go back to the frenzy and frustration of town life.

After feeling a momentary balancing of the scales, Michael's persevering mind returned to the issue of a certain missing boy. A journalist should keep himself one step removed from the story. He couldn't allow the beguiling Moonlight Cove to distract him.

So where did Jeremy go next?

He wouldn't have clambered down the cliff just to clamber out again. There didn't appear to be any caves anywhere in which he could hide. The beach didn't expand up the coastline. There was only the crescent-shaped sands and the waves that lapped at their edge.

Michael strolled towards the sea. He pictured the small footprints, washed away soon after by the tide. Jeremy must have walked over to the water because there was no other place he could have gone.

But where *then*? Would he have carried on, walking into his grave? Would a six-year-old boy even have a concept of suicide at that age?

Following the trail of those ghostly steps, Michael soon arrived at the edge of the shore as it hugged the cove closely, hiding many of the rocks scattered across the sea. Their unsubmerged tips were but small islands that would not provide any lasting habitation for anyone; perhaps just the occasional mermaid that would pause on one to comb its hair.

This was where Jeremy's journey must have ended.

The mystery churned over and over in his mind. The Rubik's Cube would form a collection of colours on one face, only for Michael to turn it over and see a multi-coloured mosaic on the opposite face. He had all the pieces, but they would not come together in a way that even began to make any sense.

A boy goes to a secluded cove. He walks over to the waves because he has nowhere else to go. What does he find here? *Who* does he find here? Why would he come here if he was looking for a Halo of Fires agent?

Where? What? Who? Why?

Michael could sense the answer was right in front of his nose but he could not see it, like he was searching for his glasses when he was already wearing them.

Where does he go next? Where, where, where?

'Lovely little boy he was. Never met a boy quite like him before. And not since. He had these eyes, such absorbing eyes. So clear you could see yourself in them.'

Michael felt a spot of rain. He knew what that meant. It told him where *he* should go next, back to the flat. Unfortunately, it was time to abandon the mystery until another day.

As a wave of disappointment passed through him, Michael turned from the waters and started walking back across the sands.

Had Jeremy's footsteps also gone back to the cliff face? Is that how the story continued? There had to have been some point to this part of the story.

As he was alone, and as the mystery tantalised him so much, Michael stopped walking, turned back to the necromantic waves and said, 'Where is he? Where on earth is he?'

The surf continued to roll and froth at the shoreline. A few seagulls swooped from the sky to attack a crab that scampered from the water. The rain continued to fall in bigger droplets.

No spirits appeared. No ghosts or banshees or wraiths or anything manifested from the ether to answer his question. It was just himself and an attractive section of coastline that inspired the imagination.

He turned away. The rain was pattering against his white jacket and soaking into his blue jeans. Michael stuffed his hands into his pockets. No answer today, but he would get there.

On the plus side, he had now found his favourite silver pen, for there it was in his pocket. All that hunting and suspecting and it was there all along.

'When will you ever learn, Dorothy?' he muttered to himself.

He held out the pen and stared at it. He stopped walking too.

His stomach fluttered, a whisper of inspiration suddenly sweeping through him to guide his thoughts. Michael whipped round to face the sea. He didn't know whether he was expecting to see something there or what, but for some reason he felt as if he'd hit on something. A quick turn of the Rubik's Cube and the tiles had gone from a random mess to a perfect alignment.

All because of his silver pen. An innocuous little object. His favourite weapon. A faithful writing implement that hadn't disappeared from him as he'd thought.

He could now use that same pen to write about the flash of inspiration that it had caused, the sense of synchronicity he was now experiencing.

Judging by the strength of the vibration he was feeling in his stomach, it had to mean he'd solved the mystery.

Part 11: Dead Ends

Chapter 11.1

The gold hands on the spire clock both reached the top of the dial and the nervy Seraph began walking through the oak doors into Saint Anthony of Padua's. Henry had been waiting outside for five minutes. Seleven must have been early.

The church was cold and mournfully quiet inside. Apart from the dull orange glow of streetlights that filtered through the stained glass windows on the east wing, the only other light within the building came from the candles that burned at the devotional altar.

Sitting on the front row was a bearded man wearing a baggy white collarless shirt, Seleven Vear. He looked to be alone, something which surprised Henry. He rested his hands on his walking stick, strange that he even had it as he never seemed to have a limp in his gait.

Seleven was the right-hand man of The Harbour Master, *his* chief messenger, problem fixer, and shoelace tier. There was a rather old conspiracy theory that Seleven was a decoy, that he was actually The Harbour Master himself, but Henry knew that was poppycock. He didn't look anything like *him* for one thing. Although Henry had met *him* only the once, he could still produce a reasonably accurate E-fit. A meeting with that individual was not something you easily forgot.

Hearing Henry's footsteps reverberating around the stone hall, Seleven said, 'Maristow.'

His voice was whispery and without inflection or emotion. Henry often wondered whether a surgeon would find only wires and diodes on opening up Seleven's head. The way he'd spoken was not really to say hello, but more as if his cybernetic systems had detected him and was merely registering his presence.

'Vear,' Henry replied.

He took a seat on the other side of the aisle. A giant crucifix of a dying Christ hung over their heads.

'Still a soldier of God?' Henry asked, peering above.

'We are all soldiers. Have you lost your belief, Maristow?'

'Can't lose what we've never found.'

'But I know you search. You at least know there's something to be found.'

Henry rubbed his eyes and crossed his legs. 'Where's the boss tonight? Will *he* be joining us?'

Seleven didn't reply. He just turned his head towards him. Whatever expression he had on his face was lost in his thick beard. Henry suddenly had an eerie feeling that Seleven's head was being manipulated by The Harbour Master like a remote-controlled puppet, and *he* was able to look on him through eye-like cameras.

'Why don't you ask me about what we really came here for tonight?' Seleven eventually said.

Henry nodded. 'Okay, hit me.'

Seleven put down his tall walking stick and reached next to himself. He picked up a black briefcase, placed it down and kicked it across the floor towards Henry. The sharp sound of leather scuffing against stone filled the church for a short moment before a void of silence fell upon them.

Henry knew what was inside it. He leaned forward in the pew, peering at the briefcase like a child about to open a Christmas present. With his hands clasped together and pinned between his knees, he could easily have been mistaken for a man begging to Christ for salvation.

If a twist to this tale was going to come, then it would materialise in the next few seconds. Perhaps the moment that Henry stood up, a pair of goons with machine guns would crash through the windows and spray him with bullets.

Or perhaps Henry's pessimism would finally, for the first time in his life, escape him. Perhaps if he was to get out of his seat right now and open that briefcase, he would find the very thing he had been searching for all these years.

'Don't open it,' Seleven said. Every word was ice cold.

'Why?'

'Henry Maristow, why do you always set yourself the impossible? Why did you think you could escape your past? Hiding behind Hammond's torch then holding it as your own all this time.'

Henry couldn't put his thoughts in order. It was like his mind was scattered across the entire universe and Seleven was taking the opportunity to slice him in the guts in the mental attenuation.

His messenger went on, 'You saw the Fires as a noble crusade to make up for your service in the Network. You thought if you could deliver punishment to everyone else, it would eventually erase your own guilt. Help those visions fade away. Floyd running around like some monster, while you just stood back and let him get on with it. No wonder you felt you had to cleanse your soul somehow.'

Henry blinked hard and cleared his throat. 'Didn't realise it was as easy as a Hail Mary.'

He got up and stood over the case.

'The end is always another step away, Maristow.'

Henry crouched down. He slid the catches and the locks sprung free. Delicately he lifted the lid.

Inside was the indigo gemstone that Vladimir had taken from the assassinated David Tovar, the same one The Reaper had then snatched from them. Dried blood speckled the chain of wooden beads.

Henry's trembling fingers reached forward and stroked the stone. Taking hold of the cord, he straightened his spine, feeling limitless. The treasure dangled in front of his face and Henry closed his eyes to hold the tears.

At first it was soothing, as though a healer had placed his hands on his head and centred his strained energies. He expected to hear a choir of angels as the winged messengers that adorned the colourful windows would come to life and fly throughout the nave, the nailed Christ above opening his eyes as the blood dripped from his crown. At any moment the church would illuminate with heavenly light.

However calming it was to hold this stone, it didn't feel that unusual, only like waking from a deep and refreshing sleep. Henry's arm began to ache.

'It's fake,' Seleven said to him.

Henry opened his dewy eyes. 'Yeah.'

He sat back down. The despair brought a peculiar calm, the knots in his neurones untying, the clouds in his brain dissipating. Releasing hope was bringing him salvation, all thanks to this imitation.

He wished that he'd listened to Vladimir. The kid was always right. Always, always.

'Why?' Henry asked, hoping for any sort of answer that Seleven might give him. Or perhaps he was talking to the saviour above. Nevertheless, the man had a reply for him.

'All this time we thought the stone had survived the sinking of the *Tatterdemalion*, but we've just been hunting that fake. Something that came out of a Christmas cracker.'

'It's not still down there,' Henry said. 'It can't be. We're chasing our tails here. The thing doesn't exist.'

'There's that lack of belief again, Maristow.'

'If the legend of the Akasa Stone sank before it started, then why are we even aware of it? How do we know that Silas had the stone on board if he didn't survive to tell anyone?'

'I thought you would have spent more time researching the story.'

'I'm not searching the sea for it. I leave that to the idiots like Floyd.'

'Yes. Floyd. The Harbour Master has underestimated him. Did you know he found the wreck, Maristow? Something even *he* never achieved?'

'I knew he was closing in on it. Or rather, Devlan was. Let's not give Floyd too much credit.'

'But Floyd is tenacious. And he has made The Harbour Master most perturbed.'

Henry stood as he held up the indigo stone once more. He shook it in his fist. 'You killed Tovar for this?'

He looked towards the empty chancel and was about to toss the necklace away so that some random member of the church choir might find it. But as he stretched back his arm, he hesitated.

'Not going to throw it away, Maristow?'

'I think I'll keep it,' Henry replied, beginning to realise

the power that even the fake Akasa Stone held.

'We think it would be a good idea if you did that. So long as Floyd believes you have the stone, then he will end his quest. It'll be just you and The Harbour Master in the search once more.'

'No. Just you. I'm out of it,' Henry said as he stepped back into the aisle. 'Good evening, Vear.'

'Maristow.'

Chapter 11.2

At twelve minutes to one that same morning, Vladimir and Jake were attending to some private business. They hovered in the beer garden of *The Rose and Crown*, a deserted ashtray-filled hovel by the time Tuesday night became Wednesday morning. It was a shit hole for skanks, weasel-faced dope heads with greasy hair, and job seekers spending their allowance on expensive beer.

It was also the pub frequented by the burly thug with the ripped jeans and the muscle-hugging shirt, the same man who curled up in a ball while Jake kicked his spine.

It had all started out as a friendly drink. A warm smile from Vladimir, a lewd quip from Jake about the barmaid's breasts, and then it flipped into a distinctly unfriendly drink.

Vladimir shot him such a heavy stare he fell off his stool. He threw some sloppy, beer-fuzzed punches at Jake, tickled him pretty good. And then they dragged him outside.

The guy wouldn't feel the bruises until sobriety seeped in much later. He'd probably have no memory of how he'd got them either. Whatever he'd knocked down his throat tonight had made effective body armour. It was frustrating that they were really beating him to shit and he didn't seem to feel a thing.

Jake knew exactly what this was all about. Vladimir's words shot like atom bombs. There was a holocaust through his eyes. It gave it all away. He was oozing the heat from a tremendous rage. It was another night for *that* old case.

The guy writhed on the ale-stained ground as he spat out a mouthful of blood. His pale fingers picked something from the goo.

'A tooth for the tooth fairy! When she comes, I'll kidnap her and steal her magic wand.'

'Now?' Jake asked Vladimir.

He nodded.

The guy propped himself up against a table and sang some sort of nursery rhyme to himself, laughing like a lunatic. He was blitzed.

'The tooth fairy was you. Yes, it was you!' He looked up at Jake and Vladimir floating above him like two risen demons who'd found a fallen angel. 'What did I do occifer? I coulda swored I only had a shouple of candies.'

Jake crouched and grabbed the collar of his shirt, pulling it from him like it was paper.

'Hey,' the drunk wailed. 'I hope you're gonna pay for that. When I get her magic wand, I'm gonna come back and turn you into a frog and sell you to a Frenchman. And your friend there, I'll turn him into a dildo and shove him up my arse.'

Rotating his fist, the guy started practising his wand waving. 'Dildous rectumus!' he chanted his spell.

Vladimir stepped closer. 'Stand up.'

The drunk looked up at him with his crimson grin and just laughed, throwing back his head and cackling like a maniac.

'You can't make me do anything. I have the magic wand and I have all power over you. You shall both be my slaves.'

'Get up!' Vladimir roared.

Jake grabbed the guy by the throat and lifted him to his feet. The half-naked drunk slumped back against the table.

'All right, all right. I'm standing. Now what do you want with me?' The mask of laughter had been torn away like his clothes.

'Just turn around you demented sack of shit,' Vladimir told him.

The man reached a hand backwards but missed the table, falling to the ground. He crawled onto his knees, turning his back to them so they would not see him crying.

It was all Vladimir needed to see.

The half-naked man continued to sob. By the time he plucked up the courage to turn around again he would discover that his new friends had disappeared.

***

The vigilantes stood back out on the vomit-stained high street. A couple of girls nearby were trying to spark up a cigarette lighter.

The young Throne paced up and down, waiting for the adrenaline to fade.

'What brought you to that guy?' Jake asked.

'The Virtues gave me some solid intel a few weeks back. We've been tracking him. Really thought it was him.'

'You okay?'

'I don't know.'

He went silent, lost within those heavy thoughts that stubbornly churned around in his mind like coagulated blood. It wasn't like him to be without an answer.

The two women both laughed shrilly at something. Drunken humour, like they'd just seen someone spill their drink down their shirt and it was the funniest thing ever.

'Back in a minute.'

Vladimir headed back inside, trying to find some badly needed quiet. He needed to breathe slower. He had to gather his goddamned thoughts and make them slow the hell down.

Barging into the rest room, he could feel that pressure cooker effect about to happen again, the blood running thickly behind his temples. Maybe if he splashed some cold water over his face it would help to stop it, help to prevent what he knew was coming, what always came after he unboxed certain emotions.

Or maybe taking a good look at himself in the mirror would distract his mind. He only ever looked at his reflection to see if his hair was in place or his clothes were straight. He never gazed into himself the same way he searched inside everyone else.

Within these grey and dingy toilets he dared a little peek. Tepid, salty water ran from his face as he edged nearer, bringing his ever so dark eyes closer to their reflection.

It happened.

Vladimir smashed his fist into the mirror as hard as his strength would allow. Fragments of glass shattered over his hand, slicing into his fingers. He rammed his bleeding fist into the broken mirror once more. And again, until he felt the glass slicing into his bones, mashing his reflection into an unrecognisable mess.

Blood gushed from his hand into the metal sink, turning the water a muddy brown. He froze as he took a deep breath, the pressure passing its pinnacle. As his dragon-like breathing decreased, he started to find his calm again. His composure was returning. He was the sublime Vladimir again, in control of everything. This was just a blip.

As he ran his bleeding hand under the cold water, brushing out the tiny shards of glass, he told himself tonight's failure was only a minor setback. He would keep searching. Nothing would ever stop him doing that. One day he would find that man with the tattoo of the black widow spider on his back, the man who'd murdered Jeremy Helliwell's brother and grandfather. When he did find him, he would redefine the word torture as he would make the rest of this guy's life a living hell by putting him through the same despair he'd put Jeremy through.

He would beat him for days on end, for weeks, for months. He'd tie him up and lash him. He'd get broken bottles and slice his skin up, for now that Vladimir had just sliced up his own hand, he knew how painful that could be.

He'd break his bones. One by one he would make them all snap. He'd chop off his limbs, even castrate the bastard. He'd get a hammer so he could pound nails into the guy's skull, under the guy's finger nails. He'd get chopsticks and hammer them into the guy's ears. And then he'd get a knife and slice off layers from his eyes.

He'd get a vice and put the bastard's head in it, oh so gradually turning it tighter until he heard his skull crack. He'd douse his feet in petrol and set fire to them. And finally he'd get a blunt machete and hack the monster's head off. Slowly.

That would be the best way to avenge his crimes. But until then he would have to carry on searching. Somewhere he was out there. Unlike Henry who searched for the Akasa Stone, Vladimir knew his own pursuit would one day succeed.

And unlike Henry's goal, searching for that inked killer was the perfect type of job for the Halo of Fires organisation. Revenge was what they were all about, not finding spiritual treasures.

They were there to help the victims of life. Victims like poor Jeremy Helliwell, the young boy who'd run away to Alan Hammond. Vladimir had seen to it that he was hidden where no one would ever find him.

The boy would still haunt him though, as he was doing now in the toilets of *The Rose and Crown*.

It can't be. You're not here anymore.

As blood dripped from his fingers, Vladimir could see the child across the room vividly. He was the same fair-haired Jeremy, wearing his beige shorts and blue shirt. In his hands he still held those action figures, like he'd just walked inside from playing on the beach. Rosy faced, full of playful adventure, gentle, thoughtful.

But no smiles on his face.

Sad thoughts. There on the surface of those haunted eyes, like a murder victim buried in a shallow grave. Rotting, putrid flesh decomposing in a lonely place.

Such a mangled, fucked up, twisted, fucked up, broken, fucked up spirit.

Fucked up beyond all recognition and then fucked up some more.

The poor boy was so lost. Clink clack, his action figures fell from his little hands. Kids' games don't mean anything. They're not real. Not like the real haunting by the real Jeremy and his real despair here.

Vladimir realised the boy had something for him tonight. Jeremy raised his arm and slowly released his clenched fist. The vigilante couldn't see what was within his palm because a brilliant purple light shone from it.

Vladimir squinted in the glare, his eyes stinging like blunt thorns had been poked into them. When he opened his eyes again, Jeremy had gone. It was just him and a dingy pub toilet that wreaked of stale urine.

Close your eyes and you'll kill the boy.

He faced the broken mirror and his multitude of shattered reflections.

'Keep it together, Vladimir. Keep it together.'

Chapter 11.3

It wasn't quite two o'clock, still early for Vladimir, yet he felt exhausted. He sat huddled against the graffiti-covered wall down White Horse Passage. There looked to be some additions to the spray-painted art since he'd last walked down there, but as usual there were no vandals around.

He examined his bandaged fingers once Jake had finished wrapping them up in lint. It was difficult to bend them. He figured he wouldn't be able to use them for anything over the next week or two. If only he'd used his right hand instead of his good left hand. Not that he ever had any presence of mind when the pressure cooker reached explosion point.

'Sure you're okay?' Jake asked as he leaned against the fence on the other side of the alley, fishing out a cigarette.

'I'm fine. It's just my hand. I have another one.'

Vladimir felt a lot calmer now, even strangely serene, or perhaps he was just numb. Jake had been with him a few times before when he'd become unhinged, had seen his composure crumble as that monstrous alter ego broke free. Possessed with that rage, Vladimir had done much worse things than this before.

'So, did you win?'

'Don't think we'll get any more trouble with that mirror,' Vladimir replied dryly.

'And who gives a damn about seven years of bad luck, eh?'

237

Vladimir laughed bleakly. 'Not when you've already had a lifetime of it.'

'Tell me about it,' Jake muttered as he turned to face the alleyway that led into a thick darkness, their route back home.

Vladimir looked up at him. In his eyes, Jake was more of a colleague than a friend to him. He had to keep a distance. Colleague first, friend second.

'Thanks for your assistance on this.'

'No sweat, Vlad. We'll keep looking for him.'

Vladimir lowered his head just as something caught his eye down the alley, from the way they'd walked. It was a distant, dull light: the dim light of hopelessness, shining like the eye of a ghostly Cyclops. Jeremy again, the lost soul whose misfortune would forever haunt him.

'I know he's out there. I know he's close,' Vladimir replied as he gazed into the amethyst glow.

'What if you never find him though?'

'I'll keep searching,' he replied with calm defiance. 'Until the day I die. I'll never give up.'

'What if he's already dead? Or what if he was sorry, and he'd changed?'

'Means nothing to me. It doesn't erase the crime.'

The illumination veered closer. He wished the boy would just leave him alone. Vladimir closed his eyes, hoping that shutting out the light would make him disappear.

Close your eyes and the boy will go...

'You think we're all perfect, Vlad? Do you think even Halo of Fires don't deserve to be visited by Halo of Fires?'

Vladimir opened an eye a fraction to see the light was now diminishing. Jeremy would leave him alone, until next time.

Make him go away. Jeremy has to die...

He turned away as Jake inhaled deeply on his cigarette. The breath of smoke obscured his face for a moment before his features slowly emerged: a curled lip pinned behind his teeth, his eyes squinting as he stared down the path ahead. He looked to be battling another of those difficult thoughts that sometimes filled his mind and demanded to be dealt with, perhaps reflecting on one of his defective characteristics that undermined his physical perfection. It was such a tragedy. He could so easily be a Superman if only he knew how.

'You know, Vlad, I could tell you stories,' he began, his words consumed by sighs. 'Go back to when I was a teenager, I got up to a lot of stuff. I could tell you things right now that would make you cringe. Things that would make you look at me differently.'

Vladimir remained silent, giving him the space to unburden his thoughts.

'But what I'm saying is: who's really above all this? Who can be that perfect that they wouldn't deserve Halo of Fires descending on them and delivering them their punishment, for whatever they've done? Are you? Can you tell me you've never done anything wrong in your whole life?'

Vladimir considered the question carefully before responding. 'No one can escape karma.'

'So there could be someone out there who might say you'd done something wrong and you deserved punishment? I mean, what about everything you do with Halo of Fires? What would your Bible thumper say about it?'

'They don't know what I know.'

'What's that?'

What he knew was too difficult to put into words, at least ones that Jake would understand.

'I'd never intend to hurt anyone, no one who didn't deserve it, that is.'

'Never?'

'No.'

'What if we ever made a mistake? Say we went and beat someone to shit and it was completely the wrong person.'

'That would never happen.'

'How can you say that? What about that guy tonight?'

Vladimir waved his hand dismissively. 'I *know* people. No one ever got something they didn't deserve.'

'But *I* don't know people. What if I got the wrong person? Would you avenge what I had done?'

'No.'

'Why not?'

'Because... because! You're my friend, damn it. You live this life like I do. You're in this with me.'

'Yeah, but...'

'What's the matter, Jake? So you were a tearaway when you were younger. So what? If the universe didn't want this Halo of Fires organisation to exist, then it wouldn't. If it didn't want people to get what they deserved through us, then they'd get it some other way. Like I say, whatever karma you have is something you can't escape from.'

'I'm far from perfection, Vlad. I'm nothing like you.'

'And I'm nothing like you. We help each other.'

'You don't need me.'

'I can't do all this on my own.'

'I still don't get it though. Why you? How do you do it?'

Vladimir's eyes shifted away. He'd said enough to him tonight. He clambered to his feet. Although he wasn't tired any longer, he wanted to get off home. That violet light may be dwindling but it was still there.

'I know you have your demons, but when I look at you I see a good soul. You probably don't even believe me yourself, but that's what I see.'

'I often wish I could be like you. You always know what's right. You make it all mean something.'

Vladimir nodded. He'd always felt that he and Jake made a good team, and right now he could see why so clearly. All-in-one superheroes were extremely rare, but Vladimir combined with Jake made that superheroic force.

With Jake's built body, Vladimir's perceptive mind, and the sapient spirit of Alan Hammond, the original Angel of Karma, Halo of Fires really was a perfect force.

'Come on. Let's get going.'

He turned away from Jeremy as they carried on walking into a darkness that neither blinded them nor troubled them. They were both well accustomed to the dark.

After a few yards, Jake had one final question. 'And what about Jeremy? Think anyone will ever find him?'

Again, Vladimir had no answer.

Chapter 11.4

In the early days of the Fires, Alan Hammond and Henry Maristow were eating lunch one late summer's day in Alan's favourite pub, *The Welby Arms*. Henry had ordered a ten ounce rump steak, but Alan was going to give him something much bigger to chew on.

The skies were cloudless, the radiant sun filling every last nook of the town, making it one of those days when one felt that anything was possible.

They'd been in partnership for nearly a year, their new enterprise finding its feet amongst those poor souls who'd been unfairly troubled and wanted a way to seek justice.

With his fedora in his hand, Alan fanned himself to keep cool as he waited for his salad to arrive.

'I've got the boy,' he said.

Henry knew exactly whom he was talking about, and he knew exactly why it had taken him this long to tell him.

'He's alive?'

Alan nodded.

'You do know,' Henry began before stopping himself. He looked around at the other people in the pub. They seemed like unassuming strangers, but, even so, he now leaned over the table and resumed in a hushed tone. 'You do know that they're looking for him.'

'No. But it's what I expected. Know why?'

'He's a witness, isn't he? And best get him before he grows up.'

'Why didn't they just kill him when they had the chance?'

'I don't know. Maybe the agent bottled it. Where did you find him?'

Alan placed his fedora on the table and leaned in closer. His blue eyes were twinkling, ready to release the details of the secret they'd been holding.

'Late one night I was at home watching the news when there was a knock at the door. When I go answer it, there's a girl, a young woman, standing there, and she's crying. Tears streaming down her face. I ask her what's the matter, and she tells me she just doesn't know what else to do. It was at that point I noticed him. He was holding her hand, but standing behind her. Shy, like the very first time I met Jeremy. I crouched down to say hello, and it was then that I noticed he looked rather haggard. Once she'd calmed down, she told me she'd found him at Moonlight Cove. She'd taken him back to her home, some small chalet up on the cliffs, I believe. She had intended to look after him, but all the while Jeremy kept telling her that he needed to find me. Helliwell must have told the boy to go looking for me, good old Ulric. When the boy started to get ill, and when he told her more about the people that killed his brother and grandfather, the girl figured it was best if she went looking for me.'

'Who is she?'

'I don't know. She never told me her name. She just said she would be back one day to come and see Jeremy again. I haven't seen her since.'

'No address for her?'

'No. Nothing.'

'Where's Jeremy Helliwell right now?'

'He's with my sister.'

'Where does your sister live?'

'Just out of town.'

'Think he'll be safe with her?'

'Well, what do you think, Henry?'

Henry breathed in wearily. 'They'll keep looking. Nowhere is safe. I know it sounds nasty, but you're putting your sister in danger.'

Alan nodded knowingly. 'Henry, this isn't just any old kid.'

'How do you mean?'

'He's different. I've known his family all my life. If he's anything like his previous generations, I think he could be one to really change things in this town.'

'Maybe someone else thinks that too.'

'That's what I'm afraid of.'

Henry looked at the morsel of steak on the end of his fork. The meat drizzled with a thin blood. 'Alan, it's not just your sister. It's us, too. If they keep looking for the boy then they'll eventually get to you and me.'

'So, what are you saying, Henry?'

'I don't know. It's a lot to take in.'

'If there's no point hiding him anywhere...'

'Then...'

'Then we need to consider an alternative.'

'We?'

'You're in this too now, Henry. I told you this wouldn't be an easy path. I tried to warn you.'

'Yes. I understand.'

By now, Henry had completely lost his appetite. He pushed his plate away and rubbed his eyes. 'What do we do, Alan? What are we going to do with him?'

His fellow Seraph put the fedora back on his head. In the shadow of its brim, his eyes now looked like a bulbous swelling of veins.

'There's only one option.'

'What?'

Alan explained. It was a plan that meant the two Seraphs wouldn't have to worry about hiding the boy anywhere, wondering when the Network agents would find him. It would be very difficult, but then Alan was never one for shying away from those sorts of decisions in life.

Part 12: The Bite

Chapter 12.1

Samuel Allington, the son of a local bigwig, a young man who had everything he could possibly want, a man blessed with power, grace and a heartwarming smile that could brighten the day of even the most manic of depressives, stood on the beach as the sun was setting on the waves and on his world.

Rooted to the same spot for the past half hour, the tide had edged its way up the sand and washed over his ankles, but the cold that pinched his feet had not yet registered in his mind.

Stella had said she was leaving him. After three years of being a couple and twelve weeks of being engaged to him, she had now abandoned their path. It had left him with such an empty, chilled feeling, much colder than the salty waters that soaked into his shoes.

He'd given her everything he could. He'd bought her all those gifts, taken her on holidays, treated her like a princess, told her she was beautiful, cooked her meals. In fact, he'd done nearly all the suggestions on the list in that GQ article, 'Gestures to keep your romance alive'.

Samuel knew he'd given her his complete heart. With him, Stella had the perfect life, complete devotion and endless happiness.

But she didn't want it. It wasn't good enough for her. *He* wasn't good enough. Where had he gone wrong? It made no sense. How could she hope for a better life with someone else? What more could they offer her?

And what was he to do with his feelings now there was no longer anywhere for them to flow? It was as if the course of a beautiful river had reached a void, the waters flowing into oblivion.

Sam, I'm so sorry. I'm in love with someone else.

That bastard student. He'd ruined everything, destroyed his life. What the hell did she see in him? Was he better looking than him? He couldn't be. Samuel knew he was attractive. He looked after his body; ate the right things, went to the gym and toned his muscles. He was a beautiful person. Yet still he didn't have the special something that home-wrecker must have, whatever it was.

I'm in love with someone else. I always have been.

It was worse than if she were to have died. It had been one big meaningless failure. All along when he'd seen that look of discontent in her eye and tried even harder, and yet she didn't really love him back. Why had she done this to him?

As he bowed his head he noticed he was standing ankle deep in the brine.

'Shit.'

White Gucci trainers. Bought only two weeks back. The pearl-trim leather still had that just-out-of-the-shoebox shine, or at least it did half an hour ago. Now he'd ruined them. It didn't matter though.

When he got walking, they would hopefully start to dry out. By the time this evening's Rotary meeting began, everyone would be too distracted by his glittering smile to notice the hems of his trousers might be damp or his shoes might be a little sandy.

Those minor details would belie the gentleman he was to everyone, they would be the only evidence of the savage black dog that ran wild inside him, clawing at his insides and tearing him to shreds.

Samuel, your spring fete went tremendously. We've far exceeded our target. Thank you so much for your efforts.

So human, so wholesome. Everyone admired Samuel Allington, the one who was always there to lend a hand, always there with a smile. The chap was just *always* happy. How the Rotarians wished their own children were like him.

We need to organise a fundraiser for the Flying Ambulance. How about it?

They all relied on him. He never let anyone down. But he couldn't contain the black dog any longer, constantly filling his mind with its clamorous barking.

I'm so sorry. I'm in love with someone else.

Lightning flickered in the charcoal sky, ozone scenting the air. A storm had approached from nowhere and was moments away from swallowing the sun. Rain would soon lash down, the deafening cracks of thunder would sound like the world was exploding, but it wouldn't be as ferocious as what was brewing in Samuel's mind, a disturbance no one would have thought could torment such a nice gentleman as he.

They'd have no idea of the dark thoughts he was now having, about the telephone call he would make later. When he got home, he would dial Lucas Duffy's number, the man whom people called The Reaper, the man who shot people and killed them.

It was his only way of answering the internal beast whose barking he could not begin to understand nor even face. Now that his beautiful, darling Stella had left him for some poncey tosspot of a student, there was nothing else to do. There was no other way out of it.

But before that telephone call, Samuel had a meeting to go to. He had a smile to put on, had another good cause to lend his hand to. Helping to fix the world for so long, he'd never appeared as someone who needed help himself.

The Reaper would see to it, though. That damned student. A bullet in his head would be the answer to everything.

Chapter 12.2

They'd been sitting on top of the scrap metal container for about an hour, the flies dancing around them in the moonlight. Larry's legs ached and he was bored with the card game. Poker was never any good with just two people, and Eddie was cheating anyway.

They heard scuffling below, so Eddie shone down the torch. It was Meriadoc. He'd dragged out a branch from the green waste skip and wanted someone to play with him.

'Has he found him yet?' Larry asked.

'Nope.'

Larry yawned.

The letter with the red wax blob remained unopened. They'd searched the back streets, the woods, the ruins of Empringham Abbey, they'd even hid themselves at the harbour for a few nights. Henry had told them that Devlan did a lot of fishing and that they might see him go out on a boat. But even when they returned in daylight hours over an entire week, still the mysterious devil man was nowhere to be seen. They decided to cross the harbour off the list.

Next was the recycling centre. They'd also been told that Devlan was something of a repairman, and that he might visit to pick up old machines and things to fix and sell on. Henry had admitted it was thin, and whilst monitoring the place, Eddie sensed the idea was as useful as the broken furniture and DVD players that filled the skips.

Eddie checked his watch. 'Wanna head off?'

'Yup,' Larry replied, yawning as he collected up the playing cards. 'Why is it I can never get out of the scrap heap?'

Eddie lowered himself to the ground and Meriadoc placed the stick at his feet. He picked it up and tossed it across the yard, the dog instantly scuttling after it. They'd been bringing him along since the start of the week. It was initially Larry's idea, seeing how he was good at sniffing out people, not that they had a scent on Devlan to begin with.

The two Guardians made their way down the lane, back towards the town. It was Larry who noticed the abandoned building in the emerging morning light, lurking from them across the wheat field.

'What's that?'

'Dunno, mate.'

'Want to check it out or are you too tired?'

'Let's take a look.'

Barbedwire ringed the grounds, but they soon found a hole in it, probably made by some urban explorers. They crawled through and waded through the field of waist-high stinging nettles. There were no doors on the ramshackle building, but a lop-sided sign hung above the main entrance.

'Cameron's Confectionery,' Eddie read as he stepped up to it. 'I guess we don't need a golden ticket to get in.'

Empty beer cans littered the inside, the remnants of a bonfire in one of the barren rooms. Definitely kids. It was more like a hellish workhouse than an abandoned sweet factory. The dust was decades thick. Broken wooden beams hung precariously from the ceiling. All the glass had been smashed from the windows.

And there were rats. Big fat ones that scampered from them as Larry shone the beam of the torch across the rubble floor.

'Hello?' he called out.

They heard the wind softly ululating through the shell of a building like a ghost's breath.

'I don't think Meriadoc should be in here,' Eddie said. 'Look at all this broken glass. I'll wait outside.'

'What? Just going to leave me alone in the bowels of hell?'

Although Eddie tried to usher Meriadoc back to the entrance, it seemed the dog would not move. His wide eyes stared ahead into the blackness as though something was on the tip of his senses.

'All right, let's carry on then,' Eddie said, Meriadoc walking precisely by his side. The dog wasn't going to leave either of them inside this place. Good old boy.

Farther on, Larry reached a corner. 'Holy...' It came out like a breathless whisper and was immediately followed by barking. It was the first time Meriadoc had spoken since that day on the common.

Two shrunken red eyes glowed at them. Larry whipped the beam up and they saw a man-sized creature sitting on a grubby mattress, pulling a hood over his long, scraggly hair that looked like a mass of snakes wriggling on his head.

The creature put on a pair of shades and slowly rose from his bed to examine what had woken him.

'Keep the light on him,' Eddie whispered as a cold spasm travelled through his blood.

'Harmless. He won't hurt us,' Larry murmured.

'What do you want?' the freak growled.

'Are you...' Larry began in a slightly high-pitched voice before composing himself. 'Are you Devlan?'

'Do I know you?'

'We work for Henry Maristow. He has something for you.'

As Larry reached into his coat pocket for the letter, Devlan sprung out of the torch beam.

They didn't see where he went, as though he'd leapt into another dimension. The light became like a disco strobe as Larry whipped it around.

'Where is he?'

More ghostly breaths.

'Devlan?'

'Why are you here?' came a growl so close it was like a voice inside their heads.

Larry lurched backwards and tripped over a pile of loose bricks. Meriadoc broke free from Eddie's grip and bounded up to the hooded man.

'Hey, don't touch my dog,' Eddie cried.

But Devlan offered the dog his hand and stroked his head. Meriadoc barked back talkatively.

Larry scrambled to his feet, fighting the urge to toss the envelope away and make a runner. He knew he had to stop being such a wimp. He was certain the other Halo of Fires members acted a lot cooler than this.

'Here. This is from Henry,' Larry said as he offered the envelope to the strange man. 'Take it.'

Two more beams of light shone on Devlan like theatre floodlights. They turned towards the entrance of the room and saw the outlines of three men.

The silhouettes stood examining the curious scene taking place in this derelict factory: Devlan in his secret hiding place, two ragamuffin youths, and one scrawny-looking mutt whose barking had led them here in the first place.

'Hello, Floyd,' Devlan said.

'Well, well, well,' Floyd began. 'So *here* is where you've been hiding all this time. You know, this place could do with a serious housewarming.'

'This wasn't a surprise party?'

A towering beanpole stepped from the glare. 'Who the hell are these two dickheads?'

'Couple of kids out walking their dog.'

'At five in the morning?'

Floyd approached Larry. He immediately saw the paper in his hand and snatched it off him. Larry should have twirled around in the air and scissor-kicked him or something, but the lights had dazzled his brain and frozen him like roadkill.

'That's for Devlan,' he stuttered.

Floyd glared back at him as Scrooge would have done to a beggar asking for spare change. He held the envelope into the light and ripped it open.

'Hey! Who the hell do you think you are?' Eddie said.

Floyd was too busy reading to register any of his words. 'I don't believe it,' he cried.

After stuffing the letter into his trench coat pocket, Floyd's jumping bean eyes fell still. He fixed them on Devlan. 'You're coming with me.' He stormed over to his goons who continued to point the lights in everyone's faces. 'And bring the bloody Mystery Incorporated gang too.'

'Even the dog?' one of them asked.

'Kill it,' Floyd spat. 'No, wait. Bring it too.'

'We're not going with you dipshits,' Eddie cried, his fingers wrapped around Meriadoc's collar.

Larry needed to do something. He needed to punch these guys, shout *Hi-ru-kin* and send a fireball at them, pull out a gun and get them in the crosshairs, anything.

As one of the silhouettes came bounding towards him, and as he wondered what Vladimir would do right now, the goon punched him hard in the face with a fist he didn't see coming.

Larry collapsed to the ground. He no longer saw any torches shining.

Chapter 12.3

Every day of the week, Michael's radio alarm was programmed to switch on at seven, waking him up to the broadcasts of the local BBC station. At that time of day they played cheerful oldies from the fifties and sixties that were easy on morning ears. After listening to Hank Williams asking what his good looking had cooking, and Dion warning about keeping away from Runaround Sue, Michael got out of bed and put on some clothes freshly ironed the night before.

As it was a Saturday, he strolled down to the newsagents after breakfast. He bought his usual selection of newspapers (and a packet of lemon bonbons), which he would spend reading either on the promenade if it was nice, or back at the flat if it was raining.

This morning was fair, the skies littered with fluffy altocumulus as a gentle wind fluttered in off the sea. Michael found a bench along the front and began perusing the first of his newspapers, *The Guardian*.

A hairy guy in shorts and vest jogged along the promenade, his iPod headphones ticking out a brief muffled beat as he darted past. A teenaged newspaper girl with a fluorescent yellow bag paused on her bike as she caught sight of a flock of geese swarming the skies high above. Michael looked up and saw the cloud of birds as they rhythmically flapped their wings. He brought his attention back to the newspaper, the pages rustling in the wind, the soothing sound of the waves in his ears. It was a perfect time to be reading.

But Michael couldn't concentrate. Something wasn't right. Far beyond the sounds of normality, the idle chatter between people, the steady roar of distant traffic, the occasional seagull that cawed as it soared over the sands, there felt to be an empty space where another sound should be: the whistling of a bomb as it fell from the sky, the crumbling boom of a building as it disintegrated to a pile of rubble.

He stood up and tucked his newspapers under his arm. Zipping up his white jacket tight to the neck, he set off back to the flat, a familiar twisting tightness in his gut starting up again, one he usually got when he was rushing to hand in an assignment on time.

Tick-tock, time was ticking. But why was he feeling it? Perhaps when he got back, he'd realise he'd left the kettle on the stove, or something.

But then he remembered he hadn't even had a cuppa yet this morning, for that was what he usually did after he'd gone to fetch the newspapers.

'Hello? Anyone home?' he called as soon as he stepped into the porch.

He just needed to talk to someone, a little natter to make him feel everything was all right with the world. Heck, even the dog would do.

As it was still practically the middle of the night for most of his flatmates, they'd all be fast asleep, but he heard no snoring or protestations at the noise he was making.

Perhaps Danny was awake. Michael trotted upstairs to his room and flung open the door. A fly buzzed at the closed window. The duvet lay in a crumpled mess on the bed. Danny wasn't under it. Either he'd got up very early like Michael, or, most likely, he hadn't even come home yet. So where in the hell was he?

That recent intuition floated back into his mind. The toast. The square reduced to a triangle.

One of us is going to die.

As those slugs crawled around in his guts once again, he cast his mind back to last night when he'd gone to bed. Being a light sleeper, Michael would usually hear his other flatmates arrive home in his semi-sleep, never being able to switch off properly until he heard them.

Last night he hadn't slept very well. He darted down the corridor to Eddie's room. Empty. He ran downstairs and opened Larry's door. Empty too. That's when he realised not even Meriadoc was there. *Everyone* was missing.

In the hallway, Michael picked up the telephone and dialled Danny's mobile number. Each ring felt like an eternity.

Eventually the ringing stopped, Michael figuring he'd reached Danny's voicemail.

'Hello?'

'Hey. Danny. It's me.'

'Hey, mate.'

'Danny, um... where are you this morning?'

'What does it matter?'

'I just wondered where you were.'

'What, are you my dad now?'

'I was just asking.'

'I'm fine. Nothing to worry about.'

'Are you sure?'

'Yes. I had a dentist appointment, all right?'

'Eddie and Diamond didn't come home last night.'

'No? Have you tried calling them?'

'Not yet.'

'Maybe they're out saving the world still.'

'They're usually home by now.'

'It's the weekend. They went to the club and got lucky with a couple of ladies?'

'They went to the club with Meriadoc?'

'Maybe not then.'

Michael paused for a moment. Listening to himself, he knew he was sounding like a neurotic old woman. 'Where do you think they got to?'

'I don't know. What we can do about it anyway? They're on the other side of the tracks now.'

'They're still our flatmates. Still our friends.'

'Some friends they are.'

Michael sighed. 'I'm worried. What do we do?'

'Just call them.'

'Okay.'

'I would do myself but I'm out of credit.'

'I'll try them on the landline.'

'Okay, Michael.'

'I'll hang up now.'

'Try not to worry so much. I'm sure they'll walk through the door any minute.'

'Talk to you later, Danny.'

'See you.'

Michael hung up. He reached into his jeans pocket for his mobile phone. He only had Danny's number memorised; the others he had to check on his contacts list. After finding Larry's number under 'Diamond' he dialled it into the landline and let it ring.

And ring. And ring.

A familiar female voice answered. 'Hello. The person you're calling cannot answer the...'

He slammed the phone down and then checked his mobile for Eddie's number. That one brought even less luck as the call immediately connected to his voicemail.

It was just like a horror film. All he could picture was another scene where a blood-stained mobile rang to nobody, its owner no longer around to answer it.

Why were his thoughts going away with themselves so fast? He was being silly. He looked up Larry's number again and dialled it. Maybe he didn't get to it in time.

It pulsed and pulsed again, the echoed ringing connecting to a phone in an unknown place, perhaps sounding through the dimensions into the spiritual plain where a murdered Larry would answer.

Michael... We're gone. Me and Eddie have jumped into the abyss and you'll never see us again...

'Hello. The person you're calling...'

Slam.

Something was up. Michael couldn't shake the feeling. He felt sick as the slimy slugs crawled throughout his guts, breeding and multiplying so there wasn't enough room and they would surely explode his innards open as they reduced him to a wreck.

What to do? What to do? What to do?

Michael had only one more idea. In a dim corner of his mind, he remembered his brother telling him another little story over a Sunday afternoon roast, something that was most probably a fanciful rumour. Right now though, he had absolutely nothing else to go on. If only he still had that damned business card. Why had he let Larry take it?

Michael zipped up his jacket again and shot out of the flat.

Chapter 12.4

Henry had planned to stay in bed all morning. He was going to carry on sleeping until whatever time he woke up, and if that was never, then never it would be. There was nothing to get up for any more.

The phone woke him though, and he grumbled to himself for not having switched it to silent.

He answered. It was Nigel at *The Cheshire Cat* and he told Henry to pop by. By that, he probably meant he should get up immediately and go straight down there. After hanging up, Henry fell back to sleep again for another hour. He dreamt of wild horses all galloping away from a storm. They were running towards a cliff and were unable to stop in time. One by one they all fell down. Henry saw the rocks at the bottom and all those doomed horses smashing onto them. The blood, the horror. He woke up again with a jagged headache and a bitter cloud in his head.

He dragged himself out of bed, put on a crumpled grey suit and drove into town. The traffic was stacked up as usual, but the jaded Seraph was in no rush. Parking at the hotel, he strolled up Eastgate.

Entering the café, he sat on a stool at the counter, and as soon as Nigel came over he asked him, 'What?'

Nigel opened the till and took out an envelope. 'This was here when I arrived this morning.'

Nigel put on a brew of Henry's special tea and then picked up his pad and pen to attend to another customer. Saturday mornings were typically busy, but Nigel remained relaxed and bright-eyed. Perhaps the antennas on his head sent soothing energies into his brain no matter how much frantic activity there was going on around him.

Henry stared at the envelope, his first name scribbled on it in a scrawly handwriting. Whoever the scribe, he knew this wasn't more correspondence from The Harbour Master.

His hand reached beneath his jacket for his chest. Through his shirt he could feel the imitation Akasa Stone.

The loser's medal. Or perhaps he was Superman with a chain of Kryptonite around his neck.

He put on his glasses and read the letter. Afterwards, he stared ahead into space for a good five minutes.

His head was empty. The chatter of Saturday morning shoppers did not enter his ears. Although his eyes were open, his brain did not register the light that they allowed in. Henry Maristow was a dead man.

Nigel returned to the counter and started pouring his cup of tea.

'We need to get the boys in. Call them up and get them to *Clarence*.'

Nigel frowned. 'Won't they be asleep?'

'Wake them up. I need them here right away.'

'I'm on it. One other thing...'

'What now?' Henry said, almost like a whisper. He no longer had the energy to talk.

'There's someone in says he wants to speak to you. Says it's urgent. Do you want me to get rid of him?'

Henry glanced over his shoulder. A young man in a white jacket hovered nearby.

'Send him over.'

Nigel nodded and Michael approached. Henry folded up the letter.

'Hello, Mr Maristow,' Michael said as he stood by the Seraph and offered him his hand.

Henry appeared to be in a trance as he stared down into his cup of tea. 'Take a seat.'

Michael withdrew his hand and sat on the stool beside him. 'I assume I'm talking to the right person if I want to discuss a matter concerning Halo of Fires.'

'Who are you?'

'I'm Michael Foxbury.'

'Now's not a good time, my friend.'

'People have a habit of going missing on you, don't they? First there's Jeremy Helliwell.' Suddenly the young chap had Henry's complete attention. 'But before we get to that, I want to know what's happened to my friends. I demand to know what's going on.'

Henry was silent, so Nigel spoke for him. 'Your friends?'

'Lawrence Stewart and Eddie Jansz.'

Henry looked down at his reflection in the gleaming counter. His face was the colour of ash; the flames that were once a harnessed force had grown too fierce and finally consumed him. 'Jeremy's dead. We're all dead,' Henry muttered.

'Please. They're missing. I need to know where they are.'

'We'll get them back soon,' Nigel said like a teacher reading a story to a class of primary school kids.

'You know where they are? We have to go to the police.'

Henry just shook his head and muttered, 'Devlan. Why did he turn them in? Why would he do that?'

Michael stood up. 'Where are they? We need to move.'

'Look...' Henry began. Although he was facing Michael now, it was more as if he was talking to himself. 'We're about to call in the boys. They'll sort it all out. Come, let's have a cup of tea, shall we?'

Michael was rigid, looking at them both, his jaw dropped open.

'Yes. Have a cup of tea,' Nigel agreed.

'Nigel,' Henry said from his croaky throat. 'The phone.'

Part 13: Hell

Chapter 13.1

The pain of the crushing headache, the relentless harrowing dreams, and the welling feeling of nausea finally dragged Eddie into consciousness. His neck ached and all his limbs were stiff, lying on a concrete floor. He didn't know where he was, but as his mind tuned in to his waking reality, he began to piece together what had happened last night.

They were at the recycling centre... and then Larry had spotted that abandoned factory... and, oh yes, that freaky guy with the red eyes! And then all those lights... That tall man with the leathery skin... Thugs coming towards them... Larry being walloped... Larry... Where's Larry?

'Larry?' Eddie called out into the chilly darkness. 'Where are you?'

He heard a grunt, a couple of sharp sniffs, that patter.

'Meriadoc! My man.' The dog pushed his wet nose into Eddie's face and licked him. 'You're all right. Thank Christ.'

He put his arms around his unfailing companion whom he imagined had watched over him all night in the strange place they'd been taken to. The nausea abated. All he had to do was figure out where they were. And Larry... Where in the hell was that muppet?

The room was small and sparse, not much bigger than his bedroom at the flat. The walls were made of breeze blocks and across from him were a battered wooden table and a set of drawers. That was about all he could see until he propped himself up and looked to his left.

This side of the room opened into a much larger area, a warehouse. It appeared to be full of... machinery? Eddie dragged himself to his feet and took a few steps towards the opening. He didn't get far before his sore head banged into an invisible force-field.

He cursed profusely as another thumping pain throbbed

throughout his skull. When it started to ease, he steadily reached out his hands to feel for the glass wall. What the hell was this place?

Lights flickered on, harsh floodlights that illuminated the entire building and forced Eddie to close his unadjusted eyes tight.

He heard a groan, human-like this time, and as he squinted his eyes open he saw the outline of a person slumped in a chair through the glass wall.

'Uhh... I don't remember drinking a thing. But I sure have the worst hangover ever.'

'Oy. I'm over here,' Eddie called to Larry as he banged on the glass.

Larry lifted his sorry head, a purple bruise staining one side. 'I get tied up and you get your own room? I think I ought to have a word with the management.'

Eddie smiled faintly, but the next voice was like ice-cold water trickling down his neck.

'Good morning, children. Did you all sleep well?'

The beanpole with the leathery face stomped up to them and Eddie slumped to the ground, feeling the energy drain from him like mosquitoes had covered his body and sapped his blood.

'I think it's about time I introduced myself. My name is Des Floyd. This, where you've both been catching your beauty sleep, is my little Chamber of Fun. How do you like it so far? Enjoying your stay?'

Eddie glanced around the chamber and saw that it wasn't machinery he could see, but fairground rides. The warehouse was full of them.

'Totally magical,' Larry said. 'A few guys in furry costumes and you'll put Disney out of business.'

Floyd grinned. 'Funny. I can see Maristow must have employed you as his court jester.'

'Yeah. Yeah, that's right. Good one. So can we go now?'

'Leave so soon? But, children, we haven't even started to have fun yet.'

'Uh huh,' Larry began. 'About that... Now, see, whatever your idea of fun happens to be, the thing is our colleagues are professional vigilantes, and now that we've both had a good look at your pretty face, and know your name, of course, there's a possibility they might get a little incensed if you decide to butt-rape us both.'

Floyd's eyes jittered as though they were having a party. He looked from Larry to Eddie and then back again, dread lingering in the silence like a poisonous gas.

He reached into the inside pocket of his trench coat and pulled out a crumpled letter with a red blob on it.

'Well then, boys, this here letter from your so-called boss is a bit confusing. I can only assume Maristow didn't tell you much about the monster it was addressed to.'

'He told us about him.'

'Did he tell you everything, all about what Devlan gets up to?'

They were silent.

'People often go missing in this town. It's a little problem we have, all because of this strange creature who, every now and again, will get a craving for human flesh. Now, if his hunger ain't met, he'll go out at night and grab folk off the street and drag them back to his hiding hole and chew on their bones and drink their blood.'

'Bollocks, mate,' Eddie spat.

Floyd laughed. 'You don't really think Maristow actually gave a shit about a couple of retards like you, do you? Here's how he was actually screwing you over: all of a sudden he wants to become buddies with Devlan, because Devlan knows something that Henry really wants to know about, and to get him on his side, to give him a complimentary food hamper, he sends along you two. He says: "Here, Devlan, here's some meat to get your teeth into. When you've finished eating, let's meet up for a coffee and talk business." You understand me?'

'That's crap,' Larry said.

Floyd stood over him, looking down on him with those small, empty eyes. Their flittering stopped for a moment, and even from a distance Eddie could see how empty they were of everything. Empty of feeling, empty of humanity. He'd never been so terrified in a very long time.

'You really don't know Henry like I know him. I used to work with him, kid, so I've seen what he's all about. I bet you don't know about the treasure he's been searching for. Seen that display in his office? All about his pursuit of the Akasa Stone? He'd do anything to get his hands on that thing and if it meant sacrificing a couple of teenagers, then he wouldn't think twice.'

'Can I read that letter then?' Larry asked.

Floyd laughed cockily as though he'd been rumbled. Instead of changing the subject, he said, 'Sure,' and held the paper in front of Larry.

Eddie waited for him to read it, waited for him to snort and call him a liar. But he didn't. He scanned it in silence and then hung his head.

The demon stuffed the letter away. 'Enough of all this. I think it's time we had some fun.' He turned to Eddie and approached the glass. 'I take it the dog is yours?'

Eddie glared back at him. He hated him more than he'd ever hated anyone. Even more than he now hated Henry Maristow, the bastard who'd been all smiles and sent them along to this horror. What a scumbag. He hated everyone. He hated the entire world.

'It went to you so I figured it was,' Floyd resumed. 'Stayed by you the whole time. I bet you must really like that dog.'

Eddie's nostrils flared.

Floyd continued, 'Some people love their pets. They'll cry more when their dog goes than when their mother kicks the bucket. Myself, I'm not an animal lover. They cost you money, give you fleas, tear your house up, and shit everywhere. They're pointless.'

Eddie lowered his eyes, ignoring the loudmouthed monster.

'But I think you like your little doggy quite a lot, don't you? I'm just curious to know how much you do actually like him. Gonna tell me?'

Eddie looked at the canine soul who sat quietly next to him. His ears were pricked, his eyes alert, ready to defend his master.

'Tell me,' Floyd went on, 'do you like your dog more than you like your friend over here? I mean, if you had to choose between them, whose friendship would you pick? The jester or the dog?'

'Go to hell,' Eddie spat from beneath his baseball cap.

'Answer me!' Floyd boomed. 'Which one would you pick? If you could only have one, which one?'

'Larry,' Eddie mumbled. It was a stupid question anyway, and it didn't mean anything.

'Interesting,' Floyd said. 'Now then, I'm going to want you to prove it.'

Floyd paused at that point as Eddie's dry throat tightened, waiting for it to fill with vomit.

'You see that cabinet next to you? Go over there and open it. Go on.'

Eddie staggered to his feet and trod over to it.

'Open the top drawer.'

Eddie did so. Inside was a gun.

'Now take the gun and shoot the dog in the head.'

A numbness came over him, but he flinched when Floyd pulled out another gun from his trench coat and fired it directly at him.

'Bullet proof glass, so don't even bother,' Floyd bellowed. Eddie instinctively patted his body to check he hadn't been shot.

The maniac bounded over to Larry and put the weapon to his head. 'Now kill the dog or I'll shoot your friend's brains out.'

He stared down at the gun laying in the drawer. There was no way he could pick that thing up and shoot Meriadoc.

'Do it, you fucking bastard! Kill that stupid mutt or I'll shoot your friend!'

He stared over at poor Larry whose eyes were open so wide they looked like they would pop out of his skull. He didn't have any quips to make now. Rigid in pure fear, Larry was like a deer milliseconds away from impact with the truck.

He turned to Eddie pleadingly. His mouth was shut so tight, bracing himself for the bullet that was about to sheer through his head and burst open his skull.

Eddie picked up the weapon and looked across at Meriadoc. He was panting so heavily as he stared back at his master, the man who'd rescued him from the streets and taken him in. The same man who would now have to shoot him dead.

'I can't do it,' Eddie whimpered. 'I can't do it.'

'Do it!' Floyd roared, his steel words booming throughout the still air of the warehouse. He pushed the barrel of the gun into Larry's head and the young man flinched, thinking he'd been shot.

An unfamiliar warm trickle slid down Eddie's face, and his lips tasted the salt. He'd never known such an awful feeling before in his life. He wished the universe would now just end, that the entire world would explode in a ball of flames, taking away the dreadful decision he had to make. Kill Meriadoc or Larry dies.

'I can't do it,' Eddie pleaded.

'Do it! Your friend is about to die,' Floyd roared again as he fired a bullet into the ceiling.

As Eddie looked through his blurry eyes at Meriadoc, he limply raised the gun and rested it behind a pricked ear. The warm-eyed dog cocked his furry head, panting, panting, confused, the worry burning his brain.

'I'm sorry, Meriadoc.'

Floyd grinned sickly as he waited for Eddie to shoot his own dog. Eddie stiffened his wrist. He closed his eyes, collapsed to the floor, wailing, a deluge.

Floyd rolled his eyes and licked his lips. 'Oh dear.'

The horror suddenly turned surreal as the tune of *I'm in the Mood for Dancing* chirped out in an electronic arrangement.

'Excuse me a second,' the maniac said as he pulled out his mobile phone from his trench coat. He answered it and casually ambled off across the warehouse.

Neither of the captives registered anything of the phone conversation. Eddie just stared at the concrete floor as he continued to cry. Larry had his eyes closed and was breathing in sharply as though he'd been running a marathon in the Sahara Desert. Meriadoc whined. They had a reprieve but it wasn't to last for long.

'Sorry about that,' Floyd remarked as he came waltzing back. 'Right, where were we?'

He approached Eddie's cell and brought out a key from

his trouser pocket. Unlocking a door, he walked in there with him.

'You idiot. Do you really think I would give you a loaded gun? Pathetic. Go on, how about you shoot me with it? Got enough guts to do that?'

Eddie pointed his gun at him and squeezed the trigger. He didn't expect there to be any bullets in the chamber, and there weren't any.

Floyd shook his head. 'Loser.'

The demon turned to the scrawny mutt who cowered backwards. 'Here. This is how you shoot a dog.' He raised his gun and shot Meriadoc in the hind leg.

Eddie screamed. Meriadoc collapsed onto his backside as he frantically tried to pick himself up again.

'See that? You pop them in the leg first just to wound them, so you can see the fear in their eyes and taste that sour charge in the air. You maybe shoot them once more...'

Bang! Another bullet lodged into Meriadoc's back.

'You turn the screw, so the pain becomes excruciating and you get that desperate look in their eye. *Please kill me. Please send me out of this meaningless life.*'

Floyd shot him again in the head and Meriadoc made a resigned bawling sound as his eyes closed. He collapsed to the ground as a pool of blood spread from his body. He flinched faintly one more time before his life evaporated away forever.

Floyd giggled as he left the room and locked up the door.

Chapter 13.2

Henry always knew this day would come. He'd tried to make his penance through Halo of Fires, and he'd tried to save his soul by finding the Akasa Stone, but neither of those forces could now save him. They were merely part of the chains he'd been forging, and now that bastard Floyd was tugging on them, dragging him to the fate that had hung over his head for so many years.

Standing alone in his office, gazing through the window across the dead end town, Henry felt powerless. The heavens were fading, a thick pollution of rain clouds sealing away the sky. He looked to his desk instead and saw a tea stain on the veneer. Dust had settled on top of the filing cabinets. He felt like kicking them all over, pulling out all the papers and throwing them out the window. They were all meaningless now. It was all a failure.

He collapsed into his leather chair and clutched his neck. His fingers found the clasp on the wooden beads. He removed the imitation Akasa Stone to look once more at the fool's salvation.

The door opened, disturbing his moment. It was Jake. Silently he approached the desk, his eyes tired, his stubble thick.

'So,' he sighed, taking a seat opposite.

'I had to wake you...'

'I haven't been to bed yet.'

A weak smile briefly appeared on Henry's lips. 'Jake, I've had it.'

Jake looked him hard in the eye then lowered his gaze, as if he'd just been told that Henry was dying of cancer. The muscles in his cheeks flexed and in defiant dismissal he said, 'No.'

'Trust me, it's over.'

'What is that?' His eyes squinted as it focussed on the item in Henry's hand. He held it up.

'Tovar's treasure. It's fake.'

'He was right then. Vladimir. How the hell did you get it back?'

'The Harbour Master.'

'And Floyd knows?'

'He's taken our two apprentices.'

'Did they find Devlan?'

'I would guess so. But instead of coming to me, he took them to Floyd.'

Jake rubbed his chin. 'Bastard.' He stood up. 'All right, let's go sort them out.'

'We'll need to wait for...' Henry began, before he realised that Clint was already by the door.

'Standing by,' Clint said. 'But I don't see the Boy Wonder yet.'

'We couldn't get hold of Vladimir,' Henry said.

'Shouldn't we wait for him?' Clint asked.

Jake started to make a move. 'Come on. We'll be fine.'

'Look, I just think, whatever the plan is here, whatever shit on whatever fan, whatever lightning bolts The Harbour Master will send our way, it's always useful having Vladimir with us. He's our lucky charm, our amulet. I think it's worth waiting just five or ten minutes more.'

They weren't listening to him. Wearily, Henry stood up. He rubbed his chest again, even though he was no longer wearing the imitation stone. 'Come on, chaps. Let's go.'

Chapter 13.3

The dog had been dead for over three hours, but poor Eddie had not stopped crying. He cradled him in his arms, his clothes soaked with blood. Meriadoc's soul had departed, but the youngster could not let go of the vessel that had contained it.

Larry was in the breeze-blocked cell with him now. Sitting against the opposite wall, all he could do was stare at his bleary-eyed friend.

He knew Eddie could not be fixed. It had taken Larry seven years to even begin to compose his own fractures again. Picking up the pieces only cut one's fingers.

Besides, they were still locked up in this strange place with this sadistic lunatic. Any second now he would be back for more torture. Larry had tried to break the glass wall, but despite throwing the set of drawers at it, despite throwing *himself* at it, the glass was evidently the same type used in Hannibal Lecter's cell.

Yet why was their psychopath on the other side of the glass here? Larry could not comprehend how Floyd was left running around in society, that someone who was obviously completely insane had escaped the shit filter.

Floyd wasn't even worthy of being called a human, could not be of the same species as he and Eddie. How would someone like this operate in normal day-to-day life? How come nobody had noticed this man was a complete nutcase? Now he knew exactly why the Halo of Fires organisation existed. With sickos like this, the world would be lost without a force to fight them.

Eddie's sobbing suddenly stopped and his head stiffened, as though his mind had been hit with a chilling premonition. 'We're going to die.'

Larry shook his head. 'No, Eddie. We're going to get out of here. I need you to hold on.'

'Why did they do this? What did we do to them?'

'I guess maybe we should have opened that letter.'

Eddie nodded. 'That was the test. You know, whatever I do, whatever choice I make, it's always wrong. Every time. I can never win.'

'We're going to win this time. Come on, dude, don't give up.'

Eddie turned his head away. 'He's back.'

Larry heard clanking footsteps as heavy boots trampled across the concrete floor. The leathery-faced demon trailed up to the cell, his trench coat streaming behind him like black wings. He was accompanied by an icy-eyed thug with irises as grey as a frozen lake, and a gangly looking youngster who lingered in the background with a cold smile. Larry picked up on the genetic similarity between this lad and Floyd, although he couldn't imagine him to be Floyd's son. There was no way any woman on the planet would want to reproduce with that monster.

Floyd walked up to the glass and crouched down to speak to his captives like a boy about to feed his frightened hamsters to the cat.

'Now then, children. Here's where things start to go downhill. Last night was a bit like going to Tesco. You go out for something, but then you see the offers on the end of the aisle, and with a three-for-one deal you know it's something you can't possibly do without. So here's the bad news for you: I only really need one of you. Only one of you gets a chance of living, and even that is a bit of a thin chance in all fairness. But the other one is definitely going to die, and it's going to be really, really nasty for them. So you'll have to decide between yourselves in the next minute which one of you gets to live and which one gets to die.'

He sprouted up again and darted out of view. Larry looked back at Eddie as the next sickening twist to their ordeal sank into the murky waters of his mind. There was nothing in Eddie's face though, his eyes cloudy like marbles; there was only one decision he would make here. Eddie wouldn't even fire an unloaded gun at that stray mutt to save Larry's life.

Larry closed his eyes and shook his head. His mind was only equipped for going out drinking, shooting pool, and handing in essays too late. There was no place in it for this sort of stuff. He didn't even realise this shit went on in his world, at least not in *this* backwater of a town.

He heard squeaking wheels and the groan of rusty metal. The demon and his cohorts were now wheeling in some strange piece of machinery, but this one definitely wasn't a fairground ride.

'So then, children, can any of you tell me what this little contraption is? I got it from an old business associate who used to run a pet food factory not far from here. I've never got round to using it yet. Waiting for the right moment. But it seems that moment is before us. This here machine is a meat mincer. Nice and big, as you can see. Just about big enough to pass a human through. So, who's going to be the one to test it out for me?'

'I think the fat one,' the grey-eyed thug squealed as he banged his fist on the glass next to Larry.

Closer up to him, Larry could see that his manky brown teeth had most probably never seen a toothbrush in his life. His droopy eyes and splodge of a nose made him look like his whole face was melting, as though his body couldn't even be bothered to hold itself together. Greasy, receding hair. Scraggly stubble. He was probably fifteen years younger than he looked. He wore muddy Wellington boots like he'd just stepped out of a farmyard. Not that he would have been working there, most likely screwing the goats all day.

'You're not killing either of us,' Larry shot back at them.

Eddie sat in a forlorn heap on the ground, his eyes staring past the floor to the hell that was supposed to be beneath them.

'Let's take the fat one.'

'You come in here and get me you sick sack of shit!'

Floyd approached the glass, glowing with pleasure at the fiery agitation he was creating. In contrasting calm he said, 'Come on, children, you're supposed to be deciding which one of you tries out my mincing machine.'

'You're not putting us in that thing, you sick fucker!' Larry screamed back at him, hammering his fists on the impenetrable glass.

He stared into Floyd's dead eyes like a boxer waiting for the bell. When the bastard came in the cell, he would lunge at him and tear his eyeballs out with his fingernails, bite his nose off, smash the sicko's face into the wall.

'What do you think then, Zero?' Floyd asked the thug. 'Want to get rid of the less pretty one?'

'Yeah,' he replied.

'And what about you?' Floyd then called over to the gangly milquetoast who continued to float around in the background like a grinning imp. He offered a faint nod in reply. Evidently he was incapable of speech.

'The fat one it is,' Floyd said as he reached into his trench coat for his gun. He walked round to the corridor and as soon as he opened the door, Larry ran at him with his arms outstretched like a zombie, reaching for the demon's throat. He didn't care anymore about getting shot. He didn't care about dying.

Floyd fired a bullet that whizzed past Larry's head. He clutched his head, thinking he'd been hit as a confusing pain rang in his ears.

Zero the thug grabbed his elbow to drag him out, but Larry flung his arm and sent him flying into the wall.

Floyd fired his gun again, this time hitting Larry in the shin. He collapsed to the ground in such a pain that he didn't know could exist.

Through his roars he could see Eddie staring back at him, almost calmly. He didn't seem to care, looking on like he was watching it all taking place on television.

'They'll miss you more than me,' Eddie said to his friend. He stood up and stepped towards them. He removed his baseball cap and tossed it to the ground. 'Take me.'

Floyd looked over him for a moment while the cogs trundled in his head. He then grabbed Eddie by his neck and they dragged him out of the cell.

'Eddie. Eddie, no!' Larry hopelessly roared through his screams.

The grey-eyed brute stood behind Eddie and wrapped his arms around him like he was about to lift the carcass of an animal. Floyd switched on the machine and it whirred into life.

With the help of the gangly accomplice, Zero lifted Eddie off the ground.

'Wait... You're going to shoot me first, aren't you? Fucking Jesus! Fucking kill me first!'

Larry saw Eddie kicking his legs, the two thugs edging him closer to the brutal apparatus. A few items slipped from Eddie's jeans pockets as though fleeing the approaching mouth of the mechanical beast: a bunch of keys, some coins, a green Yo-Yo that bounced along the ground with its trailing string.

'Larry! Shit, help me! Larry, tell them to shoot me!'

Larry scrunched his eyes shut tight. He couldn't watch. As the tone of the machine turned a higher pitch and Eddie's piercing scream filled the building, he knew exactly what was happening.

He heard the slopping of flesh as they fed him in feet first. All the psychopaths laughed as they slowly pushed him down into the revolving metal cutters.

With his legs cut to shreds, the screams got even louder, and Larry's whole body shuddered. They held him there for a few moments and then shoved his midriff into the grinders. The screaming became gargled, blood gushing out of Eddie's mouth.

Larry opened an eye just as they fed the rest of Eddie's body into the machine, and the howling suddenly stopped. Red flesh piled out at the other end, mixed up with strands of fabric from his clothes and shards of black rubber from his shoes. They were his indoor football boots he'd bought a couple of weeks ago for their five-a-side matches.

It had taken only a matter of seconds to turn Eddie into nothing more than a splattering of flesh, blood and bones. Larry's body spasmed as his throat wretched up the contents of his stomach. He hadn't eaten anything all day, and so only spat up stinging bile which jetted all over him, the fire and the venom that burned within.

That slop of blood was his friend. Now a pile of shredded meat. Dog food. Larry felt so hollow. In this living hell, life had no value at all.

A worn out, blood-splattered Floyd sat down next to the glass as he caught his breath. He was spent. 'Fucking brilliant,' he panted out.

'You sick son of a bitch,' Larry spat.

'Ain't it great?' Floyd replied, turning to him. 'Just you and me now, fat boy. How are you liking your stay at the Chamber of Fun so far?'

'I'm going to come back for you. I'm going to slaughter you mercilessly and you'll burn in hell for eternity.'

'Now, that's bullshit, boy,' he said knowingly. 'You know where I'll be going if you kill me? You'll be sending me to heaven. Everyone goes to heaven. Right now Hitler's up there partying with six million Jews. Osama Bin Laden's eating hotdogs with three thousand World Trade Centre workers.'

'What's with you? Are you some demented Bible freak or just fucking insane?'

'I'm as sane as you are, boy. You know what The Harbour Master says? He says good and evil share the same realm. They serve the same purpose. They come together like old friends. You dumb fuckers at Halo of Fires, you're neither one nor the other. You walk some midway line in a no-man's-land and it don't achieve a thing. But evil? Evil is good's best friend because it powers it. Without evil, there is no good. Evil is just good in another form. God loves me for what I did just now. And you know what? It's much more fun than being good.'

'You're sick,' Larry shouted once more, but his words were pointless. His anger and insults only seemed to feed the demon before him.

Sitting on the cold concrete floor next to him was Eddie's baseball cap. He picked it up and put it on his head; the raging volcano needed to be contained.

He noticed the icy-eyed thug was still standing by the pile of shredded flesh, leaning over it in fascination.

'Relax, Zero,' Floyd called out to him. 'I'm pretty sure he's dead.' Giggling, he turned to Larry. 'Not the sharpest blade him. Once took an IQ test and came out for a duck.'

'It was difficult finding the wrong answer every time,' Zero protested.

'I don't know. Never met anyone else who tried so hard to be a slob. If it wasn't for me,' Floyd prattled on to Larry as he got to his feet, 'this idiot would be sponging off society, collecting disability allowance and God knows what, and sitting on his arse all day watching *Cash in the Bloody Attic*. But now I've got him doing something. So there's some good I *do* do.'

'Are we going to eat? I'm starving,' Zero said.

'You didn't want any Shr-Eddies?' Floyd giggled as he grinned at Larry.

The monster then walked off as Zero gazed down at Larry with his cold stare. 'We'll be back later,' he said to him softly.

Part 14: The Clouds of Karma

Chapter 14.1

It was all candyfloss sweetness and dancing rainbow lights at Floyd's public amusement park where Henry and his two Powers searched out the park's owner. With every minute that passed, Henry felt his heart getting tighter and tighter in his chest, while Jake and Clint were like two lager cans shaken up and dying to be opened.

All they found were normal people. Pockets of hormonal teenagers acted cool in front of the girls, old women in beige cardigans gazed vicariously at the rides as they licked ice cream, toddlers whined in their buggies. Nothing out of the ordinary.

No Floyd. No Devlan. They charged into Floyd's office, but the only guy in there, a pale-faced kiosk worker munching a packet of crisps on his break, was clueless. Even after Jake had grabbed him by the throat and pinned him against the wall, he had no information to spill on Floyd's whereabouts.

They continued to patrol the amusements and arcades as the minutes accumulated into hours. What else could they do? Henry phoned Nigel at *The Cheshire Cat* every five minutes to find out if any more letters or phone calls had been received, or if that elusive Vladimir had finally appeared.

As Henry got back inside the black Mercedes, he undid the top two buttons on his shirt and loosened his tie. He rubbed his chest. He felt so hot. Floyd was making him sweat, twisting his nerves, making him burn. He should have done something about this monster years ago.

Alan would have done it. Even with no first-hand experience of Floyd's monstrosities, Alan knew enough that he would have organised his disposal. But Henry hadn't gone for that. He'd been too afraid. Destroying The Harbour

Master's creation would have brought about serious repercussions.

'What do we do, Henry?' Jake asked as he sat down in the driver's seat. 'Where can we go?'

Henry's eyes focussed on the smear of dead bugs on the windscreen. No matter what, they had to find him. Yet within these hours of fruitless searching, he feared the candle had already burnt out. It was the same old story. He never found what he searched for.

'I don't know,' he muttered.

'There's no telling what Floyd's going to do.'

'My head isn't in the sand now, Jake. Believe me.'

'This shit goes way back, don't it? Right back to Forseti.'

'You know what happened.'

'Yeah.'

'I've been standing back ever since. All these years. It's easier to do nothing. This is all my karma.'

'Floyd wasn't your responsibility, Henry. You didn't make him.'

'No, but I left him out there.'

'We'll get him.'

'It's already too late.'

'Then even more reason.'

Clint got in the back seat, panting after a fretful walk along the promenade for the fiftieth time. 'That punk ain't anywhere. We need Vladimir. Sure he'd have some input on this.'

'Of course. Vladimir always has the answers,' Henry replied with truthful sarcasm. He looked across Floyd's playground and watched a boat from the log flume being dragged to the top. Beyond the ride, the sun was setting on this awful mess of a day. That hollow sensation of dread soured his mind, Henry sensing it would be the last sunset he would ever see.

The log flume scooted around to the drop. The passengers, a father and his toddler son, screamed excitedly as their boat careered through the river, the spray of water raining down on them. Henry envied their fun, envied their ignorance.

But that wasn't his life; Henry had seen beneath the

mantle.

'I got bad vibes,' Clint whined. 'Can feel our luck running dry this time.'

'Should we go back to *Clarence*?' Jake asked.

'No. Let's wait,' Henry said as he closed his baggy eyes.

'We can't just sit here,' Clint piped up again.

'They'll come to us. I bet they're watching us right now,' Jake said.

A silence lingered for a few moments until Henry opened his eyes again. 'I must face Floyd alone.'

'Why?' Jake asked. 'What do you want us to do?'

'I want both of you to see to Devlan. I tried to give him a chance, but I guess he's the blood-drinking freak that everyone thought him to be. It's time we rid this town of him, time to rid this town of both its monsters.'

Jake nodded.

'Devlan? How can we...?' Clint started before something interrupted him.

Henry reached into his jacket pocket and pulled out his ringing mobile phone. He didn't recognise the number, but he sure as hell recognised the voice on the other end.

Chapter 14.2

Devlan hadn't been to the repository in a long time. He slipped in through the fire exit door at the back; it was still broken, not that he'd ever mentioned this to Floyd. Wandering through the cold corridor to the main warehouse, he saw the refurbished rides were still there collecting dust.

He wondered why his boss had asked him to come here, but looking around he couldn't see anything amiss. His olfactory perceptions told him differently, though. The scent of the skinny kid's deodorant, the oils in his dog's pelage. He could smell blood too, a lot of it. Stronger than blood.

'How did you get in here?' Floyd asked as he bounded up

275

to him.

Devlan silently continued to decode the smells of the warehouse. Floyd's stench had hit his nostrils the moment he'd stepped inside.

'You told me to come.'

'Don't know how to knock?'

'Where are they?'

'Scooby-Doo and co? I got them all locked up.'

'Yeah, right. Why do you always think I'm as dumb as you, Floyd?'

'I don't. I think you're even dumber.'

'How so?'

'Because you follow me around.'

'Dumb as a bag of glass hammers,' Devlan replied blankly as he meandered farther into the secret collection of fairground rides. 'What have you been doing to this place?'

'Nothing.'

Devlan peered over his shades. He recognised a lot of these roller coasters and merry-go-rounds, remembering the work he'd undertaken on their mechanics to get them running again. But why hadn't Floyd sold them on? He sensed that something was out of place, as if he was looking at a familiar room and trying to guess the missing object.

'Why are they all still here?'

'Don't worry your little head over that right now. I need you to do something for me.'

'Floyd is clicking his fingers again, is he?'

'You already came here, like the faithful chap you are. Or maybe it was because you had no choice.'

'The second one.'

Floyd made a cocky laugh that was more irritating than usual. 'Henry and his crew are out looking for me.'

'They know what's going on?'

'Sort of. Henry knows it's him I want.'

'Always knew there was something between you two.'

Floyd's brain was too much on one track to detect the wisecrack. 'So I need him down here now,' he went on. 'Go and get him for me. Bring him here.'

'Where is he?'

'My lookout saw him down at the amusements.'

'He's on his own?'

'No doubt the turncoat Jake and Clint the Brave might be around. I'm sure you can take care of them if they prove to be a problem.'

'Why? Do you think they will be a problem?'

'I don't,' Floyd replied, pausing, shifting on his feet. 'Henry will co-operate. He knows the deal.'

'So simple then,' Devlan said. He wandered back to the fire escape feeling like a plastic supermarket bag blowing aimlessly in the wind, waiting to be swept up and thrown away.

***

Floyd observed him closely as he left. Devlan always was a cagey sod, but it seemed he was playing along.

It was all part of the plan. Floyd had no idea how to bump him off, other than by sending him to Jake and Clint who would surely pulverise him. Thinking it was Devlan who'd turned in the two youngsters, the old freak wouldn't stand a chance, not against those two.

It was a bit of a shame to be losing Devlan's services after all these years, but he had to fulfil the orders from The Harbour Master. Devlan knew where that cursed *Tatterdemalion* was and so was a loose end that needed dealing with.

Zero interrupted his thoughts, 'Here, I got you a quarter pounder.'

'Let's eat,' Floyd replied. 'And then it'll be time for some more work.'

Chapter 14.3

Not even a quiet five minutes inside Saint Anthony's provided Michael any comfort. Two of the votive candles burned, one for Larry and one for Eddie, but as he stared at the flames, he had the gloomy feeling there was only one person he could rely on right now.

Michael stepped out of the church onto the crepuscular street. It was an hour after closing time, the town in that lull between serving shoppers and serving drinkers. He didn't know where to go any more, didn't know where else to search for his friends. He found himself walking back to the café, anyway.

The place was closed, but the manager with the trim beard and the wild hair was still standing behind the counter, going over the day's takings. Michael tapped on the glass door. Nigel looked up, hesitated, then walked over to him.

'Hello again,' Nigel said to him as though he was greeting an old friend.

'Are you one of them? Are you one of the Fires?' Michael asked.

Nigel's eyes twinkled. He peered up and down the street, then back at his visitor. 'Come in.'

Michael took his seat by the counter again while Nigel picked up his tickets. 'I have to go through all these. Add them all up, make sure it all correlates with what's in the till. I know a few pence here and there doesn't really matter in the grand scheme of things, but it gives my mind something to do.'

'Don't let me disturb you.'

Nigel wasn't looking at the tickets though, staring into space as his head lolled from side to side. 'Every day. Have to keep occupied. I don't like to stop.'

'Look, I just came here because...'

'Because *then* I start to think.'

'About what?'

Nigel locked his eyes with Michael's. For a moment he didn't say anything, just shook his head then put a finger to his lips. 'Seven o'clock. Let me try Vladimir again.'

He reached round and picked up the phone, an old-fashioned Bakelite hanging on the wall. He dialled and waited. It seemed nobody was picking up today. He replaced the receiver.

'Hmm,' Nigel said, prolonging the syllable probably so that the vibrations might soothe his inner organs.

'Vladimir. Is he the one in black, the highly strung one?' Michael asked.

Nigel nodded, his focus returning to his calculations. 'Eleven eighty-four.'

'You got an address for him?'

'No. I'm sorry, I must do these.'

'Yeah. Yeah, carry on. I just want to wait here for him.'

'Five fifty... That's not right.'

It was Michael's last hope. When Vladimir turned up, he'd demand his help and he would have no choice but to co-operate, especially when the mysterious vigilante learnt of the bargaining chip Michael was holding.

Chapter 14.4

Vladimir had gone wandering. He would sometimes do that when he slept. He understood why it happened and he knew how to stop it, but he also accepted that despite how haunting and harrowing it could get, it was something he yearned for. There were things to be found in his travelling, revelations to be uncovered in this realm of the absolute.

All day he'd been at the park next to the woods, the same area that had been bulldozed to create a new housing estate. But right now, it was back to being a park again.

He observed his footsteps stepping on the occasional horse chestnut leaf, emitting very satisfying crunches. Why had his soul been drawn here today? He remembered all the different playground apparatus: the climbing frame with the monkey bars, the old wooden roundabout, the green seesaw that whined like a donkey as it went up and down.

As interesting as it was to revisit this place, he couldn't work it out. He wouldn't be able to escape, though. Here he was trapped until the message presented itself.

He looked up through the awesome trees that stretched up trying to reach for the heavens, and he could see the sky had turned a thick grey. It would soon start to rain, and he knew it would be quite a storm.

Vladimir noticed two people had appeared. A young boy sat on a swing while someone pushed him. He'd only given him a few feeble shoves before the grey-haired man sat on the swing next to him. There was a third chair; Vladimir slowly approached.

He knew who they were, but, even so, it was very strange. It was just that Ulric Helliwell had never haunted him before. The boy was Jeremy. No surprise that he was here again.

Vladimir sat down next to them in the empty swing, listening in on their chatter. Eventually Ulric noticed him and turned round. The side of his face had that horrible, open wound on it, the flesh ripped apart and a crispy line of blood all the way down his neck.

'Here he is, Jeremy. Vladimir got here at last.'

'I've never seen you before. All this time and I've never seen you,' Vladimir said to the ghost.

'I knew they would get me one day, but I made sure I was ready for it. They weren't going to stop me.'

'Why are you here?'

'Wanted to find Jeremy, didn't I?' Ulric replied as he turned to the silent boy.

Vladimir dared a peek at him. His reflective face stared back, but his eyes weren't haunted today; instead they shone with a purple glow.

'But it's hard to find Jeremy. Hard to find him since you killed him.'

'Jeremy had to die,' Vladimir replied. 'He was weak. It was for the best.'

Ulric placed a hand on the boy's fair hair and ruffled it up. 'We all meet again though, don't we? I found you.'

'I knew it. Right away I knew that was you...'

'That's quite some perception you have, young man.'

'And that's quite a trick you performed. I should start paying more attention to the animals I encounter.'

'Alas, my canine form is no more. I have slipped away from you again.'

'Is this what you came here to tell me?' Surely the appearance of this figure signalled greater meaning. Ulric had lost his life by the brutal hand of the black widow killer.

Vladimir could see the picture forming in his mind as the dots joined up.

It's not him. He's not the killer you're looking for.

'I wish that were all,' Ulric replied before dragging in a weary breath. 'You came here to understand that one of the new Guardians is also dead, the other is still alive, for now.'

'And will you tell me who is responsible for all this killing?'

'I think you already know.'

'It's Floyd, isn't it? He killed you?'

It started off faintly, but the bobbing of Ulric's head eventually became a distinct nod.

This time it wasn't just a nudge. This time it was a shove.

The walking dead man got to his feet. 'If only we could believe that everything that happens in this world transpires according to the will of the universe. That we can't lose. Can't fail. Despite everything that is thrown at us.'

Vladimir shook his head. He didn't want to hear philosophical talk right now. He needed fire and fury, a call to arms before hunting down the killer that had evaded him for so long. 'Wait. How do I find them?'

'Follow the boy,' Ulric replied. He stared up into the sky as large raindrops smacked against the tarmac. 'This one's going to pour. I know how to tell now. It's come to drench you. To extinguish.'

The ghostly grandfather strolled away from them, fading, leaving Vladimir alone with Jeremy. He couldn't look at him, couldn't face the child.

Somehow he had to crawl his way out of this. He realised it was only a dream, that he wasn't really in this park that wasn't a park anymore. He knew he wasn't really there with this young boy whose spirit had been extinguished many years ago.

The young boy whom he had murdered.

He knew he was back at home in his bed. He could feel the bedsheets against his simmering skin. With all of his might, he tried to pull back his eyelids to rescue himself from this haunting. It took all of his effort to prise them open just a fraction and see a blurry bedroom through his eyelashes.

But still Jeremy stood by his side, staring at him. As the grey clouds swarmed the sky and sucked away all the radiance from the sky's ball of flames, the purple glow from Jeremy's eyes shone over Vladimir's body until it was the only light he could see. The rain poured and poured, gushing, drowning.

If only he could break out of this nightmare. If only he could move a limb and wake into the world of the relative again. No matter how hard he tried to control his arm, it remained dormant. Vladimir feared he might be stuck in this paralysis forever, never able to walk around in his real world, never do his work again.

Rain splashed against the bedroom window and suddenly he was awake. He sat upright and saw the sprays of water smashing against the glass like a tidal wave. He checked his digital alarm clock. It was thirty-seven minutes past nine in the evening. Just how long had he been sleeping?

He sprang out of bed and flung open his wardrobe. Each garment hung there neatly and he reached first for his black shirt. As he grabbed the hanger with his left hand, he winced in pain. His weeping wound had stained the bandage while he'd slept. It really needed changing, but he didn't have time.

As he assembled his Halo of Fires suit on his body, he felt himself becoming the immaculate Vladimir again, slipped into his role of karmic angel.

Death had already visited today; he had to get going before any more of his comrades fell away from his world.

Chapter 14.5

The rain lashed down relentlessly like the tears from a defeated army of angels, an army that was now retreating for it had given up on the town. It had chased away the last of the daytrippers long ago as darkness engulfed the seaside amusements. If there were any other stragglers, then the sight of Devlan and his glowing red eyes emerging from the mist would have easily been the deciding factor in convincing them that *Floyd's Amusements* was not the place to be right now.

Wandering around the complex, the rain soaked Devlan's clothes, and the sea wind bit against his face like a ferocious animal. He hated being wet. He really, really hated it. Too many bitter memories. He could still feel those miserable shiverings in his bones to this day.

Whenever he got involved with Floyd's foolish schemes, he always ended up in these tragic situations. He should have known better. Perhaps there was a part of him that knew all this from the start, born of a tired hopelessness. Devlan just wanted something to do, wanted to feel needed again.

He knew the Fires were coming for him, and they would intend to kill him. Amongst the putrid smells in the warehouse, he'd also smelt Floyd's deceit. No doubt The Harbour Master had asked *his* servant to dispose of Devlan. If there was a job too difficult for Floyd, he'd just get someone else to do it.

Devlan stopped his meandering. They'd get to him sooner if he stayed in one place. He removed his gloves and tossed them onto the drenched tarmac. Holding a hand in front of his face, he squeezed his fingers into a tight ball as the raindrops fell from his fingertips.

Coarse hair sprouted all the way up his arms and his fingernails were like thick claws of flint, curling round into sharp points. They were hideous, but good for defending himself, as they had proved so many, many times.

Two burly figures appeared from out of the streaming black rain, as though two of the angelic warriors passing overhead had fallen with the raindrops. One of them stood downwind, the bitter smell of whisky carrying through the slimy air. The other flanked the opposite side like a sprinter at the mark, ready to run away. He was that giant meathead Clint; the other was Jake.

Either of them on their own would not have been a problem for Devlan. Both of them together maybe balanced things. Nevertheless, he much preferred it didn't come to that.

'Where's Maristow?' Devlan asked, his voice muffled by the penetrating wind. He made sure to pull back his lips to project his words, the large canines protruding from his rows of teeth.

Neither of them answered. The shadowy figure of Jake began gliding silently towards him. Clint did the same.

'We shouldn't be getting caught up in this,' Devlan carried on. 'This is all between Maristow and Floyd. Why don't we just let them sort out their thing and we can all go our own ways?'

'We know what you did, Devlan,' Jake said.

'Floyd's playing you. You want me to take you to him? I know where he is, where he's keeping those two lads.'

'We already know where they are. Henry is on his way now.'

'Whatever he's told you, it's all lies,' Devlan fired back, a familiar sinking sensation in his chest. He hated himself for not anticipating Floyd would stitch him up as the fall guy.

'Those kids had gone looking for *you*. You kidnapped them, and we know why. You're a sick, blood-drinking freak, that's what you are.'

Devlan shook his head and lowered his dimming red eyes to his feet, struck by a painfully old feeling.

'We know what you are, Devlan,' Jake went on. 'You're that killer, Old Shiner. We've let you live long enough.'

'No,' Devlan growled.

'Just look at yourself. What the hell sort of freak are you?'

Devlan made that guttural sound, like the purr of a motorbike engine ticking over, before it erupted into a growl. Jake covered his eardrums while Clint's entire body flinched.

Clint fumbled into the back pocket of his jeans and brought out his knife. He took a lunge but it was a sloppy move, Devlan easily darting out of the way, grabbing a clawed hand on the back of his head and pushing him hard against the concrete

Jake was quicker, however, his right fist flying into his

ribcage. Usually the grunt put people in a crippled heap on the floor with such a move, but Devlan remained standing, catching the fist after the impact and then swiping forward with his other hand.

The brainless Power recoiled as the salty sea air seeped into the parallel lacerations down his neck. Devlan stepped closer and was about to spring when Jake flung his body into him, slamming them both to the ground. With a grimacing jaw he pinned Devlan against the tarmac, but Devlan stared back, his eyes burning, his mouth wide open ready to tear into some flesh.

Jake's limbs shook as though they were about to give way. At the edge of his vision, Devlan noticed Clint had found his feet again, and also his blade, his lumbering frame stumbling towards them. He growled, and with a strength that defied the fibres of his muscles, he threw the gargantuan warrior off him. Jake collapsed into some railings winded and gasping for air.

In a lightning move, he was back on his feet and eyeing up the other Power. He could smell his fear, could see his hand trembling as he held the knife before him.

Clint considered his buddy writhing on the ground, and it seemed to destroy the little courage he'd mustered. Making the most of his hesitation, Devlan stormed after him, clawing against Clint's hand and sending the blade flying into the darkness. Another claw swiped for his face, but Clint flinched out of the way. He wasn't fast enough for Devlan's next move, though. Launching himself at him, his claws pierced into his flesh, his teeth sinking into his shoulder.

Clint screamed. It wouldn't be the pain that made him yell, not with this sissy. In his panic he span around, clattering into the panels of the helter-skelter.

Still Devlan held on. Clint roared even harder, erupting every ounce of his fear in a desperate throe. Devlan sunk his teeth further into his neck, the claws rooting into his flesh like burrowing mites. Devlan would drain Clint's nerves until he died of fright.

Somehow the oaf managed to reach for Devlan's eyes and he pressed his thumbs into them. His grip unlocked and he slopped to the ground. A leather boot slammed into his ribs.

Not that Clint's assault could illicit any pain. Devlan was very quickly back on his feet and snarling as he stared back at the terrified Power. He felt indestructible.

He took a pace forwards, Clint stepped backwards. Another step and Clint was now turning to run.

No matter how hard he managed to pump his meaty legs, the Power wasn't quick enough. Devlan pounced onto his back and pinned him down. As he frantically tried to wriggle free, Devlan grabbed his head with both hands, arched it back, and then smacked it against the ground, sending him away into blackness.

One down, one to go.

***

Jake had found his breath again, a stream of blood down the side of his face. Just as he clambered to his feet, he saw the figure of Devlan standing before him. He looked around for his partner.

'Just me and you, Jake,' Devlan murmured. 'Going to run away like a little girl too?'

'I'm not afraid of you.'

'The mighty Jake don't fear anyone, does he?'

Jake clenched both of his fists. He was ready to fight the monster before him, ready to destroy him. Jake, Power of the Fires, never lost against anyone, and so Devlan could be no exception. This was Jake's chance to prove he was the greatest, that he was the champion of Dark Harbour. Devlan's scalp would immortalise his reputation of indomitability.

With an unsteady breath, he stepped forward.

Chapter 14.6

Vladimir slid his fingers through his wet hair and shivered

as the stinging rainwater trickled down the nape of his neck. The cold was such a crude sensation, an irritation that came with being a member of this realm. But it was easy for him to switch it off, such were the abilities he had.

Jeremy was bone dry, of course, completely unaffected by the restless elements. The ghostly boy with the purple eyes walked in deathly silence about ten feet ahead, a lost soul who was not of this world and who therefore could not absorb the pellets of rain that insisted on aiming down at them.

The vigilante had followed the boy down the sodden path through the fields, along the riverbank where the ducks nibbled at algae, and past the caravan park on the outskirts of town. It was an unusual route, but it gradually became apparent that they were heading towards Eastgate.

It seemed like treading across yesterday's battle zone as Vladimir walked up to *The Cheshire Cat*. The café was deserted. His fellow soldiers must have answered the call to battle and were fighting the dreadful disturbances or lying dead in the field. Where was Vladimir when they'd needed him? Lying in a nice warm bed as he'd wandered the other plains.

There was nothing here, nothing but a reminder of his failings. Such was Jeremy's spite to lead him up this dead end. Just as he was about to turn his back on the ghostly boy and carry on into the town centre, he noticed someone... a face, slightly familiar. He sat like an abandoned rag doll across the street, staring blankly as the raindrops danced like aqueous fairies in the murky puddle before him.

The shower continued to snap against his slickly drenched coat while Vladimir tried to remember who this person was: sharp eyes, personable face, clear voice. As the wind swept by him like an angel had just flapped its wings, Vladimir could see exactly who he was. In another universe, Vladimir's soul could have followed the same path as his. He crossed the road.

He remembered the nature of their encounter, the altercation they'd had in the pub where he'd grabbed his throat to shut him up.

Michael looked up as he approached. 'You must be Vladimir.'

'You're the pacifist, right?' Vladimir asked as he stepped into the streetlight.

'You remember me.'

'What are you doing here?'

'As much as I hate to say it, I need your help. I'm looking for my friends.'

'You know Larry and Eddie?' Vladimir sat down on the pavement next to him.

'I bet I'm too late.'

'No,' Vladimir lied. 'We can still find them.'

'Tell you who I did find, though. Managed to solve one of Dark Harbour's greatest mysteries. Remember I was looking for that young lad Jeremy? Well, I know where he is.'

Vladimir nodded and swallowed hard. 'I had a funny feeling you might work it out.'

'Although, he wouldn't exactly be a young boy anymore, would he? By now he'd be all grown up, probably settling down with a wife and thinking about having kids and all that sort of stuff. But I don't think it's worth taking your advice. I don't think he would tell me if I asked him who murdered Simon Helliwell and his grandfather.'

'Believe me now it wasn't Halo of Fires?'

'I found out the Fires were protectors. They were too late for Ulric and Simon, but when it came to Jeremy, they had to try differently. They didn't want to simply hide him, they wanted him to be able to look after himself as well, turn him into the same force that protected him. Plus, it's easy to hide things sometimes when they're right under your nose.'

'So what do you plan to do with this information?'

'This was supposed to be for my Journalism assignment. Supposed to help in getting myself a first.'

'A true Kolley Kibber, eh? So this was all goddamned college work?'

'Wouldn't be a good idea if I broadcast to the world where Jeremy is. There's a reason he's hidden, after all.'

'Maybe certain people have worked it out by now, but even so, I'd appreciate it if you didn't.'

'Are there many others that know you're Jeremy?'

'Only a few.'

'Why? I mean, why did you become who you are? Where's the young boy my brother met?'

'Do you really think I was supposed to see my family murdered and not turn out this way? Every day I miss them, and every day I see their killer in my mind. I won't rest until I've found him. I won't rest until there's no one else that suffers like I did.'

'They turned you into a revenge machine. The perfect candidate, just like Larry. You were exactly what they needed for their organisation.'

'They were exactly what I needed for me. You think you know what to do to save someone like me? You think I even want it any other way? Answers in your book?'

'I'm sorry.'

'Don't be. I don't need your sorrow. Don't need anything from anyone,' Vladimir said as he got up again. He gazed down the street.

Michael got up too. 'I need to help my friends. I need to save them. Please.'

He nodded. 'Your brother... He knew my brother?'

'He did.'

'Simon had a friend called Oli. I met him once.'

'Oliver. That's him.'

'Good kid.'

'He's dead too.'

Vladimir looked him hard in the eyes. 'I'm sorry.'

'I won't tell anyone what I know,' Michael said. 'You have my word.'

'Thank you,' Vladimir replied.

'You never know, maybe one day I'll need to call on you to return the favour.'

'I doubt that.'

'Just help me find my friends then.'

'Yeah,' Vladimir replied before turning away. 'Follow me.'

Chapter 14.7

As promised, Floyd was there waiting for him. He held a green Yo-Yo which he examined as though looking at an alien artefact. He twitched the disc from his hand, but it only returned halfway up the string. He yanked it again, too hard, and it completely uncoiled and span messily. Floyd tossed it away in annoyance and then clocked his old acquaintance.

Henry's eyes followed the toy as it slid across the ground and disappeared beneath one of the many old fairground rides within this strange curiosity barn.

'I got it off one of your young apprentices,' Floyd said. 'Where did you find those two? The funny farm? Are they part of some government scheme to get retards into employment?'

Henry fixed his gaze firmly on Floyd as though his eyes were trying to cut into the monster's brain. 'Where are they?'

'You're so noble, Maristow. Doing this knight in shining armour thing. Kids!' he called out. 'He's come to rescue you, kids! Everything's all right now.' His whole body now jittered around in a bubbling excitement, as though performing again for his ungodly audience, shining like a true master of destruction.

'What did you do to them, Floyd? Why? Why did you take them?'

'You know goddamned well why.'

The old Seraph nodded. 'Okay. Let's put an end to your silly game.'

He reached into his trouser pocket and brought out the counterfeit indigo treasure. He held it up for him. 'Here it is.'

Floyd approached silently, squinting his eyes like a magpie eyeing some silver. He snatched the gemstone from Henry and turned away to examine his acquisition. His body suddenly stiffened up. He stretched out his arm and the necklace dangled from his hand. As though flicking some mud off his fingers, he tossed it to the ground, raised his size 13 Doc Martens boot and slammed it down, instantly crushing the stone to dust.

Floyd laughed. 'The look on your face! I was dying to see that.'

Henry felt like a bear parading through the woods, only for the jaws of a trap to clamp around his leg. 'Where are they?' he repeated.

'What's up?' Floyd asked through his coarse roars of laughter. 'Going to negotiate their release with a Christmas cracker toy? Oh Henry, you useless idiot. They're gone. Both of them. They died horrendously painful deaths, and these were the hands that did the dirty.' Floyd tilted both of his palms towards Henry. 'And they both bit the dust thinking you'd betrayed them. You should know with me I don't do good news.'

Floyd brought out a letter from his pocket and handed it to Henry. 'Here. I saw your letter for Devlan, so I rewrote it. Couldn't believe they bought it.'

After Henry read it he threw it away and said, 'Where's the real one?'

'Devlan's got it, ain't he?'

'So... what then?' Henry stuttered. 'Why?'

'What's this all about, you mean? The Harbour Master came crawling back to me. He finally decided it was time to take his revenge on you. Time for you to atone for your fuck-up.'

'You could have done that years ago.'

'I've been waiting for the call ever since that day at Forseti's. But it seemed *he* wanted you alive all this time. Seemed *he* had a reason for you to live, a purpose you were serving *him*.'

'What?'

'Your search for the Akasa Stone. Must have impressed *him*, because it was enough to convince *him* to leave you to it. But then once you'd found it, your time would be up, and the big guy would come and take it out of your stiff hands. Ha! Said your very salvation was your destruction.'

Henry shook his head.

Floyd carried on, 'Yeah, *he* was never one to get blinded

by revenge, the old gaffer. I don't know, maybe there's a lesson in there for you guys.'

'What changed?'

Floyd grinned. 'Why's *he* suddenly called in the collectors? You're going to love this. You see, Henry, there's no reason for you to carry on searching like a total loser.'

'Why?'

'Because... Because, my old matey... The Harbour Master has found it. And in finally popping you off, *he* said *he* might even give the stone to me.'

'Where? Where the hell did *he* find it?'

'Where did *you* find it, you mean?'

'What...?'

'Your idiot Vladimir. Had it in his hands but surrendered it to The Dim Reaper.'

Henry looked to the small pile of indigo dust at Floyd's feet.

'The Harbour Master swapped it, you plank! Yes, your boy had it. Didn't even put up a fight for you. Right bunch of wet-ends you got there, Henry.'

Henry was silent for a moment. 'You really think *he* would give you the Akasa Stone if you kill me?'

'Trying to talk me out of it, are you? I don't care either way. I've earnt my redemption with *him* now. Floyd and The Harbour Master are back in business. And besides, I have something else which is much more important than the Akasa Stone.'

'What could you possibly have?'

Floyd's rusty breaths became empty of words briefly, his sluggish brain trying to catch up with his express train mouth. 'I suppose I can tell you. I suppose I can let it all out the bag. Waste time explaining our grand scheme while the cavalry has time to turn up and take me out. But wait! No one knows where we are. I have all the time in the world.' He stepped closer to Henry, but already he was becoming coy, the odious arrogance calming into a peculiar earnestness. 'We have knowledge, Maristow. Knowledge.'

It seemed The Harbour Master had reignited the madness in *his* servant once more. Faced with that, Henry was resigned to the fate they'd delivered for him.

'Anyway, Maristow, let's get on with things. See my rides around you?' Floyd raised both of his arms in pride. 'Which one would you like to go on? I shall let you pick your ride to hell.'

'You crazy son of a whore,' Henry said. It was a useless attempt at a parting shot and he realised it before all the words had left his tongue.

Instead, Henry reached into his coat pocket. It was one of Alan Hammond's tenets that members of the Fires should only use guns as an absolute last resort. But right now, Henry knew it was time to bring out the Koch P7. This would serve him much better than any insults he had to fire.

Before he could even aim the gun at him, Floyd brought out his own firearm. With a swift, well-honed skill that was a million times more impressive than spinning Yo-Yos, he fired at Henry and nicked him on the knuckle. He dropped the Koch and fell to his knees as he clutched his hand to contain the blood.

Floyd slowly approached, the gun pointed at Henry's head. 'Now then, Maristow. Time for you to choose your death.'

Chapter 14.8

Vladimir appeared to be in a trance as he led Michael through the saturated town. Occasionally he would pause on a street corner, unsure which way to tread next, but whenever Michael asked him if he knew where he was going, Vladimir would distractedly mutter that yes he did in fact know where he was going thank you very much.

The prying young journalist dared to ask Vladimir some searching questions, but none of them was a key to Vladimir's brain, none could even provoke the slightest outpouring of emotional affliction that might reside behind those black button eyes. By the time they'd crossed Seagate Road and headed past the council offices, Michael gave up on his probing.

Once or twice, when Michael looked close enough, he could have sworn that a faint purple glimmer momentarily swelled within his eyes, like a firework igniting the lonely night sky and then fading away.

He seemed a different person to the one he'd met in *The Cape* that evening. As though he'd been staring at one of those magic eye puzzles, Michael now saw definition in the darkness. Perhaps somewhere within the cosmic wasteland, the young Jeremy still roamed.

***

Beyond that stiff and distant face, Vladimir was thinking back to those days in his other life when he used to be Jeremy, those painful memories that had been stirred up within his impenetrable vault-like mind. He thought in particular of that day when he sat at the television playing with his action figures while Simon was in the next room playing Columbo.

Simon may have made Jeremy anxious, but Vladimir looked back on it differently. His older brother realised he had to do something and so had tried to take action. His nosiness and perseverance had ultimately given Jeremy some invaluable information.

Alan and Henry would have known who'd killed Ulric and Simon. Or rather, they would have known for whom the killer worked. What they were not aware of, what they never could have imagined, was that the young Jeremy knew this as well. They'd probably spared Vladimir the truth, for fear that one day he'd seek revenge against the one who lurked behind the shoulder of this child killer.

But thanks to the feisty Simon who'd rummaged through Ulric Helliwell's desk and found that letter, Jeremy had heard those mysterious three initials with which the letter had ended: T.H.M. Vladimir was nine years old when he'd eventually worked out what those initials stood for. He was far through the metamorphosis by then, his fair hair darkening into the heavy black crop he had on his head now, colourless pigment flooding into his hardened eyes. It turned out he never did get round to advancing on to his brother's comic books.

He would overhear Alan and Henry sometimes talking about a certain person in the underworld, and had come to understand that Henry had in fact worked for *him* at one point. Vladimir eventually put the pieces together one day to work out that T.H.M. stood for a name that, when spoken, usually made people bristle with fear: The Harbour Master.

For Vladimir, the image that forever burned away in his mind was that hourglass of blood constantly telling him that time was slipping away. Vladimir's prime search was always for that man who carried the depiction of that deadly arachnid. Alan had vowed to help Vladimir find this murderer, and until his passing he had done so.

He'd made no promises about searching out The Harbour Master, though. This would be Vladimir's second objective once he'd exterminated the black widow, something he'd kept to himself. Not even Henry or Jake knew about that one.

The Harbour Master was quite a different matter, but Vladimir didn't fear facing *him*, didn't fear the unknown. He would deal with *him* somehow. Whatever *his* feud with Ulric Helliwell was about, Vladimir intended to find out. He was accepting of the fact that, no matter how much he loved his grandfather, there was no telling how much trouble the old boozer had got himself into. Had The Harbour Master arranged for his termination or was the black widow man out proving his own point and got carried away?

It had to have been the case with poor Simon. The feud was nothing to do with him. He was just an innocent bystander dragged into these dreadful circumstances, and Vladimir's heart had pulsed with a vengeance-seeking beat ever since he'd seen Simon on the beach that day... stabbed... killed... murdered.

By that evil bastard. That knife-wielding demon who would discover his remaining life would be more torturous than any punishing realm of fire and damnation. Now Vladimir was the karmic angel, searching for the sinner, waiting and waiting to burn the black widow with all the wrath and all the hate he'd ignited within him.

So was tonight the night? He could feel a buzz in his limbs, his blood simmering under his skin. Deep down, had he perhaps known all along it was Floyd? He was aware he'd been the deranged henchman who used to work for that overlord. Why had Henry insisted it wasn't him? Perhaps because he feared the repercussions, just as he feared Vladimir knowing about The Harbour Master's involvement.

It all made sense, suddenly all fitted into place. Was Floyd old enough? Check. Murderous capabilities? Check. Tattoos? Check. And was Vladimir ready to exact some ferocious revenge? Check.

Vladimir's hand was stinging again so he relaxed his fist. There was more discolouring of thin blood on his white bandages under the fiery glow of the streetlight.

He paused again. Michael stopped beside him and waited for him in noisy silence. Vladimir could practically hear his impatient thoughts.

'How do you know them?' Vladimir asked.

'Larry and Eddie? I live with them.'

'I guess that was awkward then, when...'

'No kidding. You desperadoes are always giving me a headache.'

'What about your other friend? Daniel Adams. Has he stayed away from Stella?'

'I don't think so. Why?'

Vladimir sighed and shook his head.

Down a dirty road ahead was Frawley Holt Industrial Park, a cold and soulless area of town that smelt of burnt vegetables. A car sloshed through the puddles on the main road and sprayed a graceful arc of water over their feet. Michael sighed and wrapped his arms around himself in protest even though they were already soaked from the continuing rainfall.

'How do you know where to go?' Michael asked.

'Do you always ask so many questions?'

'It just looks like you're making up this merry stroll as we go along.'

'You want me to find your friends. I'm doing that.'

'Is there a trail of breadcrumbs I've missed somewhere?'

Vladimir's piercing eyes stared up the road ahead, like a soaring owl that had seen a mouse stir in the fields below.

'He's being held in one of the units.'

'Who? Both of them?'

'Yeah. When we break in there and find them, I want you to take him away. You have to take Larry and Eddie, and get them the hell out of there, then I'll do the tidying up.'

'Okay. You think they'll be... you know... hurt?'

'Yes.'

'Who's holding them?'

'Someone who will soon be very sorry for what he's done.'

'You're going to kill him?'

'Now, look. I don't want any coppers turning up here. You got that?'

'I'm just going in there to get my friends. And you know what? Don't expect them to turn up to work again tomorrow.'

'It was their choice. I didn't make them do anything.'

'Yeah, rubbish.'

'Are we going to stand around arguing? It's your friends in there.'

'You're the one leading the way, Jeremy.'

Vladimir carried on walking. Silently, Michael followed in his pale shadow.

Chapter 14.9

The freak had disappeared again. One moment he was there with those razorblade claws, the next he was flying off into the dark. Jake looked around, searching for the two orbs of smouldering ember, but only the dead eyes of wooden horses stared back at him.

He'd never been so tattered and bloody before in his life. But he was holding up. Just. In the Network, he'd studied under the very best. The Harbour Master had insisted on it.

Teachers who would test your strength and endurance far beyond what a sane mind could cope with. No one in this town was more equipped to handle the monster Devlan.

He felt claws sinking into his neck once more. The gargantuan Power shook him off as he fell to the ground for the hundredth time. Grazes all over. He scampered to his feet just as Devlan was finding his. A quick swipe caught Devlan on the chin. Another right hook got him round the jaw and he stumbled backwards. It was a firm strike; he'd stunned him. Jake should be making the most of his daze but exhaustion was creeping in.

No matter how hard he'd gone at him, Devlan fought back with equal strength. Doubt now seeped into his mind; the fear had done so from the start. But he had to keep going. Jake never lost. Everyone knew it. Why didn't Devlan?

As the warrior raised his fist, he saw the blood dribbling from his knuckles. He swiped at Devlan but the freak deftly rolled out of the way, Jake effecting just a pitiful spray of blood drops that rained over the tarmac. His frustration now releasing in a hoarse growl, Jake reset himself and lunged a desperate boot towards Devlan's crouching frame, but it was sloppy. It wasn't how he'd been taught to attack. How his teachers would be frowning.

Devlan clambered onto the platform of the gallopers. The chomping faces of the garish wooden horses watched as Jake followed him. The beast came at him again and Jake staggered into the central control box. As he fumbled upright, fairy lights flickered on, the horses slowly bobbing up and down, the haunting sound of the band organ filling the air.

I do like to stroll along the Prom! Prom! Prom! Where the brass band plays Tiddley-on-pom-pom!

As the ride built to a spin, Jake threw the monster off him and they both collapsed to the floor beneath the hooves of the springing horses. Jake noticed there was also a bizarre-looking cockerel galloping amongst the troop, yet he was worried for himself for even noticing it. Where was his focus?

'Give up yet?' Devlan panted.

'Still standing, aren't I?' Jake replied as he writhed on the floor.

'You can't kill me, Jake. Just walk away. Save yourself.'

'You're a sick murderer.'

'And what are you? Nothing but a brainless mercenary.'

'People change.'

'You were the same with The Harbour Master as you are with Maristow. Same old dog, just a different kennel.'

'That's not true.'

'Look at you. You're an animal.'

Jake got to his feet again. Devlan did the same.

'Why so mouthy, Devlan? What's up? Nerves?'

And there's lots of girls beside, I should like to be beside. Beside the seaside! Beside the sea.

The rain drummed down on the roof of the gallopers. Devlan's red eyes glared unblinkingly back at him.

'Sensing defeat has finally found you?' Jake asked.

'It's found me before.'

Jake smiled. 'Took a beating, did you?'

'Yeah. So I know you're nowhere close.'

'Well, well. No one ever told me.'

'Because after a hundred years most people are no longer around to tell the story. But yeah, I was once a cocky bastard like you. We had a big problem back then. Something that would make you Fires go screaming home to mummy. But that was a time when even I cared about making a difference. So I faced it, the only one who would.'

'Who?'

'Night-Shines Nick. The one you *think* I am. I tell you if I was, you'd already be dead by now.'

'Apparently he's no longer around to confirm that.'

'For now. Still you idiots mix me up with him. After I tried to help this town but then they...'

'Then they what?'

'Who cares?'

'So you're not indestructible. Just wait till this gets out.'

'Jake, trust me. It won't.'

Devlan sprang forward at the bleeding Power like a deranged jack-in-the-box, his mouth open wide, his claws fanned out. Jake was too slow for him, too relaxed from

Devlan's story-time, and he tumbled into one of the wooden horses, crashing through it, losing his footing on the edge of the platform, falling. On the puddled tarmac, he smacked his head.

The salty rain fell into his eyes and blurred his view of the two demonic eyes that hovered over him. They burned like brake lights on a car. Slowing, stopping, the end of the journey. His vision began to fade.

Chapter 14.10

Zero walked into the cell and flashed his manky brown teeth at Larry as he sat on the floor clutching his blood-stained leg. The gormless thug closed the door and locked it.

'Wanted to put you 'frew the mincer. If I coulda' picked. Your mate was nice.'

Larry stared blankly at nothing, his face frozen hard as stone, his lips pursed as though he was about to break down and cry at any second.

'I see you likes the pies. I realise I can't talk,' Zero patted both his hands against his bulging guts. His blood splattered T-shirt didn't even cover all of his stomach, exposing a line of yellow skin and wispy chest hair beneath it. 'Still, don't mind nailing the whale. You'll do.'

Larry broke his gaze to find Zero smiling vacantly at him. It was less of a smile and more a smirk. The door behind him was shut, not that he could make a run for it with this leg wound.

The slob took two steps closer to Larry and crouched down. Even from a few feet away, Larry could smell his foul breath like a diseased rat had crawled down his throat and died.

'I prefer 'em a lot younger. But yous have to take it while yous got it. So are you going to roll over for mi then, lad? It'll all be over soon. And then you'll get to go.'

'Go to hell.'

Zero grabbed Larry's mouth, but before he could connect

his lips with his, Larry flinched away from him and cowered back against the wall. With a heavy, almost choking wheeze, Zero stood up and kicked Larry's leg. He screamed as he felt that burning pain again.

'Roll over, fatty. It's this or I'll get my hammer and smash your skull in.' He pulled the tool out from his back pocket and pounded it in his thick palm.

'Then kill me.'

'I'd most probably do you, anyway.'

Larry then watched as the blob of walking flesh removed his T-shirt, revealing his flabby man-breasts. His skin was sweaty and flaky and Larry knew he would have to be dead if that thing was going to press his body against his, if the nightmare of his youth was to be repeated.

He began to cry. Lifetimes weren't supposed to have this much horror in them. Larry now knew there was no God.

Zero knelt down beside him and grabbed Larry's belt. He wheezed as he unbuckled his belt. 'There, there. You'll like it really. They all do. Even the little ones.'

As Larry wailed, he didn't hear the door to his cell being kicked in. With his eyes shut tight, he didn't see Zero turn around and receive a sharp blow to his face from the intruder.

Larry screamed harder when he felt him touch his shoulder, shaking him, grabbing his mouth. He knew he'd descended into insanity when he dared to open his eyes and see that Zero had turned into Michael.

'Larry! It's me. You're okay, Larry.'

Larry could not form any words on his tongue. He saw Vladimir behind his flatmate clutching his fist. Vladimir. Now he definitely was all right. They'd come back; they hadn't abandoned them to the horrors of Dark Harbour.

'Take him,' Vladimir said. 'Get him out of here.'

'Larry, where's Eddie?' Michael asked.

But still he couldn't talk. He just looked at the dazed slob of flesh quivering on the ground next to him.

'Larry... I need to find Eddie.'

'He killed him.'

Michael went numb. Larry hobbled to his feet.

'This sick bastard killed him,' he said as he grabbed the

hammer and stood over the thug. He cried, 'This sick motherfucker killed him,' and in between each word he dealt Zero a blow to the head with the hammer. With all of his strength.

Michael went to stop him but froze when Vladimir grabbed his shoulder. He could only watch as Larry took out all of his fury on the murderer beneath him. Larry kept going until he'd cracked the bastard's skull apart and brains splattered all over, until that annoying smirk was wiped from his face because the bastard no longer had a face, and with his head smashed to pieces, Zero was as dead as Eddie but Larry kept hammering away to make sure he was dead and dead again.

When the bloody mallet clanked to the ground, Larry stood silently as he looked down at what he'd done.

'Larry,' Michael said as he gingerly put his hand on his shoulder. 'Let's... Let's go.'

Larry turned to look at his friend. He recognised that compassion on Michael's face, the same one he'd seen that time when he was drunk and singing in the street. The same friend. A different Larry.

'Come on, Diamond.'

Larry followed him. Michael paused when he reached the door and turned back to the silent vigilante.

'Are you coming?'

'No. Now I have to find my friend.'

'Will you be okay?'

'Yes. Go.'

Supporting the lame Larry over his shoulder, Michael headed out of there, back to the refreshing world of normality outside. Vladimir, however, had more work to do. Somewhere in the warehouse there was another demon that needed to be destroyed.

Chapter 14.11

Shooting Henry dead apparently wasn't part of Floyd's plan.

No, the sicko wanted to strap him into one of his old amusement rides, some mini roller coaster. But Henry wasn't going to go down easily. He fended him off as much as he could despite the welling pain in his chest.

It felt like an elephant was standing on him, and Henry seemed to remember hearing that comparison before. He'd read it in a magazine, or maybe some doctor was talking about it on breakfast television one morning. It was the sign of a heart attack.

Floyd clobbered him with the butt of his Glock. 'Get on the ride, you arse.'

'Get lost,' Henry wheezed.

The pain swelled even more. Not just an elephant. Now it was an entire building. Henry smiled at Floyd, knowing the cardiac arrest would thwart his silly final plans.

'My boys... they will come for you. They'll come...' he said and then collapsed to his back.

Floyd kicked his legs. 'Get up! You useless idiot!'

But Henry was dead.

***

Just as Floyd was about to shoot a petulant bullet at Henry's body, he caught a black shape in the corner of his eye.

'Too late, Vladimir. You're...'

'Drop the gun,' Vladimir ordered.

An impish grin formed on the agent of destruction's face. 'Just you, is it?'

'I said put the gun down.'

'Well, well. I guess I have another Fire to put out tonight.' He raised his gun.

Vladimir stood like an angelic statue as Floyd fired three bullets at him. And then three more. And then the rest of the bullets in the clip.

At Vladimir's feet, rooted to the ground as firmly as ever, was Henry's Koch. He picked it up and pointed it at Floyd.

Confused, Floyd reached into his pocket and brought out his other Glock. He fired more bullets, but again they had no effect.

'Zero!' he cried as he started receding.

Vladimir aimed his gun at him. In all of his work as an Angel of Karma, he had never before shot at anyone. He could see the rotten, black soul before him, malignant energies swarming in his aura like flies, and yet strangely it felt like he was holding a gun to himself. He lowered the muzzle and shot Floyd in the kneecap. It was as though the bullet had seared through his own soul.

Floyd toppled over. He giggled through his groans of pain like a schoolboy whose playground stunt had gone wrong. Slowly he dragged himself away, leaving a wet smear of blood over the concrete floor.

With the demon dealt with, Vladimir knelt beside his master and saw the nothingness in his eyes. Henry's face was now the same colour as his slate suit. He'd seen that stagnant complexion before on his brother and grandfather, like some prosthetic model in a Hollywood studio that could never fully look like a human being without having an aura. Without having a soul. But, again, this was no movie.

Vladimir's hands curled round into fists, and as he was about to hammer them into the concrete, he thought about his bandaged left hand and the nasty pain that would cause.

There was nothing to do with the anger. Another loved one taken away from him. He would not accept it.

And he didn't have to.

Not with the powers he had. The special gift that had been given to him. The gift that had unlocked the door.

Vladimir placed one hand over Henry's chest and another over his forehead. His life-force had just left him and so he only had to reach into that infinity and draw him back, somehow channel those vibrations back into this realm.

The violet glow exploded in his eyes, swirling around like spirits in the ether, every atom in the universe within his perceptions. It was as though every soul he'd ever known was sweeping through him.

His hands suddenly felt warm, as though he were holding them over a flame. Vladimir saw the colour filling Henry's eyes again, felt the beat under his palm. A sudden gasp of air passed through the old Seraph's lips and

Vladimir gasped in exhaustion.

'Vladimir...' Henry murmured.

'It's okay now.'

'I saw lights... colours.'

'What the hell?' Floyd boomed.

Gathering his breath, the karmic angel rose and turned to see that Floyd had propped himself up. His grin had transformed into a hateful sneer.

'What the hell happened?' Floyd demanded.

'You search for enlightenment, Floyd?' Vladimir asked him as he floated over.

'He was dead.'

'Why were you looking for the Akasa Stone? Why? Someone like *you*?'

'To destroy everyone's dream. Make them think there's no hope in this world. It's the will of God.'

'So it's the will of God that I'm going to shoot you,' Vladimir said as he raised the gun.

'Go on then.'

He paused. 'Questions first, Floyd.'

'Want to find out if I've got the Akasa Stone, do you? It's not here. So go ahead and shoot me. Either way, you lost. The Harbour Master has it. Took it off *you*, you dipshit.'

'That what *he* told you?'

'*He* wouldn't lie to me.'

Vladimir smiled then knelt down beside him. He shook his head. '*He* is lying to you.'

He undid the top buttons of his black shirt. Pulling the fabric away he revealed a violet gemstone hanging from a cord of wooden beads.

'You bastard,' Floyd hissed.

Vladimir stood, holding the gun at Floyd's face. It was time to kill him, time to send this black soul into oblivion. He knew for certain the monster had murdered Eddie, and just what other murders was he responsible for? Yet somehow Vladimir still couldn't make his finger pull back that trigger. Not even when Floyd began laughing.

'Oh, you hero. Get this, everyone! Vladimir...' But the agent of destruction never finished his sentence.

Floyd's left eye exploded in a mush of blood as the bullet

tore into it. The monster collapsed limply to the ground. Extinguished.

Vladimir didn't realise his gun had fired, but then noticed Henry standing behind him with a Glock in hand.

'I was going to do it.'

'Yeah,' Henry replied, his eyes immediately focussing on the gemstone around Vladimir's neck. For a long moment silence hung in the air. 'You had it all this time?'

'I just needed another second.'

'How long?'

Vladimir turned back to Floyd's body and now shot him. 'See? I can do it.' Another hollow stillness followed the sound of the gunshot, and Vladimir watched a trickle of blood spreading from Floyd's leg.

It was time to reveal the truth about this psycho, to understand his crimes fully. Vladimir crept up to the corpse, kneeled down beside it and shoved it over so that Floyd now lay face down against the concrete.

With his back to Henry, Vladimir could not see the expression on his face, just heard the sigh.

'You never trusted me, did you?' Henry said. 'Why didn't you believe me?'

'Need to see for my own eyes,' Vladimir replied as he held his knife firmly in his hand. He slid the blade underneath the collar of the trench coat, and like he was hacking through the blubber of a whale, he ran it along the material. In one smooth motion he'd made the necessary rent; he was an expert at this now.

Placing his knife down, he grabbed the torn clothing and peeled it back to reveal the naked flesh of Floyd's back.

He slumped backwards. That crushing feeling. Not even a thousand mirrors to smash would offer him release from this frustration.

'I tried to help you, Vladimir. Tried to guide you. Why did you never return the favour with my search?'

'You know what they say. If you find it, don't tell anyone.'

'How long have you had it? Can you tell me that?'

'I've owned it since I was a teenager.'

'How in God's name did you get it?'

That was another secret hidden behind those black button eyes.

'I don't...' Henry said, shaking his head as he looked at the Akasa Stone. 'You had it. All this bloody time.'

'Yes. It's what saved me, and it's what enabled me to save your life too just now, so save the indignation.'

'You lied to me, all this time. How could you do this to me?'

'Henry...'

'You betrayed me. I can't believe you betrayed me!'

'I did what I had to do. Just leave me alone.'

With that he got to his feet and stormed away. He heard Henry calling after him but nothing would stop him now.

Chapter 14.12

The defeated Power lay in a puddle of blood and rain, motionless, like a whale washed up on the shore. The Goliath slain by a greater power. Devlan noticed he was still breathing, so he put one of his claws to Jake's throat. One effortless twitch would make a deep incision.

The Adam's apple was right between his fingertips and his claws sliced into the skin like a carving knife sinking into the Sunday roast. Once he nipped open the artery, the blood would slowly pour out of him, washing away with the rainwater, his life-force draining into the sewers.

It felt cowardly to kill a man like this, but Devlan knew how to look after himself. To survive in this town, he'd had to be ruthless. He'd learnt about the cold spirit of humanity long ago, people's prejudices thrown in his face all the time, like splinters of glass injected into his hardened heart. When they looked at Devlan, all they saw was a wretched devil, someone who should belong in a horror film.

Something caught his eye: a shard of wood from the galloping horse. Devlan's shoulders sagged. This was an antique, an 1890s classic, built by the renowned fairground ride manufacturer Savages. He was well versed with its pulleys and pinions gears, having maintained the ride's smooth operation over the years, making sure it worked each summer for the tourists that flocked to the seaside.

Looking at the fragments scattered across the ground, he could see this would be some repair job, not that he'd get a call from Floyd in the morning asking him to come patch it up.

Poor Perrin. That was the identity of the broken horse, its name inscribed down the side of its mane.

Devlan got to his feet and approached the carousel. Hopping back onto the moving platform, he went over to the control chamber that he and Jake had smashed into earlier. That didn't look too bad. At least all Perrin's friends continued to bob up and down rhythmically to the music that cheerfully thumped and tinged.

A strange reverie suddenly swept through him like a ghostly breath in a still room. He imagined what it must have been like if he'd had a normal childhood, if his mother had taken him to the seaside amusements like all the other kids. He wondered what it would have been like to sit on this ride and go round and round. If only his soul had landed in a different life instead of this aberrant mess. If only he had a *normal* soul.

It was such a peculiar feeling, one that soon turned to sadness. He reached forward and pressed some buttons, killing the ride and the band organ. Just as the music stopped and the carousel slowed, he felt something grip around his neck.

Something very strong.

Devlan slashed a claw behind himself but only swiped at thin air. Whatever was holding him was just slightly out of reach. As the sides of his windpipe pressed against each other, and as he stumbled between the twisted poles of barley, he realised that, incredulously, there was no way he could shift this person.

Peering back over the tarmac, he saw that Jake was no longer lying there. The bastard. How had he woken up so quickly? Devlan cursed himself for not anticipating it. He should have kept an eye on him, especially as he'd been upwind.

He couldn't speak, couldn't say the words to surrender.

Can't breathe...

Devlan jerked his body around, but Jake would not budge.

What's he doing? Doesn't he know when a fight is over?

Flashes of Devlan's long life appeared in his mind. Endless days of cold and rain. Stalking rabbits in the woods for food. The shaky whispers under the breaths of strangers.

What is that freak? What in God's name is he?

They'd known that Devlan had never fitted in anywhere. They'd known he'd never woken up on Christmas Day to find a stocking full of presents. He'd never had any happy birthdays, no telegram from the King when he'd turned a hundred, no token of the remotest sign of affection from anyone.

And now there's not even any air.

Just the cold horrors that inhabited his mind like flies crawling over a carcass. In a world where love showered down like raindrops but drained away into the gutters.

As Jake pressed even harder against his neck, Devlan could feel his mouth smiling. It was a strange possibility he hadn't hated life as much as he'd thought.

The glow of his eyes began to fade. There was nothing he could do, and so his limbs went limp. Jake held him for a few more seconds before releasing his iron grip, and Devlan's body collapsed to the ground like a sack of concrete.

Chapter 14.13

Henry stuffed his handkerchief over his mouth. Flesh still dribbled out of the other end of the mincing machine, a splattering of blood beneath. He knew that Floyd had put at least one of the two lads through it, but it was impossible to tell which one.

He approached the cell, the door to which hung on a single hinge. In the corner of the room was a dead dog with numerous gunshot wounds, and next to him was some guy who was also clearly dead as his head was too bashed in for Henry to even recognise him. Seeing as Vladimir had bottled it when it came to shooting Floyd, he figured this wasn't his work.

Had the other Guardian escaped? If only he could talk to Vladimir and debrief him. He thought about phoning him, but then smiled wryly to himself when he remembered that it was National Nobody Pick The Fucking Phone Up Day.

At least Jake had been dependable and as solid as ever. Good old Jake. Worry filled his mind about how his mission might be going, remembering he'd sent him to take care of Devlan.

He grabbed his phone and called him, slowly walking back towards the main warehouse, away from the stench of raw death. His mouth got drier as the phone continued to ring. Maybe it was a stupid decision sending them after that creature. What had he been thinking?

The call connected.

'Hey, Henry.'

'Jake. How's it gone?'

'All sorted, mate.'

Henry went silent for a moment. He lowered his eyes to the corpse at his feet.

'How about you?' Jake asked.

'Floyd's dead,' he replied, prodding him with his toes. 'Not sure about Eddie and Larry. One of them was killed. I think we got the other one out.'

'You think?'

'Vladimir finally turned up. It appears he rescued him, before he then came to get me.'

'Good man. So where is he?'

'I... I don't know.'

'Is he okay?'

'I hope so,' Henry said as he crouched down to inspect the corpse. 'We argued.'

'He gets wound up sometimes. Always calms down again.'

'So you really... You really got Devlan?'

'That's what we wanted, wasn't it?'

'He's dead?'

'He'd been working with Floyd. Been working for him for ages. Peas in a pod.'

Henry peered around the warehouse at all the old rides: the roller coaster with the tunnel that was clearly too low, the pirate ship with the carpet of sharp spikes beneath it. It was an evil hellhole, and Henry knew that Floyd couldn't have made this place on his own. Devlan was the mechanic.

'Good work, Jake.'

'Want to meet back at HQ?'

'Yes, as soon as I've finished here,' Henry replied. Immediately he heard some distant sirens. 'Actually, that'll be sooner rather than later. The police are coming.'

'You call them?'

'No. But I think I know who did.'

'Who?'

Henry didn't answer as he continued to put the pieces together in his mind.

'Okay, look, I'm going to hang up. I'll see you back at *Clarence*.'

'Okay, Henry.'

'Wait, what about Clint? Is he still with you?'

'Yeah, he's here. I think he's going to make it.'

'Great. Speak to you later, Jake.'

He hung up. The police cars were already right outside the warehouse.

He should have started running, but instead he knelt beside Floyd's body sprawled over the cold concrete. His trench coat was open and he spotted a piece of paper sticking from the inside pocket. He took it out, the red wax blob immediately catching his eye.

Idly rubbing the Halo of Fires seal with his thumb as though he were feeling dried blood, all he could say to himself was, 'Shit.'

***

Clint continued to hold his head, propped against the helter-skelter. Jake sat next to him as he checked his own cuts and bruises. It felt like a maniac had gone at him with a

Stanley knife. He took a deep drag on the cigarette, and then offered it to Clint.

'You're a silly tosser,' Jake said. 'Getting yourself knocked out while he goes all Freddy Krueger on me.'

'Thanks. I could have been dead here.' Clint took the cigarette and inhaled.

'Well, what? You'd want me to be arranging your funeral instead?'

'Took your sweet time, didn't you?'

'Hard work when everyone else is having forty friggin' winks.'

Clint shook his head. 'Tosser.'

'You the tosser.'

'Want a drink?'

'Right behind ya. Come on,' Jake said as he got to his feet, flicking the cigarette away. 'Think we've earnt it.' He pulled Clint up.

'Before we go, I want to see your work. I have to see this for my own eyes.'

'Sure.'

'And I'll be taking a picture on my phone. I remember that time you threw a one-eighty but, lo-and-behold, no one was actually around to confirm it.'

'He's right over there on the merry-go-round.'

Clint shuffled over there. He still looked dizzy, so Jake hovered around him in case he needed a prop.

'You were just going to leave him there? Let some poor kid find him when he gets on one of the horses tomorrow morning?'

'No, I was going to take him to a bloody taxidermist.'

'You should put his head on a plaque. Hang him in your living-room. That would be different. Make a lovely talking point for you and the ladies.'

'Yeah, because I take them home to *talk* to them.'

'Don't kid me, Jake. I bet all you ever yap about is Oprah's book club and what new shoes you just bought.'

'How hard did Devlan hit your head?'

They arrived at the carousel and stepped up onto the platform of speared horses.

'I think the real question is,' Clint began, 'how hard did

312

he hit yours?'

Clint could see the evidence of a violent scuffle, but nowhere amongst the wreckage could he find Devlan's body.

Part 15: Endings

Chapter 15.1

In Daedalus Fields, amongst the arching willows and the empty cider cans, is a boulder the size of a car. Now a place for young lovers to etch romantic proclamations of their everlasting conjugations, the rock is the only thing that remains of Dark Harbour castle, which was demolished during the Elizabethan age, the stone being used to build the town hall and other such buildings.

Samuel Allington sat huddled against the rock, waiting for The Reaper to arrive. He clutched the leather briefcase, partly because it offered him a small degree of protection from the cool midnight breeze, but mostly because it was filled with fifty thousand in notes.

It had taken him longer than expected to get to this point, but in a matter of minutes they would confirm the deal. Stella had moved out. He'd assumed she'd move in with that student, but that hadn't happened, at least not yet.

She'd been continuing to rendezvous with the tosser, of course. Having continually tracked them, Samuel spied on the joyous couple as they'd walked down the river. He saw him hold her hand. And kiss her. She was evidently in such awe of her new toy as she gazed into his eyes, laughing at all his jokes, twiddling her hair.

The day after that riverbank stroll, he'd seen her go to the student's flat to deliver a letter. Samuel noticed it protruding from the letterbox, and so after she'd left, wearing his black beanie hat, he crept up to the door and snatched it. Once he'd read it, he knew there was no way she would ever come back to him.

The slut. That's all that women were. How could she be engaged to him one moment then frolicking around with some random student the next? How could she suddenly be *in love* with him?

That had always astounded him with women, how they never mourned the death of their romances. They just jumped into bed with the next guy and everything was like an episode of goddamn *Hollyoaks*. They didn't give a shit about the one they left behind and the devastation they caused him.

That's why Samuel had to seek this other revenge, this *better* revenge. The ever-dependable Fires had seen to it the first time, but unfortunately that wasn't enough. After going back through his father's contacts book, he'd found The Reaper's number. As he'd searched the office, he'd also looked to see if his father had a gun. Maybe he could do the job himself.

It was better in the hands of a professional, someone who wouldn't lose their nerve. The Reaper would exact such a delicious revenge, something that would scream in her face of the terribly cruel thing she'd done. She'd be sorry then, the bitch.

'Do I find your name on here, anywhere?' came a grating voice. 'Sam and Stella in the tree, K-I-S-S-I-N-G.'

A short man with a lopsided trilby resting effortlessly on his head walked around the rock. Duffy went on in his dry tone, 'And they say that once you write your names on here, your love will last forever.'

Samuel shook his head. 'And I say you write your name on a ruin, you're asking for it.'

'My, oh my,' The Reaper said as he put a hand on his hip and leaned against the boulder. 'What an evil thing is love. All those broken hearts. All those unplanned conceptions. All those Westlife records. What a bane it is.'

Samuel looked away from the psychopathic motormouth as he suddenly thought about their song. *With or Without You* had been playing on the jukebox when she'd walked into the room, a haunting tune to mark her entrance, as though the angels had sent her to him.

And right then their eyes had met for the very first time.

And instantly Samuel had known he was in love.

'I don't suppose *you* ever fell in love,' the young man said.

'Who says? You should hear my verses. I like to describe

my amorous liaisons. There once was a girl from Nantucket, who had a twat like a...'

'No thanks.'

Duffy shifted off the rock in faux offence. 'De-diddly dee, de-diddly dee,' he muttered, trying to bait him, but Samuel was silent. 'Even a horse, she would screw it. I'm still working on it. Got some lines missing.'

'It's beautiful. How about she met The Reaper, and he had a small peeper?'

Duffy slowly cocked his head. As his eyebrows were halfway up his forehead, Samuel figured he was carrying on with his act, but then the assassin reached into his jacket pocket and whipped out his SIG Mosquito.

'Hey,' Samuel cried. 'Calm the hell down.'

Duffy laughed. 'Oh wait. Is that why she left you? Always the same. Women are such shallow creatures.'

'Like you'd know,' Samuel muttered to himself, burying his head in his folded arms.

Duffy put the gun away. 'Anyway, I guess the fact you brought the dinero means you want to go through with this.'

'He's not so dim after all.'

'Want to open that up for me?'

Samuel unlocked the briefcase. The assassin peered inside and picked up a wad.

'Fifty... One hundred... One hundred and fifty...' he said in a slow, childlike voice.

'Fifty percent now. I'll get the rest for when you do it. Are you listening, dipshit?'

'Two hundred. Two hundred and fifty...'

'What, you think I'm trying to rip you off?'

'This will go a lot quicker if you'll stop interrupting me. Where was I? Two hundred and fifty... Three hundred...'

Samuel rolled his eyes. 'Jesus.'

Duffy put the wad back in the case and slammed it shut. 'You got the directions for me, Romeo?'

He explained it all to him precisely, where and when and how he wanted it doing. He even knew what clothes he would be wearing. The Reaper sat looking at him like a nodding dog and Samuel couldn't help but wonder if he was taking it all in or if his mind was composing more crude limericks.

'That sounds agreeable, my friend. Drummond Road is quiet that time of night. I'll be parked up early.'

'And remember,' Samuel added, 'no matter how much he pleads with you to spare his life, no matter what he says, you shoot him. You got it?'

'I hear ya. Jees, you ever known me to miss? You coming to watch this?'

'Yeah, I'll be there.'

'Good. I'll get the other fifty then.'

'You will.'

With that, the love-troubled man stood and ambled his way through the willows away from the romantic ruin, melting into the night.

Chapter 15.2

Larry hardly said a word on the train journey back home. He sat opposite Danny and Michael, holding the order of service, his crutch rattling against the armrest. Three weeks on and he was still severely shell-shocked. His leg burned with pain every time he put any pressure on it.

'You don't have to move out, you know,' Michael said. 'We don't mind you staying. We'd prefer you to stay.'

Larry looked up briefly, before his eyes fell back to the picture of Eddie on the front of the order of service. 'No, thanks.'

After he'd read the eulogy in a thick voice, and as they'd sung *Abide With Me*, Larry reflected on the events in that warehouse and realised that although he'd escaped the horror of that mincer, the experience had completely mangled him up on some other level. Having been away since that night, he intended to find answers now he was back in town.

'Come on, Diamond,' Danny chipped in. 'Where are you going to go?'

The train was slowing as Larry glanced out of the

window and saw the Dark Harbour sign. 'It's sorted,' he said as he propped himself up.

He manoeuvred into the aisle as the other passengers began to get out of their seats.

'What about your things? Your DVDs? You're going to lug all of them out of the flat?' Michael asked.

'I'll be back later in the week.'

'Okay.' Michael looked like he was running out of things to say. 'Do you want to play pool on Friday?'

'Yeah,' Larry said in such a weak way that he may as well have said no. The passengers began bustling up to him so he hobbled down the gangway.

'We'll see you later then.'

'Take care, Larry,' Danny added.

'See you later.'

***

He was gone. Swallowed by the crowds. Just another stranger again.

Once the passengers had trickled clear, Danny and Michael made their way onto the platform. It was a comfortably warm day here, as it had been in Eddie's hometown. The sun glistened down, and the air smelt rich with summer. Another year of college would soon be over and the town would be alive again in the merry carnival of seaside holidaying. More moving on.

Danny loosened his black tie. 'Just you and me again. We're not really going to see him any more, are we?'

Michael knew exactly what he meant, but he didn't want to agree. He'd had that feeling before, when friends move on. One day that connection would be there, that interchange of energy that happens as each person gives to the other, learns from the other, and then one day it's all over. Suddenly the friendship is dead, served its purpose. The ink run dry and the paper filled.

Thinking it over, Michael realised he'd spent too many occasions squabbling with Larry, telling him to tidy up or to help him out round the house. Is that what you would really call a friendship? Even so, Michael was already beginning to miss him.

'They always come back,' he muttered.

***

The café was almost empty when the wounded Guardian hobbled in. The only customer was some guy in the corner buried in the local newspaper, the front-page headline: 'Youth Attacks Man With Cricket Bat'. Behind the counter, Nigel refilled the sugar pots. It seemed it was a slow Friday afternoon at *The Cheshire Cat*.

Larry delicately propped himself on a stool and Nigel began pouring him a drink. He needed something to revive him after the day he'd had. What better than a cup of tea? It was all the Fires seemed to do when they were sitting around. The tea was too hot to drink, but it seemed he would have to wait.

'How did it go?'

'Just like a memorial service,' Larry said bleakly.

'You know,' Nigel began in his customer chit-chat voice, 'I heard that a couple of hundred years ago there became this fashion amongst the rich that they wanted their bodies to be broken up. All cut into pieces. They believed it helped in the release of their soul from their body.'

'I guess they did that to them after they died.'

Nigel nodded. 'Souls know when they want to go. When their time is up, there's nothing we can do about it.'

'Is that right?'

'So Vladimir says. He's always going on about such things.'

Larry hadn't seen or heard from Vladimir since his rescue. Precisely what had happened to him next, nobody really knew. Nobody except Henry, that was. All they knew was that Floyd, the author of that counterfeit letter, had been killed.

He'd expected the police to come knocking on his door, sensational headlines in the *Harbour Gazette* for weeks, Hollywood on the phone wanting to buy his story.

But so far there'd been nothing. What a mystifying town this was.

Perhaps Henry had pulled his strings to make it all quieten down. Or perhaps it was the work of someone else.

'Where is Vladimir?' Larry asked.

'You'll one day learn that time is better spent not trying to solve that mystery,' the man behind the newspaper said. Larry turned round to see its reader as the paper folded down.

'Hello Henry,' he replied, his eyebrows arched. 'So you don't know?'

'I'm sure he's fine,' the Seraph said as he rose and made his way over to him. There seemed to be a stronger beat in his gait, a renewed focus in his demeanour. The windows had all been opened and an invigorating breeze of air had freshened his inner palace. Perching next to him, he said, 'Vladimir can look after himself. That's exactly what we taught him to do.'

'This is the longest he's gone missing,' Nigel said.

'He's been missing all his life. But he'll return to us. He knows nothing else.'

'What happened, Henry?' Nigel went on. 'Why do I get the impression there's more to it than you're letting on?'

Henry was silent for a few moments and then his speech took a thick, whispery tone, 'That's between me and Vladimir. And always will be.'

'You got him though, didn't you?' Larry asked. 'That bastard Des Floyd. You took him out.'

'And out of that box come a whole load of other evils. One evil in particular you can't yet comprehend. Floyd didn't become who he was on his own, Lawrence. He had a superior, a man they call The Harbour Master.'

'Who's The Harbour Master?'

Instead of answering, he slapped down the *Harbour Gazette* on the counter. For a moment, Larry wondered if Henry had been scanning through the paper to see if there was any mention about what had happened. That was when he noticed a small headline on the page folded open: 'Arsonists To Blame For Warehouse Blaze'.

Larry grabbed the paper and skimmed the article. The

two paragraphs mentioned how an important local figure, Des Floyd, had died trying to put out the fire in his warehouse. A private collection of antique fairground rides he'd passionately preserved had been destroyed.

'Arson? But the police got there. Michael told me he called them. How could it then burst into flames?' Before Larry could get the question out, he realised he knew the answer. Already he was comprehending The Harbour Master's influence in this town.

Henry nodded as he saw the realisation on his face. 'All the other junk is there. The drunken fights, the domestic disputes, the underage sex. *He*'s already got *his* hopeless town without people being aware of *his* true shadows.

'So what hope is there for us, anyway? At what point do we tire of praying for a better world that never comes? I fear that hope alone is useless when it comes to the malevolent forces of The Harbour Master. I've looked into *his* eyes. I know that Floyd was an amateur in comparison. I need warriors, Lawrence. Because we have an even greater darkness to fight now. And trust me, it's coming.'

Larry took a sip of tea. It was cool enough to drink, but it still zinged his tongue. It tasted rich, almost metallic.

'White Pearl. Plucked in the fields of Tibet, five-thousand feet above sea level, only when there is a full moon.'

Larry frowned.

'The tea. They all drink it,' Henry explained.

'You make them drink it,' Nigel muttered.

'This was the same one we drank in your office.'

Henry nodded. 'Special import. We have something else for you.'

Nigel reached under the counter and brought out a small black box with a gold trim. It was an oblong shape, about the length of a shoe. He slid it towards Larry.

'Open that box and it all changes.'

'What'll happen?'

'You will be a Dominion. You'll be under the command and guidance of Jake who will train you for a higher level. One day you may make a Power. That's if you open it.'

'What's in there?' Larry asked as he eyed it up.

'The future. You can leave it if you want, finish your tea, go home to your Xbox, watch *Coronation Street* and float the mainstream. You'll perhaps stay awake at night wondering if there's more to life, but you'll be safe. Or you can join us.'

'PlayStation. Not an Xbox.'

'It's entirely up to you, Lawrence.'

'Dominion,' Larry said, trying the word on his tongue.

Henry stood as he put on his bowler hat. As ever, he was dressed as though he was on his way to something important. Enjoying a night at the opera or policing the criminal underworld, both were things that the Seraph of the Fires would be found doing.

Larry took hold of the box and flipped it open. Inside was a gleaming dagger and a leather scabbard. On the handle of the knife was an inscription that read: 'Ishim'.

'Work starts at ten o'clock tonight. Jake will be waiting for you in the market square with Clint. There will be wrongs to right, a crumbling world to smack in the face, to remind about virtues and integrity. We'll do our bit, and we'll make them aware they were on the wrong path. And you? You'll never see an episode of *Coronation Street* ever again.'

Henry whistled as he strolled towards the door. Two guys in suits were approaching the café, so he held the door open for them. After bidding them a good afternoon, he continued down the street to his next appointment.

Nigel discretely closed the box to Larry's dagger as he greeted the two men. They were office workers, probably on a late lunch. They continued to talk in a hushed tone to each other, but Larry could hear every word.

One of them talked about some girl he was screwing, and it was evident he was too proud of his conquest to care if anyone might overhear him. The other one, who was grinning like a clown, then asked him if he suspected his wife knew anything about it.

Larry sipped at his White Pearl tea and he felt strong. In fact, he no longer felt any pain in his knee at all. Right now, he could probably stand up on his own and run a marathon.

This was good. It felt like he would be a busy man.

Part 16: The Lost Soulmates

Chapter 16.1

Danny started the day believing it might be the last day he would ever see. There was no sunlight streaming into his room when he woke up; the coastal skies were typically congested with gloomy grey clouds, the colour of cadavers, the same colour as his morning face.

He mostly went about his day as normal: the Friday morning meeting with his tutor to discuss the essay he would never live to finish, lunch in the canteen with Michael, and then an afternoon in the library surfing the internet. He looked mainly at viral video sites. Watching some lunatic skateboard across apartment blocks was something he had to see to make his life complete.

What was the point of doing any work, anyway? He figured he should take it easy with the little time he had left, savouring every breath of air as though it may be his last, waiting for the bullets to tear into his heart at any second. He knew it would come after what he had planned this evening.

Danny hadn't thought beyond this day at all. His mind was only on this one occasion and anything that followed was like the month of January, the void that followed Christmas. This would be the final scene, the end of the story, nothing but rolling credits to follow. Danny wouldn't be back for the sequel because he'd been written out.

But supposing Samuel didn't really have the guts to murder him and it was all just a hollow threat, he still had difficulties projecting his mind forward into the future. Where would Danny and Stella go after this evening? There just didn't seem to be anything there at all. Only that ominous void.

Once he'd had enough of viewing pictures of the crazy things pet owners put on their cats, he stuffed all his books into his bag, the ones he'd had out to make it *look* like he was doing some work, and put on his coat. He then caught the next bus home.

Michael was already back, sitting at the kitchen table, his eyes magnetised to a letter. It seemed not even an earthquake would shake his concentration from it.

For a moment, it was as though he was looking at himself reading one of Stella's letters, unaware of anything else in the universe. Despite these fleeting signs of emotion Danny saw in him, Michael remained his level-headed self most of the time. He never appeared consumed by obsession, haunted by the incessant melodies of an internal goblin as Danny was. How did he do it?

Danny glanced at the cupboard drawer, the one that contained the cutlery. 'How's Faridah?' he asked.

Michael looked momentarily startled as he tore himself away from her words. 'Oh hello. She's good. She's talking about visiting this summer.'

'About time.'

Danny emptied the kettle and refilled it, his eye still on the silver drawer handle. Maybe he would have a chance against Samuel's thugs? Perhaps if he was to take a knife with him? 'I put up an ad in the student union today.'

'Good idea. Heard from Larry yet?'

'No. He still hasn't been to get his stuff.'

Michael put the letter down. 'I know. Yes, please,' he said as he saw Danny switching on the kettle.

'Do you think we should phone him?' Danny asked.

The thought registered on Michael's face, but he didn't have an answer to give. Danny should have known better than to present him with a decision when he had other things on his mind.

'Well, pour the tea when it's done. I have to go get ready,' Danny said as he left the room.

Upstairs he showered then sprayed on some aftershave, the one Stella had remarked on one time. He dressed in his favourite clothes: a white shirt with black buttons, blue jeans. Stuff that was easy to remove. This morning he'd made sure they were fresh to put on for tonight.

As he faced the mirror, he felt his appearance looked its

best. He had to reflect her awesome yin with whatever yang he had. He didn't quite have the David Beckham figure and the George Clooney charisma that Samuel had, but obviously Stella responded to some other quality in him.

He didn't know what it was, but just the fact she'd seen something in him made him feel incredibly special. He breathed in assuredly and stared at his reflection in the mirror. If Samuel was to exact his revenge on this very night, then Danny was certainly well presented for when he would go up to heaven, or for when he'd transform into a ghost. That was unless they were killed during the act. Would he just be a naked ghost for the rest of eternity then? If he made neither of these journeys in the afterlife, then at least he would look good in the morgue.

Michael was still rooted in the kitchen when he returned downstairs. He gave up on the knife idea. It was a straw-clutcher, anyway.

'You're seeing her again this evening,' Michael said, too much as a statement to be a question.

'I am.'

'Think this is a good idea?'

'She left Sam. Why shouldn't we be together?'

'He's resigned to losing her? Is that what you'd do? Sit back and let her go?'

'It's over between them. He knows it.'

'What's he going to do to you next, mate? Have you seen him any more?'

'No. I haven't,' he said, but it was a complete lie. Samuel's tormented face had haunted him everywhere. In crowds of strangers, his reflection in shop windows, lurking in the corner of his mind with that stare of death that conveyed his destructive intentions.

Despite this looming threat, he knew there was nothing he could do about it. He knew the depth of his feelings he had for Stella, could feel the bind his soul had with hers like a pining ache in his chest. He would die *without* her.

He wasn't going to let fear dictate this. If death resulted from his relationship with her, then so be it. Maybe he'd accept that his soul had fulfilled its purpose and melded with hers, releasing itself into the eternity. Perhaps Stella knew it was fate that something destined them to come together like this.

'What if he comes for you again?' Michael asked.

Danny sighed dismissively. 'What if this was you and Faridah? What would you do?'

Michael's eyes lowered to his letter and he drummed his fingers over it. The kettle had boiled some time ago, and the water was now going cold. Danny stepped towards the door.

'See you later, Danny. Take care.'

Danny paused and just gave a vague nod in reply. He didn't want to say any more and so he left, walking out into the fading light.

Chapter 16.2

He beamed a smile as she sat next to him at the bar. Stella smiled back. No words passed through their lips for a few minutes; no words needed to.

That internal goblin resumed playing that sweet, heavenly music he'd started on the beach. Danny would now experience the rest of that tune. He no longer despised that creature within, for it was his ever-persistent playing that had led him to her, had led him here. The goblin was now his friend.

She really was the most beautiful person in the world, flawless. Her perfectly proportioned cheeks that no geek could outshine with some computer-generated imagery, her flowing eyebrows that curled like waves above her violaceous eyes. Oh those eyes!

Danny ran his fingertips up the naked flesh of her arm as she delicately picked up her glass. Her skin was so deliciously creamy and Danny wanted to run his palms over her. All over. And he knew he would do so later.

'Do you still want to know the truth about us, my lost one?' she asked as she sipped her vodka and lemonade.

'I do.'

'Course you do. Here we are, two ships that have been

floating along the lonely waves, and here we meet.'

'Feels like I've been sailing a long time.'

'I know you have, Danny. I sense your thirst. I want to feel it, feel it completely.'

Danny's words spilled from him like seeds from a dandelion head, teased out by her electrifying presence. 'Stella, I...'

She placed her soft fingers to his lips and he stopped. 'You don't need to say anything, Danny.'

He took her hand in his. For too long he'd been holding onto the words in his head, and he knew it was time to voice them. Tonight he would release everything.

'Stella, do you believe the universe guides people together, that they're *meant* to be together? Do you believe in links between souls?'

'You mean, do I believe in soulmates?'

'Yes.'

Her head nodded softly, and she lowered her gaze to her glass. Danny saw her eyes welling with tears, pricked by a profound sadness.

'No. I do not believe. I know.'

They sipped at their drinks, a patient wait before the final step. Nothing but a jealous bullet could stop it now. Danny suddenly pictured himself back at school, waiting for the last bell to announce the start of the summer holidays.

He swallowed the rest of his whisky and they stood up to leave. Outside, pinhead stars filled the coruscating sky, a panorama that enticed contemplation of the depths and mysteries of the cosmos. Stella held Danny's hand as they walked along the seafront street. It was as though he could see every constellation in the sky tonight, all the patterns coming together, the balance of the universe in perfect harmony.

He had no worries, was aware of nothing else but the moment. Buddhist monks might spend years meditating to reach this tranquil mental state, but all Danny had had to do was hold her hand. As she led him down the street, it was as if she were leading him beneath the veil into another dimension, where Danny was aware of the universal energies that bound every atom in existence. Connecting with her fully could only heighten this sensation.

Her apartment was in the last building on the street. She'd been in there only a week, a room with a sea view. As they walked inside, the spicy aroma of jasmine greeted them. She had candles out here and there but not much else; most of her stuff still seemed to be packed in boxes.

She led him into the melancholic moonlight of her bedroom. Dropping her bag onto a chair, she stood by the window. The calm waves were a rich shimmering purple and as Stella gazed upon them, Danny could see a glowing swell of even brighter violet in her eyes, as like a necromantic reaction to her desolate aquatic dominion.

'Nobody should have to wait this long,' she whispered.

'I'm here,' Danny replied as he ran his hand up her back, beneath her golden hair, feeling the peachy skin of her neck.

'I know you are, Danny. And I'm here for you, here to show you the way.'

'I've waited so long too.'

'I know how it must seem. But I'm not as young as I look, you know.'

Danny had always figured she was a few years older than he. But so what? She could be ten years older and it wouldn't matter one bit. Age was meaningless if people were supposed to be together, when it came to the desires of the soul.

'With age comes experience,' he said, stepping closer to her, smelling her fruity skin.

She smiled at him. 'Perhaps I have lots of things to show you then.'

'I hope so.'

He kissed her warm lips and she pulled his shirt from his trousers. Her breathing quickened as she began kissing his cheek, biting his neck. He could sense her frustrations burning within her. Danny wrapped his arms round her, holding her tight.

'Stella...'

She stopped kissing his neck and looked at him. 'Yes, Danny.'

'I love you.'

She was silent, her face nodding gently. No doubt they

were words she'd heard many times before. Only beautiful people like her would ever get bored of those three words, but Danny had uttered them with complete truth.

Everyone's in love with her, someone like her. Hard not to adore someone like her, isn't it?

'I thought you might say that,' she replied.

Danny didn't know what she meant by that, but he knew what she meant when she began to unbuckle his belt.

'Get my clothes off,' she said to him, almost as if it was an order. Danny removed her top and then swiftly unclasped her bra. She edged her way to the bed and then eased herself onto it. He climbed on top of her, kissing her all over.

After she pulled his shirt from him, she then arched up her waist so Danny could remove her skirt and panties. There in the pale light of the room he tried to take in her naked perfection.

It felt so unreal, as though Danny were watching a film. He never would have imagined the universe would have this role for him, that he would get the girl, *this* girl, the most beautiful girl he could imagine.

'It's all in the eyes,' she said to him. 'Windows to the soul. There you can see everything.'

And so his gaze rested on her eyes, so their souls could be unveiled to each other, as naked as they were in the flesh.

'Keep looking, deep inside me. Then you'll understand.'

He slid into her, and both of them gasped, releasing such deep, pent-up feelings. She seemed so hungry for him.

Danny continued to search her sunset eyes. Within them, the violet exploded into a kaleidoscope of colours and he felt as though he were looking into the depths of infinity. He could see his entire life all at once, how the tides of the universe had flowed through him, carrying him along to this very moment, being inside the girl he loved.

He pictured an island, far away from him, lost within the cosmic currents, a paradise just out of reach. But he couldn't understand why he was floating elsewhere. The girl he loved was right here in his hold, underneath him. This was the moment. It was all about this moment.

He closed his eyes, a wave of sadness passing through him. The goblin missed a few keys as he played some discordant notes. Stella was the island. She always was. She was the beginning and the end, the alpha and the omega. He could not imagine loving another person as much as he loved her now.

'Danny...' she whimpered.

And Danny looked into her eyes once more. And suddenly he felt he almost knew what she was trying to show him. It was right there. Right at the edge of his mind's fingertips.

And Danny knew the revelation would destroy him. But not even that thought would stop him from enjoying this moment; Danny was already destroyed.

***

Lucas Duffy, the man who didn't have the name The Dim Reaper on his birth certificate, the man who didn't have any compunction about shooting people and killing them, the man who didn't mind parking in zones reserved for residents, was sitting in his BMW M3 Saloon, a newspaper resting on the steering wheel. The paper was three weeks old, but he wasn't really reading it, only doing a crossword.

A song had ear-wormed into his head, something that was on television this morning. He'd been watching some kids show as he often did. He found them so colourful and trippy.

'This old man, he played one, he played knick-knack on my thumb,' he uttered in a William Shatner style singing voice.

His trilby was positioned on the passenger seat. Beneath it was his silenced SIG, fully loaded. This afternoon he'd been shooting pigeons off the tree in his back garden for target practice.

'Oh, this old man. He played two. He played knick-knack on my shoe,' he sang, livening it up half a notch. 'With a knick-knack paddy-whack, give a dog a bone. This old man... is a motherfucking Al Capone.'

***

Danny reached the ecstasy as she did. He collapsed on top of her in a pile of perspiring flesh. Although she was still beneath him, she suddenly felt distant.

He crawled off her and slid under the duvet. Stella did the same, placing an arm around his waist.

'Now, my lost one,' she panted, 'now do you understand?'

'Two ships sailing along the waves...'

'...and now they will sail on.'

Danny sighed. 'I don't want anyone else.'

'We are lost souls, but you are not meant for me, and I am not meant for you. We are both lost to others.'

He closed his eyes solemnly. 'We're meant for whomever we choose.'

Stella nodded. She turned away to face the window. 'And I have already chosen. A long time ago.'

Danny leant up, the confusion writhing in his head. 'Who? Who can it be? Sam? You left him.'

Stella shook her head as soon as she heard his name. 'I told you, I've waited for so long. Believe me I've tried to fight the loneliness. I have tried other ways.'

'It's not Sam?'

She shook her head again.

'Then who is he? It's not me, it's not Sam. Who the hell is he?'

'You're only aware of this fragment of the journey your soul is making. Those we have walked beside before, in other times, in other lives, they are our true soulmates.'

'But I love you. It's you I want.'

'Somewhere out there you have a true love. She's the one you truly yearn for, from your lifetimes gone by. But you'll find her, as long as you keep searching. It's the gift I've given to you. You'll know now as soon as you see her. You'll know she is the one.'

'It's you.'

'No.' She sat up and started picking up her clothes off the floor. 'I'm sorry, Danny. One day you'll understand. One day you'll know what I've done for you.'

331

He knew then that it was all over, that no matter how hard he tried to fight it, she would fade away from him, like petals on a flower shrivelling up as night inevitably descended. He felt so empty, the magic of the universe now just a sadistic illusion, fate just randomness, the goblin just natural chemicals in the brain. There was no pattern to anything. Stars were just stars. Stella was just a beautiful girl with fortunate genetics.

And Danny was some unfortunate nobody who was ready to welcome whatever fate Samuel had prepared for him.

***

Samuel was indeed waiting for him. Wearing his black beanie hat, he paced up and down the pavement, his nerves on edge. He was only minutes away now and then it would all be over. Simple. It was all arranged. Nothing could go wrong.

In his hand he clutched the briefcase that contained the other fifty thousand. Samuel checked his watch. Seconds away.

He carried on pacing, dodging the dirty puddles that lurked here and there. He couldn't be ruining another pair of expensive trainers.

He knew this would make quite the story in the *Harbour Gazette* next week. Nobody would have seen it coming, and it would shake them to their cores. They never would have known that Samuel Allington was the type.

Staring skywards, he stopped pacing. He watched his crystallising breath floating upwards into the night air like ghostly vapours. One or two drops of rain fell on his face and it felt refreshing, for he was sweating like mad. His hands were shaking too, ripples of faint spasms going through his body, as though he was about to disgorge the delicious meal he'd eaten tonight. Steak and chips followed by chocolate ice cream. His favourite.

He looked up the street. Any second now.

***

Dressed once more in his white shirt and blue jeans, Danny slung on his jacket. Stella had gone to the kitchen to get him a drink of water, but she was taking a long time. He just wanted to go, wanted to get out of there and face Samuel's wrath.

He crept out of the bedroom and peered through the kitchen door. She was rooting through one of the packing boxes, probably looking for a glass. Danny knew that would be his final look at her. His final image of the girl whose beauty had haunted him for so long and led him to this fatal cataclysm.

There he left her. Danny tiptoed out of her flat and stepped inside the elevator. Down he went, back to the ground and the sobering salt air.

The clear skies had sucked all the heat out of the night, and Danny shivered. He felt worse than any hangover he'd ever had, as though someone had doused his soul in gasoline and set fire to it.

What a lucky man he would be to make it back home, to sit and watch the ten o'clock news with Michael. Or perhaps he should get on with his final essay that he was supposed to hand in next week. There was work at the chip shop tomorrow to think of too. He couldn't be having a late night tonight.

Back at the flat there was an ordinary life waiting for him, and that's what Danny was feeling once more. Ordinary. Average.

But after this evening he longed for that ordinariness more than anything, as much as he'd longed for Stella. If Samuel was about to kill him, then he would have to plead with him that there was no longer any point. Stella and Danny were over; Samuel could have her back. Not that she apparently wanted him, not that she wanted *either* of them. No, there was someone *else* she had her eye on.

His breathing shallow, his heartbeat hasty, Danny quickened his pace as though he was late for a lecture. It felt like time had run out, that the world had been going on without him. He just hoped that with the little composure he had left he could make it back home...

***

'This old man, he played seven, he's gonna send you along to heaven.'

Lucas Duffy could see him. He was there just as he said he would be. Son of a bitch was even right about what clothes he was wearing.

He hurried up the street. There was no one else around. A quick shot to the head and he would be on his way.

He felt the SIG Mosquito in the holster under his jacket and flicked the decocker. Just as he approached the silent figure, he whipped the gun out and pointed it at the guy's head.

But he did not shoot.

Something wasn't right, and when the guy turned round, he saw exactly why.

'Holy shit,' Duffy cried.

He quickly hid the gun away and put his hands on his hips, looking around to see where the target was. 'Fack, when you said what he'd be wearing I thought you meant what *he* would be wearing, not *you*. Jesus!'

Tears were streaking down Samuel's face. Duffy continued to search the streets, thinking already that tonight's job was well and truly botched.

Samuel slung down the briefcase, and then Duffy raised his eyebrows.

'Wait. No. No way,' he gasped, a peculiar grin appearing on his face. 'That's totally messed up.'

Samuel cleared his tight throat. 'I had your word.'

'Why didn't you do it yourself?'

'I can't. I tried. I failed at everything, I even failed at that.'

'This is wild.'

Samuel Allington closed his eyes for what he hoped would be the final time.

'The rest is in there?' Lucas asked.

'So dim.'

With that, Duffy shrugged, put the silenced SIG to the front of Samuel's head and blew his brains out all over the pavement. He picked up the briefcase, wiped the spray of blood off the leather with his sleeve and then skipped off down the street.

'With a knick-knack paddy-whack, give a dog a bone. This old man came rolling home.'

Chapter 16.3

The cove had called her back again as it had done throughout the years, throughout the endless sunsets that had burned onto her doleful gaze. It was the same place where her heart had been broken. The same place that had tried to reconcile her searing pain. It was a place of bitter loss and bitter discovery.

Broken people were often called here. It was somewhere that could show them the things they dreamt for, if they truly believed that asking the waves could manifest the destiny they imagined. Stella knew this because it had worked for her. It had manifested exactly what she was looking for.

And here he was back again, the forlorn lost soul who'd stumbled into her arms all those years ago. He was her soulmate, lost in another life, but found in this one.

The day she'd lost him was the same day she'd obtained the tool to find him again. It had taken a while to understand her new powers, but eventually she realised what new perceptions she had, that she could wander the world and look into the eyes of every person she met and know exactly who they were. She knew that if she carried on looking long enough, then she would find the particular soul she had lost that day.

Once she'd harnessed those powers, she was able to freeze her life-force, her soul in stasis as she wandered around like a living ghost. Time brought no lines to her face, no fading of her honey hair, her springtime energies held firmly within her grasp like an amaranth, until it was time to let go. Until she would finally look into that pair of eyes and find the one she was looking for.

Twenty-six decades later and she did just that. The lost little boy who'd emerged out of the darkness and silently walked up to her shores. She'd seen that he was broken, as he'd remained until now, even though she'd passed on the stone so he could look into her, into himself. To align everything.

'Hello there,' she said to him.

Vladimir did not react to her voice, staring numbly at his feet planted in the glistening sands.

'Keep finding you here, don't I?' she added as she stepped next to him.

At last he looked up at her, but only briefly, not the penetrating way he would stare at other people; Stella was a soul that he dared not search. She was a breeze that threatened to blow out the flame.

'You still have it, don't you?' Stella said as she saw the cord of the Akasa Stone around his neck. 'Why don't you use it for what you're supposed to use it for? The reason I gave it to you.'

He shook his head listlessly.

'You know who I am, don't you, Jeremy? You know what we are. Why won't you look inside me?' She moved closer to him, stepping within his jagged aura, trying to pull his eyes up to look at hers. As ever, they were like buttons, holding everything inside.

'I waited forever for you. When I lost you, it was a pain I never stopped feeling. And I know you feel that same pain, Jeremy. I know you're still hurting so much. But I can help heal you.'

'I don't know who I was, Stella. You're talking about a lifetime that I don't even remember.'

'Why won't you try and remember? Why don't you just search yourself?'

'I know who I am.'

'Who are you, Jeremy?'

'I am Vladimir. Throne of the Fires.'

But all Stella could see before her was the lost little six-year-old, the one she'd swept into her arms as she'd wept with such elation.

'If that is so, then why are you here?'

Vladimir closed his eyes and then sank to his knees in the wet sand. With both his hands he grabbed the hair on his head as though trying to pull it from his scalp, his knuckles turning white, his left hand beginning to weep with blood once more.

'Love me, Jeremy. Love me again. Abandon this dark path and come with me. I love you.'

'I don't love anyone,' Vladimir cried.

She knelt next to him and put an arm around him. A wave crawled up the beach and swarmed through them. She could feel his black walls crumbling at last, a chink of light through his impenetrable fortress. She gently took his arms and pulled them away from his face.

'Look at me. Just look at me.'

And he did. And she felt that sweet rush of air on her face like someone had just opened the door between dimensions. The brush of an angel's wing.

Vladimir closed his eyes tight.

'Now will you follow, my love?'

'No,' he replied as he pushed her away and stood up tall. Throwing back his head, his roars echoed off the clouds as he once again screamed, 'No!'

His black button eyes said it all. He was Vladimir, Throne of the Fires, Angel of Karma, and he had another soul to search. That hourglass of blood that burned in his mind every single moment of his life. This was his soul purpose, that even in this moment he would feel was going unfulfilled, his time slipping away.

He turned away from her and walked towards the town, back to where he intended to make his own destiny.

And Stella remained kneeling by the shoreline, staring at the reflection of her moonlit face in the swirling waves. And just like that day twenty-six decades ago, the waves would carry away the tears that now fell from her eyes.

Afterword

Have a thirst for more? Fear not...

The journey continues in *Night Shines*, the sequel to this book. This is the tale where things get even darker, when an old nemesis makes his terrifying return...

As the creature of the night starts murdering unfortunate individuals one by one, the townsfolk turn to the Halo of Fires organisation to rid the town of its menace.

But no one has ever succeeded at this before, and the Fires have never seen themselves as heroes. Yet when destiny comes calling, the Fires realise another nemesis has been manipulating them into the danger zone...

That Mailing List Link You Were Looking For

To get your hands on the free *Dark Harbour* bonus material then sign up to my mailing list here:

www.josephkiel.com

Do that and I'll send you another *Dark Harbour* tale, the eBook of *Into The Fires*. This novella is a prequel to this book, a standalone tale that gives the backstory of Ulric Helliwell and what initially brought him to the town. The book explores the critical decisions he'd made to trigger his misfortune, and introduces one or two new characters.

Also on my mailing list, you can learn about my future releases, offers, information about my other books and projects, not to mention news on my negotiating the option rights to the *Dark Harbour* series with those top Hollywood producers (we haven't started yet but you'll be the first to know when we do).

If you enjoyed reading this novel then please do leave a review on Amazon, no matter how brief, to help spread the word. Post a 5 star review and who knows, somewhere in Dark Harbour a street may be named after you, or maybe the mayor will put up a statue of you, or something. In all seriousness, reader reviews can make a big difference to authors and help increase visibility. They make a real difference.

Thank you for picking up my book.

"Night Shines" PREVIEW

(Book 2 of The Dark Harbour Tales)

Part 0: A Love Set Sail

Chapter 0.1

Something dreadful has happened here. The sorry town is like a devastated battleground, drained and numbed by the attempt to exorcise the harrowing evil, with only this book to make sense of the visitation.

It's not the first time this has occurred, but, even so, you never have any idea what to do about it. The constant fear as you timidly peer up at the heavens, wondering if that feathered fate is about to pounce upon your failing existence. Forever facing the mirror as you examine your ugliest and most pitiful features. And the feeling of despair that quietly taps you on your shoulder, suggesting you just surrender, that your flawed spirit shines feebly, like a cold and distant star.

Those were the thoughts that infected the psyche of this town. Was it better to give in as the folk had done so often before, or was there anything worth fighting for? What would be left of the soul of the possessed town, assuming the exorcism succeeded? And what would be the cost?

Perhaps these are questions for which the answers will not come readily. In the pubs, the regulars will sip silently at their pints, while the children go home straight after school and stay safely indoors until the following morning. Fear is everywhere, taking each person from the strange creature of the night and leading them directly within, right to their own languid soul.

It would not be advisable to broach this subject with anyone here, not for the time being. Read this tale, understand their affliction, and take comfort that you haven't yet found this gloomy town, that you didn't encounter this horror. Be satisfied that you never experienced a brutal microcosm of hell operating in your own world, as it has done here, a place where something can burn more fiercely than a Fire.

To find that creature Night-Shines Nick, first you must go back... to the fog of one early morning of November 29th in the year 1753. A golden time for some, another tribulation for others, those of a certain secluded seaside town of England.

Salvation sailed the waves... the same waters whereupon it sank.

**

Trent stood on the forecastle as the creaking vessel glided towards the harbour. The fog was getting thicker, but certain members of the crew held an equal amount of longing and dread as they approached their home.

He glanced down at the flowing hair on the figurehead as she appeared to fly above the waves, and for a moment he imagined the young girl to be singing. She was an urchin dressed in rags with a cheeky smile, and perfectly summed up the character of their vessel, an ageing Dutch Indiaman with tatty grey sails.

Shivering beneath his sea cloak, Trent kept watch, even though he couldn't see a damned thing across these misted waters. Six members of a Harbourian brotherhood had set off on the long voyage, but only four of them were returning. They were subordinates to Captain Silas and his ragtag band of pirates, voyaging on a mutually beneficial quest. It was to be Silas's final adventure, the raiding of the Védena Temples, a distant place spoken of in ancient tales. A magnificent bounty of treasures was guarded there. The greatest treasures.

It was more like pillaging than piracy, but Silas's crew, and particularly the brotherhood, were a determined bunch. They couldn't allow anything to get in their way. Too much depended on it.

If news was to break on the brash operation they'd performed, the monstrous *Tatterdemalion* was well equipped to deal with any attacks from rogue pirates as they sluggishly trailed back to England. Only one Brigantine, *La Pereza*, had attempted such impudence, and now lay somewhere at the bottom of the Atlantic Ocean.

Another sea cloak-dressed figure approached the front of the ship. It was Drood, a member of the brotherhood, their default leader since the incident with the Brigantine.

'If there's something I've learned,' Drood began, 'it's that I'm not a man of the masts.'

'Nor I,' Trent agreed. He followed his gaze back across the vessel, the unspoken thought about to be spoken: 'Do you have it yet?'

'No.'

Trent sighed. 'Let me go in there with you. And Hawker and McDay. Let's all of us go.'

'Silas's men outnumber us five to one. Let's not cause a commotion. Allow me to employ my diplomacy.'

'Then go back in there, man! Remember your oath.'

Trent remembered that occasion vividly, just days before they had set sail. There, within the circle of torches, the six agents of the brotherhood had made their pledge.

'I saw...' Drood began, as his eyes now looked in the direction of the captain's cabin.

'What?'

'I saw Finlay.'

Trent swallowed salty air down his dry mouth. 'Finlay's dead.'

'He was in there. As plain as I am here now. I saw him.'

He should have continued to protest Drood's obvious delirium, but the truth was that he felt his mind was descending into a peculiar state as well. Ever since they'd acquired their treasures, things had turned a strange shade, the curtains of the theatre of perception beginning to lift from a twisted stage of freaks and illusionists, within which they were now wandering amongst.

'We'll soon be back home. And what then?' Trent asked.

Drood wiped a film of moisture from his face as he looked to be summoning the courage for their grave task.

'The lighthouse!' a coarse voice echoed from across the vessel. 'Point her to the lighthouse!'

They observed the first mate remonstrating with the helmsman. Somewhere through the fog was the faintest smear of light penetrating the sky.

'Fine. I'll talk to him,' Drood replied. 'Stay here.'

Trent watched as he clambered back down to the deck. Just at that moment he heard it again. He glanced towards the figurehead and half-expected those wooden lips to be moving, but fortunately his madness hadn't descended upon him that much yet.

There was no denying the melody in his ears though, the beautiful voice that hung in the frigid air like a spray of perfume. He could almost make out the song. Tilting his head, his body gently listed towards those murky waves, that aquatic wilderness that the *Tatterdemalion* continued to glide across.

Printed in Great Britain
by Amazon

17099673R00200